WHEN I'M BAD I'M BETTER 2

When I'm Bad I'm Better 2

K.F. Johnson

One Ironwoman Publishing

Contents

One Ironwoman Publishing
Grayson, GA 30017

Cover Art: Christine N. Davis

ISBN-13: 978-1-954469-03-7

1

Valerie

"All right! All right! All right! Where are all my ballers and shot callers at? Get your wallets and your big faces out for the next dancer coming to the stage! She's the prettiest, sexiest taste of heaven you're ever going to get. Welcome, The Man Trap's own, Angelica!" Primo announced as the beat to Rae Sremmurd's "Throw Sum Mo" started, and I hit the stage to Nicki Minaj's voice.

Licking my lips, I grinned sensually at the sea of nondescript faces lusting after me by the stage as I circled it, jiggling my apple bottom on beat. Slinking my way to the pole, I climbed it almost to the ceiling, then raised my lower body in a slow, erotic grind until it was parallel to the floor.

Even with my level of inebriation, I was a beast on the pole. Courtney, said the routine made me look like an angel hovering over the stage, and actually coined my stage name. I was resistant of it at first because Angel was also the pet name Brent had for me. She quickly erased my apprehension after brainstorming all of the angles I could work to make myself stand out.

We found a costume store that carried huge sparkling over the shoulder angel wings in multiple colors and I bought five. Next, I went online and ordered a bunch of rhinestone bra and thong sets in various colors to match my wings. I switched up every night I danced with a wig in the same or similar color, and I made an impression instantly.

I doubted any of the drooling onlookers could tell, or even cared that I was actually a Juilliard trained dancer; but I hoped my talent exuded that. I liked to think I brought more to the stage than simple raunchy moves.

Between watching YouTube videos and Courtney's help with my techniques, I easily incorporated what I already knew, with what was required to transition into being an on-stage seductress. Even though I'm generally conservative, dancing naked in front of a crowd turned out to be rather easy.

Growing up, I idolized Josephine Baker, who danced with little more than bananas on her waist, just as much as I revered Janet Collins, the first black ballerina to dance with the Metropolitan Ballet. My body is toned and well-proportioned for my size, so once I got out of my own head about the stigmas, I was proud to show it.

My mother didn't agree, and thought I was having some sort of breakdown when I told her I was stripping until I found other professional work. She stressed that a good, morally stable woman wouldn't prance around naked for money and strangers to ogle.

Of course, she had to end it with a guilt trip of how my father would've reacted if he was alive. There was no use in arguing with her once she was convinced she was right about something, so, I didn't bother.

She was a totally different person since my father died. She seemed to have an opinion about everything and everything out of her mouth was negative. I guess since misery loves company, she was trying to enlist everyone else. Instead of letting her continue to drive me up the wall, I let it drive me out of her house only a month after I moved in.

Thankfully, Courtney took me in without hesitation, and I've been paying half the mortgage and utilities at her place since. Staying with her was a breath of fresh air compared to the claustrophobic way I felt around Brent, my mother and my cousins before. They always said I was quiet, but that was partially because I couldn't get a word in edge wise even when I did have something to say.

Over the last few months, I've become closer to her than I am with Amina or my other kin anymore. Courtney's a free spirit who thinks too many people don't do things for fear of what other people will say. When I asked her why she was stripping, she didn't try to sugar coat it. She cited the hours, the money and the attention as reasons with a straight face.

Another perk of living with Courtney was that she was completely off of Brent's radar, so he couldn't track me down to her place. In the beginning, even after my brother whipped his ass, the two-timing, bald-headed bastard was stalking me like I was the last woman on earth when I lived with my mother.

I had to change my number, my habits, and my usual haunts, just to avoid him mysteriously showing up wanting to talk. He couldn't get it through his thick head that no amount of flowers, money, gifts or apologies would make me take him back. I almost put a restraining order on him, but since Courtney said I could live with her, I decided not to. He wouldn't know where I was to harass me.

I hadn't seen or heard from him since I moved in, and though I'm not on social media, Courtney told me she saw pics of him hanging with a socialite a couple of months ago. I was just glad he finally gave up chasing me. I hated to admit it, but Vanessa was right when she said he was a control freak. Of course, that was before I knew she was letting him control her pussy too.

She also might have been right about my former prudish ways being part of the reason Brent and I fell apart, but I would never tell her that. Since I've been stripping, I have felt a certain amount of freedom and confidence I never felt before.

My usual introverted nature, and currently jaded view of men, still conflicted with the necessity for coquettish and intimate contact with potentially weird or scuzzy men though. Consequently, I suppressed my nerves with a few shots of Vodka or swigs of Hennessey each night and put on my game face to make this money.

Admittedly, I've been regularly drinking my feelings into hibernation since Daddy's funeral six months ago. Yesterday was the first

Thanksgiving ever that I wasn't able to call or spend with my father; and my heart ached. My mother wasn't herself anymore either, and these days I barely wanted to speak to her at all, so I didn't.

That being said, I drank a little extra to numb the pain and worked at the club instead of attending the family dinner last night. I was fed up with other people trying to dictate how I should live my life, and I wasn't going anywhere that my whole family could pass judgment in a group.

Twenty-fifteen gave me little to be thankful for, and I didn't feel like faking it just to get some home cooked turkey and yams. What was left of us wasn't much of a family anyway since Yasmin and Vanessa's penchant for sleeping with their sister's men was exposed.

Tamika still hates Yasmin, I still hate Vanessa, and everybody else rides the fence. Once our loyalties were lost, so were our tight bonds, and nobody cared enough to attempt mending them.

Swinging around the pole and doing tricks both upright and upside down, I removed my bra as seductively as possible. When I came down, I crawled, twerked and contorted my body in front of each extended hand offering money with a sensual smirk.

I'm still green to the business, so I didn't realize that holidays were slow for strip clubs. Still, because I was only one in a hand full of us that was working these days at The Man Trap, the money wasn't too bad. Thanks to a celebrity birthday bash for a local rapper and a large bachelorette party, tonight's crowd was good.

I was nearing the end of my six-hour shift, and 2 A.M. couldn't come fast enough. The liquor was making me sleepy and my heels were killing me. I squatted by the edge of the stage in front for ankle relief and bounced my butt cheeks in isolation, all while swiveling my hips.

Looking back provocatively at a guy sliding a Jackson in my thong, I noticed a disturbance brewing behind him. The crowd suddenly started shifting, which made me stand up abruptly to see what was going on.

Security was tight, and we rarely had any altercations to speak of, but I spotted at least three brewing in the same proximity. Tempers were heated between a group of guys and the lesbian ladies at the bachelorette party. The husky female wearing a "Groom" sash was barking angrily at a lanky man, while waving a champagne bottle in her hand.

My eyes bulged as the groom cracked the bottle into ole' boy's face, instantly splitting his cheek open and sending him stumbling backwards into his boys. Security was on her before she could take another swing with the now jagged bottle, but it was too late to stop the melee that ensued afterwards.

People were fighting while others scattered to avoid the chaos and a bunch of them hopped on the stage to get away. My half-drunk ass didn't want to get trampled, but I definitely grabbed my cash from the floor before hurrying towards the dressing rooms.

I was hurrying down the hallway to the dancer's quarters when someone gripped my arm from behind.

"Hey," he called spinning me halfway toward him.

I don't know why my heart rose into my throat at the sight of his arrogant face, but I felt like a kid caught with my hand in the cookie jar.

"Get your God damn hands off me," I growled, staring at his hand like it was made of feces.

"No. You need to stop running from me and talk to me," he replied clutching me firmly. "Why are you working here?"

"I said, get off of me!" I shrieked yanking free, causing some of my money to fall to the floor.

Bending to pick it up, I felt his eyes burning through me like lasers. Embarrassment seeped in, making me nervous and clumsy, despite my not owing him any explanations.

"I can't believe you're in here whoring yourself out just to make a point Val. I told you I was willing to go to therapy or whatever you wanted to get us through it, but you're too stubborn. You can't be happy sinking this low. We both know you're better than this."

"Whoring myself out?" I sneered. "You're the only whore I see here Brent. I'm just dancing. If anybody's a whore, it's your community dick having ass!" I yelled, standing to my full height to glare at him. "Who are you to judge?"

"I swear I must really love you," he chuckled smugly, sizing me up and resting an elbow in one hand and rubbing the stubble on his chin. "This isn't you and you know it. I come here to celebrate my frat brother's birthday, and this is what you're doing?"

His egotistical demeanor mocked my growing anger as I ran my tongue across my teeth in disdain. The thought of going back to him made my blood curdle. Especially with him acting like he would be doing me a favor when he was the one that messed up.

Everything about him that I used to love, now repulsed me like a cockroach in my food. His once piercing almond shaped eyes looked hollowed and his smooth skin looked ashen. I don't know if it was his actual appearance, or just how he appeared to me, but I didn't want anything to do with him.

"Brent, go away. I'm not your concern anymore. It's over! I don't care what you think, and I don't want you! Stop stalking me. Go screw my sister or some other whore that cares. Leave me alone!" I rapid fired angrily.

"Stalking you?" He hissed, addressing me like an insolent child. "Don't be ridiculous. Seriously Val, you need to grow up. Men cheat. Your father probably cheated on your mother, and his father probably cheated on his mother too.

It happens. It doesn't mean that I loved you any less. It's a carnal need that men find hard to control. Especially when I was getting more action from my palm than my own fiancé. I acknowledge that I hurt you. But you weren't innocent in this and if you would just talk to me, you would see that.

I haven't seen your sister since that night Val, and I'm sure you know that too. It wasn't love I had with her. She probably doesn't love anybody but herself anyway. I just can't believe you would rather do this, than humble yourself and come back to me."

My eyes almost burst from their sockets.

"Humble myself? Negro, are you sick in the head? I don't owe you anything. You're dead to me," I spat turning to leave, only to be yanked back toward him again by my bicep.

"Don't walk away from me. I'm not done with you and you're not done with me. You were cold and preoccupied after your injury and you need to own your part in this just as much as I do. Once you can do that, we can move forward. You know if your father were alive and knew you were doing this, it would probably kill him."

"I said get off of me."

"I'm not letting you go until you agree to meet me somewhere and talk," he scoffed with the stench of consumed liquor on is breath.

"Kiss my ass Brent. I don't have to do anything. Let me go."

"See? Do you see how you've changed? Cussing like a hood rat and dancing for chump change when you know I can give you the world. All because of one slip up? Is this really the life you want?"

"What I want is a man that can be faithful, and you were not capable of being that, so miss me with this intervention speech."

"I am perfectly capable of being faithful. Are you capable of giving a man a reason to be? You act like you caught me banging a different hoe every week. And I could have, being who I am. But I didn't. At least it was with your identical twin."

"At least?" I snarled. His declaration jolting me like an uppercut.

He sighed like he wished he could reverse his words back down his throat and I wished he could to. With the assistance of my foot.

"What I'm saying is. If I was going to cheat, which I shouldn't have, at least it wasn't because you were lacking anything physically. She a gold digging, glammed up, flashier version of you, but she looks just like you. Now, I never required you to stay dolled up, but I did expect you to start acting more wifely, once I put that ring on your finger.

Instead, you acted like you didn't appreciate the fact that I was willing to give you my last name and make you the mother of my children. You didn't put me first. What did you expect to happen? I owned up to my part. Now you have to own up to yours."

My chest rose and fell heatedly as his words sunk into the pit of my stomach and festered in my soul. Without pause, I yanked my arm from his grip and slapped his disrespectful face all in one turn. The money in my hand fell to the floor and I glowered at him hatefully before bending to pick up my earnings.

"Stop acting like a mongrel and keep your hands to yourself," he growled stepping back and massaging his cheek. "You're lucky I don't hit women. You and your brother have a problem with self-control."

"Only when it comes to you. Now get your ass out of here before I call security, or let Victor know he needs to beat the brakes off you one more time."

"I'd actually like that. I've been training in Krav Maga. Believe me, Vic doesn't want to see these hands or these feet. I'll have him buried right next to your father if—"

The wad of spit propelled from my mouth onto his nose and upper lip before I even thought about it. Unlike when I spit on him after catching him cheating with Vanessa, the rage it incited made me instantly regretful.

His hand clenched my throat as he drove my back into the wall and leered at me through slits. His top teeth bore into his bottom lip while his hands attempted choking me into an eternal sleep.

Tears squeezed from my eyes as I clawed at his hands, writhing kicking and gasping for breath. I was about to die.

2

Yasmin

Warm tears and the sound of my own whimpering woke me as I slowly opened my eyes to the glow from the television screen. Using the back of my wrists as tissue, I dried my eyes and took a deep breath.

Nightmares have plagued me since my attack, and no amount of meditation, green tea or prayer prevented them from invading my slumber. My nights were already restless due to the small blessing in my belly, but the nightmares had me dreading sleep altogether.

"It's okay Sophie. We're okay," I whispered, massaging my protruding tummy to soothe her tossing.

I smiled foreseeing the day I would finally hold my daughter in my arms. I just needed her to hold out the remaining four weeks until her December 28th due date. This doctor ordered bed rest was trying for both of us.

My pregnancy was high-risk because of my past medical issues anyway. Compounded with the trauma Malik's savage attack caused my body, Sophie and I were both lucky to be alive.

I would never, in a million years, have predicted that my husband would've reacted so violently toward me. Common sense dictated that he would be hurt and angry when he found out about me and Dwayne; but trying to stab me to death with a steak knife? I *literally*, never saw it coming.

Everyone was at my uncle's funeral, and nobody was talking to me anyway, so I would have easily died in a pool of my own plasma if not for my nosy neighbor Octavia. Thank God she was in her yard when Malik rushed from the house in bloody clothes with an arm full of luggage and raced off.

My car was in the driveway, so she had every reason to believe I was home. The way I heard it, she trotted over to check on me as soon as he sped off. When her knocks and ringing went unanswered, she peeked through the glass on the side of the door and saw blood on the carpet, so she called 911.

Malik withdrew as much as he could from his credit and bank cards at an ATM and got ghost. The police speculated he cut himself in the frenzy because his blood was mixed with mine and trailed all through the house. I was stabbed eleven times. If not for the knife jamming in my back and the handle breaking off, I'm sure he would have stabbed me to death.

He's been on the run ever since, and I'm convinced his sister and mother have been helping him. Fatima loves her baby brother like her own son since she's 10 years older, and if his mother had two nickels to rub together, she would give them to her precious son. Even while living in assisted living.

Knowing Malik is still at large has kept me away from my house since the day I was discharged. I was on doctor ordered bed rest anyway, and I needed someone to help care for me during my recovery and pregnancy.

To Tamika's dismay, my daddy took me in for the sake of myself and his grandbaby. He picked up what I needed from the house and went by once or twice a month to pick up my mail, turn on the faucets and make sure everything was still kosher.

Recuperating from the damage done during the attack has only been exacerbated by anxiety and the stress of pregnancy. On top of everything else, Daddy's diabetes has been flaring up, leaving him too fatigued to do much more than rest and order take out.

My aunts bring food by sometimes, but believe me, it's a hard pill to swallow when family you've always been there for turn their backs on you when you need them.

I know what I did hurt Tamika dearly, but I still can't believe she could write me off so easily when I was potentially *dying*. No matter what she ever did in life, I wouldn't want her to die for it. She hadn't so much as made a phone call or stepped foot in my room the first few days I was in ICU, nor during my entire hospital stay. Hell, even Vanessa's trifling ass found time to come check on me then.

Nicky's traitor ass wasn't much better. She came over from time to time to get her mail and made small talk with me, but it was easy to see she was team Tamika. I tried a couple of times to get her to intervene and get Tamika to hear me out, but she flat out refused; and *we* ended up arguing.

I hated that everybody seemed to be placing the brunt of the blame for the affair on me when Dwayne seduced *me*. Realistically, the whole family knew that Dwayne stepped out on Tamika before, including her.

She was checking his phone and whereabouts way before we started messing around. Her insecurities were four years in the making. Holding me accountable for their ruins when I had only been with him a couple of months wasn't fair.

You would think Tamika whooping my ass like a runaway slave in front of Kamari and everyone at her salon would be enough, but the tramp was still mad. I'm convinced that Malik and I would've been able to get passed everything if Dwayne hadn't done what Malik couldn't seem to do our entire marriage. Get me pregnant.

It's like everybody wants to make *me* out to be the villain, while these violent halfwits are labeled victims. If I really wanted to be petty, I could've pressed charges against Tamika and had her black ass locked up for assault, but I didn't.

If not for my nephews, and the shame of the entire situation, I probably would have too. I *definitely* thought about it after she dimed me out to Malik. Lucky for her, I was too busy grieving the loss of my uncle and my marriage to focus.

I never wanted to be the reason Tamika and Dwayne broke up, but it was always doomed to happen. Dwayne's been living with his homeboy Cortez since she threw him out, and he's working sporadically in Cortez's barber shop, COOL CUTS.

I don't know what's up with that guy, but he can't stand me. The abhorrent way he eyes me under whatever Cali team baseball cap he's usually wearing makes it obvious. He never says more than two sentences to me if he can help it. I don't know if it's because he disapproves of me in general or just how Dwayne and I got together.

To make things worse, the day after our one and only Lamaze class, Dwayne messed around and got his car towed and driver's license suspended for unpaid tickets. Because of that, Cortez has been chauffeuring him everywhere he doesn't Uber to since September. So now I see Dwayne even less, and when I do, I usually have to see Cortez's scowling face too.

I stopped caring about being friendly with his weird ass after my first few genuine attempts were met with curt answers or essentially ignored. Dwayne claims he's just the introverted type, but I'm of the belief that he's just an asshole.

Either way, Cortez has been dropping him off or sitting in the car instead of facing me at Daddy's house recently, and I'm perfectly happy with that.

My growling belly reminded me that food cures all anxieties as I hoisted myself from the bed, and pulled the hem of my nightgown down. Grabbing my cell from the nightstand, I swiped the screen and pressed the last number called as I waddled down the staircase.

"What up Shawty?" Dwayne answered on the second ring in his typical slow drawl.

"Can't sleep. Nightmares got me and your daughter hungry."

He chuckled. "You always hungry Shawty. Don't be blamin' my baby fo' yo' piggish ass.

"Shut up," I laughed.

Even if he was more right than wrong about that, he didn't need to say it. I was sure I gained way more than just baby weight in past months, but so what. What did anybody expect when I can't exercise and have to stay in bed the majority of my waking hours?

Scrolling social media and comfort foods had become my companions, and I knew I would regret it after Sophie was born. Still, for the time being, I didn't care one damn bit.

"Were you already up?"

"I wasn't 'sleep yet, but I was on my way. What you 'bout to stuff yo' face wit'?"

"Leftover Thanksgiving dinner."

"Oh yeah? What y'all had?"

"You would've known what we had if you came over for dinner like I asked you to," I sassed reaching the landing and heading to the kitchen.

"Pshhh. C'mon Shawty. I told you I wasn't comin' from jump. Yo' daddy already can't stand me comin' by to see you on a regular day. I know that man ain't want me eating dinner wit' him. Plus, Mika would flip that whole house upside down if she knew."

I huffed. "Well Tamika didn't show up, and she didn't bring the boys by either, so that wouldn't have been an issue."

No matter how Tamika felt about it, Dwayne was about to be the father of my child, and she needed to accept it. Maybe I wasn't thinking rationally, but I hoped he would come to dinner as a support for me on Thanksgiving Day knowing how forlorn my family had me feeling.

Of course, he didn't show and didn't even bother to return my text messages asking if he was coming. This would be my first Thanksgiving without Malik by my side in almost a decade, and the guilt about that had me longing for a replacement companion to ease my discomfort.

No matter what happened, I knew Malik and I would never be again, so I filed for divorce in July. Ideally, I still wanted a nuclear family for my daughter though. Dwayne wasn't the type of man I would've ever chosen, but he was Sophie's father, and a viable choice.

To my knowledge, he hadn't been dealing since the media insinuated he might be into illegal activities when my stabbing hit the news. For a while, they were even researching the possibility of a connection with my carjacking, but nothing panned out.

Truthfully, as awkward as I knew it would be for the family, and specifically for my nephews to understand, I had serious thoughts of trying to make it work with Dwayne. We touched on the topic on occasion in conversation, but neither of us tried to set anything in concrete thus far.

"She's going to have to accept reality eventually Dwayne. Everybody is. We're going to have a daughter together, and we might end up together too."

"Yeah well, Mika ain't *gotta* accept nothin'. Have you met yo' sista'? I'm glad she ain't been blockin' me from seein' the boys, but she don't make it easy neither. Kamari ain't messin' wit' me no more though. Lil' nigga don't got one word to say to me."

"He's petty like his momma. He'll come around. You've been the only father that boy has ever known. Hell, I've been just as much of a mother to those boys as Tamika has any—"

"Aight. Chill Yas. Don't do too much wit' all that. Tamika's always been a good mother," Dwayne set me straight.

I pulled the phone away from my ear and screw-faced it before speaking back into it.

"Umm, excuse me, but I've been helping my sister for years before you came along. Me, my dad and Nicky have helped her *become* the good mother you think she is now. Don't forget, she's my *older* sister.

She used to care more about getting high, chasing her baby daddies and going to parties than her boys. I was the one babysitting, playing, and taking them to parks while she ran the streets at all hours. *While* I was in law school I might add.

Kamari is not the smart, strong minded and opinionated teenager he is because Tamika sacrificed hanging out to help him. Shoot, neither is Nicky. My big sister got to shirk her duties after my mother died to do what-the-hell-ever she wanted to do.

If anybody's in a place to talk about her mothering skills, I am," I retorted, taking out the Tupperware bowls with macaroni and cheese, and yams from the fridge while swiveling my neck like he could see me.

"Aye Shawty. Stop actin' like you betta' than people," he said in a stern but low tone. "I told you I don't like when you talk like that. You ain't been in her shoes as a mother Shawty. Yeah, she made some mistakes. So what? You been perfect all yo' life?"

People made me sick assuming that because I didn't have children of my own, I was clueless about mothering. When my mother died, Tamika abandoned us for the streets and my father left me and Nicky to our own devices while he grieved.

Uncle Vernon, Aunt Di and Aunt Pam were there as support for us, but *I* was the one who stepped up. At fifteen years old, *I* was the woman of the house. Not Tamika, who's four years older. I had to be there for my dad. I had to be there for Nicky. *Somebody* had to be the responsible one while Tamika was experimenting with her reproductive organs every few years.

I sucked my teeth and took a plate from the cabinet, grabbing a big serving spoon from the dishrack. Movement outside caught my attention from the large window over the sink. I stopped and gazed out at the shed tucked away in the backyard, lit only by the moon and the slight light from the kitchen.

"No, but I've been close to it until I started sleeping with you," I replied haughtily.

"Cut the drama," he laughed sarcastically. "Stop puttin' on Shawty. That ain't cute. I know you *and* I know Mika. Ain't none of y'all flawless. Real talk, Sometimes I think you always talkin' down on her 'cause you light weight jealous."

"Jealous? Tuh! Of what? Too much body fat, three baby daddies, and struggling to pay my bills every month? I'll admit my life isn't perfect, but I'll pass on trading places with her too."

"You coldblooded Shawty," he mocked.

"So, have you thought more about opening your own barber shop like we talked about? I can't have my child's father getting locked up for selling drugs," I asked switching subjects so's not to elevate my blood pressure any more than it probably already was.

"Oh. You done talkin' 'bout that huh?" he snickered. "Naw. Not really. Why?" he asked, letting out a cough that was probably weed induced. "You 'bout to buy it fo' me?"

I was listening to his words, but my attention was now on what looked like footprints in the light cover of snow that fell earlier in the evening. I brushed the bangs that had long since grown out of my pixie cut from my face and squinted.

I wasn't sure they were footprints. The patches of grass causing gaps made it hard to tell the difference exactly. The shed was fifteen or 20 feet away from the house, so my eyes could've been playing tricks on me, but I didn't think they were.

"Buying it for you? Hell no. I will not be your sugar momma," I quipped, setting the plate on the counter and leaning closer to the window to scan the yard. "You are definitely smoking too much"

Daddy didn't live in the hood, but it wasn't the safest place to live in America either. Break-ins occurred occasionally, which is one reason Malik and I bought our house elsewhere.

I preferred to be able to live where I could mistakenly leave my doors unlocked and expect everything to still be in my house when I got back.

"I'm smokin' 'cause you called a nigga at two o'clock in the morning', and I needed to be doin' somethin' while I was talkin' to yo' bougie ass if I'm gonna stay up," he joked.

"Whatever. You're always looking for an excuse to smoke. I swear if my child comes out with any birth defects, I'm blaming you," I answered, ready to chalk my paranoia about a trespasser up to lethargy.

That is, until the shed door creaked open and a slow-moving figure emerged maneuvering a motorcycle through it. Stumbling backwards with a yelp, surprised there actually *was* a prowler on the premises, I inadvertently banged my elbow against the counter, and sent the plate crashing to the floor.

"Yo Shawty, what happened? You aiight?"

Liquid fear trailed from my inner thighs as the intruder's face became clearer under the illumination of the moon and kitchen lights.

The hatred radiating from his eyes was undeniable as they momentarily locked with mine.

The hairs on the back of my neck stood at attention as I gripped the phone tightly to my ear and whimpered into it.

"Oh my God Dwayne. It's Malik. He's going to kill me.

3

Amina

My hips rotated wildly beneath the pressure of Cedric's suctioning mouth on my pearl as his tongue slid skillfully between my moist slit like a snake. His hands grasped my butt cheeks with his face dipped between my thighs, pinning me against the picture window with the Las Vegas skyline watching.

Images of Donovan's face subconsciously replaced Cedric's behind my lids with every thrust I drew closer to orgasm. It was pathetic really. Considering that I've never seen Donovan naked and the only sex we had was in my dreams. Still, I thought of him while Cedric and I had sex, and whenever I masturbated alone.

My fingers tightly entwined in his thick, graying curls, I rode Cedric's face into ecstasy like The Lone Ranger into the sunset. If you can't be with the one you love, love the one you're with. Right? Not that I ever loved Donovan, but I felt like the potential that was there had been dashed away too soon.

After being emotionally closed off for so long, it was frightening, yet exhilarating, when I started feeling comfortable enough to open up to him. He broke down my barriers while helping to nurse me back to health and in the process, broke my heart when he bailed so easily. As hard as he pursued me, was as hard as I had started to fall for him.

The dreaded day my uncle was buried, and I came home to chaos, was the day he distanced himself from me with the quickness of a shot put. My phone calls went unanswered and my texts messages ignored, all while I coped with the aftermath of the B&E in secret.

What I hadn't noticed initially was the rest of the damages to my property. The word WHORE was also spray painted on my $400 bedspread and bedroom wall, and SLUT was sprayed across the custom-made brick wall in my great room. I was livid, and it was a no-brainer that the video and derogatory graffiti had to be related to my former occupation.

It might seem crazy, but calling the police wasn't an option. Even though my back door was busted open and somebody vandalized my house, nothing was stolen. I didn't want to risk something being discovered that would lead to me being investigated or arrested in the future, so I erred on the side of caution.

Yes. Escorting *is* legal in the state of Georgia as long as there is no exchange of money for fondling, oral, anal or genital penetration. The problem was, that video showed Todd eating my box, though they would have to prove he paid me to do it. For all I knew it was him.

Begrudgingly, I called Jamie that night and solicited her help. She didn't make it easy for me, and I hated asking knowing she was still salty about our split, but I had nowhere else to turn under the circumstances. Within three days I had everything previously defaced repainted, the backdoor replaced, and a new state of the art security system installed with surveillance cameras around the property.

By day four, Jamie came through with the identity of the vandal, and I couldn't have been more shocked to hear it was Todd's wife! Partly because I never knew she existed, but mainly because she was nearly 1000 miles away and knew my true identity, which Todd didn't even know, but also where I lived.

Turns out, my wealthiest and longest standing "boyfriend" wasn't the big BP exec he claimed to be. Instead, he was the kept husband of a wealthy Texas heiress who also had some mental issues. Jamie reported the woman spent a few lengthy stints in mental institutions over the past five years which left him in control of her private companies, and her money.

This time, she hired a PI to investigate Todd's affairs, spending habits and whereabouts while she was "regrouping". Which led her to me. Whatever slimy PI she hired must've paid a hotel employee to let them in and set up a camera to get video of us. Per Jamie, Lesley, Todd's wife, admitted to him that she personally trashed my home.

He disappeared that weekend and deducted a large amount of money from their account, which she thought he was bringing to give me. How she knew I would be out of the house was as much of mystery to me as it was to Jamie. Because my house was a new build back then, only a few of the homes around me were occupied. Most homes were still being completed, or hadn't been sold yet, which made the fear of witnesses, slim to none.

If Jamie hadn't confirmed it as fact, I wouldn't have believed any of it, but I guess expecting a certifiably crazy woman to make rational decisions was asking for too much. Jamie assured me that Todd had his wife back under control and he had her pass me $25K for the inconvenience and my keeping law enforcement out of it.

Lesley swore she wasn't behind my shooting, but I wasn't convinced. I wasn't out here making a lot of enemies, and it happened on the last night I was meeting with him. Coincidental? I didn't think so.

On a positive note, nothing else has happened like that since, but last night, Jamie left a message saying she needed to talk to me about something. The two of us had sort of made up, but if she wanted to talk to me about something, it had to be about business, or a continuation of this situation. She wasn't the type to call for social reasons.

I appreciated that she came through for me in the clutch despite the tension between us after our business split. So, if she wanted to talk, we would. I just hoped that whatever she had to say, it would put me more at ease than I have been.

I was still as paranoid as a schizophrenic sometimes, so I didn't go out as much as usual and always had my head on a swivel. Honestly, it was exhausting. The all-expense paid invitation Cedric extended to Vegas for Thanksgiving week was just what I needed to escape the anticipated misery of the approaching holiday.

We tore through every popular show, restaurant and club on the strip we could manage since Tuesday evening, and now he was tearing into my center in the penthouse of the MGM like Thanksgiving dinner. Even at almost twice my age, Cedric made a hell of a seat filler for Donovan.

His wealth, charm, sexual appetite and laid-back attitude made age totally irrelevant. I think everybody looks like somebody famous, and Cedric wasn't the exception. I don't know what Tina Knowles new husband's name is, but Cedric resembles a shorter, darker version of him.

I met him at the Cartier store while getting a battery changed in my watch, and his eyes were on me the instant I walked in. He was buying and asked me to help him decide between two watches. Afterwards, he asked me to dinner. My days had been filled with nothing but painting, decorating, gun range practice and training my guard dog, so I accepted.

He's turned out to be a great distraction from my worries, and I haven't ever enjoyed myself with a man like this outside of my previous professional obligations.

"So sweet," he said smacking his lips with a devious smirk as he lowered me down to eye level.

I simpered, swaying my dark tresses behind my shoulders, and kissed my juices from his lips licentiously. He released my legs so I could stand and wrapped his arms around my waist.

I was actually surprised and impressed by his stamina. I'm no slouch in the bedroom myself, but we had been going at it for a couple of hours with few breaks. He was fit and toned for a man in his fifties, but he was beating my kitty up like a man in his twenties.

"I'm glad you came with me," he spoke into my ear while licking the rim of my lobe.

"Oh. Believe me. I came a lot."

"No," he chuckled. "Not like that. With me to Vegas."

"*Ooh*," I grinned foolishly. "Me too. But now I need you to *cum* with me too," I teased shoving him playfully back towards the bed licking my lips.

I was still tipsy from the bottles of champagne and mixed drinks we consumed earlier. Cedric's private jet was scheduled to pick us up from North Las Vegas airport at 9 A.M., and all I wanted to do was screw these last hours in the city away before we fell asleep.

"Your wish is his command," he replied gesturing towards his stiffened tool before falling backwards onto the bed and splaying his arms wide.

Making sure my eyes never left his, I dipped my back, giving him the perfect view of my plump rump, and made his dick disappear down my throat like a magician. His face contorted with wayward pleasure as I slowly bobbed up and down, licking and slurping with every motion.

The effects of my own lewd behavior made my juices churn as my fingers massaged the aroused ache between my thighs. Cedric's open mouth drooled as he propped himself up on his elbows in admiration of my deep throating technique. He's the only one I've let inside my pink walls since I was shot, but I never gave him awesome top like this before.

I felt it was the least I could do for the good time he was showing me. At least it gave me good reason to miss Thanksgiving dinner at Uncle Jerry's. I had zero designs on eating with the skeleton crew that was going to show up. This was a crappy year as it was, and a dreary Thanksgiving dinner with all the missing heads was just going to be a reminder of that.

Mika was definitely not coming or bringing the boys. She hadn't been by Uncle Jerry's once since he decided to let Yasmin live there until she had the baby. I couldn't blame him since Yasmin needed somebody to tend to her while she was on bedrest, and nobody else was going to do it.

I'll tell you what though, the bad blood was still thick, and Mika would sooner see Yasmin on a gurney than at her father's house during a visit.

Val's been conveniently MIA since she turned into Diamond from *Player's Club*, so I doubted she went either. She was huffy and indignant when we last talked, so I'm sure she wasn't going to be warm and fuzzy even if she *did* come. I didn't even think our argument was that serious, but since she didn't give me her new cell number and hadn't called me, obviously it was.

Vic was visiting his fiancé Zaria's family in Memphis for the holiday, but he usually split his visits between his mom's house and Uncle Vernon anyway. With my Uncle gone, and the family drama brewing, he probably would've passed even if he didn't have other plans.

I heard Vanessa had a show at *The Tabernacle*, so she wasn't coming. She's still beefing with Aunt Di and Val, so if she did come, it would've only been to get under their skin and flaunt her new fame in Val's face.

That left my brother Mark, my mom, Aunt Di and Nicky to show up. My brother has spent the last four Thanksgiving's helping at the homeless shelter with *Hosea Feeds The Hungry* all day, so if he came, it wouldn't be until late.

My mother and Aunt Di were supposed to be cooking, and though they can throw down in the kitchen, that wasn't enough to erase my dread of going. It would've just been me, them, Uncle Jerry and Yasmin making awkward small talk since Nicky already said she wasn't coming.

She told Uncle Jerry she had to work, but that heifer's job wasn't open last Thanksgiving, so I knew she was lying about it being open this time. There wasn't actually any benefit in me snitching on her, so since I wasn't going, I just let her live.

It was probably the most pathetic Thanksgiving dinner *ever*, with everybody pussyfooting around Yasmin's over emotional ass. I love my cousin, and I'm glad she's still alive for me to even be able to judge her stupid ass, but I'm simply not here for Yasmin's victim act. I mean, she did get her ass whipped by Tamika, which she deserved, and she was stabbed by Malik, which was going too far, but she's not exactly innocent either.

She tried to justify her snaking around behind Tamika's back with Dub to me while she was recovering in the hospital, but most of it was a pile of bull. What she did was just as grimy as what Vanessa did to

Val, except worse, because now their kids were going to be cousins *and* half-siblings.

Yasmin was *still* up in Mika's face pretending to hate Dub and listening to Mika whine about his cheating, the whole time she was one of the tramps sneaking off to hotels with him.

They told me how Mika flipped out in the waiting room the day I got shot when she saw them there together. They weaseled their way out of getting caught that day, but Yasmin came clean to me that she was laid up in the hotel with Dub right before she got car jacked.

All these men out here they could've chose, and they picked their sister's men? No ma'am. That had to be on some type of "get back" in my opinion, and nobody can convince me otherwise. Valerie and Vanessa always had a sibling rivalry, and the same with Yasmin and Tamika.

I used to say we're all more like sisters than cousins, but if *this* is how sisters do each other, those tricks can keep their siblingship. I was about to say that at least with Mark, I don't have to worry about him sleeping with my man, but from what Donovan saw, maybe I do.

With everything that's happened in the last six months, it never seemed like the right time to ask my brother about Dana. I haven't seen him that much face to face and frankly, I've been too busy dealing with my own problems to worry about getting in his business.

I felt Cedric throbbing in my mouth, coming closer to climaxing, so I quickly climbed up on the bed and straddled him like a jockey. He cupped my large breasts with both hands while nursing one taught nipple like a newborn to its mother.

His length was hitting all the right spots, forcing me to balance myself with my hands planted firmly on his chest. Our bodies synchronized in the frenzied heat of sexing, he gripped my waist and flipped me on my back with force.

Burying his face in the crook of my neck with my legs now clamped together at the ankles behind his back, Cedric pummeled my sopping box with determination to bring us both to sexual bliss.

We groaned, grunted and emoted every animalistic noise our bodies commanded as I closed my eyes and rode the wave of my approaching orgasm. Every orifice convulsed simultaneously as I finally hit my peak and squealed into the air.

"Arrgggh!" Cedric roared right behind me, delivering two more powerful thrusts before all movement ceased.

I opened my eyes just in time to see his roll up into his head, his face strangely contorted, as his right hand gripped at his chest and his jaw went slack. I stared confusedly at him. Not sure what exactly I was witnessing.

"Cedric?" I called out, covering my mouth with a gasp as he teetered backwards, stiff as an ironing board, eyes glazed over, and hit the floor with a thud.

4

Vanessa

"You look familiar," the middle-aged black dude changing the front door locks stated while chewing his gum annoyingly like it was the last supper. "Are you a singer or an actress?"

"No," I replied trying to veil my impatience as I sat on a step near the bottom of the staircase scrolling IG from my phone.

The locksmith's attempts at small talk had been relentless, and at nearly three in the morning, I wasn't here for it. I usually love being recognized, but not while I'm trying to be incog-negro.

I wore my Prada cat eye shades, a plain black baseball cap with the bill hovering just above my eyebrows, and my purple hair was tightly wound into a bun at the back of my head. I needed to be inconspicuous, and I was happy he hadn't asked for any ID from me to change the locks since I was already inside when he arrived.

Regardless, for all the money I was paying his Forrest Whittaker looking ass to come out at this time in the morning, he needed to focus on changing all these locks instead of me. To keep him on task, I unashamedly held up the Gucci Plexiglas bracelet watch Gavin bought me for Christmas to view the time.

He took the hint and continued doing what I was paying him to do, but didn't stop running his mouth.

"I swear you look like somebody famous, but I just can't put my finger on it right now. I'm really good with faces, so it's going to keep bugging me until I figure it out. Maybe if you weren't wearing glasses I could tell. Do you get compared to any celebrities a lot?"

I was two seconds away from cussing this nosy fat bastard out, but thought better of it, knowing it would only defeat my purpose."

"No, I don't. Listen sir, it's really late and I'm not feeling too talkative at the moment if you don't mind," I answered, standing and brushing lint from my *Seven* jeans as I descended the steps.

"Oh, I'm sorry. I completely understand. Usually when I get called out like this, it's because somebody just got kicked out and whoever is changing the locks is pissed off."

I presume he was baiting me to get me to open up as to why I was having the locks changed myself, but he had the wrong one.

"How much longer do you have to go?" I asked yawning.

"I'm almost done."

"Good," I replied forcing a smile as I stepped away from the cold doorway and ran a warming hand up the side of my cashmere shirt.

"Vixen!" he exclaimed pointing a screwdriver towards me. "That's who you look like. That new singer who's sleeping with the producer who shot his wife."

He stared at me with a satisfied grin as my smile turned to a scowl faster than Jesus turned water to wine. If he was going to recognize me, he needed to put some respect on my name.

"Y'all resemble *a lot*. Maybe you're related?" he queried with a raised brow.

"No. I don't even know who that is," I retorted curtly.

He gazed at me suspiciously for a moment more, but quickly got the drift that he needed to get back to work. Clearing his throat, he tore his eyes from me and took some screws from his toolbox.

Sweeping the top row of my teeth with my tongue in irritation, I briskly stalked toward the kitchen mumbling the correction to myself.

"She's not his *wife* either."

Snatching the rubbing alcohol and cloth from the countertop, I cut through to the downstairs half-bath and closed the door behind me.

Without warning, a dreadful feeling overwhelmed me, and Val invaded my mind. Not only was I struggling to breathe, but I actually had to steady myself against the door as I closed my eyes to let it pass.

It was over almost as quickly as it came, but I still had to take a moment to collect myself. Something had to be going on with her, but I had no idea what, and I wasn't going to call to find out. Sometimes being a twin was a bitch. Simmering down, I sat the supplies on the edge of the sink, removed my jeans and relieved myself in the toilet.

I couldn't wait until my name was no longer synonymous with Delia's damn case. Her shooting dominated the news for months, and the only reason coverage had died down now is because her condition hadn't changed. Everyone seemed to be pulling for her full recovery, except me.

Leave it to me to shoot the luckiest hoe on earth. Not only had she survived a bullet at point blank range to her chest, but the thick brush below cushioned some of her rocky descent and landed her in the middle of a Boy Scout camping ground.

Good thing I went with my first mind and didn't look over the edge or I could've been seen. My only regret in hindsight is not shooting her in the head instead. She sustained severe head injuries, broke several bones, lost the baby, and has been in a coma for six months. The problem is, she's still not dead.

I read that there's usually brain damage when a person is comatose for more than four weeks, and she already had head injuries, but doctors haven't *officially* said that. Every day her heart beats puts my future at risk, so my anxiety's been at an all-time high waiting for her to croak.

Delia and Brand's followers have been holding vigil for her at the hospital like she's a major celebrity, so I went up there once just for damage control. I never got past the waiting room since her visitation list was limited to immediate family, but I made sure to shed tears for the cameras and feigned disappointment before I left.

The police questioned me for hours two days after her "accident" about my whereabouts on that day and my relationship with her and

Brand. I knew Brand was the one who pointed them towards me as a person of interest, but I wasn't going to let him off easily either.

I didn't hesitate to throw his rapist ass under the bus right beside me. I showed the cops the explicit texts and pictures sent between us in my phone and explained that he was *my* man *first.* We just never stopped seeing each other.

Tabloids stirred the rumor mill with speculation about us long before Delia was shot, so admitting to it couldn't sully my reputation any more than it already had. Furthermore, I snitched on his harem of hos I knew he screwed from coast to coast too.

I didn't even think about telling the cops what he did to me at the studio because I knew it would be pointless. It would just be my word against his, and he would make sure to ruin my career before it even got off the ground.

I've had nightmares about that night and how he forced himself on me, and each time I woke up in tears with vengeance on my mind. I hoped they would eventually nail Brand for Delia's attempted murder since I used a gun I stole from his desk draw at the studio to shoot his preggo bride to be.

I hoped he had it registered so it would come up in a police search that he owned a gun the same caliber as the one that shot Delia. Unfortunately, no such finding had been leaked to the media thus far, so I could only speculate that the gun had been dirty.

Just to fuck with him, I told the cops that Brand suspected the baby wasn't his and that he expressed to me how angry he would be if she confirmed it. Of course, that was all a lie. I knew from the way he shut me down when I even *suggested* the thought that he didn't question the baby's paternity. But, so what.

My grieving state of mind on the day of my father's funeral, and my attendance as an alibi panned out well for me during my interrogation. For the first time in ages, I was grateful to be an identical twin.

Us dressing somewhat alike for the funeral and my plain Jane look after crying most of my makeup off, made me look more like Valerie, and played up our twin-ship. We both wore dark sunglasses, and I took my purple extensions out that morning, so people probably got us mixed up there.

I doubted anyone knew I ever left, but once I was back, I made sure people saw us both in the same room, at the same time too for good measure.

Val still snubbed me with her childish self, but one of the drawbacks of being identical twins is the involuntary emotional connection we share. Believe it or not, I *do* love my sister. Our relationship with my mother is very different, but we were both Daddy's girls, so I know how bad losing daddy hurt.

I almost stepped outside of myself and attempted to make amends, but her grimacing face as I approached, changed my mind. I know what I did with Brent was foul, but what *should've* mattered was that he took the bait. Engaged or not, Valerie knew her relationship with him was weak *way* before she caught us together.

She didn't appreciate or even want most of the money and gifts he showered her with, and if Brent actually cared about her, he would've found out what she really wanted instead. But he didn't. He just supplemented the love he claimed he had for her with monetary stuff, which I was too happy to take off of her hands.

I think Brent was just in the market for a pretty, low maintenance, submissive wife to bare his children, and Valerie fit the bill. She ignored all of the red flags me and my cousins tried to point out to her when she moved back here from New York.

If you ask me, she was just going through the motions like she does everything else in her life. Except dancing. She's always been docile, introverted and naïve. She didn't even know that Brent was doing coke and probably still doesn't.

You know, when we were young, *I* was always the one protecting her and making sure nobody took advantage of her good nature. Yeah, we rolled tight with my cousins, and my brother Victor would mop the streets with anybody threatening me or Valerie. But when it was just the two of us, I was the defender.

I'm the one who spoke up for her when she was too shy to speak up for herself. *I'm* the one who encouraged her to coax my parents to let her take the African Jazz class that led her to her dance career. *Nobody* had her back like me. *Nobody* knew her like me, and nobody ever will.

I don't care how close she is to Amina or to anybody else, they'll never share the twin telepathy we have sometimes, or the emotional link our DNA gave us. Without me, she's just prey to the vultures in this world. She's already proved it by letting some skank convince her that stripping is a good career for a classically trained dancer.

I know my mother was probably nursing a mental breakdown when she found that out. Not her golden child! That was something she would expect *me* to do, but not her precious Valerie.

Even though *my* career is the one that's popping now, my mother still looks down her petty nose at me. She called interrogating me a couple of days after the funeral like she had a badge under her nighty because *E! News* mentioned me while talking about Delia.

She didn't even pretend to care how I was holding up after losing my father. The first words out of her mouth were, "Vanessa. I'm sitting here watching *E! News* and they're talking about you. Please tell me you weren't sleeping with Delia's fiancé too? Lord child. Are you seeking out other women's men? They saying that man might have killed her for you."

I was so livid that I didn't even bother to entertain her chastising. I hung up, turned my phone off and went about painting my toenails like I had been doing before her call.

Keeping it real, Delia's near death was the best thing that ever happened to my career. The publicity on me was crazy. My latest song, *"Take Your Man,"* was all about me telling another woman I could steal her guy. Ironically, it mirrored the real-life drama people speculated was going on between Delia and I.

Radio and television talk shows wanted me on for controversy, and just like that, my song was in heavy rotation. At first, Black Twitter and

Delia's fans tried to drag me on the net, attacking me with meme's and #ShootYourMan tweets parodying my #TakeYourMan ones.

I clapped back on a lot of them in the beginning, but after a while, I just ignored their antics. What was more important was that whether people loved or hated me, *I* was trending. Suddenly, rappers and singers with star power wanted to work with me, and I welcomed the popularity.

When I heard that nine-time Grammy winner, Gavin The God wanted to work with me, I was ecstatic. We started working on a couple of songs in August, and by September, not only were we an item, but our new song, *"Top Shelf"* was blazing up the charts like wildfire.

Shortly afterwards, negotiations to leave *Brand Good* were set in motion considering the recent tensions between me and Brand. It wasn't a smooth transition, but a deal was made, and in October, I became the latest artist on Gavin's label, *Kingdom.*

For the first time in a long time, everything in my life has been falling into place. I've got two current radio hits, my name and face are ringing bells in the industry, and Gavin and I are the new *"It"* couple in R&B and Hip Hop.

I haven't felt this way about a man since my last serious boyfriend before Brand in 2000. Of course, my feelings aren't all the way in, because I don't believe in that anymore. But it feels good to have my own man to claim who publicly claims me for a change.

When we're not working separately, we're inseparable. I'm at his place more than I'm at my own most of the time. So much that he gave me a key and the security code to his house so that I can move freely in case he's not home.

The only relationship thorn in my side has been his baby's momma Daphne. He broke up with her early last summer, but the way she tries me and flirts with him constantly lets me know she wants him back.

Daphne's a decent looking tall woman with some Tyra Banks features that she tries to play up with make-up and long hair weave. She doesn't hold a candle to me, but she doesn't seem to realize that when we're in same company.

Their four-year-old son Davin is the spitting image of his chocolate drop daddy, with dark eyebrows, big brown eyes, a defined jaw and a deep chestnut complexion. He has a few facial features from his salty momma too. Luckily for him, she's mostly ugly on the *inside.*

She's always using the boy to try to manipulate Gavin. I swear, Daphne calls about everything she can, and uses every excuse in the book to get an ounce of his attention. If Davin sneezes too hard, she's calling or texting Gavin like the kid has Typhoid so he can come over.

It irks me like nothing else.

"Miss!" the locksmith called outside the bathroom door, snapping me from my thoughts while washing my hands. "I just wanted to let you know that I'm done."

"Okay. I'll be out in a minute," I told him saturating the cloth on the sink with rubbing alcohol.

I made sure to wipe down everything I touched and did the same with the doorknob when I exited. Forest handed me the keys to the locks as I approached him. I took the wad of money from my back pocket to pay him and put the keys in there in its place.

"Thank you for coming out," I told him at the door as he retrieved the rest of his tools from the porch.

"You're welcome. Here's my card if you ever need my services again. *24 Hour Locks,*" he replied handing the card to me with a polite grin. "You have a good night."

"You too," I retorted closing the door behind him.

Exhaling hard, I scanned the interior of Daphne's quaint little four-bedroom home from the foyer laced with envy and disdain. The decorations were gaudy, incongruent and tasteless in my opinion, but it still put my little apartment to shame.

I got the alcohol and cloth from the bathroom and proceeded to wipe down every lock, knob, door, bannister and surface I or the locksmith touched while we were here. I paused momentarily, mentally playing back my movements, and nodded to myself. Satisfied that I hadn't left any evidence that could be traced back to me, I checked my Movado, ready to leave.

Meandering down the hallway, I scrutinized the various framed pictures covering the wall with a snarl. Daphne's vanity was so apparent, and though she's pretty, Gavin definitely upgraded when he started dating me. There were more pictures of her around the house than of Davin.

I would understand it if she was a new mom, but the boy is four years old. What mom has more pictures of herself in her house than of her own kid? One photo particularly incensed me, and there was no way in hell I was leaving with it still intact.

Gavin's smiling face agitated me as he stood shirtless in white linen pants, embracing a pregnant Daphne, dressed in a flimsy, white linen dress. They were facing each other on a sandy beach somewhere at sun set, looking like the cover of a romance novel.

I sneered at their portrait and turned around, looking for something to smash it with. Marching out of the hallway into the great room, I snatched the statue of a dolphin from the mantel and stomped back to the picture.

I felt like Daphne's jovial expression was mocking me, therefore, her stupid face was my first target. The glass shattered in the frame and the picture shifted, now hanging on by one hook instead of two. Swinging at it with the full force of my jealousy, I smashed it until the picture lay beside the fragmented glass on the floor.

My adrenaline flowing, I decided not to stop there. Recalling how pissed Brent was when Valerie plowed through his wall of expensive paintings, I thought I would evoke the same emotions from Daphne.

Every framed picture in my path was demolished as I attempted to avoid being cut by flying shards in the process. I was delighted that a few of my swings dented the plaster on the walls too, since damaging her property was my ultimate goal.

When I was finally out of targets, I paused with the statue in my hand, bent over, out of breath and sapped. Once recomposed, I carefully made my way through the destruction, wiped my prints from the statue, and placed it back on the mantle.

Looking over my handy work from the foyer, I laughed maniacally, imagining her appall when she came home to this mess. That is, whenever she could actually get back inside the house at all. This'll teach that heifer not to brag so much.

I was livid when I found out via *MEDIATAKEOUT* that Gavin bought Daphne this house last month. I understood his reasoning once he explained it to me, but the fact that he didn't tell me in advance still hurt. He didn't like the high crime neighborhood Daphne's mom lived in.

Since Daphne and Davin were living there after they split, he worried about Davin's safety. By default, he felt like he needed to take care of Daphne too, to ensure his son was out of harm's way. If she hadn't already been taunting me on social media with digs meant to make me jealous, I might not have cared about the house. But she was.

She couldn't wait to flaunt her new come up with tag lines blatantly claiming Gavin would always love and take care of her. She was doing the *absolute* most to agitate me, and it was working.

I was already lucky I hadn't been arrested and jailed for the fire or Delia as yet, so I couldn't react as aggressively as I wanted to. Still, what I wasn't going to do, was take another female trying to make me feel inferior lightly. What I *would* do, is destroy her property just for my own amusement.

Alcohol and cloth in hand, I used the cloth to press the buttons and rearm the alarm with the new code I changed it to. My thick, long sleeve cashmere shirt wasn't doing much to shield me from the winter wind, so I hurriedly trotted to my car at the end of the driveway and got in quickly.

Tossing everything into the passenger's seat, I blew into my palms and cranked the heat on high as soon as I started my BMW. Her neighborhood was still asleep and there wasn't a single sign of life besides me on the street.

Her house is nestled on a rural street in an affluent area of Brookhaven where I imagined people named Carol and Mike Brady probably lived and walked their dogs. If it was me, I would've expected a mini mansion from a man who owned an estate with servants. If I ever pop out any rug rats for Gavin, he will definitely be catering to me.

Yawning, I strapped myself in and put my car in gear, preparing for the 20-minute ride back to Gavin's. I was as sleepy as a Seventh Dwarf, but if I wasn't there when he arrived back from L.A., I was going to have some explaining to do.

5

Valerie

Maaco swaggered in as I held the door open while rubbing my chilled arms and stifled a yawn. Courtney was having loud, obnoxious sex in her room upstairs, and the thin walls of her house made sure we knew it.

Locking the cold out behind him, I caught his lustful stare raising from my partially exposed butt cheeks. Playfully pulling the hem of my Cami down over my matching cotton panties, I sleepily led Maaco to my downstairs bedroom.

It was a little after eleven in the morning, but that was early for me to be up given the night I just had. With the blinds still drawn and the overcast outside, the house was dim. Maaco draped his winter coat over the armchair in my room, kicked off his Jordan's and began undressing under the weak light from my window.

Launching myself on the bed, I crawled back under the covers and sunk into the warm spot I recently vacated.

"You worked?" his baritone voice inquired as he slid in bed clad only in boxers, spooning his hard body against my backside.

I grunted confirmation, spinning to face him and snuggling into his embrace. Shutting my eyes tightly, I was ready to drift back into slumber, but he kept talking.

"I missed you," he continued, kissing my lobe, then gently taking it in his mouth.

"Uh uh. I'm tired," I whined half-heartedly as each kiss coaxed me further and further out of my desire to sleep.

"Aww. I've been gone all week. Are you sure you're too tired for me?" he grumbled into my ear before his tongue molested it.

"*Maaaaaco*," I cooed feeling my nipples harden while my body involuntarily grinded into the swell in his boxers.

"Didn't you miss me?"

"Mm hmm."

"I know you did. I missed you too."

My head fell back, exposing my neck as his tongue sensually attacked the crook of it until I winced.

He stopped instantly and I felt his hard gaze on me without even opening my eyes. His fingers gently traced my throat before I grimaced again and opened my eyes.

"What happened here?"

The Ibuprofen I took when I got home had worn off and I imagine the contusions on my light complexion were even more visible now than before.

"Brent saw me at the club."

"And what? Are you telling me Mr. Harmless, did this to you?"

Inhaling deeply, I nodded, allowing shame to control my emotions. The *new* Valerie is supposed to be strong and confident. The *new* Valerie isn't supposed to be getting assaulted at work by her Ivy League ex-fiancé. The *new* Valerie is supposed to be in control of her life. *Supposed to*, being the key words.

"We got into an argument and he tried to choke me," I answered leaning back against the headboard.

"In the club? What was security doing?" he carped touching my face and inspecting the damage more closely.

"There was a brawl on the main floor that had the whole club scattering. They were handling that when he caught me in the hallway to the dressing room."

He sat up in the bed, rubbing the top of his head with one hand and looked back at me in dismay. Maaco warned me that Brent's stalking meant he wasn't as innocuous as I claimed, but I had shrugged it off.

I never thought Brent would physically hurt me before tonight. Clearly, that was just one more thing about my ex-fiancé that I was delusional about.

This was one reason I was afraid to open up fully to Maaco. For all intents and purposes, we were not a couple and could rightfully see whomever else we choose. If I had been so vastly disconnected with someone I was going to marry, what did that say about my relationship skills?

I didn't feel ready to commit to anyone else anymore and I didn't have a guess as to when I would. Maaco and I have history, and he's been fully transparent about his feelings for me, but risking falling down the rabbit hole again was terrifying.

"Explain to me what happened."

I ran my tongue across my top teeth and aggravatedly recapped the events. Maaco's eyes stayed silently fixed on me, but the veins visibly tensing in his neck and his clenched jaw spoke volumes. He didn't speak until I stopped talking.

"You got these bruises on your neck and your left eye is red like you burst a vessel in it. I know you don't just expect me to let this go. Where does this bitch-made nigga live?"

I dropped my gaze abashedly and looked off with a shrug. I didn't want Maaco to get locked up for beating Brent up in my defense, but I did kind of enjoy his protective nature. He reminded me a lot of my father in that way, and I missed my daddy.

"It's already handled. Pauly got him off of me before he did any real damage and he ended up getting arrested anyway. I'm fine. Really. It was scary for minute, but I'm fine," I pled touching his face.

Maaco had been up to the club enough times to know some of the bouncers, and some of them worked alternating nights at the strip club Jamie owned across town.

"You're not *fine*. He needs me to jam my fist down his throat and you need to stop working at that club if they can't provide proper security for you."

"It wasn't that. Pauly slammed his face into the wall a couple of times when he pulled him off me. You should've heard Brent threatening to sue with a busted lip and blood in his mouth before he got arrested. He sounded like a kid with a lisp," I grinned trying to lighten the mood. It didn't work.

"I told you that dude was crazy. Arrested or not, if I get a chance to get my hands on him, it's going to be lights-out for that pussy," he huffed pinching his bottom lip between his thumb and index finger in vexed contemplation.

"Well, hopefully he'll have this whole weekend in jail to think about what he did unless his lawyers are good enough to get him out sooner. I really just want him to leave me alone and live his life. I don't want to see him, and he shouldn't want to see me," I said before a thud overhead startled me into a yelp. "What the hell?"

It sounded like Courtney and her guest either fell on the floor or knocked something over in the heat of passion. I would have been worried if not for the fact that their moans only got progressively louder.

"Damn," I whispered with an envious frown and the bud between my legs throbbing at the thought of what they were doing. "They're really going at it."

Maaco rubbed the back of his head and exhaled as my mind, and vision shifted down to the flaccid, but still ample knot in his boxers. He may have been engrossed in thoughts about retaliating against Brent, but now that I was fully awake, I just wanted to feel as good as Courtney was feeling.

"I'm *o-kay* baby," I reiterated getting up on my knees, grabbing his muscular arms, and wrapping them around my waist. "I promise. I'm fine. But I could be better."

Cupping his face, I placed my mouth on his frowning lips, and force fed him my tongue. He reciprocated immediately. We hungrily devoured each other through groans, groping and gyrations as he removed my Cami and panties with skill.

Inserting two fingers between my folds, with his tongue dancing over my breasts, he massaged my pulsing walls and kneaded my taught pearl with his thumb.

Moans escaped my mouth into his as I pushed him back on the bed, still humping his fingers. Lowering my face to his crotch, I tugged at his boxers until his rod sprang out and into my mouth.

"*Yeeeah!*" he sibilated closing his eyes and thrusting deeper into my throat. "*Ohhhh.* Just like that," he coached with one hand on the top of my head.

As of late, I was enjoying giving oral sex as much as I did receiving. I've never been a head doctor, though I've done it in previous relationships, but it was always a chore I did my best to avoid.

I especially dreaded giving oral when I was with Brent. His dick was long and thick with a deep curve that usually triggered my gag reflexes before I even got mid-shaft. His disgusted attitude with my novice abilities made me so insecure that I didn't even want to attempt it most times.

Since my evolution over the last six months, I'm no longer too timid to try. I googled techniques, watched some porn stars at work on video and started practicing on a dildo I bought from a sex shop. Once I understood what was required of me, learned to relax my throat and my mind, I started trying it on Maaco.

Judging from the loads of unborn children he's since released into my mouth, I've learned very well. I kind of enjoy the control it gives me over his pleasure, and his confirmation of my skills strokes my ego the way his fingers were now stroking my clit.

Just as my mouth picked up a steady rhythm, he grabbed me by the waist and turned me until we were in a sixty-nine with my dripping center over his face. His lips French kissed my lower ones while I tried not to lose focus on my task and his dick punished my tonsils.

Electricity shot through my core as he suckled and lapped my folds while strumming my clit. Just as I felt an orgasm building, his large hands grasped my ass tightly and spread my cheeks wide for his tongue to thrash and slurp a trail from my pussy to my chocolate star.

I started pulling away immediately. That was unchartered territory that I wasn't sure I wanted him to explore now, or ever. Even the thought of him putting his huge member or anything inside my anus had me spooked.

"Umm umm. Umm umm," he protested clenching me in place with his hands as his tongue stiffened against my sphincter and penetrated it slow and deep.

My back now arched, I couldn't deny the euphoric feeling it induced.

"Oh my God Maaco!" I cried out as he alternated between tonguing both holes and licking a slippery path in between.

The sounds of our sloppy foreplay and lustful moans reverberated through the room, and probably the house, until he finally brought me to a shrieking climax.

As soon as I regained my faculties, I was determined to make him feel as good as he made me. I resumed licking his girth through my spasms with vigor. Trailing my lips from the base of his shaft to the tip of his mushroom, I plunged my mouth down onto his tool and consecutively milked it with both hands.

Maaco pumped his hips faster in and out of my mouth and I could feel him thickening with his natural elixir. The flesh inside my cheeks was getting raw, but I sucked until he finally exploded a flood of semen with a guttural growl.

When his seeds subsided, I licked the remnants away and rolled off of him and onto my back. Through my own heavy panting, I noticed the silence upstairs. Courtney and her guest must've finally spent themselves too.

"I swear you tried to suck the soul out of me?" Maaco jibed through bated breaths.

"Something like that," I laughed shutting my eyes while I steadied my breathing.

Before I knew it, I was jolted awake by pounding on my room door. Somehow, I fell asleep, and apparently Maaco had too because his eyes shot open just like mine had.

"What?" I yelled wiping sleep from my eyes while Maaco stretched and tried blinking himself alert.

"Brian's blocked in. Can your man come move his car please?" Courtney bellowed from the other side of the door.

I sucked my teeth with a sigh as he climbed over me getting out of bed.

I glanced at the late afternoon time on the clock and cleared my throat.

"Okay. Give us a second."

"I put that ass to sleep huh?" Maaco quipped putting on his sweats and boots as I got up grinning and getting my robe from behind the door.

"Hmph. You were sleeping too sir."

"Because you fell asleep. Snoring all hard an everything. I didn't want to wake you up, so I went to sleep too."

"Whatever," I scoffed. "I know you're lying now."

"You were."

He pulled me in for a kiss before I could protest further, and when we broke, I licked my thumb to wipe my dried juices from the circumference of his mouth.

"What are you doing?"

"I'm all over your face." I smirked.

"Oh. I'm a messy eater," he laughed patting my butt before retrieving his keys from his coat pocket.

We played grab ass as I squealed and swat at his hands walking the hall towards the front room. My eyes involuntarily rolled when we came up on Courtney with her back to us, clad only in lace panties and a tank top.

Maaco had seen her in way less at *The Man Trap* before, but I still hated her lack of modesty when she knew my man... well, my *company*, was in the house.

"Hey," I greeted her and Brian, who was leant up against the front door typing on his phone.

He was regular company for Courtney, so I knew him by name and by sight. Brian was easy on the eyes and easy to remember. He stood six feet with a clean-shaven caramel complexion, and a black ski hat pulled down to his ears. His ginger brown eyes were focused on his phone, but he grunted a hello and shoved it in the pocket of his black bomber.

"My bad," Maaco said to both of them, passing me and dapping Brian up at the door. "I wasn't even thinking when I pulled in."

"No problem," Brian answered pulling keys from the front pocket of his jeans. "Hit me later Fox," he told Courtney as he opened the door.

He never called her anything but Fox or Black Fox, which let me know their connection was made through the strip club because that's her stage name. Her bedroom's been a revolving door of suitors, but I saw Brian the most. I think it's because she likes him best.

Just then, a familiar-faced pretty, butter scotch bombshell came strutting downstairs in a thigh-high peach dress and high heels. She was a tall buxom chick I recognized as a sometimes dancer at the club. I looked at Courtney curiously and she returned a mischievous grin before sticking her tongue out lasciviously.

"Bye Brian. Hey Maaco. Funny seeing you here. Long time no see," she greeted with something slick in her smile that I didn't like.

I almost caught whiplash when she said my man's… Maaco's name. The way she instantly sized me up let me know they were more than casual acquaintances and I felt self-conscious standing before her looking tousled. Brian tossed up two fingers on his way out, but Maaco totally ignored her.

"Val, this is Capri. Capri this is Val," Courtney introduced, fingering a track in her weave and oblivious to the building tension.

"Hi," I greeted dryly as her eyes dissected me.

"How long did Uber say it was going to be?" Courtney asked.

"Like ten minutes. Val. Yeah, I know you. Angel, right? I've seen you a couple of times on nights I've danced at TMT before. You wear wings and dance all bougie," she added placing one heavily ringed hand on her hip still looking me up and down. "You and Maaco look real cozy. Are y'all supposed to be like... A thing?"

I craned my neck and returned her audacity. Who the hell was this strange THOT questioning me? I was working off of barely five hours of sleep and I so didn't have time for random crap from random women right now.

"Why?"

"Why? Bitch, because I asked is why."

"*Bitch?*" Courtney and I sang in unison.

"Hold on now girl. Why're you poppin' off on my homegirl? Chill out," Courtney asserted stepping in between us protectively.

Capri sucked her teeth at and turned her loathing gaze back to me.

"Whatever Fox. If she was any kind of *real* woman, she would make sure he sees his son."

6

Yasmin

I swear my life was starting to play out like a cheesy *Lifetime* movie. Malik hadn't actually tried to harm me, but the hate in his eyes staring back at me, and the fact that he hadn't fled Georgia certainly left the door open.

It took me hours to calm totally down from my bout of hysteria, even after Daddy searched the perimeter with his Smith and Wesson and called the police. I was in disbelief that Malik had resurfaced after all of this time. Albeit to retrieve the motorcycle I discovered my dad was supposed to repair for him last spring, he was *still* back.

The police didn't do anything but repeat what Daddy had already done, get my statement and update the APB that was out on Malik already. Once they left, I dragged myself to the shower to wash away my tears and shed the humiliation of soiling my pajamas.

I had no one. Well, I had my father, but he wasn't enough. Six months ago, I could've called either of my sisters or cousins and cried till my heart's content into their phones. Now, I knew I would either get their voicemails or end up being the only one talking.

Even more hurtful was Dwayne's lack of concern. He hadn't called back or tried to come over after Daddy took the phone from me and confirmed what was going on. I was the mother of his child for Christ's sake. Didn't he care?

The more obstacles I hurdled alone during this pregnancy, the more foolish I felt for getting myself in this predicament. I was truly feeling stupider by the minute for ever drinking the Kool-Aid and even half-way believing the things Dwayne said to me at the hotel that day.

"I ain't never want no woman like I want you before. Wit' yo' sexy ass," Dwayne grinned making me blush. "We so different. But you pro-lly jus' what I need."

"You make me do things I never thought I would do before. It's like with you ... I can be who I am without worrying about you judging me. I wish we could just run away together and never look back," I told him raising on one elbow and looking him in the eyes.

"Shawty you know we can't do that," he replied placing one finger gently below my chin. "But as for judging you ... nah, judging is for people who think they betta' than the next man, ya' feel me? I'own care where a man or woman's at in they life right now ... They eat, shit and die just like e'rybody else. Ya' feel me Shawty?

But you and me on another level tho'. We got somethin' can't nobody else recreate. You know I ain't no mushy kinda dude. I'own say I love no chicks easy or nothing but ... I got love for you Shawty. More than anybody else 'cept for my kids."

Pshh! He had a strange way of showing it. I was definitely regretting sacrificing my marriage for Dwayne now, but I wouldn't have Sophie growing inside me if I hadn't. Maybe Dwayne had a good reason for not calling me back or coming to see me right now. Maybe he didn't want to ruffle my father's feathers by coming by so early in the morning.

Emotionally drained, miserable and hungry, I climbed in bed laying on top of the duvet, eating a turkey leg with a butcher knife tucked under my pillow just in case Malik came back to finish me off.

Daddy eventually went back to bed, and I spent the rest of the wee hours in the morning sobbing softly about any and everything while watching old episodes of *Law & Order* and finally crying myself to sleep.

"Wake up Auntie," an impish whisper cajoled as I was shaken awake by the shoulder.

Dazed and unsure if I was dreaming, I opened my eyes, reaching under my pillow for the knife before focusing on the beaming four-year-old face of my nephew.

"Waynie?"

"Hi Auntie!"

He shouted way too close to my face for him to be so loud. But I didn't mind. I couldn't believe he was actually here in the flesh and I was ecstatic to see him after so many months. Struggling to sit up, I scooted to the edge of the bed and hugged him as tightly as I could around my stomach, and kissed his chubby cheeks.

"*Heeeey* baby! What are you doing here?"

"We came to see Papa," he replied revealing a snaggle tooth smile with his eyes fixed on my extended belly. "You got fat Auntie Yas. Your belly's big like Santa's."

I tittered and hugged him against my stomach again as he tried wrapping his tiny arms around my waist. I really did miss my little munchkin, and like almost everything made me do now that I was pregnant, I started tearing up.

The only difference is that for the first time in half a year, they were tears of joy.

"I'm fat because I'm carrying a baby in my tummy. I don't think Santa has the same excuse. You're going to have a little cousin soon."

"Oooh! A baby! Miss Laura's fat with a baby too, except her baby kicks a lot. She let me feel it one time."

"Who's Miss Laura?"

"My teacher."

"Your *teacher?*" I questioned playfully, realizing that he would've started kindergarten this past August. "Oh my goodness. I forgot you're a big boy now. I can't believe you're going to school already," I tried cloaking my dejected feelings with a smile as he nodded proudly, teetering back and forth on his heels.

I had always been involved in the boys first days of school. Even when I was still a teenager myself. I was the one taking pics of them in their new clothes and helping Tamika see them off. It hurt my heart that I missed Waynie's first day of kindergarten and I resented her keeping the boys away from seeing me this long too.

"Does the baby make you sick?"

"Sometimes. Why?" I asked perplexed.

"Because you don't come see us no more. Mommy said it's 'cause you're sick. But you don't look sick. Are you better now?"

I tongued the inside of my cheek and shook my head at Tamika's pettiness. I'm sick huh? Sick of her crap.

"Yes. I *am* better. Did you miss me?" I asked, reaching out and tickling him under his arms as he squirmed and chortled.

"Yes! Yes! I missed you!"

"You want to feel something?"

Waynie nodded and came closer as I took one of his hands and placed it on my stomach over my nightgown. "Do you feel that? You feel that moving? That's your little cousin Sophie."

"Soapy!" he yelled into my belly, gently patting my stomach.

"So-*fee*," I sounded it out. "Named after your great-great-grandmother. She's going to be your Cousin Sophie."

"*Hiiii* Cousin *Sophie*," he repeated. "When you come out, me, and you, and Niko are gonna play, okay? But I run fast so you can't catch me, but I'll come back. Kamari, he don't play wit' us little kids, but he might come look at you."

Sophie thumped the area under his hand and delivered some additional kicks to my bladder that awakened my frequent urge to pee.

"I feel it! Soapy kicked my hand Auntie!" he shrieked snatching his hand away and giggling wide eyed with his palm splayed. "Right there! She kicked my hand right - there!" he prattled.

Waynie's mini dreads flung around his little head as he bounced up and down and I basked in his glee. I really loved kids and couldn't wait until my little one was born for me to hold.

"Her name is So-fee, baby. Not Soapy," I laughed. "Are Niko and Kamari here too?"

"Niko is," Tamika replied insipidly from the doorway, causing me to involuntarily jump in surprise.

"Oh my God. I didn't see you there," I replied with a hand to my chest.

"Kamari didn't want to come."

"You're looking good," I offered trying to break her icy front while raking my mane with my fingers as I often did when nervous.

No words left her glossed lips as she leered at me with a hand on her hip and an elbow leaned against the doorframe. If she intended to look intimidating, she succeeded. Her eyes dropped from mine to my stomach, then back again with a look of repulsion filling them.

She actually looked better than I'd seen her look in a long time. Either she dropped 15 or 20 pounds in the last six months, or the black-on-black turtleneck and leggings she wore gave that illusion. She was still thick and curvy, but maybe a size or two smaller and definitely more toned.

Her hair was neatly coiled into thick Bantu knots and huge silver bangles hung from her ears, complimenting her round face. My sister had always been pretty, but her snarling expression distorted her face as she plucked at her stiletto nails like she wanted to stab me with them.

"Mommy, Auntie Yas has a baby in there like Miss Laura. My cousin Soapy," Waynie whooped running to her and pointing at my belly with a wide grin.

"Umph. Your *cousin* huh?" she answered cutting her eyes at me. "Go downstairs with Papa and Niko baby."

"*Nooo* Mommy? I just got here," he complained poking his bottom lip out. "Wanna touch Soapy kicking?"

"No. I don't. Now do what I say. Go downstairs. Papa's making grilled cheese sandwiches too. You said you were hungry right?"

He nodded, then turned to me.

"You comin' Auntie Yas?"

It felt good to be wanted. I loved my little munchkin.

"I'll be down shortly honey."

Tamika watched him trotting down the hall before directing her attention back to me.

"He's gotten so big," I stated, deciding to try another affable route in hopes she would bite.

She dismissed my statement with a huff and stepped inside the room to lean against the dresser.

"So, listen. Daddy wanted to see the boys, and I decided to stop punishing him, and them, just because *you're* here. Seriously, I've been walking around hotter than fish grease at how you and Dub did me, and you know what? I need some answers. I *deserve* some answers. And I decided, *you're* going to give them to me," she stated as a matter of fact.

My heart pounded with alarm and I watched her apprehensively, knowing how irate Tamika could become if the conversation didn't go her way. I was nervous about protecting myself and my unborn from the unpredictable beast that was my sister.

"What you acting all jumpy for?" she furrowed her brows like I was already getting on her nerves.

"The last time I saw you, you tried to knock my teeth down my throat. How did you expect me to act?"

She rolled her eyes and smirked.

"How did *you* expect *me* to act when I found out my, 'holier than thou', baby sister, was doing my man? Believe me Yasmin, I didn't do half as much as I wanted to do to you, *because* you're my sister. Malik wasn't the only one mad enough to kill you. He's still not."

It hurt that she could talk about me being stabbed so casually, as if I hadn't actually almost died. As if I wasn't still suffering from my estranged husband's assault every day. I was wrong to cheat with my sister's man, and I own that, but I don't deserve to die for it.

My guilty eyes glared at her as I massaged my pregnant belly and thought about the knife I was hiding under my pillow. Sister or not, if she made a move on me today, I was going to gut her like a trout.

The funny thing is, she reacted *exactly* how I thought she would if she found out. Which is why I never intended for it to happen in the first place.

"I have kids with that man Yasmin. We were living together. Why, of all the guys out here you could've cheated on Malik with, did you choose him?" she questioned angling her head accusingly.

I wanted to remind her that only one of her three was biologically his, but thought better when I saw the rabid look in her eyes.

"I didn't. I didn't plan on cheating on Malik. *Especially* not with Dwayne. It just… Happened."

She threw her hands in the air and laughed sarcastically.

"Oh, *'especially not with Dwayne'* huh?" she mocked. "You're a piece of work."

Obviously, nothing I had to say was going to be right, but I didn't see how apologizing could go wrong. So, I tried that.

"I'm sorry Tamika. I know I've said it before, but I really am. I swear I never meant to hurt you *or* Malik. I… I jus—"

She raised her hand cutting me off and exhaled like she was trying to control her anger.

"Don't even try it. You didn't give a single, solitary, remorseful fuck about hurting us. You know how I know? Because you sat up in my face day in and out, talking about, *'Tamika you deserve so much better than that low life drug dealer.' 'You know he's cheating on you.'* Skank," she admonished, spitting my former advice to her back at me derisively.

"The whole time, your bougie ass was telling me to dump my man, *you* were creeping with him behind my back."

"Tamika, he was cheating with other women way before me. You know that. I was wrong. Yes. We all know I was wrong. But it's not like it *started* with me," I was fed up with being the scapegoat for all of his cheating.

Her eyes bucked and her head snaked indignantly with attitude.

"Oh *really?* So, you just figured, what harm would *one more* random pussy in the mix do, right? Forget that I'm your sister. Forget that you were *married.* Forget that he's the father of your nephew! Right? Right!" she spat aggressively, now hovering over me.

Her expression eerily resembled Malik's maniacal one when I peered at him through the kitchen window. It was a tortured brand of hate. One with roots derived solely from my affair with Dwayne. Still, as remorseful as I was for what I had done. I wasn't going to continue to shoulder all the blame for what Dwayne and I had done *together*.

"Listen Tamika. He came on to *me*. I didn't go after him. I would never have gone after him. I didn't even think he was my type. I was in a messed-up headspace and… And he was giving me attention I wasn't getting at home.

Malik and I were going through it. I didn't tell anybody, because I was embarrassed, but… He cheated on me. Malik cheated on me with one of our clients, and I found out."

Malik claimed he merely kissed the woman he stepped out on me with, but I didn't believe it, and needed to embellish, whether it was true or not. The chances of Malik ever being able to refute my claims was slim, and I had to say whatever was necessary to support my actions to my sister.

"I was angry. I was hurt. I was irrational. I wanted to pay him back. I wanted to feel… Desirable again. I don't know. I wanted *a lot* of things. I should've rejected him when he came onto me, but, I was vulnerable. For whatever reason, that day, Dwayne—"

"*Dwayne?* Why do you keep calling him Dwayne? What are you, *too good* to call him Dub like everybody else? Tuh! You know what? I'm so sick of you always acting like you're so morally high and mighty. Better than me," she fumed poking me in the shoulder, causing me to flinch.

"No, I don't. I never thought I was better than you. I just thought you could do better than you gave yourself credit for. I still do. And, me calling him Dwayne is just because I hate his nickname. I always did. You *know* that. I've said that before."

I stopped talking. The way she was looking at me, I knew she wanted to take my head off, and I didn't want to lose it.

"Before what? Before you started cheating with him behind my back? Yeah. It figures. You really think going to college and getting a law degree makes you Michelle Obama or something don't you? I almost thought you were just as perfect as you wanted us to believe too.

But you ain't," she criticized, jabbing the air in front of my face with her index finger.

"I never claimed to be perfect," I interjected, inexplicably choking on the tears that seemed to be rising from my throat.

People insisting that I thought I was perfect could only be because they thought I was close to it in my opinion. Otherwise, why would multiple people keep saying it?

"Oh, you didn't? I sure couldn't tell. Always parading your marriage, your job, your big house, your money, your *designer clothes* around like you were perfect. But the truth is, you're just as grimy as any other hood whore out here. Just *sneakier.*

Now, you got my son out here about to have a *sister-cousin,* because you couldn't cheat with *any other man* in Atlanta besides *his* daddy, or use condoms. How long have we been sharing dick Yasmin? Huh? That's what's really eating at me. How long!" she demanded.

"Please Tamika. Just calm down for a second," I begged leaning away from her and beginning to panic.

Her close proximity and her heightened fury had me contemplating calling my father to come save me. It's already been established that I'm not a fighter, but I hoped she wouldn't be crazy enough to attack me at eight months pregnant.

"*Please?* Please what? I'm just asking you a simple question. When did it start?" she asked, slowly pacing in front of me.

"It wasn't that long," I whimpered averting my eyes to the floor. "Since, mid-March."

"Wow," she said touching her forehead and sucking in her lips as her eyes became glossy. "That long. So, let me ask you something else. The day Amina got shot… Were y'all together that day too? When I busted y'all sneaky asses in the hospital lobby?"

I thought about lying, but changed my mind. Tamika was a fact checker and if she was *finally* deciding to talk to me about this now, she would probably talk to Dwayne about it later.

I stood with one hand planted in my back, intending to go to the bathroom and get away from her interrogation for a minute, before reluctantly answering, "Yes."

Her eyes instantly dropped to my belly and a rogue tear leaked from the corner of her left eye before she quickly wiped it away.

"So... The baby. Did he *want* you to keep it?"

"Umm," I shrugged. "He just said he would go with whatever I decided. I thought about having an abortion, but... I just couldn't. *You* know, all of the problems I've had trying to conceive. The doctors told me I would probably *never* do it naturally. So, this baby was a miracle for me."

"A miracle," she scoffed. "What were you going to do about this *miracle baby*? Pretend like it was Malik's while y'all kept screwing behind our backs?" she asked folding her arms against her heaving chest.

"I don't know. Maybe," "I just found out the day I went to tell him at the barber shop. We barely got to talk about it before everything was out in the open."

"So, what are y'all doing now? Are y'all supposed to be a couple?" she snarled invading my space.

"No. I don't... I don't know," I pled placing a fearful hand between us as I looked into her fiery orbs, now filling with tears, and hoped her fists wouldn't soon be triggered. "We're just focused on the baby right now. Can you... Back up?"

"How many times did y'all do it?" she growled ignoring my request. "Did y'all screw in my bed?"

"Tamika, can you stop? I don't want to talk about this anymore. I just want to move passed it. Plus, I have to pee."

"How. Many. Times?"

"I don't know. *I don't know Tamika!* Four. Four okay! Four!" I screamed deciding to underestimate it lower than the number that sent Malik into a stabbing fit.

As soon as the last word left my mouth, I felt the sting of her hand against my cheek. My impending scream was instantly stifled by a second slap that prompted a gush of fluids to surge from between my legs.

Tamika backed away from me as I cupped my aching face with one hand. Thinking I peed myself *again*, I stared down confusedly at the small pool of excretion on the carpet beneath me in horror.

"I can't believe this," she cackled flailing her hands out like the psycho she is. "Your water broke."

7

Amina

"You all right?" my brother asked glancing at me with slight concern as we hit I75 North from the airport.

He was killing the winter in a beige lambs-wool, shawl collar sweater over dark blue Givenchy jeans. One thing my brother and I had in common was our eye for fashion, despite us growing up without the money to afford it.

He was actually a director of human resources, but he dressed like he had an appointment with a magazine shoot most of the time. Since I found out his girl was playing hide the sausage all this time, I've been wondering whether his fashion sense was correlated to his hidden sexual preferences. I'm just saying. Gay men usually have a heightened fashion sense.

I sighed, trying to shake the glumness from my spirit, methodically concealing the windows to my soul behind my black Butterfly Runway Chanel shades. Even though Cedric was little more than a wealthy distraction for me, I *was* fond of him. I'm sure his three kids will miss him dearly.

Initially, I was visibly flustered, and somewhat ashamed that I didn't know the answers to nine tenths of the routine questions hotel staff, paramedics and the police bombarded me with afterwards. Having a man die inside of me was traumatic to say the least.

Additionally, insomnia kept me awake the majority of the seven-hour flight I had to book back to the A because I had no way of contacting Cedric's pilot. Every time I closed my eyes, the vacant look in Cedric's haunted my thoughts, along with the memories of Franco Diamati's dead man's stare all those years ago.

No. To answer Mark's question, I wasn't all right. But I would pretend to be.

"I'm fine. Just tired. Ready to go home and lay down."

"I bet. Did you have to pay a lot for your flight?"

"Not really. It was about 300 and some change. I'm glad I brought my credit cards, or I would've been calling you to book me a flight home too." I adjusted the seat to accommodate my long legs and sunk back into it.

"You know when you said you were going out of town with a friend to Vegas, I assumed you meant the guy you brought to the funeral. I didn't know you had already broken up with the brother."

"Donovan and I didn't *break up*. We were never together. He was just a friend being supportive at the funeral."

I answered smartly as he glanced at me skeptically.

"Umm hmm. Well, Ma was practically picking out names for your kids after he brought you that get-well gift up to the hospital," he claimed with a huge smile. "You know she's dying for you to find a man and make her a grandma."

"Go to hell Mark. *You* make her a grandma. You're older," I huffed sucking my teeth.

"Don't hold your breath waiting on me. I'm not sure I even want kids, but *your* biological clock is ticking. You better get to work if you want some before your eggs shrivel up."

"I beg your pardon? My biological clock is perfectly oiled, and my eggs are nowhere *near* shriveled up. There is no rush for me to push out anybody's babies, anytime soon. Taking care of Linx's spoiled behind is more than enough for me right now," I assured him. "Speaking of which, I gotta pick him up from the kennel. You wanna swing me by there to get him first?"

"No. I don't want no dog hairs in my ride," he sneered.

"Oh please. He's a Doberman. It's not like he's got a lot of hair to shed. C'mon sweet brother of mine," I whined. "I really don't feel like having to go back out after I get home. You could save me an extra trip."

"Nope. I already had to rearrange my schedule so I could come pick you up. I don't have time to do all of that too."

"Do all of *what* too? It's only like two or three exits passed my house. We'll be in and out of your car before you know it."

He shook his head more vehemently, making me want to smack him upside the back of it.

"C'mon big brother. *Pleeeease.* You know I'm still traumatized from what happened," I pouted.

He cocked his head towards me in a blasé fashion.

"You just sat here and said you were fine not five minutes ago. Now all of a sudden you're traumatized because you screwed some elderly sugar daddy into early entry to the pearly gates like Celie's daddy in *The Color Purple?*"

"He was *not* elderly, asshole!" I squealed melodramatically as a grin involuntarily crept upon my face, matching his. He could be an insensitive jerk sometimes, but we both had dark senses of humor, and I really wanted to laugh.

"I knew I shouldn't have told your childish ass that part. "He was only 51, and for your information, he *looked* like he was forty, and handled me like he was 20. *Ooh* and the way he ate the box…" I emphasized licking the rim of my top lip licentiously for effect.

"Mimi! Knock it off," he ordered, his jovial expression morphing into one of revulsion. "I'm the *last* one who wants to hear all that extra information. Ill!"

I giggled while reaching to turn down the latest rap garble V103 was playing for the millionth time. Mark's hand swat mine like a pesky gnat before I could.

"You're a *passenger.* Stay in your lane. Don't touch my radio," he warned wry faced before I could get a word out.

"Psssh," I let my hand linger defiantly by the volume button. *"Boy,* I don't care whose car this is. I don't wanna hear this mess. Aren't you too old to be Nae Naeing anyway?" I quipped referencing one of the dances Silento' was singing about in his song, *"Watch Me",* blaring through the speakers.

"You're going to be *Nae Naeing* your little ass right out there on the curb if you don't remove your crumb snatchers from the controls."

"Who are *you* calling little?" I taunted snaking my neck. "I've been taller than you since the tenth grade. *Little brother."*

"Please. You act like that measly inch really means something. I don't care how much taller your black amazon Barbie ass is than me. Respect – your – elders!" he barked playfully pushing my hand again. "Sit back and ride. Boujee girl."

My eyes rolled dismissively behind my shades as I waved him off and sat back comfortably in the bucket seat of his Camaro. He's always been bossy, stingy and selfish with his things. That's why I used to go in his room and purposely rearrange all of his toys when we were kids to drive him crazy.

Still, I don't know what I would do without my big brother always around to get my back. Sure, he's a consummate clown, but he's as loyal as they come, and I wouldn't trade him for the world. He definitely inherited his zany personality from our mother though. Both of them mask nervousness, insecurities and awkward moments with humor, but are hard to calm down once angered.

I also got my humorous disposition honestly, except I'm not as campy as Mark. When it comes to family however, we're all fiercely protective.

"Whatever bruh. If you're going to listen to rap, at least let it be Jay-Z, Drake, T.I., Jeezy or somebody else you can actually understand what they're saying. Most of these songs sound like little whining, illiterate babies got hold of a microphone and a studio."

"Like I said, you don't control what plays in my ride. That's probably why Donovan broke up with your ass anyway. Your bossy behind doesn't listen."

"I told you he didn't break up with me, because we were never together. *Moron*," I laughed.

"Umm hmm," he jibed. "So what was wrong with him?"

"Nothing," I shrugged looking at my nails, thinking about what color manicure I needed to get next.

"Nothing? If it was nothing, then why did you stop seeing him? He seemed like your type."

"What do *you* know about *my type*?" I quizzed.

I hadn't had a boyfriend or brought any guys around my family in over six years, mainly because it conflicted with my escorting, so what could my brother know about my type?

"I know exactly what your type is smart ass. I've been cock blocking ninjas away from you for practically your whole life. You don't think I paid attention to be able to head those fools off at the pass?"

"All right, so let's hear it," I challenged placing my elbow on the middle console and perching my chin on my wrist.

"Tall. Gotta be taller than you. Brown or dark brown skin. Lean, but muscular. He's gotta be a confident, take charge kind of guy. Maybe even cocky, but he's gotta have a thick skin to fend off your slick mouth, and he's gotta be financially stable. Hell. Better than stable for your spoiled ass," he affirmed, seemingly pleased with his analysis.

I huffed like he hadn't just hit the nail on the head and used the hand I was leaning on to rake my hair. It was embarrassing how accurate he was when I was still trying to figure out when he started liking chicks with dicks.

"Or, maybe I'm wrong," he continued snidely. "*Maybeeeee* your type is rich, elderly men, with private jets, high sex drives and bad hearts. So they can leave you millions in their will."

"Kiss my ass Mark. Don't start back on that elderly mess again," I asserted.

I mean, he was partially right there too, but I wouldn't admit it. Though I was harboring some secrets about my private life myself, it was really eating at me to know that my brother had been hiding his homosexuality from me all this time. I needed to know why, and now was as good of a time as any to ask him.

"Well, since you're all in *my* business, let me get all up in yours. What's up with you and Dana? Anything big happening? Wedding bells coming? New developments."

"We're good," he answered flatly, as if *that* was going to be the end of my inquiry. Ha! Hardly!

I gawked at him through my tinted shades, knowing he hated being stared at. I knew he couldn't actually see my eyes, but it would get under his skin just the same. He pretended to be unfazed and immaturely stared straight ahead while I peered holes into the side of his face.

"*Wwwhy* are you staring at me, big head?"

"Did you hear my other questions or are you going deaf?"

"I answered. What do you want me to say? *We're good.* There's nothing to report. Marriage isn't even on the table right now. Nosy."

"Oh, *I'm* nosy? I'm sorry. Were you just in the car with me when you were all up in *my* business two point two seconds ago?"

"Nah. I wasn't being nosy. I was just getting clarification on why you started dating elderly men."

"You're such a douche," I chuckled flipping him off. "I'm just saying. Y'all have at least a year under your belts right? Do you think Dana is *the one?*"

"We broke up for a little while there, so it's not quite a year. As far as her being *the one,*" he answered tonguing the inside of his cheek. "I don't know yet. The jury's still out on that."

"But you really like her a lot?"

He shot me a puzzled glance before focusing back on the road as he took the highway off ramp.

"Why? Since when do you care about how me and Dana are doing or how much I like her?"

I crossed one leg over the other and decided to rip the Band-Aid off. There was no use beating around the bush about it at this point.

"Since I found out she had a dick," I replied calmly as he hit the brakes harder than necessary at the first red light.

His eyes bulged in their sockets and his mocha brown skin turned pale as panic and vacillation registered on his face. The car was silent for a multitude of seconds, sans his constant throat clearing and the sounds of Future and Drake's *"Where ya at"*, on the radio.

"Who told you that?" he finally asked sedately.

"Does it matter? If it's true, I wanna know why *you* didn't tell me? Do you know how crazy it was to find out that my own brother is in the closet from somebody else?"

"I'm not *in* the damn closet!" he lashed out flexing his jaws angrily. "I'm not *gay*. Who told you I was gay?"

I scoffed dubiously and leaned back towards the passenger side door. If this wasn't a serious moment, I would've hit him with 'You ain't got to lie Craig' from the movie *Friday*. Like dude, if you *and* the person you're voluntarily having sex with both have dicks, you're gay.

I'm sure my thoughts were written all over my face because his eyes dropped with guilt, then back to the road. After nervously palming the bottom half of his cleanshaven face multiple times, he banged the same hand against the steering wheel.

"*Fuuuuuck!*" he hollered without warning as he turned onto my street in the subdivision. "Nobody was supposed to know. *Nobody.* That's not even *her* anymore."

"What do you mean that's not her anymore?"

"I mean… She's not a man anymore. Everything on her is female. Everything. Dana is *100 percent* female."

I could see it in his face that he was desperate for me to cosign, and I was starting to feel guilty. I assume in his book, her having her penis surgically removed qualified her as 100 percent female. There's a need for a lot more other natural born requirements to make that true in *my* book, but hey, this was his life to live with her and not mine.

"Since I've met her, she's always looked, dressed, talked and acted like a *woman*. I mean, she's tall, but so what? A lot of women are tall. She's not *freakishly* tall. A lot of supermodels are 5'10". You're almost 5'10". There's nothing suspicious about a woman being tall.

I *never* had a clue she used to be a man Amina. *Never*. I'm not gay. I don't like men like that. I never have," he avowed. Words spilling from his lips like a running faucet.

"Mark, seriously. I don't care if you like men, women, half-and-halves, black, white or whatever. I'm going to love you no matter what. I know Ma and the rest of the family would too. I'm just hurt that you would keep this a secret from me. I thought you trusted me."

"It's not about trusting you," he said shaking his head with his eyes downcast as he parked in my driveway. "Nobody was ever supposed to find out. *I* wasn't even supposed to find out! She was hiding it from me too. She had me thinking she was practicing that stupid Steve Harvey, ninety-day rule thing at first.

I've never been a pussy hound like that anyway. You know that. I'm at a point right now where I'm looking for a wife. So, I wasn't pressed about it. Then, almost four months in, she opened up... Well, I *thought* she was opening up, and told me she had a medical condition."

"What kind of medical condition?" I asked petulantly.

"Endometriosis. It supposedly effects your ovaries, fallopian tubes, intestines and stuff like that."

"I know what it is." I wondered how lying about having it was helping Dana any.

"Well, she said it made her have her period multiple times a month and caused severe abdominal pain sometimes. She went on to explain that that was the *real* reason why she was stalling me on sex, but then, she told me she was going to have surgery for it.

So, you know, I was trying to be understanding, because I didn't want to be an ass about something she couldn't control. Plus, I really was starting to fall in love with her. I just wanted to know when there was going to be a light at the end of the tunnel. I'm not a saint. Eventually, not having sex would become an issue. You know?

She started crying, telling me how she maxed out her insurance benefits, even with the discounts she gets working at Piedmont, so she had to put off surgery until the end of May. *May* Mimi. This was like, mid-January at the time."

I listened, impressed that he liked her enough to even contemplate sticking it out that long without sex. Personally, I would've kicked her to the curb after two months of no sex myself. Hey, just because I'm a woman, that doesn't mean I don't have needs.

"Anyway," he said wiping sweat from his forehead. "Long story short, fast forward to February. I'm at her place, and the toilet in the guest bathroom is broken, so I have to use the one in her master bedroom.

While I'm in there, I see she has all these medications lined up on the sink, so I start reading some of the labels. Now when she first told me about her endometriosis, I Googled it. You know, so I would know what she was dealing with and what to expect.

Well, nothing I saw said anything about having to take a bunch of meds. So, I got paranoid. I screenshot them and got to Googling the names on the prescription bottles while I was in there. Cyproterone acetate, spironolactone, and a few others I could barely pronounce.

I was really blown when they kept coming up in relation to hormone replacement and male-to-female therapy. When I realized they were all gender reassignment meds, I went ballistic. I mean… I lost it!

I damn near flew out the bathroom and went straight for her neck. We fought for a minute until she got away from me and locked herself in another room. I just snapped out Mimi. I tore up her place, broke out windows, and messed up her door trying to kick it in."

"Damn," was all I could muster. "That's a hell of a way to find out something like that."

"Somebody ended up calling the cops and I almost got arrested. Crazy enough, if it wasn't for her pleading with them not to arrest me, and refusing to press charges, I definitely would've gone down. Instead, they just made me leave the premises. Which I did, because you know I can't be going to jail," he said with a smirk.

"No," I cosigned. "You're definitely not built for jail."

He stared off like he was remembering the night.

"I was all jacked up in the head about it. I couldn't believe I had been kissing, groping, and developing feelings for a *man* all that time. Even if he wasn't going to *be* a man for much longer, I felt like I had the right to know that from the beginning. You know?"

I didn't want to be the one to break it to him, but he was *still* kissing, and groping on a man, even if he was no longer anatomically correct. But, since my opinion on that was not solicited, I didn't offer it up.

"For two months, I stayed away from her. No calls. No texts. No nothing. I hated her, but I loved her too. I couldn't stop thinking about her. As much as I didn't want to, I had already fallen in love with her."

"I just can't quit *yooou*," I spat out in my attempt to duplicate Jake Gyllenhaal's twang in the movie *Brokeback Mountain*.

He stared at me blankly, then cracked a smile and shook his head in amusement. I guess I'm just as much of a clown as my brother is. I couldn't resist an opportunity to lighten the mood.

"I swear I hate you sometimes," he snickered. "That's from that gay ass western, isn't it?"

"Yeah. You know everything ties back to movies and celebrities in my mind. I couldn't let you get away with that. Especially under the circumstances," I replied touching his arm lovingly. "Seriously though. I understand. *I've* never loved anybody that much, but you do. I'm not judging."

He nodded slowly and folded his bottom lip under, slamming his head back against the headrest. As dismal as he looked, I could tell it was a relief to be able to tell someone. I had been there but hadn't quite done that yet.

"I know you think I'm crazy for staying with her knowing she used to be a man. Shit. Maybe I am. I almost wish I would've just let it play out the way she planned it and kept me in the dark."

"No Mark. That's too big of a secret for anybody to keep from some-one they're in a relationship with. *Huge.* You had a right to know a long time before she actually told you."

"You know what?"

"What?"

"Sex with her feels normal though. It's just as tigh—"

"Mark! Oh my God! *Whyyyy* would you think I wanted to know that?" I screeched a laugh while taking my keys from my bag. "Asshole."

He chuckled as I pressed the fob and my garage door began to lift. I was usually driving, so I was accustomed to entering that way, and with my roller bag, it would be easier.

"You need me to help you take your bags in?"

"No. I got it," I advised kissing his cheek and hitting the door locks.

"Okay. I'll call you later."

He honked and waved before backing down my driveway as I rolled my bag through the garage past my Jag. Opening the door to the kitchen I was instantly alarmed when it chimed but the house alarm didn't go off. I mean, there *was* a small possibility that I had simply for-gotten while rushing to meet Cedric on time, but I doubted it.

I was especially cautious about security since the prior home inva-sion. The only way I may have faltered on it was by regularly leaving the door to the garage unlocked. Linx was usually on guard inside and there was no way for some random to know that though.

I surveyed my kitchen for signs of intrusion and debated whether to play *Charlie's Angels* or not without a gun. I had left it tucked in a shoe box in my closet instead of toting it since I didn't know Vegas's gun laws and I didn't think I would need it anyway.

I shot my brother a text asking if he had been in my house while I was gone and tested the alarm just to be sure it was working. It did. I mentally retraced my steps before I left on my trip, and within minutes, Mark texted me back that he hadn't.

Deciding I was overreacting, I adjusted my bag over my shoulder and drug my carryon down the hall, peering into the great room, half bath and den on the way. Everything looked normal, but I still felt uneasy. It had taken a lot of time for me to get comfortable in my house again after the video thing and that alarm slip up had me on edge again.

I traipsed into my upstairs bedroom with a sigh and dropped my bag on the bed. Still holding the handle to my roller bag, I stared at the open door to my walk-in closet with angst. No way had I done that. My closet door was always closed unless I was inside of it. I hadn't been in it since the night before our flight, so there was no way in hell I mistakenly left it open.

Goosebumps rose on my arms as I appraised my room, then gawked back towards the closet. Besides my car, the two most important things I owned was in there. My gun and my safe. My heart thud in my chest intensely as I cautiously drifted inside the closet. Eyeing my clothing and the shelves that housed my shoes stacked in boxes of threes across it, I wearily glanced over my shoulder again.

Nobody was there, but I felt like somebody had been. Somebody else had been in my home again. In my room. And it wasn't Mark because he didn't have any reason to be. Pulling a shoe box from the middle of one stack, I was relieved to see my gun and two boxes of ammo just where I left them.

Removing its contents, I reached up to put the box back in place and paused in confusion. Squinting, I leered at the small square shaped object stuck on the outside of another shoe box on the shelf. Pulling the box down and inspecting the gadget, I looked in the direction it was facing once I figured out what it was. It was a camera. And it was trained in the direction of my safe.

8

Vanessa

Gavin's tongue assaulted my clit as bestial moans escaped my lips and reverberated off the tiles of the shower walls. The steamy water from the rainfall showerhead threatened to drown me any time I tilted my head back, but it felt like the powerful orgasm building in my loins would be worth it.

"Ri-Right! Right there baby! Right *therrrrrrrre!*" I squealed thrusting my sex deeper into his mouth as I shuddered and released all the juices he craved into it.

I barely had my bearings when he stood to his full height and spun me around to face the wall.

"Now let me feel that cum all over my dick," he ordered slapping my ass, guiding himself into my slippery opening from behind.

Unease slowly crept up on me as my cheek pressed against the tile while he drilled passionately inside of me. Flashbacks of Brand pushing my face into the brick wall in the alley clouded my thoughts as tears drained from my eyes, disguised by the shower drops.

"Yeah. Throw that ass back baby," Gavin commanded feverishly, totally oblivious to the internal meltdown I was experiencing.

Squeezing my eyes tightly shut, I desperately tried to recompose myself and enjoy the long stroke I usually relished. This was crazy. We had sex all over the house and in practically every position imaginable before without me thinking of what happened even once.

Something about *this* position though, it triggered memories of the one night I vowed to forget. I hadn't told Gavin or anyone else about it and I never would. Nothing could reverse what he did, and I was too strong to let him make me into a victim.

On the upside, I was already getting the best revenge. His happily ever after with Delia was snatched by my hands while Gavin and I were on our way to being a musical power couple. Life was good.

"*Yees* Daddy! Make this pussy cum all over that big fat dick!" I screeched, forcing myself to get back into it while peeking at him through the rush of water splashing my face.

His features warped into an agonizing expression that I knew was the precursor to his ejaculation. The more he looked down at his dick pistoning in and out of my dripping box, the tighter my walls squeezed around it.

"*Ohhhhh* Vix… I'm about to cum all in that pussy girl!"

I couldn't say the same, but I was just as eager for him to finish so we could get out. I only had four hours sleep before he came home waking me up and ready to grind. I didn't and wouldn't *ever* complain about that. It was simply par for the course. I could sleep when I was dead.

This bout in the shower was our third go-round as I threw my ass into his torso, moaning and bouncing it up and down on his tool like a porn star. Within seconds, he exploded inside of me with a grunt and fell back against the wall.

Grabbing the body wash from the hanging rack, I lathered us both up with it, and washed his back with a loofah. I admired every curve of his muscular body as the suds and water ran between each crevice, and I mentally pat myself on the back for nabbing him.

I stood on my tippy toes and kissed him on the back of the neck as I maneuvered the soapy loofah around his shoulder blades.

"Earl scheduled us to do the video for "Top Shelf", and we're going to be on *The Breakfast Club* on Power 105.1 next week," Gavin said wiping a splash of shower water from his eyes.

I couldn't help the huge grin that instantly captured my face. That was one of the top radio shows in the nation, and an appearance on it could be epic for my career.

"'Bout time," I arrogantly scolded, handing him his loofah to do the front and grabbing my own. "As much trash as they talk about me, it's only right that they actually have me on to get the real story."

Gavin shrugged and shot me a look I couldn't read.

"What was that look?" I asked with a frown.

"I just need you to be chill when we get there. Speak your peace, clarify anything you think has been misunderstood, but don't flip out like you did on Rita Rasaad's show."

"Are you serious? That mealy-mouthed ho deserved to get flipped on. The way she asked every question was disrespectful. If we weren't on camera, and I didn't have a reputation to keep up, I would've dragged her right there," I argued almost getting hype all over again thinking on the insulting way she interviewed me.

She undoubtedly believed I was a homewrecker in the Delia and Brand situation by the way she coined each question and either grunted or side-eyed me after each answer. That bum ho was lucky I had more to lose by dragging her than by cussing her out.

"Believe me. Anybody watching it could tell," he said with a slight smirk as I stepped in front of him to squirt more soap on my loofah. "Bae, you gotta stop being such a hot head. People are going to take shots at you in this business whether you're involved in a scandal or not. You better get a thicker skin."

I rolled my eyes and rotated my neck to look at him like he was delusional. Had he just met me? I'm far from fragile.

"Oh, I have a thick skin already. If I didn't, your sidelined baby's mom would've ran me off with the crap you let her do and say to me. It's not that I *can't* take it. It's that I refuse to."

"Hold on now," he said raising his hands defensively. "I don't *let* her say or do anything. Y'all are both grown women. You both know where you stand in my life, so all that cat fighting between y'all is just your hormones.

She's always going to be Davin's mother; therefore, she's always going to be in my life. At least until he's eighteen. Either you can deal with it, or you can't. I'm with you instead of her for a reason. Act like you realize that."

I nodded in agreement as I washed around my nipple rings, but inside, my blood was boiling. Was this jackass serious? *Either you can deal with it, or you can't,'* I mocked him in my mind. I've already been dealing with it. The problem was, he wasn't checking her when she needed to be.

That's what I *wanted* to say to him, but I held my tongue. I had to keep looking like I was open to being friendly with Daphne if I wanted to stick around. His son was everything to him, and jeopardizing his relationship with Davin would only diminish all the progress I had been making.

"I have been baby. Every time we get into it, *she* starts it. Daphne's the one who ran up on *me* at HOT 97.1 last month with her THOT-bots threatening me and dogging out our relationship. You know the only reason I didn't pop her in the mouth is because of you right?"

"I know. I know," he said grabbing me around the waist and pulling me back under the water with him. "And I got in her ass about that too. Both of you are hot heads, but I'm not with her. I'm with you. So, you're who I'm asking to reel it in. Okay?" he asked before kissing me deeply.

All of that went in one ear and out the other, but again, I nodded in phony agreement after our lips separated. When we got out the shower, I wrapped a towel around my head, dried off, and sauntered into the master bedroom.

I loved the feel of the heated floors beneath my bare feet on such a chilly winter day. I never liked to be cold for any reason, and the recent time I spent in California promoting myself had me contemplating a move.

If I hadn't already promised to meet up with Red Sonja for a late lunch today in this cold ass weather, I would still be in bed trying to catch up on lost sleep. Someone started ringing the doorbell like a maniac as I clicked on the flat screen television and squirted some *Victoria's Secret* Pure Seduction lotion into my palm.

"You expecting somebody?" I questioned with a frown, sitting on the edge of the bed as Gavin exited his walk-in closet, shirtless and wearing basketball shorts.

"Nah."

"Well, whoever it is, must have the gate code because I didn't hear the intercom buzz," I called behind him as he flung the room door open and disappeared down the hall.

Of course, I already knew who it probably was acting a whole entire ass at the door, and that brought me joy. Letting the towel on my body drop onto the bed, I rubbed lotion onto my legs and waited for all hell to break loose.

It wasn't long before a loud commotion downstairs let me know that either Gavin or his housekeeper, Mrs. Cox, had let the culprit in. Not even a minute afterwards, angry heels clacked up the stairs as its wearer argued with Gavin.

"No! No Gav! I don't play these games and I'm not about to start playing them with your new bitch either! What if Davin had been with me? You're going to just let that crazy whore lock your son out of his own house?" Daphne's screechy voice complained.

"Chill out Daph! You jumping to conclusions. Chill the fu—"

"Move Gavin! I'm not jumping to conclusions! Nobody but her stupid ass could've done it! Vixen! Vixen," she screamed as they got closer. "Or should I call you *Dicks-in* since you're such a slut? Huh Ho! Huh?"

I chuckled to myself. Totally unbothered by her name calling or antics. If my grin got any wider, I would've needed an extra face for it. This was going to be fun. Watch me work.

"Bitch! And you sittin' up here naked! You..." Daphne hollered through spittle, cutting her own rant short at the sight of me as she struggled with Gavin to get in the room.

Faking surprise, I clutched my chest dramatically and forced a perplexed expression watching Gavin trying to keep her at bay.

"What? What the hell is wrong with you? What're you talking about?" I questioned in my best exaggerated victim voice.

"You know what I'm talking about you *psycho!*" she claimed through hitched breaths, temporarily stunting her attack mode.

She's got me by an inch or two in height, but Gavin's six feet still towered over her.

"You changed the locks on my house and vandalized it!" she yelled as he blocked the doorway with his body.

This was pure comedy. Daphne's meticulously madeup face was screwed up like the devil herself, as her 22" curly weave flung every which way but loose. Her black swing coat swished around her as she kicked out at me in jeans and the exact black Manolo Blahnik ankle boots I ordered from Bergdorf Goodman online yesterday. Damn!

I swear I can't stand this chick. That's why it gave me even more pleasure to antagonize her in all of my naked glory. Nipple rings freshly gleaming from the shower, clean shaven kitty out and all. Gavin told me it was her extreme jealousy that broke them up, so I knew seeing me so comfortable at his place was only making her angrier.

"You're crazy. I swear I don't know why you think I'm even thinking about you. Gavin what is she talking about?" I asked using the towel on my head to dry my hair.

"See? I'm telling you she did it!" Daphne continued flipping out. "She's too calm. It was her!"

"Vix, did you go over to Daphne's house and ha—"

"Wait a minute. Why are you even questioning me if I did whatever the hell she's accusing me of? I've been busy promoting and recording pretty much every day for the last month. When I'm not with you, you know where I am, which is usually here.

On top of that, I don't even know where she lives to do anything to her house. Don't you live in a gated community with surveillance cameras and security like we do? Check the video dummy," I retorted with major attitude while cackling inside.

"*We* do? Ho *you* don't live here!" she growled nearly shaking with rage as crocodile tears scurried down her cheeks. "She changed the security code on the alarm system too Gav. For real. You need to do something about this hoe. It had to be her. You can't be buying this innocent act she's selling."

My nonchalant attitude was undoubtedly fueling her ire, which in turn, elated me. She could accuse me all she wanted to. Unless she could prove it, her only recourse was whining about it like she was doing.

"Unlike *you*, I actually have a career besides Instagram modeling. I ain't got no time to track down your house and climb the gate to vandalize it or change the locks, or whatever the hell you said I did. Ask your housekeeper. How did she get in? Maybe *she* did it?"

Out of gas, Daphne was no longer fighting to get at me. She just stared at me furiously, trying to calm herself down while I did my best to look guiltless.

She didn't have a gate to climb, a housekeeper, or any of the luxuries I threw out there. Pretending I thought she did could only make me look more innocent. Right? Even more so, I knew I was getting in her head. Making it seem like I *expected* her to have it diminished the importance of him buying her that little abode because she *didn't* actually have them. I loved it!

"Calm the hell down! You can't be bustin' up in my spot screaming and acting a fool. Come talk to me downstairs. Let her finish getting dressed and we'll figure out what happened," Gavin said finally losing his typical cool.

As he attempted to guide her away by the arm, she snatched out of his grasp and sneered at him.

"Don't *touch* me. I can't believe you're taking this Ho's side over me. She either did it, or had somebody else do it for her. I *know* it was her. Unless it was *you*, nobody else has a key to the house. Your dumb ass probably got my spare keys and stuff around here somewhere and she found 'em."

I stood from the bed with a deep sigh, turned my back to the doorway and bent over, vigorously towel drying my mane, and giving her and Gavin a full view of my beautiful undercarriage.

"See… She thinks she's cute!" Daphne hollered, followed by a lot of grunts and scuffling, which I'm sure was the two of them wrestling as Gavin tried preventing her from charging in the room to attack me.

"Daphne! You about to make me snap on your ass now! Go the fuck downstairs so we can talk God damn it! Or else I'm gonna put you *all* the way out! Let's go!" he barked slamming the room door shut with them on the other side.

I giggled audibly and stood up as I considered what caption to use in my next IG post to needle her further when I was fully dressed and fly. The T.V. was on *E! News,* which I almost never watched. I wasn't even listening to what they were saying until a huge picture of Delia's face was shown in back of the hosts and a *Breaking News* caption came up on the bottom of the screen.

I missed the beginning of the broadcast, but I prayed they were reporting that she had finally expired. I grabbed the remote and turned up the volume just as Maria Menounos was repeating some of what was previously said.

"Again, sources close to the family have confirmed that Delia De la Cruz *has* come out of her coma. We're told that her fiancé, Brand Beats was there when she opened her eyes, but no other information about her mental state or whether she's spoken has been released so far. I'm sure everyone's prayers are with her and Brand."

Oh. My. God.

9

Valerie

My heart was in my shoes by the time Maaco came back in blowing warmth into his chilled palms and rubbing them together. All eyes were suspiciously on him when he closed the door and turned to face us.

His eyes toggled apprehensively between us before locking with mine in confusion.

"Why y'all looking like that? What's up?"

"*What's up,* is that you abandoned me and your son, and now I see you in here playing house with this bougie hoe. Then you wanna ignore me like I didn't try to be civil wit' your stupid ass," Capri spat immediately getting in Maaco's face.

If looks could kill, the icy glare he beamed down at her would've murdered her instantly and set the body on fire. I waited with bated breath for him to impugn her claim, because as far as I knew, Maaco didn't have any kids.

"See. Here you go with the BS. I didn't abandon *anybody.* Talk to me when you're ready to do the paternity test. Until then, I told you we ain't got nothin' else to talk about."

"Oh, we got plenty to talk about. Avoiding my phone calls and banning me from PLATFORM ain't going to make him *not* be your son either. Just because you got a little money now, that don't mean you can treat the people that's been there for you like trash."

"Can we talk about this privately?" Maaco asked nodding towards my bedroom.

"What you need privacy for? 'Cause you never told her about us? Oh, I'm sorry. Did I let the cat out the bag?" she mocked with a cynical laugh, the jealousy and ire seeping through her pores. "Our son Jordan is four months old, and you've only been to see him twice. *Twice.* He kicked me out on my ass while I was pregnant too. This who you wanna deal with?" she asked me.

"Four months?" I blurted out glaring at Maaco as Courtney 'oohed' in surprise beside me. "You have a four-month-old son and you never said anything?"

He let out a frustrated sigh and glanced up at the ceiling as Capri stood akimbo with a satisfied smirk.

"Listen. I don't know that that's my son, and she won't consent to a DNA test. I did kick her out on her ass while she was pregnant, because just like right now, she was out spreading her legs to everybody who wanted it like holiday joy."

Capri spazzed out instantly. Jumping in his face and punching him in his chest and arm, bumping the table by the door.

"Uh uh. Uh uh! You gotta go! Ain't nobody going to be in here fighting and tearing up my place but me," Courtney scoffed switching her half naked ass over to the coat closet and snatching out a black heap of faux fur.

"You got me messed up!"

"Stop!" Maaco grabbed Capri's wrists and shoving them down to her sides as she cussed and writhed in his grasp.

"You trying to be cute and show off for this broad? You loved these spread legs when you were the one I let between them! You know Jordan is your son! He don't need no DNA test to prove that! He looks just like you!" Capri spat quivering with anger.

"Me and whoever else you let bust in you behind my back," he sneered hatefully.

I was stuck in my jealousy, feeling like an idiot as they argued about this "maybe baby" and she writhed in his grasp.

"Uber can pick you up outside," Courtney stated extending the coat to Capri whose hands were still anchored by Maaco's grip.

"Get off of me then! How I'm supposed to get my coat if he got my hands? Bitch!"

"Bitch?" Courtney repeated snaking her neck. "Girl don't get your ass beat. Maaco let this hoe go so she can get the hell up out of my house."

Once again, I felt like another woman was telling me something about my man that I didn't know. I was always the idiot in the dark while these hoes were out here winning. My life had become a broken record of relationship discovery. Things I thought I knew but didn't. Things I should've known but didn't. Surprise! It's a threesome!

What I knew for a fact, was that if Capri *was* his baby's momma, I was done. She just showed me the fool she could act, and I was not here for it. For some reason, hoes always knew how to fight, and I didn't plan on having to fight to be with Maaco. With the bad night I had, and my history with THOTS, I couldn't deal. I just needed a few things right now to make it all better. Vodka, cranberry juice, and ice.

Remembering an unopened bottle of peach vodka in the cabinet that I hadn't yet acquainted myself with, I departed from their bickering and went to get some. Maaco called after me whilst subduing the shrew, but he was ignored. My mission was already chartered.

Being a fool for these men was getting *sooo* old. Maaco's baritone voice continued dwarfing Capri's shrill in the front room as I infused the ingredients to my favorite drink and gulped it down to drown them out. Alcohol burned a trail down my throat as I closed my eyes and meditated on it.

Sitting on a stool at the island, I replayed the many conversations and nights I spent with Maaco in my head and downed drink after drink in thought. He didn't talk a lot about his previous relationships, and I could only remember him elaborating on two of them.

The woman he was in love with while he was in the Airforce's name was Andrea. I couldn't remember the exact name of the girl he lived with who cheated on him, but it started with a P, and he never mentioned any potential baby mommas.

"V? You okay?" Courtney asked startling me from the stool with her ginger-footed ass. "My bad. Didn't mean to scare you. How many drinks did you knock back already?" she asked inspecting the less than half full bottle of vodka.

I shrugged, sipping from my glass and stared off out the kitchen window at the view of her patio. I watched two baby squirrels chase each other around the deck in amusement and let out a chuckle.

"They're cute."

"What? The squirrels?"

I nodded.

"Eww. They ain't nothing but tree rats. They are *not* cute. Anyway, Uber came and got ole girl before me or Maaco had to whip her ass. Her mouth was getting real reckless, and the fool kept trying to come for me. He let her go to put on her coat and she swiped everything off the table.

Then, the heifer was talking about I need to douche. *Chile*, the way she was swallowing my clit last night, she knows she's talking fraud. I almost bust her in the mouth, but I promised myself I wouldn't get arrested in 2015, and Maaco carried her ass outside for me."

I side-eyed her, having no idea that she had been arrested so much that she needed to make a resolution to avoid it. I knew she had a big mouth and got raunchy when we were out, but she didn't strike me as the career criminal type. Then again, she had told me a few stories about her past that probably could've resulted in assault and battery charges.

"So, what you about to do about all this?"

"Nothing. I'm done with him," I replied nonchalantly pouring myself another glass.

Courtney frowned disapprovingly and leaned her elbow against the island.

"Done with him? Without even hearing his side?"

"What side? I don't want anything to do with that freak. So, if the kid is his, I'm getting off this ride right now. Either way, he kept it a secret from me."

"But y'all weren't exclusive right? I mean, yeah, he could've told you that her son might be his, but he didn't *owe* you that. He obviously don't even think the kid is his anyway, but it's not like you're his girl. Like he said, he's waiting on the DNA test.

If the baby is really his, then why's she stalling on proving it? She was over here letting me and Brian use her like a blowup doll but she ain't had time to get the kid's mouth swabbed so he can know his daddy? Nah. She's being shady."

I didn't respond. I already told her it wasn't just because he might be a daddy, but I didn't feel like repeating myself. I really just wanted her to shut up so I could enjoy my liquor and vacant thoughts.

"Where did you find this hoe anyway? I didn't see her at TMT tonight," I wondered aloud.

"We chopped it up before when she danced at TMT, but me and Brian saw her at this swinger's club off East Ponce called, THE DUNGEON."

I rolled my eyes and shook my head as her face scrunched in response.

"Don't judge my extracurricular activities sweetheart. Especially not while you're over here gettin' *lit* as a Christmas tree at 2 o'clock in the afternoon like a big lush over nothing," she teased glancing at the digital clock on the stove.

"Nothing?" I scoffed. "Maybe it's nothing to *you*, but it's not nothing to me. That's all I need in my life is some community pussy type using her child as a pawn and trying to fight me."

"Well, Ms. Vincent. Don't forget *you* pop pussy for a living, so before you get on your high horse, you better make sure it has legs," Courtney retorted cocking her head in offense.

I stared at the floor with a slight attitude, saying nothing. I knew I didn't have *a lot* of room to talk, but it still felt like I had *enough* to speak on it from the upside. Dancing naked for money, and sleeping with random strangers as a hobby *is – not – the – same – thing.*

"Look Val. If she is, then you'll just have to deal with it. What are you going to do? Let their past mess up your future and give him over to her on a silver platter? He's practically all you talk about when you're not talking about yourself, and believe me, that's *aaaaaaaa lot.*

Sometimes, I just throw in random facts about myself when we're talking just to remind you there's another person in the room," she joked making duck lips before biting the apple.

I giggled, but still dropped my eyes to the marble island top and rested my forehead on it in shame. She made me sound so shallow. Somehow, I lost my balance and nearly toppled over, making Courtney laugh harder as I steadied myself back onto my seat.

"Drunk ass," she teased.

"Am I really that bad Court?" I murmured, hoping she wouldn't confirm that I had become some obnoxious version of Tamar Braxton.

"Yeah. You look pretty pissy."

"No. Not that. Self-centered."

She shrugged.

"You're a sweetheart, but yes, you *are* that bad. Nicky told my sister how quiet you used to be, and I was like, 'When?' Your ass sure ain't quiet now; and your favorite subject is you and your problems. Believe me, if Maaco is still rocking with you, with all your baggage, it's because he cares about you. Didn't you say he told you he loves you?"

I sucked my teeth and poured another drink, frowning at the scarce amount of cranberry juice left in the carton. It was starting to look like I was going to have to finish off the rest of the vodka solo after this round.

"You listening to me?" she questioned snapping her fingers in my face while chewing like a horse.

"I hear you, but I'm still done. Who knows if the negro has other kids out here he's keeping a secret? I'm *Done!* I'm glad he took his black ass home before I had to throw him out too!" I claimed accidentally spilling liquor onto my robe.

"Who said he went home? Dude is sitting in your room waiting for you to come talk to him in private Ms. Tough girl," she snickered. "I told him I would come buffer you first, but I didn't know you were in here getting white girl wasted. You probably need to slow down."

"Whatever," I answered finishing off my drink and reaching for the bottle to start another.

"Val, stop drinking and go talk to the man," she said tugging the bottle from my grip. "Listen to his side of the story before you cut him off. He deserves at least that much for sticking with you through all these games you be playin'."

I pointed at myself in surprise.

"*I'm* playing games? How sway?"

Courtney cackled, placing the vodka bottle back down on the island.

"Say what now? 'How sway'? Chile… You in here cussing and using slang like you about that life. 'How sway?'" she mocked again. "Who did your prim and proper ass pick that up from?"

I leaked a small smile.

"From the girls at the club. Did I use it right?"

"Yeah, but you still sound too proper saying it," she told me tapping my hand playfully while taking a bite from her apple with the other. "But anyway, go talk to your man. I need to hit the shower and wash my ass."

"He's not my man."

She rolled her eyes and rested them back on me in agitation. "Then why're you mad?"

When I didn't answer, she continued, "I thought so. Stop acting like a brat before you lose your man, or whatever you wanna call him. At least know the results before you write him off."

She drew me into a hug I didn't realize I needed until the comfort settled. I used to have this with my cousins. Especially Amina. I'm sure Courtney's advice was just as good in this moment, but there was nothing like family having your back. Too bad I lost my faith in that when Vanessa crossed me.

"Let me go find my phone before I go into withdrawal," she joked leaving the kitchen as I exited behind her, but in a different direction. Maaco sat on the edge of my bed with his elbows on his knees and his head in his hands. It was a familiar position that Brent had taken many a time before he fixed his lips to manipulate me back into the fold, and I was determined not to be so naïve for Maaco.

I ran a hand through my hair and glided haughtily to my bedside table, picking up my cellphone, and looking down at it as I opened the Instagram app and sat in the chair his coat was draped over.

He lifted his head with a forlorn gaze fixed on me and brought his hands together in front of him as if he was going to pray. I intentionally kept my eyes down on my phone, but I slyly observed him in my peripheral.

"Val."

I lifted my gaze with a mean mug and answered with a comparable tone. "What?"

"I'm sorry I didn't tell you. She's lying, so I didn't see the point. I told you how she played me when we were together. I haven't had anything to do with her since the day Jamie showed me those pictures of her cheating on me and I put her out.

I didn't even know she was pregnant at the time, and I don't think she did either. She came to me two months later crying wolf about that baby, but I don't know who the daddy is. I told her to holler at me after she had him for a paternity test, but she won't consent. So I left it alone.

Believe me. If I *truly* thought he was mine, we wouldn't even be having this discussion. I wouldn't trust her hoe ass to raise my son without me, but she's lying. As soon as Pri saw that I got the club up and running she was back claiming the little boy was mine.

I did go to see the child a couple of times, in case I was wrong. I just wanted to see if he looked anything like me, but he doesn't. I know that doesn't prove anything, but with her refusing a paternity test, that's all I have to go on."

Pri. That was the girl's name. *Duh.* I remembered him telling me about her now. He dated her in Miami when he got out of the Airforce and they moved to Atlanta together a year later. When she got busted cheating, she claimed it didn't mean anything and she was just bored and lonely while he was out grinding.

"Are you going to say anything?" he asked while I mulled over his words in my head.

"Whether you believe her or not, it's still a possibility, right? You were still together at the time."

"It's not impossible. But—"

"Well then you should have told me. Why keep it a secret?"

"It wasn't a secret. I wasn't hiding it from you. There wasn't anything to tell. She's trying to use her son as a way to guilt me into getting back with her. She's crazy. She's my past and I've been trying to leave her there."

I scoffed, looking down at my now vibrating cellphone and inhaled hard. My mother's picture and face flashed on the screen, and I let the call go to voicemail.

"How am I supposed to trust you if your way of communicating is by not saying anything at all?" I asked him.

He frowned.

"I have been communicating. I've been crystal clear that *I* want to be with you. You're the one who keeps saying you're not ready. You can't expect me to open up 100% to you while you're still being guarded though. As soon as you hear anything you don't like, you're ready to cut me off. You've already done it twice since we reconnected. You want girlfriend privileges but not the title. Let's be fair."

"I am being fair. What good would a title be if you're still being shady? I've already been down that road and I don't want to do it again. I don't want any parts of lying, cheating or pop-up baby mommas."

"I haven't *lied* to you about anything. I spent a holiday week closing down Jamie's club in Miami and tying up paperwork, *by myself*, and still found time to call you. You know the mess I'm going through with my sister right now and I make time for you through all of it.

The first thing I did when I got off the plane was come straight to see you. I have my own club to run Val. But tell me I don't still find time to check up on you at TMT when I know you're working. I don't give you any reason to question who I am, what I do, or how I move. I've *been* all in. I'm just waiting on you to stop wasting time being too scared to let me love you. So, what's this really about?"

"What it's about is you keeping secrets. Is that *not* what we're talking about right now?" I replied snippily. "You can be everywhere I am. Call me every hour on the hour if you want to, but if you're keeping secrets, I still can't trust you. You let another woman tell me something about you that I didn't know. That I should have known!"

He blew out a breath and folded his bottom lip under annoyed. The veins in his neck tensing as he rubbed one side.

"We're talking in circles. This is another reason why I didn't say anything. Do you realize that we're arguing right now about me not telling you that I *didn't* get another woman pregnant? I knew you were going to act like this if I would have said something."

I huffed and laughed cynically, rubbing my still sleepy eyes.

"How am I acting right now?"

"Unreasonable."

"You know what? Just forget it then Maaco. You're right. You're not obligated to tell me about anything. I'm not your girlfriend and you don't have to tell me anything. We're both clear on that for sure. You can leave now," I dismissed him.

As far as I was concerned, Maaco could take his readymade family and bounce the hell on. Maybe it was time for me to be single for a while. Besides, the liquor and the stress of the long night were still weighing on my eyelids. I just wanted to go back to sleep.

"That's not what I said, and that's not what you want Val."

"Oh, and you're an expert on what I want?"

He inhaled deeply, taking his bottom lip between his teeth in thought as his eyes bore into me and his broad chest rose and fell with agitation.

"No. I'm definitely *not* an expert on what *you* want. But neither are you. You're just trying to do whatever you think is going to prevent you from getting hurt again, and I know that. That's why I would never intentionally hurt you.

I don't want to go. I came over here because I wanted to see you. I'm still here explaining my case to you right now because I want to be with you. I would never do anything to hurt you," he promised coming towards me.

Kneeling down in front of me, he searched my reddened eyes for a sign of forgiveness as I tried my hardest not to give him one. Jealousy was winning over everything. Her striking looks, the probability of her having his first born, and the fact that her freak-o-meter was obviously way higher than mine. Even with my new enhanced skills in the bedroom, I was *never* going to have a threesome.

I couldn't bear to invest my heart into another man who would betray me for a more interesting piece of pussy. I certainly wasn't going to compete for him with Capri or anybody else either. Losing my fiancé to my sister, who was basically just sexing him to prove that she could, was enough humiliation for me this year. Thank you and good night.

"I'm sorry," he apologized softly kissing my lips as I stared passed him in thought. "I am. I should've told you, and I promise there's nothing going on between me and Pri if you're worried about that. I don't ever want you to feel like you can't trust me. I made a mistake, and I'm sorry baby."

Focusing in on his pleading eyes, I saw nothing but sincerity. But what did I know. I was confused, drunk and tired. Not that my judgment of character had been hitting on much lately anyway.

My cell vibrated in my hand and I looked down at it as he gripped the back of my chair with both hands, entrapping me between his muscular arms.

"Do you forgive me?"

Not sure I actually had, I stared at the picture of my mother flashing on the screen again. It was too early to listen to her complain about me not showing up for Thanksgiving, and that's all I could imagine she wanted to do.

"Do you need to get that?" He kissed my forehead and rested his against mine.

Probing each other's faces for answers as he traced the width of my lips with his thumb. I wanted to ignore the fear, anxiety and insecurities Brent's cheating created in me. To trust and love Maaco like he wanted me to. But I'm not sure I could.

"Not now."

The vibrating stopped and we sat with our temples melding in silence. Our eyes locked, my phone juddered again with a text message.

With my phone in my lap between us, I tapped into it.

Mom: Yasmin's gone into early labor. We're at Piedmont. I expect you to be on your way.

Put family first

I was sure using my father's favorite mantra at the end of her messages was another, not so subtle form of manipulation. And it worked.

10

Yasmin

My eyes watched the rise and fall of the blip tracking Sophie's heartrate on the fetal monitor as the nurse checked our vitals and adjusted the band wrapped around my belly.

"Have you had a chance to look at the menu yet?" she asked smiling. "Believe it or not, I've heard it tastes pretty good for hospital food. Of course, you can choose to eat food brought in from friends and family if you want to too."

I knew all too well what the menu selections for each meal consisted of, and I was sure the options hadn't changed that much since I was last a patient. I would be getting delivered food from my family whenever I could get them to agree.

The weight of seeing Malik again, having my sister assault me for the *second time, and* going into labor a month early, was a lot to take in. I couldn't help but ruminate over every occurrence that put Sophie's life in jeopardy, and assign culpability to each offender.

Tamika's level of cruelty still left me reeling, and if there was ever a chance of us mending our sisterhood before, it was officially defunct now. Dwayne and I may have deserved her loathing, but my unborn didn't.

She was as cool as a cucumber while Daddy scrambled to sooth my panic and get my pre-packed bags to take me to the hospital.

Ambling passed me repeatedly as she helped the boys put their coats on and gathered her own things, she made zero attempts to apologize, assist or even acknowledge me before Daddy got me to his car. If she was remorseful at all, it wasn't apparent.

The petite nurse nodded and pat my hand kindly, brushing a strand of her curly auburn hair behind her ear. Pulling the sheet of paper that printed from the monitor, she studied it and looked back at me jovially.

"Is she doing okay?" I questioned, leaning to look at the readout with her as if I had a single clue how to read it.

"She's fine. You haven't been having any contractions, which is what we want, but we *do* need you to stay hydrated."

I pushed back into the pillows propped up behind me with a deep sigh of relief and looked down at my stomach.

"Thank you God," I whispered to the higher power.

"There's a pitcher of ice water for you right here," she continued gesturing towards it on the rolling table. "It's still early enough to have them bring you dinner. Did you want me to tell them you would like something?"

"No. My father is coming back with food for me."

"All right. By the way, I saw Dana on my way in here. Dana English. She said she's a friend of the family?" she presented as a question rather than a statement.

"Yes. My cousin's girlfriend."

"Well, isn't that nice. She's a great girl. Anyway, she told me she was going to poke her head in here to see you as soon as she finished her rounds. In the meantime, if you need anything, just use the call button."

"Okay," I answered dryly, already brooding in my own thoughts again.

Luckily, they were able to stop my labor with steroids, and would continue to do so as necessary, until the following Sunday to induce. We all wanted Sophie to be as healthy as she could be, and her wellbeing superseded my newfound dread of hospitals.

After the long stint I spent recovering from Malik's attack, I would've opted for a midwife and an at home birth to avoid it at all costs if I could've. The mere thought of having to repeat the vitals and contraction check four times a day, every day for a week made me antsy.

Rubbing my tummy to sooth both myself and Sophie, I had to admit that my room was pretty nice and spacious. The décor was basic beige, aqua blue and woodgrain, with a rocking chair, a big window, a small sofa that pulled out into a singular bed and a small table.

There was a little desk attached to the wall with another chair and some draws beside an entertainment center with a flat screen tv, and DVD player in it. The floor was carpeted everywhere except in the oval area surrounding my bed and a wardrobe closet with drawers was embedded in the wall beside my bed.

I sighed to myself and hoped everything from here on out would go smoothly for me and my little angel. The past months were mostly a blur of bad news, bad behavior and bad blood in our family. It was time for something good.

When the affair started with Dwayne, it was invigorating. Our rendezvous catered to *my* schedule and he catered to *my* sexual needs. He made me feel like I made him want better for himself, and he made me feel like I could let my hair down without judgement.

I was ashamed of myself for allowing him to dickmitize me into ruining my marriage and my relationship with my sister, but after a lot of thought, I was planning to make lemons into lemonade. Now, as time ticked away and I lay here all alone, I was finally beginning to regain my senses. He had been, and would probably always be, unreliable, irresponsible, and as of this very moment... Absentee.

Malik wasn't the perfect husband by any means, but the more Dwayne relegated my importance in his life, the more I regretted collapsing my marriage for fantasy sex and no substance.

I picked up my cellphone and tapped the screen to see if I inadvertently missed a call or text from him, or anybody else for that matter. Slamming it back down in frustration, I shook my head and raked my hair once again.

I knew this negro had to have seen my text messages about going into labor and being admitted to the hospital, even if he hadn't listened to Daddy's initial voicemails when I was first brought in.

How was it that the man whose attentions I *wrecked* my marriage for, was evading me like I was the police? Just as I picked my phone back up intending to call him and leave him a voicemail that would burn his eardrums, knuckles rapped on my room door.

"*Heeeey,*" Valerie chirped in a quasi-friendly timbre as she pushed the door open and tentatively entered scanning the room.

A mixture of shock and joy muted my voice as she neared and bent down to bestow a half-hearted hug upon me. I instantly knew it was Val and not Vanessa by her unpretentious appearance and low-key entry. Vanessa was everything *but* unpretentious and low-key.

Val's hair was in her signature ponytail, under a gray Julliard cap pulled low over her eyes, with no makeup, and small diamond studs in her ears. She wore a forest green wool coat over a gray turtleneck with black jeans and black Nikes.

"H-hi," I eked out with a wary but growing grin as I surveyed her more closely.

She didn't look much different than I was used to seeing her when she wasn't on stage with Alvin Ailey, but something about her was definitely... off. It was an air unlike the Valerie that I knew, but that I couldn't put into words, and I wasn't sure I liked it.

"What's up?" she spoke again awkwardly, darting her eyes around the room, then briefly resting them on my stomach. "The way Mommy was calling and texting, I thought you probably *had* the baby already. I'm surprised everybody else isn't here."

"Are you?" I quipped skeptically as she shifted her weight from one leg to the other without acknowledging my humor.

She had to know that most of my family had been shading me the same way she was. Even if she didn't know, it was an easy conclusion to draw under the circumstances.

"Aunt Di *was* here for a couple of hours, but she left to go pick up Vic and Zaria from the airport since his mom is still in Texas for the holidays. It doesn't look like I'm having Sophie until Tuesday or Wednesday anyway. They stopped my labor until I'm at least 34 weeks along."

"So, you're both okay?"

"We're good so far. I'm just going to have to stay here until I deliver if I want to keep it that way."

"Where's Uncle Jerry? I thought he would be glued to your hip. I remember how he was when Mika had her kids," she recalled with a contagious smile that infected my face too.

"Oh, I'm sure he's planning to be. He'll be back soon. He just went home to take his meds, pick up some more clothes for me since we didn't expect for me to have to stay this long, and to get us something to eat.

I would rather not have to eat the hospital's food unless I don't have a choice. It's not the worst, but it's not my first choice either."

"I hear you," she said grabbing a chair and scooting it over to my bedside.

"I *am* surprised to see *you* though. We missed you at Thanksgiving dinner."

"I was working."

"Working on Thanksgiving?"

"Strip clubs are open every day. Even on Christmas," she countered wryly.

"I realize that. But we haven't really seen you in months. I know your mother wanted you to come? I mean, strippers basically work for yourselves, right? Couldn't you have taken off?"

She cleared her throat and fluttered her long lashes insolently before sighing.

"I was working Yasmin. The day is already gone, so what I could have done doesn't really matter anymore *now* does it? I'm sure I'm not the only one who didn't show up."

"True. But it still would've been nice to have you there. I think it was hard on everybody not having Uncle Vernon there this year. Especially your mom and Daddy. How've you been?"

The haggard and reddened tint of her eyes already suggested that she wasn't doing too well, but I prepared to hear the lie I knew was coming anyway. Given her new profession, it was possible that the late hours were simply taking its toll on her appearance, but if I didn't know better, I would say she was toasted.

"I'm good. Can't complain. Just… Minding my business. Living my life. You know. I'm good. Yeah. I'm good," she reiterated trying to sound convincing while her eyes averted to the floor.

"I meant as far as coping with losing Uncle Vernon."

"I'm fine Yasmin. Don't I look fine?" she asked holding her arms out for me to view her.

"You look tired."

"I *am* tired. What do you expect? I work the night shift. I would be sleeping *right now,* if your auntie hadn't texted me saying you were in labor and talking about, 'put family first'. I'm sorry if you're disappointed that I didn't get glammed up to come see you."

"Okay. Okay," I backed down.

"Hell, I'm glad I didn't glam up anyway or somebody would've inevitably mistaken me for Vanessa. Reporters and camera people are swarming the parking lot trying to catch anybody connected to Delia's case."

"*Still?* I thought all of that died down months ago. I mean, she's been here for half a year already. I was too out of it when they brought me in this morning, so I didn't notice any of that, but I'm surprised."

She furrowed her eyebrows and gave me a questioning stare.

"You *do* know she woke up today right? It seems like that's all anybody's been talking about on T.V. and on the radio since."

"Who? Delia?"

"Yes. She came out of her coma."

"*Oh wooooow*. No. I hadn't heard," I replied thinking of the 100 other things I had going on today that were more important than that.

Although Delia's whodunit story had been big news both locally and nationally since it happened, I hadn't been keeping up with it much over the last few months. Rivaled only by Whitney Houston's daughter Bobbi Christina's death this summer and the rumors surrounding *her* death, the media was so obsessed with Delia's shooting that I got burned out.

Everyone was speculating about who shot her and why, but there weren't any witnesses, and the police didn't have much else to go on. Her fiancé, Brand Beats was the number one suspect according to the court of public opinion, though he remained vigilantly by her bedside.

Of course, Vanessa was right in the middle of their alleged love triangle, so she was facing the heat as the potential shooter as well. Since her songs and recently publicized relationship conquests had her pegged as a habitual line crosser, she was hated by many, but popular none the less.

"Is she talking?"

"No. Or at least she wasn't when last I heard. I bet whoever shot her is shitting bricks. If she was shot at close range, she would've seen the face of who did it. Unless they had a mask on."

I snickered hearing Valerie's treble like voice using profane words that she used to take great care to avoid so easily. I guessed she would have to evolve from her shy, chaste nature to excel in her new occupation, but I was still surprised by it.

"What?" she asked frowning.

"It's just funny to me. I can't believe you're cussing now too. I know you're dancing naked in the company of pimps and hoes now and everything..." I ribbed tapping her forearm playfully. "But this is a new side of you. It's like... like... I don't know. Like Vanessa's possessing your body or pulling the puppet strings to make you talk like her."

The way she glared at my hand as I spoke and then back to my face, her pupils might as well have transformed into shards of glass. She blew out an irritated breath and countered with a tilt of her head and not an ounce of humor.

"Hilarious. Was she pulling your puppet strings when you screwed Dub to turn you into a homewrecking whore like her too? Or was that all you?"

"Hold on a minute Val," I shot back leveling my palm to her face. After the morning I just had, I was 100% *done* letting these morally corrupt heifers continue attacking me without retaliation. "I was just *joking*, but if you still have a bone to pick with me and Dwayne about it, we can do that at another time."

She frowned and retorted, "I don't have a bone to pick with you or *Dwayne* about it. Y'all are both foul and you already know it. I just want you to remember who you are and what you've done before you open your mouth sideways to me in judgement."

"Listen. I'm supposed to be stress free right now for Sophie's sake and I'm not letting you, or anybody else jeopardize my daughter's life over your own judgmental hang ups."

"Judgmental hang ups? Me? Now *this* is what's really hilarious. The *queen* of judgmental hang ups doesn't like being judged for her *own* disgraceful behavior? Surprise. Surprise," she clapped in succession cynically.

Seeing the increase in blips on the monitor on the other side of my bed, I was unwilling to allow her to continue baiting me. My energy didn't need to be wasted on her foolishness. This was going to stop now. *Right* now.

"Thank you for coming. You can go now."

"Oh. I can go now? Tuh! Okay. You don't have to tell me twi—"

"Baby momma," Dwayne called displaying both rows of gold teeth as he bopped in pulling up his sagging jeans at the waist.

"Well, if it isn't everybody's favorite baby's daddy," Valerie mumbled standing up.

"Sup Vanessa," he tossed over his shoulder in his slow drawl, leaning down to kiss me on the cheek.

"*Valerie*," she spat cutting her eyes at me as if I put him up to misidentifying her.

"My bad. *Valerie.* Y'all know I can't tell ya' apart from the otha' one. I thought maybe you was tryin' to disguise yo'self from the paparazzi or somethin'," he said glancing at her beneath the layers of long brown dreads partially obscuring his face and hanging down his back. "How you feelin' baby?"

"I've been better," I answered trading dirty looks with Val.

Whether Dwayne was on the top of the list of people I wanted to throat punch at the moment or not, it would be a cold day in hell before I let Valerie see me sweat over him. I wasn't going to give anybody reason to parrot that there was discourse between us, if for no other reason than to prevent their gloating.

"Thanks for coming," I repeated dismissively to Val with a plastered grin.

Balking, she brought the keys she was jingling out from her pocket and twisted her lips with attitude. Dwayne's eyes volleyed between the two of us in amused puzzlement as she stalked out without another word.

"Bye!" he called behind her satirically, turning back to me with a smirk. "She trippin' cause of me, or you?"

Ignoring his question, I decided to take my built-up aggression out on him.

"Where the hell have you been? And why haven't you picked up your God-damned phone to check on me and your daughter? For all you know, me and Sophie could've died in labor."

"I had some bidness to handle, and you know I can't drive. I had to wait on my boy to get back. What you want me to do? Get locked up for drivin' on a suspended license?"

"*Pul-lease.* What *business* did you have to take care of that took precedence over potentially missing the birth of your daughter? You could've called an Uber if Cortez wasn't there. Don't come in here feeding me this crap Dwayne. Seriously, I've had enough of that for today, and forever," I spat as his nonchalant expression antagonized me further.

"C'mon Yas. If I coulda' been here sooner, I woulda' been. Now, I know they ain't got you hooked up to all this stuff fo' no reason Shawty. How's my baby doin'?"

"She's Fine. Not that you care," I hissed, shifting to relieve a spasm in my shoulder that I was often plagued with as a result of being stabbed.

"Quit bein' childish. You know I care. I'm here now ain't I?" he argued shoving both hands in his front pockets beneath the long mustard sweater he wore that matched his Timberlands.

"Aye Dub," Cortez's unwelcomed voice called out as he entered making a B-line to Dwayne without acknowledging me. "I'm about to head out bruh. You going to be good? Or you need me to circle back when you're ready to go?"

Chills sprinted up my spine as I took in the red bandana draping over the collar of his black Raiders coat and the matching cap he wore low over his eyes. The scent of his cologne wafted towards my nose like a smack in the face as my eyes began to water and my hands turned clammy.

This was the closest he had ever been to me since he started chauffeuring Dwayne around, and the uneasy realization of a deeper familiarity with him forced a lump in my throat. He was always wearing gear representative of California, but this one was particularly familiar. I had seen this outfit before.

"I'on know. I'll pro'ly hit you up in a couple-a-few hours," he answered rubbing the stubble on his chin.

"*Hello,*" Dana sang from the doorway in hospital scrubs with a huge smile on her impeccably beat face before walking in.

What the hell was going on? Fifteen minutes before, I couldn't pay anybody to come see me. Now all of the sudden, my hospital room had become Grand Central Station. I liked Mark's girlfriend well enough, but right now, I couldn't force a smile on my face if you paid me.

"Sup Dana," Dwayne replied with a head nod as she approached me, her smile fading as she passed Cortez.

I wondered if his creepy vibe had spooked her too, or whether it was just my imagination.

"Hey Dub. Cortez," she greeted as she leaned in to hug me.

"Oh you know my boy Tez too?" Dwayne questioned with a smirk.

"Yeah. How you know my name? You know me?" Cortez asked studying her as my eyes jut and my heart began beating like a conga drum in my chest.

"We've met before, but it was a long time ago. You wouldn't recognize me," Dana answered levying a small smile as his words echoed in my mind and the memory of the carjacker holding a gun to my face resurfaced.

'You know me?' The jacker grilled after hitting me with the butt of his gun that day at the Sheraton.

It couldn't be. I had to be wrong. Because if I wasn't, the person who robbed me of my car, my dignity and the secrecy of my affair was, Cortez.

11

Amina

"Amina!" The pimply faced barista called as I sashayed over to the counter to pick up my order.

Starbucks was a heaven sent on this cold November day. Since I didn't want to drink and drive, I needed some caffeine in my system to help me function. I had to push back my meeting with Jamie a few hours and I was still running late.

"Amina," another voice called behind me.

Donovan. I turned to see the deserter in all his dark chocolate glory smiling at me. Why was he smiling? We hadn't ended on good terms as far as I was concerned. His winter look caught me by surprise. His grew out his mustache and his beard was now longer but neatly trimmed, giving his bright smile a sexy backdrop. I was officially beard gang as I cerebrally reprimanded my vagina for drooling over the enemy. All pleasantries were to be aborted. Immediately!

"Hello," I replied deadpan as I skirted around him.

He gently grabbed my forearm and halted my strut, causing my coffee to slosh around in its cup. If this fool would've made me drop my triple, venti, half sweet, non-fat, caramel macchiato, they would've been mopping him up from the floor right next to the spillage. I was already on edge and this coffee was practically all that stood between me and a nervous breakdown.

I leered at him over the top of my shades and he dropped his hold defensively.

"Sorry. I just wanted to say hi and see how you were doing. How's your back?"

"Why?"

"Why?"

"Yes. *Why?*" I asked pursing my lips trying to ignore how enticing he looked in that zipped up snow white polo sweater and jeans with brown military style jump boots.

Why didn't he have on a coat? I mean he looked good but, it was too cold out here to be… Never mind. I wasn't focused.

"I need a reason to ask how you are?" he asked stepping hooking his thumbs in the belt loops of his jeans.

"You haven't cared how I was all of these months. Why care now? *I'm obviously fine.* Both internally and externally as you can see," I retorted tossing the matching scarf to my Prada bag over my other shoulder dramatically.

His face cracked. My heart pounded. I needed to get where I was going before I let him say anything to melt my icy demeanor.

"It wasn't because I didn't care. If you…"

"I have somewhere to be Donovan. You take care and have a blessed day," I curtly stated, whirling on the heels of my Saint Laurent Preja pointy toe booties, flouncing fiercely through patrons like I was on a runway.

I hoped my dramatic exit left him looking and *feeling* as stupid as I had when he darted out of my house and snubbed me forever after. Toting my Prada bag on the same arm supporting my coffee, I left with my chin held high. I was a catch, and he had thrown me back.

No matter. I had more important and bigger fish to fry, and Donovan's flaky ass wasn't on the menu anymore. Entering *CHICA'S*, a quaint Mexican cuisine restaurant, I placed my shades atop my head and stopped at the hostess podium to scan the dining area. Differing sized sombreros hung from hooks on colorfully tiled walls, while chairs and booths were decorated with depictions of birds, cacti, fish or flowers.

"Hi. I'm looking for…" I started before spotting Jamie already seated in a booth with her elbows on the table, perusing the menu. "Never mind. I see her."

I was surprised she wasn't already eating and drinking since she's always early, if not right on time. The day we met about Todd's wife, she was waiting in my driveway when I got home from grocery shopping, and I was 15 minutes early. I was thankful to have extra hands helping me bring the bags in, but she had greeted me like I was late when I arrived.

"What's up Beauty Queen? Look at you, strutting up in here with Starbucks. I know they want to kick your bougie ass out already," Jamie laughed standing to hug me.

We're both tall, but with my six-inch heels on, I was taller. The hug was unexpected since she's not the affectionate type, but I leaned into it anyway. Ignoring her hand brushing against my denim covered butt, I sat in the booth across from her.

"If they know what's good for them, they'll leave me and my little macchiato alone. Do we have to sit in this booth? I don't like sitting with my back to the door. Can we move?"

"You can always come sit next to me. Then we'll both be facing the door."

She pat the red leather cushioned bench beside her with a sly grin and I rolled my eyes. She wore bulky jeans and Jordan's with a fatigue coat that concealed the tattooed sleeves on both arms but left her neck tats exposed. Her pretty face was makeup free and her neatly braided hair hung in two pigtails passed her taped down breasts. She was attractive no matter what you liked, and she knew it.

"No thank you."

"Suit yourself, but we're not moving. I'm superstitious. I go with my first mind on everything. Don't worry about it. I can protect you. And I'm always strapped."

"I am too. That's not the point," I mumbled.

She massaged her chin nonchalantly as I plucked the menu from the holder huffily.

"Did you watch the video?"

"Yeah. Let's order first before we talk about all that. I'm hungry," she said as our dark-haired waitress approached.

She wasn't unattractive, but her big breasts were hands down, the most interesting of her features. By the way Jamie was ogling them, she wanted nothing less than to see her unclothed.

"Hi. I'm Marisol, and I'll be your server today. Can I get you something to drink or bring you out some waters?"

"I'll have a glass of water please. Light ice."

"Le'me get a Heineken, and a glass of water, sexy," Jamie shamelessly flirted, letting her tongue dance at the corner of her mouth.

"Also, I already know what I want. Do you?" I asked placing my menu back in the holder.

My stomach was nearly touching my back from hunger and as good as my coffee was, I felt like it was only making me hungrier.

"Yeah. We can go ahead and order. They don't have what I *really* want on the menu though," she emphasized eyeing Marisol like a slab of meat to a hungry tiger. "But I can find a substitute for it for now."

Marisol blushed, soaking in Jamie's flirtation, and giggled annoyingly. I rolled my eyes and shook my head. I don't understand how that sleazy ass approach gets her any play, but apparently, it does. Jamie is anything but subtle, and I hated when she wolfed down women in my presence. Clearing my throat, I placed my order to interrupt the blatant disrespect.

"I'll have four fish tacos with spicy sauce. That's it."

Jamie gave me a 'stop cock blocking' look before licking her lips at Marisol, pointing to what she wanted on the menu.

"I'll have the two-chicken enchilada special with the avocado corn salad."

"Okay. Did you want any other sides? We have guacamole, rice…"

"Yeah. le'me get a side of guac with that too," she answered biting her bottom lip and looking at the girl's thighs. "If that's all I can have."

I brought two fingers to my mouth and pretended to gag. Jamie smirked and Marisol fawned over the attention before embarrassingly remembering her ass was at work under my glare.

"I'll be right back with your drinks," she grinned.

I imparted a peeved stare in Jamie's direction as she chuckled after gawking at Marisol's wide, but flat, pancake ass swaying away.

"What's your problem Beauty Queen? Why're you hatin'? You know you can have me whenever you're ready to stop playing games. You don't have to be jealous. I can't help it if the ladies love cool Jamie."

"Tuh. Don't flatter yourself. I could care less about you and Miss Mexico."

"Don't knock it till you try it. I bet you ain't never been with a lefty before, have you? I do magic with these five fingers you ain't never felt before," she grinned wiggling the fingers on her left hand.

She fell off a ladder a few years ago and crushed her right hand on landing, so what used to be her dominant hand, wasn't anymore. Even though it apparently still worked, she tended to favor her left hand for most things now including writing.

"*I* want to talk about this, the surveillance footage I sent you from my property, and whatever you said you wanted to talk to me about on your voicemail," I grilled taking the mini camera from my bag and placing it on the table. "It was stuck on a shoebox in my closet."

It wasn't unlike ones that Jamie used on the PI side of her business to record marks and surroundings in secret, so I knew she knew what it was. This camera thing had me freaked out. I picked up Linx from the kennel, changed the security code on my alarm and made sure to lock all the doors when I left. Including the garage door.

Hopefully, there weren't more of them hidden that I hadn't found. I wasn't even sure how comfortable I would be getting dressed and un-dressed in my own home until I was sure. I did my own amateur sweep of every room but came up empty handed.

"I spent two hours checking everywhere else for cameras. I feel so violated."

She picked it up and briefly inspected it before putting it back down on the table and shook her head.

"You said you found this in your closet?"

"Yes. On the side of a shoe box."

"And you didn't notice *anything* else missing? Rings, paintings, silverware? Dude was in there for almost an hour. He had to be doing more than just planting that camera."

"All my jewelry, TV's and stuff were right where I left them. If they stole something, I haven't figured out what it was yet. I wouldn't have suspected anything if they hadn't been sloppy with resetting the alarm and leaving my closet door open."

She sniffed, swiped her nose and rubbed her chin, looking off in thought. I drank my coffee, and discretely noticed the tension in her jaw as cool, calm and collected Jamie seemed uncharacteristically on edge. I wondered if something was going on in her personal life that was causing it. Not that she would tell *me*, but I would give it a shot.

"You okay?"

"Always," she replied dryly.

It was a little annoying that no matter how many years passed, she remained as secretive and aloof as she had from day one when I've opened up. She knows enough about me to write a book while I can fit everything I know about her personal life in a paragraph or two. She's from Detroit, Maaco is her only sibling, and she joined the Marines at 18.

She did security for a few celebrities and company Execs afterwards, was an MMA fighter for three years, gambles like nobody's business, and loves women. Still, I wondered if her glassy eyes and sniffles were due to the cold weather, or the coke habit I suspected she had.

My suspicions of her drug use, coupled with her often-unpredictable behavior were just two of the reasons I wanted to split business ties with her. Her mood swings were increasingly ferocious this past year, some of the other girls complained of not getting their money as promised, and she would disappear for weeks without a word. I didn't need the headache, or the hostile work environment.

At any rate, the jetlag was starting to get to me and the day's events were making me want to cocoon myself away from everybody right now.

"So, Beauty Queen, why do you think they would put it in your closet though?" she asked again as though snapping from a trance. "You doing something else in there other than getting your clothes or getting dressed?"

I opened my mouth to tell her, but somehow, a lie fell out.

"No."

Something in my gut told me not to tell her about the safe, and I always trusted my gut. Even if I had come to her for help, I still didn't fully trust her. She looked down at her watch, then back at me.

"I can come over after we eat and do my own sweep. Some stuff can be easily missed by the untrained eye. Especially if the surface they mount it on is black or if they put it inside something like a plant or on a book. I had something else to do but, I can cancel it. You're *paying* me to help, so let me help," she grinned.

"Not tonight. I'm tired and I think I did a thorough check myself. Besides, Linx is back at the house now and I don't want to have to put him up again tonight after being away from him for so long."

Another lie. I didn't put Linx up for anybody. I might send him into another room, but I decided when I got him that I wasn't going to lock him up in a house he lived in for a visitor. I just didn't want her to come home with me.

Her face contorted skeptically as she eyed me up and down and exhaled an aggravated breath.

"Okay. I'm better equipped to look for stuff like that, but if you think you got it covered, that's on you. Dude creeping on your surveillance was clearly a pro. He knew you were out of the house and that the dog was gone, so he must've been watching you for a while.

He also made sure he was covered from head to toe so he couldn't be identified on camera. You can't even tell if he's black or white on the footage. He was prepared. He used a remote to open your garage *and* he most likely knew the code to your alarm. Or at least how to disarm it in time without it going off. That's no amateur."

She counted off each point on her fingers as I listened and thought about the bulky figure I watched sneaking in and out of my home on the video from two nights ago.

"I don't bother anybody. I don't *have* any enemies. I shouldn't be on anybody's radar to watch me, break in my house or video tape me. There's no reason for anybody to go through all this trouble to stalk me."

"Did you have any beef with the builder or somebody working for him? They usually use the same kinds of openers for the properties they're contracted for. All they need is the model number and manufacturer name to get a duplicate. You can buy them off Amazon, eBay or just get a programed universal opener."

I hadn't ever considered Donovan, but what if it was him? Maybe he found out about the safe somehow while I was seeing him and decided he wanted to rob me. As far as I knew, he was doing pretty well for himself, but maybe he was greedy. Maybe he was still mad at me. Was it really a coincidence that I ran into him today?

"Why you looking like that? You think it was old boy you were seeing?" She asked as Marisol approached with our waters and Jamie's Heineken.

Stating that our food would be out shortly, she gleamed a broad smile and darted away to another table as Jamie took a gulp of her beer.

"I don't know. I don't know why he would even do something like that. Maybe Todd's wife is off her meds again."

Jamie shook her head and leaned back, placing her free palm flat on the table and strummed her fingers on it.

"Nah. I don't think so. She was sloppy, even with the PI she had helping her out. Breaking glass to get in and all of that. She *wanted* you to know you were violated so you would leave Todd alone. This guy was more meticulous. Skilled. He was probably a hired hand, but not for her. This person didn't expect you to notice. How the hell *did* you spot this thing on a shoebox, all the way up on a shelf anyway? With all the damn shoes you probably got, dude must've thought he could hide it there forever," she snickered fingering the mini-cam again.

"It was on the box next to the one I keep my gun box in. When I went to get it down, I saw it stuck to the side. Just... Dumb luck."

"Dumb luck," she murmured with a sniffle and a smirk.

"Anyway, what did you want to talk to me about?"

She raked her teeth over her bottom lip and took another swig of her drink, swishing it around her mouth like mouthwash before swallowing.

"Kev's dead."

I gasped. "Damn. What happened?"

She sat her beer down and formed her hands into a steeple.

"Somebody put two slugs in his skull and left his body in the bushes on a nature reserve in Miami. Workers clearing out dead trees after a storm found his bones. His wallet and everything were still in his pocket, so he was easy to identify."

I shook my head sympathetically and took the last sip of my nearly empty coffee. I assumed he was in Puerto Rico or somewhere tropical living la Vida Loca. I honestly hadn't thought about him in years, but I hoped, like Jamie and I, that Kevin had turned his life around.

"Wow. I haven't talked to him in years. Wait. Did you say they found his *bones* in the bushes or his *body*?"

"His *bones*. I ain't talk to him since the last time we were all together either, but I just assumed he got brand new on me. I ain't gonna front, I was a little pissed about it too. You know me and Kev go back since we were little jits in Detroit. Even if he decided to go off the grid, I figured he would look me up from time to time. Turns out, somebody peeled his cap back, and he's been dead this whole time."

"This whole time as in how long?"

"As in seven years."

"Who do you think did it? Franco's people?" I whispered.

"Could be. Or maybe somebody closer. At least that's what Lala thinks."

"His sister Lala? You talked to her?"

"Yeah. She's the one who reached out to tell me. Last time she heard from him was on a voicemail. He told her he just dropped me off, where to pick up her cut and that you and him were about to disappear together."

I jerked my head back and frowned. I didn't know anything about Lala except that she was Kevin's sister, an escort like I was, and that Franco had gotten lax enough to open his safe in her presence while they were "dating". He made the crucial mistake of falling for an escort, and she set him up to be robbed and ultimately killed.

"Why would he tell her that? I left back to the A before both of y'all. There weren't any plans for us to disappear together. We weren't even a couple."

She shrugged and thumbed her nose.

"I'm just telling you what she told me. That was the last she heard from him. All these years she thought he was somewhere with you."

"Well, we both know he wasn't with me. She doesn't think *I* had anything to do with him being shot, does she?"

Jamie cocked her head ambivalently and leaned back.

"Are you kidding me?" I screeched.

"Lower your voice," she snapped.

"Sorry. But c'mon. That's crazy. I'm the least likely person to have done something like that. I'm not a killer."

Narrowing her eyes and wiping her nose again she gritted, "I don't know what you're implying Beauty Queen, but neither am I. You might want to watch what you say, and *how* you say it."

"You were the last one to see him alive. Why's she looking at me?"

Her menacing laugh was anything but humorous.

"It sounds to me like you're suggesting *I'm* the type of person that would off my homie. Which would be very hurtful and insulting to me by the way. Especially considering all the love I've showed you then and now."

"For a price," I grumbled.

"Of course, for a price. Nothing in this world is free. You wasn't giving up no ass for a discount," she chuckled again. "Hasn't it been worth it for you? You made money when we did business together and you paid way less for me to handle that situation with Todd than you would have if the police found out. Or better yet, if nobody put a stop to it."

I nodded as the words spilled icily from her lips and my blood curdled under her intimidating glare. I shelled out upwards of five figures for her to get to the bottom of the situation with Todd for me, and she likely extorted way more than that from him to keep her behavior discreet. I knew I was on the clock for this situation too, and she would give me the damages at her leisure.

A nervous breath hitched in my throat as Marisol approached with our orders. She suggestively placed Jamie's plate down in front of her with a flirty grin, then slid mine in front of me. Strangely, Jamie disregarded her lewd, and might I add *rude* behavior and kept her gaze on me. I must have made her angry.

"Can I get you anything else?"

"No," Jamie waved her off like a pesky gnat and began unfolding her knife and fork from the table napkin.

Marisol's face flushed, her posture stiffened with rejection as she raised an embarrassing glance and stalked away.

I watched Jamie tear into her enchilada and suddenly, my hunger wasn't as great.

"Look. I'm not saying *you* did it. I'm just saying that... It doesn't make sense for her to think *I* did. I'm not from Miami. That was my first time ever visiting. How would I know about a nature preserve? Better yet, how would I lure or lug his big ass there after killing him and get away with nobody seeing me? He was 6'5" and 200 and something pounds."

"For what it's worth, *I* don't think you killed him either. I know you ain't built like that. That boy was always into something. No telling who caught him slipping with all that money. Could've been Franco's people or anybody else. I used to tell him that he was too flashy for his own good. But he never listened."

She put another bite in her mouth and chewed obnoxiously before pointing her empty fork my way.

"Let me tell you something Beauty Queen. Money can turn a priest into an assassin."

The more the wheels turned in my head, the less I believed anything that was coming out of Jamie's mouth. Between her behaving like a fidgety addict and the loopholes in her story, I knew she was lying.

Maybe *she* was the one who didn't think the $385K we took a piece was enough money. I hadn't thought about whether her take was enough to finance the businesses she opened in Miami and Atlanta at the time. I was too young, green and afraid of her back then to ever question the moves she made. Being older and wiser now, I had questions.

"So, if you thought it was her all this time, why play these games?"

"Whoa. Whoa. Calm down. I don't know for sure it's her. The guy on the surveillance obviously isn't a woman, so she could have hired him, or he could be there for another reason. I'm just telling you who else it might be. Lala definitely wants revenge for Kev. She might even be the one who shot you."

"Wait. What? But I thought you said they just found his bones recently?"

"Nah. Nah, it wasn't recently. It was back in March. I thought I said that."

I closed my eyes and folded my hands in front of me. She was talking in circles and it was pissing me off.

"No. You didn't. When did you find out about Kevin?"

"She reached out in March."

"I called you! I asked you if you knew if anybody might have it in for me when I was in the hospital. You didn't say anything about Lala or Kevin being dead or anything."

"I was still in my feelings about how you left things with me. Honestly, I didn't know if she had anything to do with it anyway. I still don't know."

The blasé smirk on her face made me want to kick her in the teeth for holding off on this information for so long. If it was indeed, real information.

"Might not have been her. She got locked up the same week anyway."

"Locked up for what?"

"A hundred and twenty days in TGKC for slicing up a girl at a club. Then she got another 30 tacked on for fighting before she got out."

"Where's TGKC? That's not in Georgia is it?"

"Nah," Jamie shook her head while using a fingernail as a toothpick. "Turner Guilford Knight Correctional Center is in Miami."

"So, she came here, shot me, went back to Miami, got locked up, got out, and now she's back in Atlanta sneaking in my house for what?"

She grinned.

"Money. Jewels. Whatever you got in that closet. Or maybe it's not her at all. You tell me."

"How would *she* know what I have anywhere? She doesn't know me."

"I'm pulling at the same straws you are Beauty Queen. I'm just throwing out suggestions. You wanted my help, and I'm here to help you."

I sipped my water, suddenly needing to coat my dry throat as she eyed my plate. I wanted to scream. I wasn't sure which parts of what she was feeding me were lies, and I needed to sleep on it to mull it over in my head.

"You going to eat your food? You ain't took a bite of them fish tacos yet. You ain't hungry."

I waved her off.

"I'll take it to go.

She took another sloppy bite of her enchilada as I ogled the gross way she was eating.

"You need to go ahead and hire me. I'll make it all go away," she said between chews.

"Hire you? I *did* hire you and you waited six months to tell me you probably knew who was stalking me all along."

She laughed heartily.

"You never hired me for that. You hired *Femme Fatale Private Investigations* to find out who vandalized your property. That mission was accomplished. Tab closed on that deal. Technically, I was never working the shooting. Now, you need somebody to *resolve* the problem. Right?

The expertise you would need for that kind of job is gonna cost you a lot more if I have to help you resolve this little issue you're having completely. It could turn out to be somebody else, but it probably isn't."

Bingo. That was her angle. She was going to let Lala or whoever terrorize me until she ultimately came in as the equalizer and resolved the problem for me. At cost. Even if she was right, I wasn't sure I wanted to risk getting into bed with her again. Figuratively speaking of course.

I've seen up close and personal what Jamie is capable of. Watching her splatter the getaway driver's brains all over the boat still haunted my dreams, and my conscience. She had to be expecting a large payday.

She sighed, running a hand over her face like the time I was taking to give her an answer was annoying her.

"Listen Beauty Queen, here are your choices. One. You can sit around and wait for her to finally pick you off. Two. You can track her down and handle your biz yourself, which I don't think you're capable of. Or three. *I* can handle it.

I didn't give you the cops as an option because then you'd have to explain too much and open a can of already sealed and buried worms. The last thing either of us wants is for you to have to mention my name in any sentences that can lead to a felony charge. Right?" she asked sweeping her tongue over her top teeth forebodingly.

I swallowed hard, wringing my hands nervously. Groaning and shifting my gaze to my hands, I replied, "How much to resolve this?"

"Well, we can negotiate a friendship discount if you wanna trade a little pink," she stated licking her lips and pausing poignantly for my response.

I sucked my teeth and glared at her, noting the broad and perverted grin taunting me.

"All right. Your loss Beauty Queen."

"*How* much?"

"$300,000."

"$300,000," I repeated jadedly now clearly understanding her motive.

"Problem solving is expensive."

12

Vanessa

"I'm telling you Vix, as soon as I catch that hoe, I'm two-piecing her in the mouth *on sight*. On sight!" Red Sonja complained banging the steering wheel as we drove up Peachtree in her cherry red Range Rover headed to the *Atlanta Fish Market*.

"I hear you," I half-heartedly replied while checking my hair and makeup in the visor as she vented about her man's baby momma's latest Twitter rant.

I cared less, but it was entertaining listening to her going off in that thick New York accent. Short and petite with a ginger complexion and a head full of long fiery red dreads, Red Sonja was *Kingdom's* premier rap artist. She was a pretty 24-year-old from Brooklyn with a foul mouth and a big personality. Needless to say, despite our age difference, we clicked instantly.

I was especially happy to be in the company of another artist who smoked cigarettes since it seemed like Gavin was just as bad as Brand had been regarding my smoking. Brand hated that I smoked because he said it could damage my vocal cords. Gavin on the other hand, was anti-smoking because his mother and uncle had both died of cancer after being long term smokers.

"She acts like I won't book a flight and show up on her doorstep ready to toss her wig back. I told Ja, he better put a muzzle on his bitch before I do it *for* him. She don't know, but these hands are just as lethal as my mouth. I'll lay that ho *down!*" she threatened, blowing through a light just as it changed to red.

"All right girl. Cuss her ass out in person, but don't kill me before we make it to the restaurant. You just ran that light, and I got things to live for," I jibed, blowing smoke from the Newport I toked out through my nostrils.

Her eyes narrowed, unappreciative of my dig at her reckless driving, as she glanced at me, then into the rearview mirror at traffic behind us.

"My bad. She got me in my feelings with her raggedy ass. Every chance she gets, she's on Twitter with my name in her mouth. Like, don't that ho have some *mothering* to do to her daughter? She's steady online thuggin' wit' her saggy titties and them ugly ass tattoos on display."

Yet another thing Red and I had in common was punk ass baby mommas. Daphne was a pain in my ass I was more than anxious to relieve myself of, but I couldn't think of any way to get rid of her, short of *actually* getting rid of her.

"Listen. Don't let jealous hos knock you off your square girl. Do like I do to Daphne. Just keep stuntin' on them hoes with the latest labels and looking happy. That hurts them more than anything else to see you living happily with the man they lost. That's why I haven't blocked Gav's nosy baby momma from my accounts.

I know every time she looks at a picture of me with Gavin, in his house or wearing something he bought me, it *pains* her," I advised dashing out my cigarette in the ashtray with a grin and caressing the mink hairs on my fur coat.

It wasn't cold enough for mink, but I was glad it was at least a windy 46 degrees to justify. I had been waiting since June to flex the gift Gavin bought me for my birthday.

Everything I had on was ripe for a photoshoot. I wore a pink *Dolce & Gabbana* tie front cardigan, embellished *Dolce* jeans, and black *Ferragamo* ankle boots paired with a mink *Ferragamo* envelope purse. I looked and felt expensive.

My hair was in big barrel curls and my makeup was as flawless as the curves on my body. Thanks to Gavin's frequent generosity, and the regular use of his black card, I never wear or buy *anything* that isn't recognizably pricy anymore. Unless I have to pay for it myself that is.

My days of needing to pilfer the unworn expensive clothes Brent bought Val from her closet were long gone. Now, I was flaunting my come up on the *Gram* and *Snap Chat* daily for hater's and fellow label whores like my cousin Amina to envy. Image is everything, and mine was going to hurt jealous ho's feelings.

Red screeched into the lot for the *Atlanta Fish Market's* valet and threw her car in park like a getaway driver about to hop out and run from the cops. All eyes were on her truck as I gathered my purse, and an attendant helped her step out in green floral printed thigh high Balenciaga boots.

His grin was as wide as Red's hips as he watched her curves sashay to the curb in a black latex bodysuit. While her boots were banging, I had no idea who designed that porn star bodysuit she had on, but if nothing else, it was definitely turning heads.

The *Atlanta Fish Market* was usually packed out on Saturdays and today was no different. It's a popular Buckhead landmark and one of my favorite places to eat. The wooden bar, tables, chairs and leather seated booths were outdated and lacked imagination, but the décor never stopped the crowds of people, including myself, from spending money on their pricy seafood.

We had reservations, because I wouldn't be caught dead waiting in line for anything anymore with my new-found celebrity. While Red spoke to the hostess, a chubby teenage girl with microbraids approached me so quickly I jumped a little.

"Oh my god. Are you Vixen?" she beamed.

"Yes," I answered matching her smile, running a hand through my purple tresses.

"I knew it! Oh my god! I can't believe you're right here. I was just listening to *"Top Shelf"* on my phone. I *love* that song. Oh my god. You're my favorite. Can I take a picture with you?"

"Of course," I answered coyly, posing cheek to cheek with her as she snapped one picture, then another with her cellphone.

"I can't believe I'm really meeting you."

"What's your name?" I asked pretending to care.

"Shelley."

"Nice to meet you Shelley. I'm glad you like my music"

"Who do we have here?" Red asked turning back towards us as the hostess got ready to seat us.

"Oh— my— god," Shelley mumbled palming her cheeks with her phone still in one hand like she was having excitement overload. "Red Sonja!"

"Oh, you know me *too* Lil' Momma?" she asked flinging her dreads back and posturing so that her booty commanded an audience from anyone else looking.

I smirked because the girl was taller than me *and* Red with our short selves, but she was calling her *Lil'* Momma. Even funnier was how the eyes on one of the adult men in the group Shelley left bulged out of his head while staring at Red's butt.

"Oh my god. Yes! I'm Shelley. I know all of you guys songs. Can I take a picture with both of you?" she squealed pouring it on thick.

"Sure. We can take a few snaps," Red replied wrapping an arm around the girl's waist as I leaned in from the other side for the group photo.

She got two more pictures with different poses from both of us before an older woman, who resembled an older version of Shelley interrupted.

"Okay. Thank you so much ladies for taking pics with my daughter. She loves you guys. Let's go Shell. I'm sure they're ready to get to their table."

"Thank you!" Shelley shrieked happily, damn near gliding away while looking down at the pictures on her phone.

A few other patrons stopped us to speak or ask for pictures as we made way to our table too, and like the hams we are, we took every one. I loved the attention from fans. Hell, that was one of the perks I loved the *most* about becoming a celebrity. The recognition, unless I was doing something I didn't want to be recognized for, was half of my motivation.

"I am *sooo* hungry," Red said right after our waitress dropped off our drinks and went to put our food orders in.

"Me too. I haven't eaten anything but oxygen today."

She laughed.

"Don't y'all got a chef up in that big mansion to keep your belly full?"

"Yeah, but Gavin was beatin' it up from the time he got back from New York until the time I left. I ain't have time to put nothing but his dick in my mouth."

Red and I were cool, but I decided not to tell her about the incident with Daphne. I was done talking about that ho for the day and I didn't want to get Red back yapping about her guy's baby's mother either.

"I ain't mad at ya. That millionaire dick deserves to be serviced when he's lacing you in Minks," she jibed knowing he got me the coat for my birthday.

I nodded and looked down at my vibrating phone when I felt a presence looming over me. Looking up into the familiar face, I cocked an eyebrow. I hadn't seen her in almost a year, so I wasn't sure how to receive her presence.

"Hey Van. I thought that was you," she greeted me and leaned down for a hug I semi reciprocated. "How are you?"

"I'm great. Just taking a break to eat with my friend."

"Hi. I'm Rachel," she said extending a hand out to Red.

"Sorry. I don't shake hands before I eat when there aren't any wet wipes at the table. No offense to you of course. Nice to meet you," Red replied in a phony smile and tone I recognized.

Rachel slowly withdrew her hand and used it to sweep hair from her Chinese bob from her face before clearing her throat and turning back to me.

"So, long time no see. Correction. Long time since you've seen *me*. I've been seeing *you* all over the television and hearing you on the radio. I'm so proud of you girl."

I smirked while sizing up her appearance and mentally picking it apart. The orange long sleeve, *Bodycon* knitted dress she wore did her typically stick figure shape justice by making her small breasts and booty look perkier and fatter.

Other than that, she didn't look like her lifestyle had upgraded much since we last saw each other. Rachel, Delia and I were thick as thieves since the ninth grade, and probably still would be if Delia hadn't betrayed me with Brand Beats. Once Rachel sided with her, she was curbed too.

"Thanks."

"I actually thought I saw you dancing last night at *The Man Trap*, but then I realized it was your sister. She was really good, but, what happened? I thought she danced for Alvin Ailey in New York?"

I maintained my pokerfaced expression and glanced at Red for a quick second before replying.

"Well, obviously not anymore. What were *you* doing at the strip club? I thought that wasn't your thing? At least it wasn't when we hung."

"Oh, believe me, that hasn't changed. It's *still* not my thing, and even if it was, it wouldn't be after last night. My cousin Joyce is getting married and she had her bachelorette party there. Her and her rowdy ass grooms-maids got into it with some other drunk ass negroes and ended up going to jail.

I'm glad the wedding isn't until next weekend or she would've been missing hers today."

"Your cousin and her *grooms-maids*?" Red interjected bewilderedly.

"Yeah," Rachel nodded. "My cousin's a masculine type lesbian, so sort of as a partial joke. She's been saying she's the groom and calling people standing on her side grooms-maids. Four of the five attendants are women, but they're just as butch as she is."

I sighed twirling the straw inside my rum and coke. This disloyal broad was still on my "do not call" list, and she knew it. Yet she was over here yapping like we were still besties.

"I hope your sister is okay too. I heard some guy got arrested for choking her. I guess people were losing their damn minds last night."

I couldn't hide the shock on my face. Whether we were cool or not, she was still my sister. That explained the small spell I experienced at Daphne's house that night. I hadn't heard jack about anybody choking her, but that had to be what I was feeling.

"I beg your pardon? What guy was choking her?"

"I don't know. I didn't see it happen. Some of the dancers were talking about it when we were all out in the parking lot trying not to get arrested too. At least I was. One of the girls pointed him out when the cops brought him out in cuffs, but I didn't get a good look at him."

"And she didn't tell you?" Red commented like anybody was talking to her or asked for her nosy ass opinion. "That's crazy. You should call her. I know if a bastard puts hands on one of *my* sisters, me and the goons are running down on him like Storm Troopers."

"Simmer down Darth Vader. It must not have been that serious if I haven't heard about it yet. I got a couple of missed calls from her last night, but I haven't had a chance to call her back yet," I lied.

Not only hadn't Val called me, but I wouldn't recognize her number even if she had, considering the fact that I was never given her new one. I was thinking about making a call to Mommy Dearest and asking for it now though. I would feel like shit if she somehow died before we ever made up.

"She's probably fine," Rachel said placing a caring hand over mine. "I'm sure she'll tell you all about it later. And... You know Van, I really came over to let you know how proud I am of you. I know how hard you have worked to get your career off the ground and every time I see you on television or hear you on the radio, I can't help but smile.

I know we kind of fell out after you and Delia got into it, but I really do miss you. Maybe we can meet up another time and talk about it."

"Talk about what? I'm over it. I've *been* over it. In case you didn't know, I'm in a relationship with Gavin The God now. She chose Brand, and you chose her side over mine. It's all good. Everything happens for a reason," I answered moving my hand from under hers and cocking my head.

She straightened her posture and glanced uncomfortably from me to Red, who was watching us like an episode of *Love and Hip Hop Atlanta.* If there had been a bucket of popcorn on the table, I'm sure she would have eaten from it.

"It wasn't like that Van. I know it seemed like that to *you.* But it wasn't like that. I know now isn't the time to talk about it. But... It wasn't like that at all. You know I've always been ride or die for you *and* Delia both. If you'd let me back in, you'd know that. I just feel like we should move past it. Especially since Delia is awake now. Don't you?"

Evidently, the blank stare I was bestowing on her was taken as a cue to continue rather than to wrap it up. I didn't need anybody eavesdropping in my business and Red didn't need to be present for this discussion either.

"I gotta believe that me seeing you here is more than a coincidence. The last time Dee and I talked, she was saying that she was going to reach out to you again and try to mend fences. Once upon a time, we made a pact to never let a man come between us. You remember that?"

Oh brother. This was the same mess she spewed on the voicemails I ignored before she finally got a clue and stopped.

"Once upon a time, we were in *high school* when we made that pact. Let us not forget that I'm not the one who let a man come between us either. You and Delia did."

She sighed and folded her lips in with a poignant stare.

"Okay. Well, while I've got your ear, I also wanted to give you my condolences for the loss of your father. I know it was months ago but, he was always nice to me and Dee growing up. We sent a reef to the funeral when we heard.

I wanted us to come to the services to support you too but, we weren't sure if you would be okay with us being there. You know if anybody knows how you can get, *we do*, and we knew you weren't above cussing our asses out in front of your whole family if you felt like it," she giggled.

I smiled genuinely too as a momentary phase of nostalgia encompassed me. I could see the sincerity in her face about my dad, and I appreciated that. I missed him all the time and I hated not having anyone around that I could talk to about him who would share the sentiment.

Rachel was right. At one time in our lives, no one knew me better than she and Delia. Not even my sister or cousins. I didn't have anybody in my life that close now, and as a rising celebrity, I probably needed people like that in my corner. Maybe I *should* reconnect with her.

"True," I threw her a bone and a half-smile. "That day was a little crazy. I might have let y'all slide by that time since you were coming in good faith."

"You know what's really crazy? Knowing what we know now, if we would have actually come, whoever shot Delia would have missed their chance to hurt her."

I nodded. She was right again. I would have had to come up with *another* date and time to blow Delia away had she shown up to Daddy's services. I only wished I had executed my plot better in the first place. I was supposed to leave her as a corpse instead of a patient.

Two waitresses approached with our food on trays and Rachel moved to the side as they set them on the table and asked if we needed anything else. I didn't want anything, but Red asked for extra cocktail sauce and dug into her food like there was no one but her and the plate in the room.

Rachel glanced her watch when the servers left and then in the direction she was originally headed.

"Well, I'm going to let y'all enjoy your meal and get back to my date before he sends out a search party for me. It was good seeing you again Van. My number is still the same if you can ever etch out time in your busy schedule for one of your ex best girls.

Maybe we can go see Delia together or something when they start allowing her visitors again."

"I don't think that's a good idea. I tried to go see her in the hospital already, and thanks to Brand, I'm on the block list. So, I'm just going to have to wish her well through prayers from a distance."

"Wow. Really? Well, I can't believe she would want that. Despite everything, she still loved you and hoped you could work past this riff. I hope that for you too. God willing, we'll all have plenty of time to talk it out and get it right this time. All we need is time an opportunity."

I nodded, averting my eyes to the drink I was now sipping through a straw. I hoped that by some miracle Delia would be dead before that opportunity arose, and just like that... Rachel had overstayed her welcome.

"Rachel. Girl, you better get back to your date like you said. I know if I was in his shoes I would be two seconds away from leaving by now," I said picking up a knife and fork for my New Zealand King Salmon. "We'll catch up some other time. I don't want to be rude to Red. You take care girl."

Red and I were cool, but we were still getting to know each other. Rachel's diarrhea of the mouth was only going to lead to probing questions from Red later I wasn't sure I would ever answer.

"Oh. Okay. Yeah. Well, call me. Or, I'll call you. Nice meeting you Red," she said with a small wave before slowly walking off.

Red placed a piece of crabmeat in her mouth as the waitress dropped off the requested extra cocktail sauce on her way to another table.

"So, you, this Olive Oil looking chick..." she said using her fork to point in the direction Rachel went between chews. "And Delia used to be close huh?"

"We did," I chuckled.

"Are you thinking about being friends with her again since she extended that flimsy little olive branch?"

"Maybe."

"I wouldn't. I mean, I don't know that bird from any of these other pigeons out here, but she seemed fake to me. Jane Jetson told me to be careful of old friends trying to become new ones again when you get famous," she warned and I nodded in agreement.

Jane Jetson had been a platinum selling singer on Epic Records in the early 2000's before coming to *Kingdom* two years ago. If anybody knows about fake friends, it would be her. Her feuds and court cases with friends and family members were highly publicized at one time, and I didn't want that for myself.

"On God, after hearing her talk, she doesn't even seem like your type of chick. Don't get me wrong. I know we haven't been down for a long time either, but she comes off like a lame, stay in her lane, never out the box type. Am I off base or nah?"

I looked up at her prying face while chewing my food and debated whether or not to elaborate. Red Sonja and I were cool, but *how* cool was still yet to be determined. I've never hung too tight with females other than Rachel and Delia, unless you count my sister and cousins.

Other women rarely had the same objectives as I did and eventually, we ended up butting heads over something. Money, men and fame are the only things that make my world go 'round, and most of these vagina toting coat tail riders can't adjust.

"Let's just say... she's a Michelle," I answered after swallowing my food.

"A Michelle? Michelle who? Obama?"

"*Heeeeell* no," I snickered. "A *Michelle*. Like from *Destiny's Child*. If me, Delia and Rachel were *Destiny's Child*, I would be Beyoncé, Delia would be Kelly, and Rachel would be Michelle."

"*Soooo*, y'all could sing better than her?" she curled her lip up confusedly.

"*Noooo.* It's not about singing. Delia wasn't a singer. I'm saying metaphorically. If we were them, she'd be the Michelle to us. *The lame one.* The one that nobody ever wants to be for a costume party. *Like that.* Fits in, but never as fabulous. She was a good friend for the most part, until she took the wrong side," I scowled.

Red nodded as my phone began vibrating again and I remembered that I hadn't checked to see who was calling me earlier. The number that came through wasn't private, but it didn't belong to anyone saved in my phone either.

Unlike a lot of people, I don't have an aversion to answering unknown numbers. Now that my money was up, I didn't have any bill collectors to worry about, and before I signed with *Kingdom,* the primary connections I made came from numbers I didn't already have.

"Hello," I answered taking a sip of my drink.

"Hello, is this Ms. Vanessa Vincent?"

"Yes. Who is this?"

"This is Detective Drew Randall with the Fulton County Police Department. We have some new developments in the death of Lamar Freeman, and we would like for you to come in and talk to us about it as soon as possible."

If my heart had legs, it could've jumped out of my chest and sprinted away.

13

Valerie

Tuesday

After several of the slowest moments on earth, I finally heard the locks on the custom wrought iron double doors turning before one of them swung open.

"Hey," I stated with the biggest smile I could muster, hoping to influence the deadpan gaze my cousin greeted me with.

"Hey," Amina replied dryly.

I could tell by her high ponytail, splattered long sleeve T-shirt and leggings that I had probably interrupted her in the middle of painting. A big, black Doberman stood intimidatingly on guard by her side as I took a cautious step backwards.

"Oh shoot. When did you get a dog?"

"How can I help you?" she answered with one hand lingering on the door in preparation to shut it on me.

Uh… Did she hear my question?

"How can you help me?"

"Yeah. What can I do for you? Did you and that Foxy Black chick fall out or something? Are you looking for a place to stay?"

I swear my cousin is petty. I knew she would be mad, but I didn't expect her reception to be *this* icy. If not for the faint sounds of Christmas music playing in the background reminding me why I was there, I would have followed her petty lead and screeched out of her driveway.

The thing is, I missed my cousin. I missed my family. Hell, I missed my Daddy, and it was time I stopped fighting reconciling with everyone before I lost someone else I loved unexpectedly. Tomorrow isn't promised to anyone, and the days I've had to think about that gave me reason to be at Amina's doorstep now.

"You're funny. I don't need a place to stay, and even if I did, I can afford my own place now, thank you very much. P.S. her name is Black Fox, not Foxy Black."

"Peachy. So, what do you want?"

"To come see how my cousin is. My Bestie that I haven't seen in months. That I miss very much," I smirked, hoping to penetrate her frosty exterior with a little charm.

"Girl bye. You haven't *been* missing me. You didn't even give me your new number when you changed it. So why are you here? I'm busy."

Damn. If my face was made of glass, it would have cracked and shattered all over her porch along with the light cover of snow, and my ego.

"Wow. You're that mad?"

She didn't answer, but the slight tilt of her head, and twist of her glossy lips did. Hell yeah she was that mad.

"Well, can I at least come inside and apologize? It's cold as a witch's titty out here."

"You don't have to come inside for that."

I thought the November wind attacking my face was cold, but sheesh! It didn't have anything on Amina. I glanced awkwardly over the lay of her property, again debating on fleeing, then back into her unforgiving eyes.

"Okay. All right. I can apologize here. I'm sorry."

"For what?" she asked folding her arms indignantly across her chest.

"For... shutting you out. Not giving you my new number, and not coming to see you sooner."

"And."

"And... What?" I frowned.

I was sorry, but I wasn't about to be out here groveling and getting sick to stroke her ego. Just like she was my best friend, I knew I was hers. She could play tough all she wanted to, but whether she was mad at me or not, I was sure the missing was mutual.

"*And*, for accusing me of wanting your man and deserting me while I was still recovering from being shot, and not even checking up on me even once."

If my guilt-ridden expression didn't say it all, my mouth was about to. I said a lot of stuff during our argument that I didn't really believe, but she knew I wasn't in my right emotional state then. I did owe her an apology for not checking up on her recovery though. She was definitely there for me when I was going through it with my Achilles injury, and I owed her that much.

"And for getting in my feelings and accusing you of wanting Maaco. *Aaaaaaaand* for deserting you while you were recovering. From the pits of my soul, I'm sorry. I was selfish. I admit it. It's not because I didn't care though. You should know that."

"Whatever," she replied stepping to the side to let me in.

I stopped just inside the doorway and waited beside her while she locked the door. There was no way in hell that I was about to try that Doberman while he looked like he was fantasizing about chomping my jugular. He hadn't taken his eyes off me yet, and I was afraid any wrong move would seal my fate.

"Does he bite?"

"Of course," she answered snobbishly, typing a code in the security pad and leading the way to her great room with an attitudinal strut. "That's why I got him."

I rolled my eyes behind her back and unwrapped the scarf from my neck. Taking a seat on the white leather sectional, I observed the colorful pictures, statues and artwork strategically placed in the room as Amina disappeared into the adjacent kitchen.

"I love what you did in here. I'm loving the elephant tusks over your fireplace too. Are those real or manmade?" I called after her.

There was a veil of silence for a short while before she reemerged with a mug of what smelled like coffee with the dog on her heels. Smugly sipping from the cup and peering at me over the edge of it, she sat in the loveseat across from me, and the dog laid on the floor beside her.

"Real," she finally answered and placed the mug on a cupholder on the table between us.

Where was the hospitality? For the love of God, the heifer didn't even offer me a sip of tap water, and I was thirsty. My nerves were already bad, and the two shots of vodka-cran I had before leaving the house were starting to wear off.

"So, tell me why you dipped on the whole family Val."

I sighed and looked around her living space as if something in it would give me the inspiration to say what I wanted to say.

"It was just a lot. Tearing my Achilles tendon, losing my spot at Alvin Ailey, catching Brent and Vanessa. Then losing Daddy..." I rubbed the back of my neck agitatedly. "I just needed an escape where I could live my life, dance and take a break from the drama."

"Okay. I just don't understand why you had to cut everybody off to cope with what happened when all any of us wanted to do was be there for you. At the very *least*, you knew *I* would have your back."

"I know you would have," I answered ashamedly. "I didn't want that though. Everybody's so used to me doing what *they* want me to, or what *they* think I should do. I just wanted to do *me* for a change. Do you real-ize that until that point, at almost 30 years old, I had never made a deci-sion about my own life that didn't include getting someone else's input on it first? Never.

If it wasn't from my parents, you, Vanessa, Yasmin, Nicky, Tamika, Uncle Jerry, Aunt Pam or Mark, it was from Brent or Uncle Derek when I lived with him in New York. That's *a lot* of people behind the controls of my life.

I'm not blaming anybody but myself for it, but the truth is, I was enabled to keep functioning like that all my life. I was *literally* afraid to make decisions alone. How pathetic is that at my age? I started to feel suffocated."

"Well. Mission accomplished. You've been making all the decisions without any of our inputs," she stated draping an arm across the top of the loveseat.

"It wasn't personal Amina. I mean it *was*, but it wasn't like I only alienated you. I was in a different headspace then. I realize now that I don't have to shut y'all completely out to be my own person. Don't misunderstand, Vanessa is still as far out on the curb as a trick can be, but the rest of y'all don't have to be.

I'm truly sorry if I hurt you or made you feel like I didn't care about you, but… I was just trying to find my way out of a lifelong, mile deep, rabbit hole. Maybe I'm having my mid-life crisis early. I don't know what it is. I just needed to do what I did."

"All right," she said twirling a random tendril from her ponytail around her finger.

I don't know what I expected her to say or do after I poured my emotions out for her, but this sure as hell wasn't it. I was about to say something else, but she beat me to the punch.

"So, tell me about this great life you have now shaking what your momma gave you at *The Man Trap*," she said with every bit of sarcasm intended, pouring from her tone.

"See, while you're being all judgmental about what I do, I've made more money dancing at the club per month than I was when I was dancing with AA."

"Judgmental? Me? Believe me, I'm the *last* person who would be judging you for making your coins in the sex industry. Aunt Di and the rest of them *surely* are, but I'm not. I was judging you shutting me out, not you stripping. I don't care about that. If you're happy and it's paying your bills, that's your choice."

I studied her face for signs of deceit or mockery while taking off my coat, revealing my maroon Cowlneck sweatshirt and found none. I was starting to feel kind of guilty for boxing her in with everybody else.

We shared countless secrets from childhood on up, and though I still kept some things to myself, she never spilled anything I ever told her in confidence to anyone else to my knowledge.

"*Are* you happy though?" she quizzed.

"Sure. Once I got over the anxiety of having to get naked in front of strangers, it was a piece of cake. I mean, it's all just dancing right? And that's what I'm good at. I'm just like… A modern-day Josephine Baker," I told her trying to convince the both of us that I believed it to be true.

She raised a brow skeptically and picked up her coffee to drink as I continued my spiel.

"It's actually pretty cool. It's kind of fun getting in touch with my sexy side and coming up with new choreography to make myself stand out. I go by Angel, and I have different color costumes with wings and everything.

The only thing I still struggle with sometimes is the one-on-one time with customers off stage. You know I'm naturally introverted, but I've been getting better at acting like I'm not."

"If I was a stripper, I would do better with the one-on-one time. I'm not up for all those stage tricks and getting sweaty trying to pop my pussy all night. But, since dancing is your thing, I could see how it's not that different than what you were already doing."

"Right."

She kept sipping from her mug, and I sat uncomfortably, periodically touching my hair and scanning her place, wishing we could get our mojo back.

"So, are we good now?"

"*Pssh.* I guess your little rinky dink apology will suffice."

"Rinky dink?" I laughed. "I. Beg. Your. Pardon. That apology was heartfelt. What's really rinky dink is your damn hospitality. Where's *my* cup of coffee? You know all this begging has me parched.

Better yet, can a sista' get some libations? You didn't even offer me tap water. I mean, can you at least pour some in my hand?" I joked, trying to sound like Chris Rock in the movie *I'm Gonna Git You Sucka*, where he begged for a handful of soda at a fast-food restaurant.

Her stern exterior cracked into a bout of giggles when I cupped my palms together and mockingly held them out towards her. As bougie as she can be, her and Mark are like television and movie trivia savants. They're constantly quoting them and thinking people they meet have a celebrity twin. I knew my antics would break her hardened shell.

"Greedy."

"I'm not greedy. I'm thirsty!"

"Come on fool," she said standing, as did the dog beside her. "Did you want some coffee for real or were you serious about wanting something alcoholic to drink? All I have is wine and maybe some Champaign."

"I'll take the wine. But umm… Are you sure he's not going to bite me if I follow behind you?"

"No girl. He's fine. He's just protective, and a little bit spoiled. Linx. Make friends," she told him, and the dog immediately approached me with his head down. "Hold your hand out Val. With your palm up."

I did as she said, and the dog sniffed my hand for a brief moment before headbutting it.

"He wants you to pet him," she told me. "That's how he makes friends."

I stroked the top of his head a few times before kneeling on one knee to rub the side of his face and under his chin when he leaned into it.

"Hi big boy," I cooed. "Are you your mommy's protector? Huh big boy? You make sure nobody hurts your mommy?"

His wagging nub gave me relief as he nudged his head further into my hand and even licked it once. As an animal lover, baby talk has always been my secret weapon to get on their good side. But I'm no dummy. I wasn't going to try it if she hadn't assured me he would be receptive.

"Come on animal whisperer, if you want that wine," Amina interrupted after a few minutes of watching Linx and I get acquainted.

"When did you get him?"

"A couple of weeks after Uncle Vernon died. Since *you* deserted me, and I was still cooped up in the house for the most part all by myself. I thought I'd get a companion. Believe it or not, he's only 10 months old."

"Damn he's big for 10 months. He seems well trained though," I told her while washing my hands in the kitchen sink and ignoring that blatant dig.

"He has his days. Believe me. He's too smart for his own good sometimes. He's learned how to open room doors if you don't lock them. It takes him a while, but his black ass can get out."

"Open doors? Like, turn the knobs?"

"Umm hmm. I got him from a guy that trains security and police dogs for the Atlanta PD so he goes straight for whatever weapon you have. Like I said. He's smart. Me and Mark worked with him a lot to get him to where he is now. He's friendly but he'll rip your throat out if I command him to."

I frowned considering how she said it while I was in the midst of petting him. She just shrugged and smirked, so I figured she was exaggerating. He was a big dog, but I doubted he was that vicious. Yet.

"What happened to Donovan? I thought y'all were an item," I asked surprised she wasn't still seeing him.

From what little I knew and saw of him when Amina and I were still talking, she really liked him, and the feeling was mutual. I felt sure they were going to be in it for the long haul. But then again, what did I know with my bleak history.

She sucked her teeth.

"To make a long story short. No. I ran into him the other day and he started texting me again, but I haven't had anything to say."

"What did he do?"

"Nothing. He was just looking for the type of woman that I'm not. And I'm not about to change."

"Oh. Seemed like you really liked him." I leaned backwards against the sink and surveyed the upgrades since I was here last.

I loved the avantgarde décor with reflective surfaces, high-tech kitchen appliances and a huge tree branch designed chandelier hanging over the island.

Noticing she never responded, I queried further while noticing a small television monitor with four split screens on the opposite wall from the one housing her 35" flat screen.

"So you haven't been dating anybody new?"

"Girl," she chuckled wearily. "I was but… Chile I don't even want to talk about it. That relationship is dead. Literally. I'm concentrating on other things, like talking to this gallery owner I know about selling my paintings."

"Seriously?" I asked shrilly, snapping my head back towards her and clapping my hands. "*Yeeeees*! You're finally going to be selling your paintings somewhere! I'm so proud of you!"

"Calm down," she chuckled as I rushed to hug her and she guardedly reciprocated. "I've only sold a few paintings and what's going to be shown in the gallery hasn't been written in stone yet."

"That's *still* huge! I told you a long time ago you should be selling your paintings in these big boutiques or online. I know Mark and Aunt Pam gotta be bursting at the seams about it," I boasted.

Even though she was clearly trying not to be pretentious, I knew painting had always been her passion and it's the only area in Amina's life that she was bashful about. Like Eryka Badu said, she's an artist, and she's sensitive about her shit. So much so that she rarely shared it with anyone outside of the family. This was a definite milestone for her, and I was genuinely happy for my cousin.

"I haven't told them yet. I'm sure they will be though."

"*Sooooo* am I the *first* one you've told?" I asked as a childish grin spread across my face.

"Yes," she answered pretending I was annoying her.

"I knew you still loved me," I playfully pinched her rump and went to inspect what the split screen television showed. "Does this show your entire property?"

"What? Oh," she answered taking a bottle of wine from the refrigerator. "Mostly. Front, back, driveway and street view. I won't get caught slipping again."

I can't say I blamed her for being cautious when her attacker was still out there. Especially when I hadn't left the house myself since I saw Brent without worrying I would see him again. I wasn't really *afraid* of Brent yet, but I was getting there.

Chewing the corner of her bottom lip, she brought two glasses down from a cabinet beside it. That lip chewing had been a dead giveaway to her anxiety since childhood and I wondered what was behind it while moving to sit in one of three metallic, high-back stools at the island.

"Did you know Malik was in Uncle Jerry's backyard?"

"What? When?" I balked noting her impromptu subject as she filled our glasses halfway with wine.

"He snuck back there at like two or three in the morning the same day Yas went into labor. He came to get his motorcycle that Uncle Jerry was supposed to be working on. Uncle J said Yasmin saw him out the kitchen window and damn near pissed herself."

My mouth hung open speechlessly as she nodded in affirmation. I didn't even think that man was still in the state. He had been on the run since he stabbed Yasmin and I felt sure he had either offed himself or fled somewhere far away by now.

"Wow. I can't believe nobody told me."

"It's not like you've been the easiest person to reach."

"Whatever Amina. I just saw her on Saturday. She didn't even tell me."

"Yeah, I heard about that. Yasmin said you came up there half drunk, cussing like a sailor and snapped on her when she said you were looking tired," she informed passing me a glass half filled with wine.

"Half drunk? Are you freaking kidding me? I was not. And of course, I looked tired. I had just finished working all night, and instead of sleeping, I drug my tired ass up to the hospital to see her.

My mother called and texted that she was having the baby so I went up there to see Sophie, but her fat ass was still pregnant when I got there."

I was livid that Yasmin was spreading that BS to my family. I can only imagine the crap she would have spread if I hadn't been wearing a turtleneck and she had seen the bruises on my neck.

"You *have* turned into a trash mouth though, and you *do* look hella' tired for only… Three o'clock in the afternoon. Did you work last night too?" she laughed looking at her wristwatch as her eyes fell over me briefly in summation.

"What do you think? I have to make a living, don't I? What's wrong with how I look?" I touched my face self-consciously and looking down at my clothes, knowing I hadn't been to work since Brent attacked me.

Not only was I offended, but I was baffled too. The one thing I *was* getting a lot of, besides booze and Netflix, was sleep. Maybe I wasn't as put together as Yasmin and Amina looked on an average day, but then I never was.

I've always been a casual girl. Sweatpants, sweatshirts, leggings, long T-shirts, and jeans always made up the majority of my wardrobe. Maybe I could have rolled an iron over my clothes one more time, but my hair was neat.

What was with these broads all of the sudden harping on how tired I looked? I was starting to wonder if how I felt on the inside, was starting to show on the outside.

"All right. Don't get snippy," she said flippantly sipping her wine.

I gulped down more of mine with an attitude and closed my eyes as it's warmth soothed my angst.

"My bad. I'm sorry. I am tired, but nobody wants to keep hearing that they *look* it," I said forcing a smile. "Especially after hearing the other stuff Yasmin said about me. I swear if she wasn't pregnant and I was a fighter, I would have smacked her."

"Mm hmm. Well, Mika already did that."

"I know but that was a long time ago."

"A long time ago? No, it wasn't. That's how she went into labor."

"Stop lying! For real?" I exclaimed cupping my mouth.

"Hand to God," Amina said raising it. "Yasmin didn't tell nobody either. Mika told Uncle J yesterday. That's how you know Yas must've been in the wrong or else she would have been telling *eeeeeverybody*."

I leaned over and grabbed the bottle of wine. Filling my glass to the brim, I gulped down a third of it and Amina sat on the stool beside me.

"*Wheeewwwww!*" I squawked squeezing my eyes shut and flailing my hands as the liquid saturated my organs. "This tea requires *alcohol*. What did she do this time? I didn't even think they were dealing with each other anymore."

"They weren't. Mika came over to leave the boys with Uncle J and decided to go ask Yasmin questions she knows damn good and well she didn't really want to know the answers to."

"*Ooooh* boy."

"Umm hmm. She asked her how many times they slept together, and Yasmin told her four."

I just shook my head from side to side skeptically.

"I'd bet money it was more than that."

"I was thinking the same thing!" Amina screeched as we high fived each other. "She *is* a professional liar you know. Lawyers are trained in deceit. I talked to Mika myself and she said Yasmin kept calling him Dwayne too like she was too good to call him Dub."

"Girl, I never heard anybody call him that until she said it at the hospital. I totally forgot his name was Dwayne, even though I know Waynie was named after him."

"Shit. I forgot too."

We laughed.

"I can't with the two of them. I'm *soooo* glad Vanessa didn't get pregnant by Brent. I would *not* have been able to handle it."

We both nodded and sipped our wine in contemplation. I love Tamika's kids to pieces, and plan to love Sophie the same way, but I can't say I would be able to stomach a reminder that my sister slept with my ex-fiancé if Vanessa had gotten pregnant by Brent. I think my hate for them would trump my ability to love their child.

"It's times like this that I'm happy I don't have a sister," she joked, and I laughed with her. "I went up there Sunday for a couple of hours and it was awkward as hell. I barely know what to say to her. I almost feel like I don't know who she is anymore."

"I almost feel like I don't know who *anybody* is anymore."

I was glad Amina and I were reconnecting again, and that yearning I've had for a sense of belonging was slowly starting to dissipate with every minute I was here. Still, I felt like something between us was re-miss.

"That's because you've been MIA for so long."

"Even before that," I said seriously.

Taking a sip of wine and repositioning herself on the stool she said, "So, catch me up on you. How are you and Maaco doing? You know I haven't talked to him since you left me in the dust."

"We're *not* doing. We're kind of just trying to figure things out right now. I'm not sure I'm ready to jump into anything anytime soon after what happened with me and Brent."

"Girl please," she sucked her teeth and glided the nails on one hand back and forth across her thumb. "Don't let your bad relationship with Brent deter you from a good thing with Maaco," she said playfully nudging me with her shoulder and I smirked.

"Oh, he's no saint. He has red flags too."

"Like what?"

"Like he might have a four-month-old son and never told me."

"What do you mean *might*?"

I drank more wine, even though I didn't feel like it was doing anything for my nerves. I wanted... No, *needed* something stronger for this conversation.

"The mom won't take a paternity test."

She mulled over my words and stared into her wine glass for a long moment before speaking.

"What's the maybe-baby's momma's name?" she asked in a tranquil tone that gave me pause.

"Capri."

She nodded slowly.

"You knew about her before?"

"I knew Jamie busted her cheating on him and I knew she was pregnant, but I didn't know it was supposed to be his."

"Why didn't you tell me?"

She screwed her face up and stared at me like I was crazy.

"Tell you when? You haven't even been talking to me. Besides, what was I supposed to tell you? She was before y'all got back together. Plus, I don't know whose child that hoe had. If it was his, why wouldn't she want to prove it?"

I hissed and finished off my glass of wine. This conversation felt like déjà vu. Courtney had virtually said the same thing to me in the kitchen, and now I was wondering if I really was overreacting.

"The way he keeps secrets, for all I know, he could have a whole family in Miami. He just spent a week *supposedly* closing down one of Jamie's clubs, but how do I know that's all he was doing? Seems like a lot of days just for that. Right?"

Amina frowned and put her hand up to stop me.

"Hold up. Maaco went to Miami to close down Jamie's club?"

"Yeah. Quiet as kept, her gambling has been getting out of hand, and he's had to step in to try to help her get right again."

"Oh really. How long has her gambling been out of control?"

"I don't know," I shrugged. "He just started talking to me about it a couple of months ago, but I think it's been pretty bad for *waaay* longer than that. Why? You think he's lying about that too? Exaggerating her problems so he can use it as an excuse to have to bail her out and go out of town?"

Amina drank the rest of her wine and wiped her mouth with the back of her hand.

"No. No. I was just curious. Did they own that together or was that just hers?"

"Uhh… I don't know. I didn't ask all that."

"But they *both* own *Platform,* right? They're still partners in that?"

"Y-yeah. As far as I know. What does this stuff have to do with any-thing?"

Was she trying to help me figure out if he was cheating or figure out if his finances were in trouble?

"Nothing. Never mind. Are you upset because you think he's cheat-ing, because he didn't *tell you,* or that he actually might have a baby with this girl?"

Twiddling my fingers, I deliberated on her questions and looked to the ceiling for wisdom.

"You don't even know do you?"

"I *do* know," I snapped. "I'm upset because this secret might just be the tip of the iceberg. I don't want to be hurt again. I can't take being hurt again."

"I know sweetheart," Amina said touching my knee sympathetically. "But Maaco isn't Brent. He should have told you that girl is claiming her son is his, but he's not Brent. He's nothing like Milk Dud.

Maaco's just private. For the record, he's not even the one who told me about Capri. Jamie did. Just… Don't push him away if you really want to be with him Val. It's not easy to find a good man out here. If you want to be with him, do it."

"Me wanting to be with him doesn't make him right for me. I thought Brent was right for me at one time too and the negro slept with my sister, then tried to choke me out."

"Wait. What? You never told me he choked you. I thought you were only fighting Vanessa?" Her faced balled into a frown as she refilled our glasses.

"No. Last night."

Her face stayed contorted as I pulled my collar to show her the bruises on my neck and ran down our encounter at The Man Trap. By the end of it, she was off the stool and pacing heatedly.

"I hope you're planning to let Maaco whip his ass. Did you tell Vic? Oh lord. Vic is gonna kill him this time."

"Hell no I didn't tell Vic. He was already lucky Brent didn't press charges on him after the funeral. I don't want him or Maaco getting locked up behind this nonsense."

"Well, if you need me to run up on him, I can get him *alll* the way right."

I chuckled. "You know Brent is not a street guy. I think he got the point when he got arrested. I hadn't seen him in months before last night."

She waved me off. "Do you have a gun?"

"A gun? Girl no. He's not *that* dangerous. This is Brent we're talking about. Prep school. Trust Fund Baby Brent."

"Did you expect Prep school, Trust Fund Baby Brent to damn near choke you to death?"

I stared into nothingness in contemplation.

"None of us thought Malik would try to turn Yasmin into Sharon Tate either, but he did. Sometimes you have to anticipate the worst, and prepare to protect yourself."

"That's what the police are for Amina. I probably couldn't shoot him even if I *did* have a gun."

"You never know what you're capable of when forced."

I raised a brow, watching her slightly tremoring hand pour more wine for us. She was chewing her lip again and avoiding eye contact, and I was wondering what was up.

"Yeah… I guess. Speaking of the police, have they gotten any leads on who shot you?"

She shook her head sideways and drained her glass.

"What about Jamie?"

"Why would *she* shoot me?" she asked strangely defensive.

"*Chiiill.* That. Was. Not. What. I. Meant. I'm saying, what about getting her to investigate? She *is* a P.I."

"Oh. Yeah. Sorry. My bad. I thought… Never mind."

Her face relaxed and she gazed off discomfited, which was even more confusing to me. Maybe it was the alcohol affecting her brain. Or maybe, it was something else. I stared at her and rested my elbows on the island until she finally looked back at me.

"You already know who did it, don't you?"

Sighing, she looked passed me in thought, confirming my suspicions with every second in silence.

"Why haven't you told the police?"

"Because I can't."

"Why not? They might try it again."

"Not if I get them first."

"Amina!"

"*What?*" she asked snapping her head around so fast I thought she might give herself whiplash.

"Are you crazy? Why aren't you letting the police handle it? I don't understand. Who do you think shot you? Talk to me."

Out of nowhere, her eyes became moist with emotions.

"You have no idea how much I want to. But I can't."

"You *can.* You can tell me anything. If you don't want me to tell anybody else. I won't. I swear. But please Amina. I love you. Please tell me what's going on."

Seconds passed as she studied my face and decided whether she would trust me with her secret or not. Finally, she fingered tears from the corners of her eyes and licked her lips.

"Okay."

14

Yasmin

"Mmmmmmmmph!" I grunted squeezing Dwayne's hand as the shards of pain stabbed at my groin and lower back like a savage attacker.

"Are you sure you don't want to get that epidural? Those little blips on the monitor are spiking like crazy," Aunt Di asked concernedly.

Unable to speak through the agony, I shook my head no, vigorously and tried to concentrate on the serene sound of Jill Scott's voice singing about taking long walks on the portable iPod player Daddy brought for me.

I didn't know if I would ever be a biological mother again and I wanted to experience every part of the process, no matter how painful. They started the drip at noon and the labor process had slowly begun to creep up on me from that point.

They still had me and Sophie hooked up to machines, but my doctor said I could still have a natural child birth unless they determined she was in distress, and for now, she wasn't. I definitely didn't want a C-section, so I was going to endure whatever Mother Nature threw at me as long as Sophie was still safe.

"I just couldn't even go in to work today. I feel so guilty too because I was cussing him out over text the whole holiday because I thought he was ignoring me," Nicky confessed from a chair by the window.

She was engaged in a deep conversation about the death of a guy she was seeing practically since she arrived. Everyone was supposed to be talking to keep me distracted from the pain, but this particular talk was depressing as hell.

Daddy, Aunt Di, Aunt Pam and Dwayne were the only ones present since everybody else was either at work, or claimed they couldn't come until later. Amina was supposedly "retired" now, so I don't know what her excuse was, but I'm sure it was bull. I didn't expect to see Valerie after our blow out the other day, but Aunt Di said she texted to say she would come after Sophie was born.

"You didn't know Nicky. Nobody knew. Don't beat yourself up about it," Aunt Pam sympathized leaning up against the wardrobe closet as everyone nodded in agreement.

"I'm sure his family was probably wondering why he didn't show up to Thanksgiving dinner too. I can't imagine the hopelessness he must have felt lying at the bottom of that stairwell. I actually hope for the sake of his suffering that he didn't live the entire holiday weekend like that."

"I don't know. I know we barely got any work done all day yesterday and the gossip around the office was that somebody might have pushed him down the stairs. The police asked a lot of questions about who else was there when he left and if he had any enemies."

"It's their job ... To ask a lot of questions. Don't read too much into it," I advised when the contractions finally subsided and allowed me to breathe like a normal human.

"But how does a healthy young guy fall down the stairs and die? I can understand breaking a leg, a rib or even hitting his head, but falling down the stairs and dying is like... Like some Lifetime movie plot. It was only down one flight. Maybe somebody did push him," Nicky stated rubbing her eyebrow distraughtly.

"Freak accidents happen all the time. Take it from an injury attorney," I managed through pants, referring to myself as Dwayne dabbed sweat from my forehead and cheeks with tissue. "Much crazier things have happened by accident."

"Ain't that your Office Manager that got shot too?" Daddy asked from the rocking chair.

"Umm hmm. Greer Patterson."

"I thought that was her," Aunt Pam commented. "That lady just can't win for losing. First her husband gets killed by his mistress, then her own father shoots her. She sure has bad luck with men."

"Wait. That's the same lady from the "Sleeping with the enemy" murder case back in 2014? I just saw them talking about that on Dateline the other night. I forgot you worked with her," Aunt Di stated.

"Umm hmm. I never liked her but even I feel bad for her," Nicky said somberly brushing a jet-black strand of hair behind her ear.

"Don't y'all have anything… Less depressing to talk about?" I questioned between pants. "This is supposed to be… A happy occasion."

"Sorry," Nicky apologized.

"Here Shawty. Take some more ice," Dwayne held a cup up to my lips.

Putting a flat piece in my mouth, I sucked on it and tried to relax. When I wasn't in pain, I was basking in Dwayne's attention. He had been coming by every day since I got admitted, watching television with me, bringing me my favorite foods and spending time with me like he wanted to be there.

Daddy still couldn't stand him and cut his visits short when Dwayne showed up, but that was his choice. I had to do what was best for my daughter, and after some heartfelt conversations with Dwayne, he agreed to make some changes in his lifestyle and to see if we could maybe be together too.

I never wanted to raise my child in a single parent household, and though I'm prepared to do it if I have to, I want to at least give me and Dwayne a shot. Since I lost my marriage and my family's respect messing around with him, I owed myself and Sophie that.

"So, what are your plans after the baby is born? Are you two an item now?" Aunt Di asked causing all eyes to look interestedly between her, me and Dwayne.

"We're still figuring it all out," I answered hoping the daggers I was shooting at her would prevent the barrage of foolery she had on the tip of her tongue. No such luck.

"Dub? Or Dwayne. Is that what you're going by now?"

"They both my name. It's whateva you wanna call me," he answered leaning in further on my bed from his chair he sat in.

"I doubt you want me to call you whatever I want to call you. Because I definitely have some names," Daddy maintained.

Dwayne snickered, exposing his gold toothed grin apathetically.

"Look here old man," Dwayne flicked his nose midsentence. "I ain't about to keep dealin' wit' yo' disrespect waitin' on my daughter. I'on say much when you and yo' family be on my ass outta respect for yo' daughter, but—"

"Respect for which daughter? The one you got a son by already or the one you got knocked up right there?" Daddy challenged with his eyebrows knitted together tighter than a Coogi sweater.

"Okay. Calm down Jerry. Not here," Aunt Di said standing from her seat beside him and placing a hand near his chest as if that would prevent him from getting up.

"Don't get it twisted Dub. I don't care if you're with Tamika, Yasmin or Mother Teresa. You better respect my daddy. I know that much," Nicky warned looking at me like I was supposed to do something.

"Only thing I betta' do is breath, eat and die. I ain't gon' give no man nothin' that man ain't givin' back to me. He ain't never liked me and I ain't never cared. That's why he's so mad. 'Cause I'on care."

Daddy looked like he was about to blow a gasket, and I prayed his blood pressure medicine was strong enough to keep him from going into cardiac arrest.

"Stop it." I squeezed Dwayne's hand hard as a contraction traveled through my groin. "Don't do this now. Don't do this at all."

"Talk to yo' daddy," he shot back as my father was still verbally coming for Dwayne's neck.

"You damn right I ain't never like no drug dealing, do nothin' ass Nigga. Especially not for my daughter! Not none of my daughters!" Daddy yelled ignoring me and pushing Aunt Di's hand out of the way as he postured to pounce.

"Oh, I do a lot. Don't let Mika tell you I wasn't helpin' her out when I was livin' there neither. For three years? C'mon on now. Unless you think yo' daughter dumb as hell, she ain't lettin' nobody live wit' her for that long, eatin' off her like that," Dwayne hissed. "You ain't got to like me Partna'. I ain't here for you."

"You wasn't doing enough Young Blood, 'cause if you was, I wouldn't still have had to give her money. Yasmin gave her money too. So what was you doin' so spectacular for Tamika?"

"I only made one of those three seeds Pop. You was already helpin' her when I got there and I—"

"Can we not do this right now pleeeease," I begged clinching my jaws as the hardest contraction yet hit me with force.

"Y'all shut up arguing. Nicky, go get the doctor," Aunt Pam demanded looking at her watch. "Those contractions are coming quick."

I heard shuffling, but my head was down and my eyes squeezed shut while I tried to will the pain away.

"Aight Shawty. Breathe. Breathe. My bad for stressin' you. Do the breathin' exercises. Haut. Haut. Haut," Dwayne soothed rubbing my back and repeating the words they taught us in lamaze class emphatically.

If I wasn't hurting so badly, I would have laughed at how ridiculous he looked when I opened my eyes to see him repeating "Haut" over and over again. Within a matter of minutes, my nurse Alana, another nurse I hadn't seen before, my doctor, and the NICU Specialist I met earlier were crowding my room. It seemed like voices were coming from everywhere trying to give me direction while prepping me for delivery.

Dwayne was already in scrubs with his dreads in the cap for his role as the baby daddy, and the rest of my family was propped up along the walls as the medical staff made way. Before I knew it, my legs were propped up, Dr. Christianson was between them, and my body was trying to force me to deliver what felt like a basketball from my HooHah.

More than a dozen pushes and countless minutes later, I was sweating like the walls of a bath house, tired beyond belief and thoroughly regretting not getting the epidural.

"You're doing good Mom. She's almost here," my OB coached as I whined that I couldn't do it anymore. "Yes, you can. Yes. You. Can. I need you to try to take a deep breath, and give me another one. You've got this Mom. You've got this."

"I can't!" I cried dropping my head back in pure exhaustion.

"C'mon baby. Sophie's right there. Right there at the end. You just gotta push one mo—"

"Shut up Dwayne! I know what she said I have to do! I can't! If I could, I would! I'm trying but I can't!" I shrieked.

It was bad enough that I felt like I was already failing my daughter in my first genuine task as a mother. Yet another thing Tamika did effortlessly with my nephews that I was struggling to do.

"She's right here Honey. Yes you can," Dr. Christianson praised as both my body and my baby bullied me from the inside to keep pushing.

Gritting my teeth, I inhaled as deeply as possible, and defiantly glared at all the judgey eyes on me. The second I glanced Nicky's grimacing face as she recorded my undercarriage with her iPhone, I lost it.

"Stop recording my pussy!" I screeched just before attempting another hard push to dislodge Sophie from my innards.

"You said you wanted the birth recorded. So I'm recording it," she answered resentfully as though I was the one violating her vagina's privacy with a camera.

"Maybe you should put it down," Aunt Pam warned as I gasped in another rush of oxygen.

"The birth! Not my whole entire vagina!" I shouted.

She lowered the phone embarrassingly, and everyone but the doctor's attention briefly volleyed between her face and mine.

"Fine!" she conceded sucking her teeth. "Crazy."

"Mom. I'm going to need you to focus. I know you're tired, but you need to give me a really, really big push right now," Dr. Christianson interjected snapping my attention back to her.

Daddy and Nicky were mumbling something between them, and I wanted to snap because I knew it was gossip about me, but the onslaught of pain in my loins and the task at hand distracted me.

Spittle spritzed between my clenched teeth as I mustered every ounce of strength I had left in my vessel and pushed.

"Raaaaaaaaaaaaaaaaaaaaaaaa!"

"I see her. I see her," Daddy's voice chimed jovially.

"Oh my God!" Aunt Di said next.

Dwayne tilted forward trying to see what everybody but the two of us saw.

"Here we go. Good job Mom. Good job," Dr. Christianson said as my body expelled what felt like every organ inside of me through my once small lady bits.

A medley of Ooh's and Ah's erupted from my family, but I was immediately concerned with one thing.

"W-why isn't she crying?" I asked blinking perspiration from my eyes and trying to catch my breath. Was she breathing?

"Is she okay?" Dwayne asked leaving my side to get a closer look.

What was probably only seconds of silence felt like an endless cluster of minutes as I watched the NICU Specialist and the nurse crowd Dr. Christianson.

"Congratulations Mom and Dad. You have a beautiful baby girl," my doctor finally announced as Sophie's cries permeated the room and my fears.

"Can I see her? I want to see her." I begged reaching out weakly towards them.

My doctor and the specialist babbled about having to take Sophie to the NICU, but all I wanted to do was lay eyes on my daughter. I watched impatiently as my baby was handed off to a nurse who took Sophie off to the side.

Seconds later, the nurse brought Sophie over in a blanket, predominantly clean of birth matter. Tears drained my ducts as I looked at my precious baby girl's wailing caramel face, and full head of jet-black hair.

"We're going to have to bring her to the NICU now. We'll come get you shortly.

I was barely listening. Sophie only opened her dark brown eyes while fussing for a few fleeting seconds, but they were beautiful. My baby was here, and she was beautiful.

"Look at my baby," I doted feebly as an abrupt wave of heat ran through me and labored breaths escaped my lips. Wiping perspiration from my brow, my head began to swoon and every grain of energy I had left felt like it was seeping out through my pores.

"She's hemorrhaging," Dr. Christianson's troubled voice announced as my baby girl's face became a blur and my lids fell shut.

15

Amina

The Uber driver jovially hummed along with the music on the radio as Valerie and I sat quietly in the backseat. She had gone preverbally mute after my wine induced confessional. While I was trying to clarify where her head was with everything I revealed, my mom called.

Yasmin had hemorrhaged and passed out after giving birth to Sophie and was rushed into surgery. Mom said Sophie was doing as well as expected for a preemie, but they wouldn't know anything more about Yas until she was out of surgery. That was all we needed to know. We were on our way.

Since Val and I emaciated a full bottle of wine, there was no way I was going to let either of us get behind the wheel and drive. I was probably tipsier than she was, but there was no point in chancing a DUI. Somebody would just have to drive us back later, or we could Uber it again.

Reading a new text message from my brother, I nudged Val's shoulder and showed her my screen.

"Oh snap. Mark said Vic told him Vanessa's coming."

She sucked her teeth disgustedly and leaned on her elbow against the door. She hadn't said more than a few words to me since I decided to spill my guts to her for the first time about my escorting, Franco and my current situation.

She took my escorting way better than I expected. Even joking that she should have chosen that over dancing given how I came up. She

152

wasn't too thrilled that Maaco had kept knowing my profession a secret from her, but in the end, she understood why he had. It was all the other stuff... The murder, the break-ins and my qualms about Jamie that caused her to clam up like a sea urchin.

"Val. What's up with you?" I whispered leaning closer.

She jerked her head back with a frown, taking offense.

"Nothing. What's up with you?"

"Why're you being so quiet then?"

"Please forgive me for not being a chatty Cathy after hearing..." she folded her lips in and ran her hands over her face. "It's a lot Amina. We've been drinking and I don't want to say the wrong thing. Just let me process it."

I swallowed past the lump in my throat and glanced at the Uber driver who didn't seem to be listening to us, but probably was. The wine on our mostly empty stomachs and my guilty conscience were probably making both of us paranoid.

On top of that, I was still discerning the news Val unwittingly provided about Jamie. Maaco thinking she was getting in over her head in gambling debts and her shutting down her Miami club was further confirmation to me that she couldn't be trusted. Her intel was already suspicious, but now for as many times as I replayed the video of the person on my property, I was starting to think it could have been her.

Sure, Jamie kept referencing the intruder as a "he", but that could just as easily have been a ploy to throw me off. She was just as stocky and masculine as my masked stalker. I hadn't told her that I would be out of town or that I was boarding Linx, but she's a PI by profession. Maybe she staked out my place or something.

Through some online research of my own, I verified that Kevin's remains were reported to the Miami PD in March like Jamie said. I also verified that Latasha "Lala" Kerry served time in TGKC during the time Jamie said too. Good thing she had the same last name as her brother.

Still, Lala's prior arrests were for assault, theft by taking, and prostitution. Shooting me, disarming my alarm like a pro and planting a camera to record me typing in my safe code seemed too advanced for her. Plus, though I never saw her in person, I was pretty sure she wasn't built like a linebacker.

Knowing what Jamie is capable of doing firsthand, I originally eliminated her as a suspect because I figured if she wanted me dead, I would have been. At this point, given the new information I'd learned this past week, I was thinking that if it wasn't her alone, it might be her in cahoots with Lala. Maybe she found out about my wall safe somehow and decided that she wanted whatever she suspected might be in it?

We were in front of the hospital before I knew it and Val was tapping me to snap out of my thoughts and get out of the car. I sighed, hating how familiar I had become with the layout of Piedmont Hospital by now. Our family was here so much in the last year that it was starting to feel like we were trapped in a never-ending episode of *General Hospital.*

The maternity waiting room was packed except for a random seat here or there, and our family occupied most of the seats on the left. While doling out hugs, Vic embraced Val, shaking her playfully in his embrace, and kissed her forehead.

"Hey Chicklet. Long time no see. I left you a message earlier too."

"My bad. I was in the middle of something. I meant to call you back, but then I got caught up."

"Umm hmm. You always have some excuse."

"That's because it's always true," Val chortled while hugging his fiancé Zaria, who always looked like she was being forced to grin at gunpoint around us.

She's a pretty brown girl, maybe a shade lighter than me, with a full figure and thick shoulder length locks. I've never had anything against her, except that she seems super boring and conservative. I could only imagine what a snooze fest married life was going to be like for them, but maybe that's what Vic wanted, given the drama women like us bring.

"How's Yas and the baby?" Val asked as I made my way back over to my brother who stood by my mother's chair with his face buried in his phone.

I hadn't seen so many of my family members in one place since Uncle Vernon's funeral. Everybody that lived in ATL was present except for Vanessa, Mika and the kids. I hoped the next time we were all together, it would be for a happy occasion. Probably for Vic's wedding Memorial Day weekend.

"Stable now. The doctor just came and said she was out of surgery. They're still monitoring her in recovery for a little while longer, but they are supposed to be bringing her back to a room soon. I think it's a new one because they asked us to take her things out of the one she already had," Aunt Di volunteered.

"Well, what did they say happened to her?"

"A ruptured uterus," Aunt Di said somberly.

"But the baby's okay?" I questioned sympathetically.

I was still salty with Yasmin for all her lies and how she did Tamika, but I still wanted her and the baby to be okay.

"She's good for a preemie. Four pounds, two ounces," Aunt Di beamed with pride like she was the biological grandma. "She's got a little jaundice and they have her under those lamps to regulate her body temperature, but she's doing good. Breathing on her own and everything. At least that's what Jerry told us. Can't nobody but him and Dub see her in the NICU right now."

"Why not?"

"Hospital rules. Grandparents can see the baby by themselves, but nobody else unless you're with one of the birth parents."

"And you know Dub's ass ain't letting none of us go in with him," Nicky sassed.

"He left anyway," Aunt Di said snidely.

"Left?" I frowned propping my elbow on Mark's shoulder to his discontent.

"I don't know what got into that boy today, but he and Jerry kept going at it. Jerry threatened to kick his ass again, he got mad and stormed out of here like a child," Aunt Di continued with a huff. "Didn't even stick around to hear if Yasmin came out of surgery all right or not."

"I'm sure he's coming back," my mother added. "They needed to be separated for a while anyway. The way Jerry was trying to provoke the boy before she went into labor, it was only a matter of time before one of them blew up again."

"Oh damn. It was like that?" I grinned.

"Uncle Jerry left too?" Val asked sitting on the arm of the chair Vic was now sitting in beside Zaria.

"No. He went to the NICU to see Sophia."

"Oh okay. Well, y'all was in the room when she delivered though right? Did you get any pictures of the baby before they took her?"

"Yeah. I got most of it on my phone and I screen shot a few pics of my little niecey-poo too. Look," Nicky glowed standing and handing her phone to Val.

"Aww. Look at all that hair," Val crooned swiping pictures. "Where's the video?"

I had only seen Tamika's kids hours after birth, and I was kind of curious to see what the whole process looked like.

"I wanna see," I whined.

Motherhood wasn't exactly on the top of my list of goals, but if they had it on tape, I wanted to see it.

"When I'm finished," Val replied without looking at me.

"Keep swiping. It'll come up. I got Yasmin's bi-polar ass screaming at me too," Nicky told Val.

"I thought she wanted it filmed?"

"She did. But in the middle of it, she turned into the chick from *The Exorcist*. I thought her head was gonna spin around. I almost dropped my damn phone," Nicky chuckled and the rest of us did too.

"You'll understand when you have kids," my mom told Nicky. "That pain can turn the sweetest thang into a beast on you, and Yasmin was already far from sweet."

"Valerie, child. Why are your eyes so red? I know you haven't been drinking this early?" Aunt Di asked with a scrutinizing look from the chair across.

Val glanced up, and tongued the inside of her cheek.

"Really Ma?"

"Really Ma what? Have you been? I worry about you."

"We were having wine and catching up at my house Aunt Di. Just a couple of drinks. Nothing hard. And we took Uber," I interjected hoping to diffuse the drama I foresaw.

"Well, I'm glad y'all had sense enough not to drive at least."

"Mommy, please. I'm grown. If I want to have a drink, whatever time of day it is, I'll have a drink. I'm not hurting anybody. I'm here right? That's what you wanted isn't it?" Valerie retorted huffily.

"Yes, that is what I wanted, but I also want you to be healthy. We barely see you anymore and I'm worried about you. I worry about you and your sister both. Is something wrong with that? You used to talk to me all the time when you were in New York. Why not now?"

"Because now... All you do is... Never mind. I gotta go to the bathroom. Does anybody know where it is?" Val asked standing and handing Nicky's phone back to her.

The heifer was supposed to pass the phone to me, so I snatched it out of Nicky's hand instantly. Nicky gave me the gas-face, but let me have it and told Val which way to go. Aunt Di tried to say something else, but Val stormed off anyway.

"*Diane*, leave the girl alone. She ain't been here five whole minutes yet and you're already on her back," my mom scolded Aunt Di. "I keep telling you you're wound too tight. Let the girl breathe a minute. She'll come around."

"Pamela, I asked *my child* a simple question. Yasmin said she smelled like alcohol when she came last time, and her eyes are red as cherries today. What if she's becoming an alcoholic? A lot of those strippers turn to drugs and alcohol to do what they do you know?"

I knew it was getting serious as soon as she called my mother by her full name. Anything other than P or Pam, and there was beef between them.

"Let her be," Mom said pursing her lips. "If she is, she ain't about to quit right now. Stop nagging for a minute? Everybody's stressed enough."

"Oh boy. This isn't going to end well," I whispered to Mark while viewing the video of Yasmin giving birth.

It was messy, bloody and made my coochie kegel just from looking at how wide her vagina spread. Aw *heeeeell* no. I might not ever have a baby after looking at that mess.

"Come on," Mark said grabbing the phone from my hand and giving it back to Nicky.

"Where y'all going?" she asked as he pulled me behind him and I shrugged back at her.

"We'll be back," Mark threw over his shoulder while maneuvering us through other people in the area to wherever he was taking me.

"Where *are* we going?" I asked once he released me so that I was trailing him of my on volition.

"I don't know. To the Café or somewhere to get something to eat. I'm hungry and I'm sick of hearing their mouths. Before y'all got here Aunt Di was grilling Zaria about her wedding. You already know she feels a way that Zaria's been turning to Vic's mom and Tamika for help planning more than she has her. It's just annoying."

"Oh really? I ain't know her and Tamika were cool like that."

"Apparently they are. Ma was telling me how Aunt Di was jealous that they went to look at flowers for the reception without her. Being that neither Vic's mom or Tamika have been married before, she thought it only right that they invite her since she's the only one that has."

"Oh lord. No wonder he doesn't visit her much. I don't remember Aunt Di ever being this overbearing and pushy before Uncle Vernon died."

"Me either, but she's a pain in everybody's ass now. Plus, I got something I need to talk to you about anyway."

"What?"

"Something Dana told me about Dub's boy Cortez," he said with a raised brow as we passed through double doors and out of the maternity ward.

I exhaled and closed my eyes briefly, not enthused about adding any more secrets to my arsenal than I already had. I barely slept a wink last night as it was. Between dreaming about Lala coming to shoot me and realizing the man I was sexing was a zombie version of Cedric, I might have slept three hours.

As for Cortez, I never met the guy, but I knew he was Dub's boy who owned the barber shop he sometimes worked in. I couldn't imagine what Mark's girl would know about Cortez, or why anybody would care, but I would hear my brother out like he usually did me.

"What about him?"

"She knows him. Well, she *knew* him. Before me. Back when she wasn't herself. Before she was *my* Dana."

I stared at him blankly, totally confused about why he was speaking in riddles. I watched him push the down button in the elevator bank and blew out an impatient breath.

"Bruh. I don't have the slightest idea what you're talking about. Between lack of sleep and the drinks I had on an empty stomach, I'm not in the mood for the guessing game. Who was she before she was *your* Dana?"

He cocked his head like I was dense and put both hands on his hips. I mimicked him and he cracked a smile.

"You *know* what I'm talking about Mimi. I told you who she was before she got with me."

I thought a few seconds, then grasped what he meant.

"*Ohhhh.* Okay. Cortez told Dub about her?"

"No. He didn't recognize her. He was in Yasmin's room with Dub when Dana went to see her. When she was with Cortez, she was still dressing like a… like a man," he whispered the last part before the elevator doors opened and we got in.

An Orderly standing behind an old man in a wheelchair and an older woman who looked like she had been crying were already in the elevator, so we halted our conversation until we got off.

"So, Cortez is gay?" I questioned as we walked.

"On the DL. He pretends to like women, but he's screwing men on the low. Dana said he has some mental issues too. She stopped messing with him because he started getting too possessive and violent."

"Wow," was all I could say.

This was interesting and everything, but I still didn't know why he cared. Dana wasn't with him anymore and he didn't even know who she was. What was he worried about?

"Supposedly, Cortez moved to Atlanta because some of the guys he dealt with in California started outing him, and he didn't want his set to find out."

"He was in a gang?"

Mark nodded as we stopped just outside one of the eateries and stood to the side so's not to block the entryway.

"I don't know how he got that barber shop, but Dana said he's got a rap sheet as long as my arm. She also told me that the last straw for her was when he pistol whipped one of her friends and took his car because he thought she was seeing him behind his back."

My eyes widened.

"Damn. That *is* crazy. But what's the issue? You think he's going to do something to her?"

He grimaced shaking his head.

"No. Like I said, he didn't recognize her. Plus, he wouldn't want her like she is now anyway. From what she said, he doesn't like men who look like women, and he definitely wouldn't want her now that she's a full woman."

I could have interjected right there, but I let my brother have that one.

"Why I'm telling you, is because of Yasmin though. Didn't Yasmin say the guy that car jacked her had a red bandana over his face and a Raider's cap on?"

"Uh… I don't know. I don't think I ever asked her what he looked like. That was the same day I got shot. The only thing I ever asked her about it was if she got her car back. By the time I got out of the hospital, the focus was on Van sleeping with Brent and then Uncle V died."

"Well, I'm pretty sure that's what she said, and Cortez is from Cali, in a gang, and pistol whipped and carjacked one of Dana's people before," Mark counted off each point on his fingers.

"That could be a coincidence. What would be his motive? I don't think Yasmin even knows him too well. He's Dub's boy."

"Exactly. He's *Dub's* boy. What if he and Dub..." Mark said jiggling his head and letting his words trail off for me to insinuate the rest.

"*Nooooo*," I said dubiously. "You think *Dub* and Cortez are butt buddies? Nuh uh."

"Pshhh," he said throwing his hands up defensively. "I don't know what they're doing, but Yasmin got jacked in the parking garage after meeting up with Dub. The guy had on a Raiders cap and a red bandana.

I know you said you never met him, but I have. Three or four times actually. He always has on some California gear. It's all too coincidental if you couple that with the past Dana said he has. Don't you agree?"

I chewed my bottom lip and stared off in contemplation.

"Well, what do you want to do? We might be totally wrong. You don't think Yas would know if it was him?"

"She doesn't have all the information we do, and she didn't see his full face. She might not have even considered him, but who knows. None of us have really been talking to her too hot anyway."

"True. So, what did you want to do with this info? You didn't want to tell her today did you?"

"No. No," he said running a hand over his waves. "Like, tomorrow or something."

"That's too damn soon." I smacked him upside his head and laughed. "At least let her get a couple of days to recover and enjoy Sophie with Dub. I hate what she did but, this is her time."

"He could be dangerous though. Ain't that who he's staying with?"

"Who?"

"Dub. Isn't he staying with Cortez right now?"

I shrugged. I hadn't been keeping tabs on what he was doing since I was barely acknowledging Yas until today.

"Look. If he's Dub's side nigga, she needs to know that. Hell, *Tamika* needs to know it too. But not today. Not tomorrow. Let's just try to have a 24-hour period without drama."

"You're right," he replied rubbing his chin. "I still have a problem though. I don't know how to tell Yasmin *how* I know what I know, without telling them Dana wasn't always *Dana*."

My stomach grumbled when a whiff of something that smelled tasty invaded my nostrils as a patron exited the café door.

"I don't know Big Bruh, but we'll figure it out after we grab something to eat."

16

Vanessa

Detective Randall was a gruff looking white man with dark hair, a full beard, a mustache and piercing green eyes. He wore a light blue button up shirt, open at the collar, with brown pants and brown loafers that looked less than 200 steps away from disintegrating.

Randall wasn't particularly intimidating, but the way he studied my every move like a long division problem didn't give me the warm and fuzzies either.

He was cordial enough throughout the interview. Offering me coffee, soda or water when we first sat and speaking in a slow and easy tone. Still, his probing eyes made me uncomfortable and I was becoming impatient with what seemed like a lot of the same questions, just rephrased to try to entrap me.

As it turned out, Lamar wasn't as dense as I thought he was. I thought I had rid myself of him and the sex tapes he was trying to blackmail me with when I set that candlestick house on fire.

Little did I know, he uploaded copies of it to an online storage account that he shared with his brother. I guess his brother didn't use the account often because he just recently discovered them, so he claims, and brought the videos to the police.

Lamar was a friend with benefits who caught feelings for me that I didn't reciprocate. When I stopped using his dick and his beats simultaneously, he let his jealousy over my relationship with Brand get the best of him.

He blamed Brand for my not wanting to use any of his tracks on songs for my upcoming album and turned on me when I cosigned. The next thing I knew, he was threatening to leak a sex tape of us that I never knew he made to *MEDIA TAKEOUT* if I didn't start playing ball.

I couldn't afford to have a sex tape of me ruin my chances at stardom or alter the way I would be branded right out the gate, so I agreed. I even pretended to understand his motives when he confessed his guilt for taking the low road with me.

After a few weeks of acting like I saw the error of my ways and catering to his schlong voluntarily, his guard was down again. Once I feigned being hype about using one of his weak ass beats on a song Brand and I had already decided wouldn't be on my album, he was silly putty in my hands.

I didn't think he would be missed too much if I killed him. He was a low-grade industry pariah whose best asset was a big dick, and whose baby's mommas hated him for neglect of their kids. My career was definitely more important than him.

I was tighter than a nun's snatch when I found out why I was called in for questioning. I didn't need anything else throwing a monkey wrench into my life right now. Of course, I pretended not to know the videos existed and expressed genuine concern about them being leaked.

I couldn't tell whether Detective Randall believed I was a viable suspect or if he was just making sure he covered all his bases. Whatever he was doing, was making me nervous, but I was doing my damnedest not to show it.

"So, after the fight, you left?"

I shook my head. "Not right away. We just kind of sat around talking about how we were going to handle the repercussions after my sister told everybody."

"Okay. Well, what time *did* you come home from your sister's fiancé's house? Was it the same evening or the next morning?" he asked holding a nonjudgmental expression that I could tell was forced.

I had already disclosed that I spent the night before Lamar's death with him at his house, and that I later hooked up with Brent at his place.

I even told him about the fight between me and Val over it to give off the appearance of being an open book.

With all the media coverage of Delia's case, it was practically public knowledge that I was also screwing Brand Beats around the same time. Believe me. Detective Randall made sure to connect the dots during his questioning too.

I wasn't sure what he already knew about me or that night, but I was only going to lie about the important things. Like me leaving a gasoline canister in the bushes at Lamar's house that I later used to ignite the blaze.

"I don't know. Like… Eleven. Twelve. I took a Uber back home so there should be a record of the times with them. It was a hectic night for me, as I just explained, so I wasn't exactly keeping track of what time it was."

"I understand. And did you go anywhere else that night?"

"No. I just cried myself to sleep for screwing up my relationship with my sister and my sister's relationship with Brent."

"Can anybody else verify that you were home all night? Did you talk to a neighbor? Anyone on the phone? Or maybe invite someone *else* over to comfort you?"

I side-eyed him, picking up on the implication that I had a revolving door of suitors. Right or wrong, he could eat a dick. I knew he was judging me. I bet if I was a man, he wouldn't be so smug.

"Not unless the Sandman can testify to it," I replied smartly, checking the time on my Michael Kohrs watch. "Listen Detective, I've got a lot of things to do today and I've answered all of your questions. I don't know how you think I can help in your investigation, but I don't know anything.

I mean, I'm pissed that he was taping me without my consent, especially because I slept with him again that morning, but I didn't even know he made them. Even if I had found out, I would have just sued his ass if he put them out.

Believe me. I'm nobody's murderer. I have too much to lose and not enough hours in the day to do what I'm *supposed* to be doing as it is already," I smirked.

"I understand completely Ms. Vincent. I appreciate you taking time to come down here and talk to me today. I just have one last question for you. Did Lamar ever mention having any problems with anybody else that might have been a danger to him?"

I shrugged and fidgeted with my fingers, wishing I had a cigarette between them.

"Not to *me*. We didn't have that kind of relationship. We worked and played together sometimes, but it was mostly work. I heard through the grapevine that his kid's mothers didn't like him, and I know he used to deal drugs. Maybe somebody in one of those circles did it."

"Okay. Well, here's my card if you think of anything else, no matter how small, that may be of help to our case.

"What about the videos of me? What's going to happen to them?"

"They'll stay in police evidence. The videos were deleted from the online storage account and are no longer accessible to anyone that way."

"How do I know nobody's going to get a hold of them and put them out? What if his brother downloaded a copy before he turned it over. Or what if Lamar had other copies stored somewhere else?"

I better not have risked my freedom by killing Lamar for nothing!

"Unfortunately, I cannot guarantee that there aren't any other copies of these videos elsewhere, but I can tell you that the copies we have will not be leaked from this office."

His response didn't sooth my anxiety in the slightest. Just the fact that Lamar's brother *ever* saw the videos had me on edge. I didn't know that negro. Who's to say he didn't make a copy too? I mean... Who wouldn't be tempted?

I left the precinct feeling uneasy and irritated as I powered my phone back on and messages began popping up like EGGO waffles.

Hiding my emotions behind my Saint Laurent shades, I walked to my car in the parking deck with fire in my eyes as I skimmed two messages from my new publicist and read a long one from Red. My heart beat like a drum as I tapped on the link she included in her last text and pulled up an article with the headline: IS R&B STAR VIXEN ALSO A VANDAL?

Great. More crap to deal with! My day already started off in the crapper when Gavin said he was going to put a groupie I got into it with before in our video. I gave no damns and less fucks if it was for a shot off set either.

Gavin can stick his sausage in whoever he wants as long as he uses protection, doesn't let me find out, makes sure I'm still number one, and it isn't Daphne.

The trick in discussion though… Not her. She doesn't know how to play her insignificant position, and for that, she will never get any shine on *my* watch.

Then, as if TMZ reporting rumors that Delia was possibly talking wasn't nerve racking enough, my brother called on my way to the precinct with more bad news. Yasmin had complications during delivery and was rushed into surgery.

It wasn't any of Vic's business where I was headed, so I didn't tell him. But I did promise to come by the hospital and see about my cousin and the new baby.

Regardless of my beef with some of my family, I still had some of my daddy inside of me. Unlike Tamika, losing him had brought out my softer side when a family member was facing possible death.

My phone automatically linked to the Bluetooth in my car when I got in and I wasted no time ringing my man's phone as I drove off.

"What's up baby? I'm in the mi—"

"What's *up* is that your ex-bitch took her muzzle off again and now she's slandering me again. I keep telling you to tell that bum ho to keep my name out her mouth!"

I barely heard his grunt over the loud music playing in the background.

"Hello! Do you hear me talking?"

"What she do now Vix?" he asked dryly.

"She did an interview with Rita Rasaad this morning and claimed *I* was the one who broke in her house. I thought you said you handled it!"

"I did."

"You *did?* What do you mean *you did? Obviously,* you didn't handle it right if Jeffrey the Giraffe is going on radio shows spreading lies!" I screamed flailing my hands as I ranted. "She doesn't have an ounce of proof that I did anything to her little hut, but you're letting her go on national radio telling people I did it!"

"I'm not *letting* her do anything. I promised her I would replace everything that was damaged, and I did. What else do you want me to do?"

His indifference made me want to slap a sense of urgency into his pussy whipped head. Whatever Daphne had put on him when they were together was clearly still strong enough to cloud his judgment.

Unexpectedly, I was on the verge of tears and I was becoming more enraged as I realized it. Maybe it was the culmination of everything I had been going through, but everything was triggering waterworks with me lately and I hated it.

"Are you serious? I don't give a damn if you replaced her stuff! I give a damn that she's accusing me of something I didn't do and you don't have my back!"

He sighed deeply. "Vix, I have your back. I'm still with you right? I don't know who messed up Daph's place, but as long as my son lays his head there, I'm going to make sure everything is copacetic for them. I can't keep getting in the middle of y'all petty beefs. I have business to handle and this isn't about business."

"Oh, really now?" I rolled my neck and glared at the speaker as if Gavin could see my angry face. "I *am* still an artist on your label, aren't I? Is allowing that boulder-headed bab—"

"Enough with the names already. I'm in the middle of a session and I can't deal with this right now. I'll talk to you when I—"

I cut his ass off just like he had done me, except I hung up the phone on him. I was sick of him downplaying Daphne's constant disrespect and not having my back. Nobody had proof that I did a damn thing! Where was his loyalty?

I banged on the steering wheel in a fury at the stop light and quickly composed myself once it turned green. If anybody could see through my tinted windows, they would probably think I was psychotic.

When I found a parking spot at Piedmont, I pulled down the visor and checked my makeup and hair. I needed a minute to calm myself down and get myself together before stepping out into the public. I had some celebrity now and I couldn't let anybody catch me slipping.

The weather was surprisingly a nice 59 degrees, so I wore a long sleeve, V-neck, beige, Victoria Beckham knit dress. I paired it with brown, calf-high Jimmy Choo boots, a Valentino Garavani Rockstud quilted shoulder bag and gold jewelry.

The outside of the hospital was decorated with Christmas decorations, reminding me of the approaching holiday that I wasn't really looking forward to. Christmas without Daddy wasn't going to feel like Christmas at all. Especially with there being riffs in the family.

My cell rang in my hand as I strode through the hospital glancing between it and the signs telling me where to go. I scowled at Gavin's pic flashing on the screen and pressed ignore. Randomly, I remembered I hadn't called or texted my publicist back. Unlocking my screen, I went to her last message and reread it to concoct how I would reply.

Focused on my phone, I collided into someone at the elevator bank. "Excuse me. Amina?"

"Oh snap," She said equally surprised with Mark on her shoulder.

Neither of them made a move to hug me, so I didn't either. Me and Valerie were twins, but you would think her and Mark were the way they mirrored each other's actions sometimes.

She wasn't her typical glammed up self, in a paint splattered long sleeve shirt and leggings, but Mark was. He was dressed preppy in a blue cardigan with a black shirt under it and jeans. They were both holding Styrofoam take out trays and staring at me like I was supposed to make the first move, but I wasn't going to.

"You here to see Yasmin or Delia?" Amina questioned eyeballing my attire.

I'm not surprised. I was definitely *slaying*.

"Delia's not here anymore," I let her know haughtily. "I came to see Yas and the baby. Isn't that why *you're* here?"

"Of course. I'm just surprised to see you. I figured you would be busy performing somewhere in the studio… Or on your back," she poked spitting that last part under her breath.

"Nah I'm standing up today for a good cause. Following your lead," I shot back slickly. "I'm surprised you're here too. I thought y'all were still boycotting her for sleeping with Dub. Or is it only me y'all want to stay pissy at for the same thing?"

"As far as I'm concerned, both of y'all are grimy in my book, and I would drag your ass on sight every time I saw you if you did it to me. But it wasn't me, so when family is in trouble, I step up and put all that aside. Even when they might not deserve it."

"Ha!" I laughed hard. "Don't you sound saintly."

"Saintlier than *you*," she snorted looking at her watch impatiently.

"How you figure? Didn't I come see your ho ass in the hospital after you got yourself shot too?" I shot back.

"Ho?"

"Ho. Call girl. Escort. Same thing," I challenged derisively.

Her eyes grew wide before she quickly pasted her typical unbothered expression back on her face and waved me off. Yeah, I knew the rumors, and now she knew I knew them too. Game recognizes game and this broad wasn't ever *just* a model or a decoy.

I've rubbed a lot of elbows in the city, and people with money talk a lot when liquor and drugs are in their system. I knew things that she definitely didn't want me to leak back to the fam, and if she stayed in her lane, I wouldn't.

I didn't have proof that she was doing anything other than what she claimed, so I never confronted her about it or tried to dime her out. Besides, I've always been willing to do whatever was necessary to secure the bag too.

Still, she needed to pipe her pretentious ass down before I let Mark know his baby sis was bartering pussy for money out here in these ATL streets.

"Chill out y'all. I hope you're not planning to act an ass when you see Val."

"Whatever Mark. You need to save that speech for *her*. I'm the only one who actually has a career to lose between me and Val, and I came in peace," I added flippantly, adjusting the strap of my bag on my shoulder.

Mark needed to shut up. He was Amina's big brother, not mine, and she barely listened to him either. I didn't expect Val to be here because I thought she was still avoiding the family like an STD, but I guess she felt compelled to come check on Yas and the baby too.

I was planning on making up with her eventually, but I wasn't planning on *eventually*, being today. I doubted Val was going to be receptive to me anyway, so the Kumbaya was going to have to wait.

I only planned to see that Yasmin was all right and get a quick look at Sophie. I had damage control to discuss with my publicist and preparation for the video shoot.

"Have you seen the baby?" I wanted to know.

"No. Only the parents and grandparents can see the baby in ICU for now," Mark answered dryly as the elevator dinged and the doors opened.

Ms. Attitude got on first and Mark and I filed in behind her. I was surprised it was empty for how long it took to come, but happy it was since it allowed us space to spread out.

"Who else is here besides y'all, Val and Mommy? Because I know my mother *has to* be here."

"Pretty much, everybody except *Dwayne*," Mark answered mockingly, smirking at Amina who reciprocated.

"Dwayne who?"

"Dub. That's what Yasmin calls him."

"Tuh! *D-wayne?*" I repeated facetiously. "Tamika doesn't even call him by his government."

Mark nodded agreeably, but Amina watched the numbers light up over the elevator door like I wasn't there. I wasn't sweating her anyway.

I let them lead the way off the elevator since I wasn't sure which direction the room was in. Plus, it was only right that I made a grand entrance since I was the only celebrity in the family.

I was confused when they led me to the waiting room instead of her room, and I looked around at the thinning crowd of people skeptically as I followed.

"Well, look what the cat drug in," my mother announced standing to hug me with a big smile.

Her delight threw me off since the last time we spoke, she was chastising me like a teenager, and I ended up hanging up on her. I was expecting either the silent treatment, or petty responses.

"I thought you would be busy."

"I *am* on a tight schedule but, I made a break in it to come see about my cousin and my new little cuz. Mark said we can't go see the baby and y'all are out here instead of in the room with Yasmin. What's the word?"

"She's out of surgery, they'll let us know when she's back in a room so we can see her. When are you going to change this *purple*? I think you look so much prettier with dark hair. I just don't understand why you girls like these unnatural colors. It's so... *Clownish*," she asked fingering the ends of my hair.

Umm hmm. Petty Betty finally rears her head. She wouldn't be my mother if she didn't have a complaint about what I was doing, how I was dressed or what I looked like.

"Well, I guess clowns are in because there's a lot of people imitating my look Ma," I retorted hugging Vic and Zaria next.

Vic had me by at least a foot and a half, looking all the way like a broad chest, hazel-eyed, younger, leaner version of my daddy. Zaria gave me the hug you give people you only talk to because you have to. For my brother's sake, I make nice with her, but I didn't feel any joy about him marrying her.

"And who better to imitate than Boyfriend Banging Bozo the Clown herself," Nicky scoffed nudging Val in the seat beside her who was looking down at her phone.

Val shot me a scalding look and wrinkled her nose like she smelled something bad.

"Listen Nicky. Don't come for me unless I send for you, wit' your Side Show Bob looking ass," I told her with a chuckle. "Don't let these Jimmy Choo's fool you. I will drag your little tail up and down this hospital just as quickly today as I always would have."

"You wish."

"All right now," my mother and Aunt Pam warned in unison.

"Don't nobody care about you wearing no damn Jimmy Choos either. Attention whore," Nicky snorted. "Especially when you're still rocking hand-me-downs that Val gave you from Brent. But then again, you like hand-me-downs since you're always screwing other people's sloppy seconds."

My stomach dropped with embarrassment right along with Val's eyes to my boots. I could see and feel her seething as I straightened my posture in a hoity toity fashion and flipped my hair.

I didn't give a second thought to where the boots came from when I put them on, and I doubted Val would ever have recognized them if Nicky hadn't pointed them out. Hell, she never even wore them before and the only reason Nicky's hatin' ass remembered them was because Val gave them to me instead of her.

"I said to stop it," my mother said firmly in a low whisper.

"Y'all are gonna get us kicked out of here with y'all mess," Mark said chomping on a barbecue wing.

"Yeah. Just... Tone it down," my brother added looking from me and back at Zaria as if silently informing her he had it under control.

"*Y'all* ain't gonna do nothing. Talk to that one with the mouth," I frowned motioning towards Nicky with my head.

It seemed like everybody was coming at me, when she was the one who started it. Nicky and I exchanged death stares before I fully looked at my sister who was steady glaring at me.

My eyes instinctively scanned her for evidence of the event Rachel claimed occurred the other night, but I saw none and she had a scarf wrapped around her neck. She truly looked a hot depressed mess to me and the bags under her eyes said she hadn't slept well in days. If she had, it was probably in the same clothes she had on.

I hoped like hell that no one saw her in all her disheveled glory and confused her for me. Still, I told myself that I was going to *attempt* to humble myself and make up with her, so I was going to at least be cordial, despite her evil looks.

"Val, I know you're still mad at me, and I don't want to do this here or now, but I do think we need to make time to talk about some things. Can we do that?" I asked trying my best not to sound pretentious.

She looked me up and down, then uncrossed and crossed her legs again with an air of revulsion that immediately made me regret extending the olive branch at all.

"We don't need to talk. I heard everything I needed to hear from you the day I caught you in Brent's bed. I don't know why you would think I want to hear anything else six months later, but I don't.

Just pretend like I don't exist and go over there somewhere," she rebuked loudly with a flip of her wrist, shifting her body in the opposite direction.

In my peripheral, I noticed not one, but multiple people seated or standing nearby with their phones up in my direction. My shades hid the panic in my eyes as I stood dumbstruck, counting each of them silently and craving a cigarette like a junky.

"I'd appreciate it if you didn't make any more of a scene than you already have," I mumbled lowly directing my gaze back to a smug-faced Valerie.

"I'm sorry. What did you say?" she asked even louder. "Are you trying to keep your fans from knowing you slept with your sister's fiancé too? Well, you definitely didn't sleep, but you know what I mean. I'm sorry. I didn't mean to let the cat out the bag in public. Although from what I've heard, your cat has been practically everywhere *but,* in the bag."

I wanted to knock every tooth in her satirical smile down her throat as she announced my affair to all the looky-loos in the waiting room.

"Ohhh snap!" Amina's chuckling voice exclaimed as Nicky burst into a hardy fit of laughter and my mother stood frozen with a hand over her mouth.

I quickly pivoted on my heels and sashayed through all the gawking and snickering buffoons in the waiting room without a word. This... Was the day from hell.

17

Valerie

Saturday

"Michael B. Jordan is *definitely* Bae now," Nicky swooned as she, Amina, Tamika and I exited the theater doors with the rest of the movie goers. "Lord knows I need a man."

"Who knew little Wallace from *The Wire* would grow up to be *sooo* sexy?" Amina cosigned making duck lips.

"Oh, he's definitely grown."

"Y'all think there's gonna be a *Creed* 2?" Tamika asked as Nicky lead the way towards the mall entrance with the rest of us in toe.

"I sure hope so. I can use another dose of him," Nicky said lasciviously.

"Okay. You're starting to sound creepy now. Freak," Amina teased, swatting her with a loose arm of her winter scarf.

Their banter made me grin, and for a moment, I almost forgot to be paranoid about the people surrounding us. Tugging my baseball cap further down on my head, I made sure to stay wedged between Amina and Tamika.

"Girl, what are you doing?" Tamika asked screw-facing me as we walked.

"What?"

"Why are you all up on us like this? You steppin' on my Jordan's, punk."

"Sorry. I'm just trying not to be noticed. You know."

"Noticed by who?" asked Nicky.

"Anybody. I don't want strangers taking pictures of me or coming up to me and asking questions."

"We got your back if they do," Tamika assured nudging me playfully. "But you still need to watch where you're steppin' while you're trying to be Waldo. I just bought these sneakers."

I did need to relax. But that was getting harder by the day after I *finally* got to see Yasmin and left the hospital Wednesday night. In less than 24 hours, videos of me telling Vanessa off had gone viral, and any semblance of privacy I thought I had evaporated.

It never occurred to me while publicly shaming Vanessa, that she wouldn't be the only one targeted by the gossip vultures. Suddenly, photos of me were being posted online next to my sister and Brent, and the scandal was trending.

I might just be paranoid, but it felt like I was being followed the couple of times I ventured from the house since the story broke. I think I saw the same silver car in my rearview, but I never got a look at the license plate to confirm. I'm not a car person, so without actually recognizing the symbol, or having someone tell me the make and model, I was dumbstruck to identify it.

When I drove to the club Thursday night intending on going up to perform, I saw suspicious looking people with big cameras and lighting out there like paparazzi. I never even knew there *were* paparazzi in Atlanta. Since Vanessa and other locally residing celebrities were caught on video and in pictures often enough, it stood to rationalize that there were, and I didn't want to be naïve.

Then, some anonymous, so called, 'friend close to the source' had been spilling tea like milk to anybody who would listen. I don't know if it was mostly speculation or if somebody was actually leaking information, but at this point, I didn't have a secret unturned now.

People knew about my fight with Vanessa, me tearing up Brent's house and lawn, my new gig as a stripper and Brent's recent arrest for assaulting me at the club. I hated knowing everybody was analyzing my failures and dissecting my life. Even worse, it was all my own fault.

"Earth to Valerie." Tamika snapped her long fingernails in my face until I broke out of my thoughts.

"Sorry. What are we talking about?"

"We're trying to figure out where to eat. You wanna go to a restaurant or to the food court?"

"Doesn't matter to me. Whatever y'all want," I shrugged.

"Three to one. Food court it is."

"*Nooo.* We haven't all hung out together in like… Forever. Let's go to dinner somewhere. I can eat at the food court every day of the week by myself," Nicky whined.

"Chile, we can all eat together at a table here in the food court. You just want us to go to a restaurant so we can cover your part of the bill," Amina replied wryly.

"One time. One time! I knew your petty ass wasn't going to let that go. I switched bags. Don't act like you've never switched purses and left something in it before."

"Not all my money. No. I haven't. Funny how you still had your driver's license when you ordered drinks though."

"So. I don't keep it in the same place I keep my money. There's nothing suspicious about that."

"You's a bold-faced lie. And you never paid me back either. But carry on."

Nicky sucked her teeth and held her middle finger up in back of her head. Amina grabbed it with one hand and bit it.

"Bitch!" Nicky spun around, snatching her finger back with a frown, while the rest of us laughed. "Freaking cannibal! And why are y'all biddies laughing?"

"*Ohhh* calm down. It wasn't even that hard," Amina cackled.

"Y'all make me sick."

Everybody split up in the food court and I headed straight to the sushi spot. I hadn't had any in a while so I might as well get some now.

"Valerie. Valerie Vincent. Is that you?"

I barely got a chance to register the face and shrill voice before I was pulled into an embrace and spritely kissed on my jaw.

"Oh my goodness Val! I thought you were still in New York."

"Nicola. Hey girl," I grinned once I recognized her beautiful doe eyes and bright smile, all wrapped in a petite milk chocolate frame. I hadn't seen my friend in years. "No. I'm actually living here now."

"I almost didn't recognize you, but that Julliard baseball cap was a dead giveaway. I can't believe you still wear that old thing."

"You know I love this hat."

I self-consciously touched the brim of my favorite cap and glanced around hoping she wasn't drawing any unwelcomed attention to us. She was my first friend at Julliard freshman year. We were both Atlanta born and bred, and her outgoing personality reminded me of Vanessa's. Which ironically, I thought was a good thing at the time.

Although we lost touch over the last few years due to our careers, I still considered her a friend, and I actually was happy to see her. She looked great. Her light brown shoulder length hair was perfectly flat ironed and her flowy winter white coat looked like something Olivia Pope would wear on Scandal. Everything she had on looked like money.

I never cared for the flashy clothes or labels anyway. I'm still just as comfortable in leggings, sweats and jeans as I've always been. The thing is, considering that she and I are both dancers, I shouldn't feel inferior in her presence. I've never felt less than *any* dancer since I became a professional, and now, I was feeling like a peon.

"What are you doing here? I heard you moved to California to do a play or something."

"I did for a couple of years, but I go wherever the job takes me. You know how it is. But actually, I'm here with my sister Tatum Christmas shopping," she said shifting the few shopping bags from one hand to the other. "I don't know if you remember her, but she's the one I told you was going to school to be a Pharmacist.

Anyway, she's still in here tearing up the mall with my father's credit card, but honey, I had to stop and get something to *eat.* Then I saw you on my way through the court, and I was like, 'Oh my God. Is that my girl?' Are you in here by yourself?"

"No. I just came from seeing *Creed* with my cousins. They're scattered around here getting food too. So, how have you been?"

"I can't complain. I mean, I could, but I *won't*," she laughed. "I don't know if you heard about this too, but I'm also engaged," she beamed holding her hand out to show me the big rock on her ring finger.

"Oh, congrats. That's beautiful."

"Thanks. I'm truly over the moon about it. It's like God keeps blessing me with good things. I got engaged in July, found out I'm pregnant Thanksgiving Day, and now, Greg and I... My fiancé, are going to be co-producing a play together after the holidays.

I waited so long for my Boaz to come into my life, and as soon as he arrived, everything else fell into place. I've never been this in love and this blessed before at the same time."

"Your Boaz. Wow. All that? That is *absolutely*... Awesome. Congratulations again," I exclaimed hugging her with exaggerated glee.

I really did want to be happy for her, but I couldn't help the nauseating sensation of envy making my stomach do flip flops. Mainly because the truth was, even before my injury, I was never as excited to be engaged to Brent as she seemed to be about her Greg. I had been happy, but ecstatic like Nicola, never.

"Thank you. So, are you dancing with AA Atlanta now?"

There was the question I was dreading just as the line moved and the lady behind the counter asked for my order. Grateful for a little more time to stall, I ordered a Volcano Roll and a Sprite while forming my reply to Nicola. With the news being what it is, I knew whether she knew about my stripping now or not, she would sooner or later.

Nicola passed on ordering for herself, her inquiring eyes brow beating me for answers as the woman made my order.

"No. I'm sort of, freelancing right now. I tore my Achilles Tendon last year and it took me a while to get back in shape. I was with Alvin Ailey for so long though. It's time for me to branch out and do something different now. I just haven't come across anything yet that's a good fit," I finagled.

"Damn I didn't know about your Achilles. That's rough stuff right there. I'm glad you're better, but I know exactly what you mean about wanting to branch out. This is my first time producing too, and that's all because of my boo. Especially since I'm pregnant now. I couldn't star in the play if I wanted to.

You said you're looking for something new. You should come audition for our play. I know you would be great for one of the leads. It's called *Birds of A Feather,* and it's a musical comedy about three friends who rob a bank."

"What?" I giggled.

"I know it sounds crazy, but I promise you, it's *really* going to be good. It's like, *Set It Off* meets *Dream Girls.* Greg has already produced two plays before back in Cali and they've done wonderfully. You see this ring he bought me," she smiled again showing me the bling.

"Okay. If you think I should. When are auditions?"

"Listen," she said taking her phone out. "Give me your new number, because I don't think the one I have in here is the right one anymore, and I'll text you all the information tonight or tomorrow. Greg knows all the when, where and what time stuff."

We exchanged numbers and lollygagged a few minutes longer before promising to talk again soon, and she went to get something to eat for herself.

I spotted Nicky and Amina at a table near the doors to the mall's exit soon afterwards and plopped down beside Amina.

"Where's Mika?" I asked taking my sushi from the bag.

"At Chick-fila, talking to her new bae," Nicky tattled.

"What new bae? She has a new bae?"

Amina and I both looked surprised as Nicky nonchalantly sipped a drink in a Styrofoam cup through a straw.

"Well, she claims they're *just friends*, but I'm not buying it. She's been working out and dolling herself up more since they started talking, and I *know* they've gone out to dinner by themselves before."

"Do we know him?" Amina pried through chews of pizza.

"Yep."

"Who is it then?" she asked looking passed me into the food court trying to see the two in conversation.

"He's not here doofus. She was talking to him on the phone while she was in line," Nicky chuckled. "Okay. Don't say anything to her about it unless she brings it up first. Which she probably won't anyway. Swear?"

Amina and I nodded mischievously as I ate a roll with chopsticks. Nicky knows damn good and well that we were going to grill her until she told us either way, so it's good that she made it easy.

"Dean."

"Dean!" I barked nearly choking on my food. "Dean Lincoln?"

"*Shhhh!* Why you so loud?" Nicky hushed me wide-eyed.

Not that Tamika wasn't a worthy woman, but let's be honest. Dean was way out of her league. No way was an ivy league college graduate *and* heir to a hotel fortune, going to be seriously interested in a woman with a GED and three baby daddies. Right? Would he?

"Sorry. Are you sure? I mean… Dean just doesn't seem like her type." I dubiously wiped the sushi I accidentally spit out off the table. "Since when did they start hanging out anyway?"

Shrugging, she answered while digging into her plate of fries with a smug expression.

"Well, if *you* had been around more, you would know why. Since Zaria's parents are deceased and she's an only child, Vic kind of recruited Tamika to help her with some things for the wedding. Even I went with Mika and Zaria to a bridal show last month with Zaria's best friend.

They've been hanging out a lot actually. Matter fact, Mika and somebody else from the shop is supposed to be doing everybody in the bridal party's hair for the wedding too."

I did feel kind of stupid and guilty that I didn't know more about the planning for my brother's wedding and hadn't been involved in it at all. I truly assumed Zaria and her clan or friends would do all the wedding planning. Traditionally, it's the bride's family that plans it anyway.

Admittedly, I hadn't made much of an effort to get to know Zaria since I moved back to Atlanta, but who could blame me with all of the stuff I was dealing with? Who could blame me for not wanting to be involved in a wedding when my engagement had just gone down in flames? And another thing. Why did it seem like everybody was getting married all of the sudden except for me?

"Dean *is* the best man," Amina reminded us. "Maybe that's why they've been seeing each other or talking a lot. It could be strictly platonic."

"Whatever. I know what I know, and the way she talks about him is anything *but* platonic. I'm glad too. Dub's moved on. Why can't she?" Nicky neck rolled with attitude. "Why're you acting like you have a problem with it? He's Brent's brother. Not Brent. Shit, if Dean can stay friends with Vic after knowing Vic whipped his brother's ass, he's all right with me."

"I'm not saying anything is wrong with him Nicky. I just... I would just like to be done with their family in total. If Dean and Tamika get together, then Brent's probably going to end up being baby four's uncle."

"That's cold Val."

"Well, she does have a history of making babies with all her beaus. I'm just saying. I don't want to be breaking bread with Brent at her next baby shower or—"

"Whoa, whoa. Slow down Speed Racer. We're not even sure if they're officially dating yet. Besides, if Milk Dud didn't get the message to leave you alone when he got arrested, I'm sure he got it now that everybody knows what he did," Amina advised balling up the wax paper her devoured pizza was served on.

"Like I said before. All this drama will die down soon and you'll be able to strip in peace," Nicky quipped. "Speaking of which. You must be raking in the money now that your name's all over the place, huh?"

"No. I haven't been back to work yet."

"Why not? You better strike while the iron's hot," Amina implored with a raised brow. "This is automatic marketing. Vanessa's the devil that slept with your man, and you're the angel, who strips in an angel costume. Men have to be salivating at the mouth to see you come out and shake your tail feathers."

"Do you strip in an angel costume for real? I might have to come down there and see what you're doing on that pole. I know Aunt Di hates that you do it, but I think it's sexy. If I could dance like you, I'd be right up on that pole with you instead of slaving at the doctor's office every day. Y'all know I'm still trying to snag me a husband," Nicky joked sticking her tongue out and snaking her body.

Nicky's antics made us laugh and I came to the conclusion then that they were right. I wasn't doing myself, or my pockets, any favors by missing work. I kept having to remind myself that I was the new Val. The fearless, do what she wants Val. I didn't have anything to be ashamed of. Why was I hiding?

"I'm going in tonight. I just needed a break after everything that happened with Brent," I told her removing my baseball cap and smoothing down my hair. "Courtney says it's way busier now too, and people have been requesting me."

"See? Get that paper," Amina cosigned as Tamika approached on her cell, carrying a Chick-fila bag and smiling like the sun was shining just for her.

Sitting down beside Nicky, she ended her call and tucked it in her coat pocket before glancing back up at us skeptically.

"What are y'all looking at me like that for?"

"Why're you smiling so big?" Amina asked slyly.

"What's wrong with me smiling? It's called being happy."

"What *I* want to know, is *who* you're talking to that's making you *this* happy though? And have you rode the dick?"

Tamika snapped her head towards Nicky and squinted suspiciously. Nicky stuffed some fries in her mouth guiltily and averted her eyes to the crowds of people in the food court.

"Big mouth."

"What?" she replied innocently.

"We're *just* friends. I haven't been riding anybody's dick. I enjoy talking to him, and he enjoys talking to me. Nicky's lonely ass just can't wrap her mind around a man and a woman *just* being friends."

"I am *not* lonely," Nicky protested as each of us donned incredulous smirks. "Okay, maybe I am. But I'm still right. Hatin' ass heifers!"

Tamika knocked her playfully with a shoulder as she unpacked her food.

"*Anywaaaay*, so what are we doing tonight? I took the day off from making money at the salon to kick it with you tricks, so we need to make this worth my wild. I got Mari babysitting his brothers tonight. So what we doing?"

"I don't know what *y'all* are doing, but *I'm* going to work. My bills aren't going to pay themselves," I answered smartly.

"*Soooo*, we're going to the strip club then," Tamika discerned without missing a beat, as though that was *remotely* what I was suggesting.

"Sounds like it," said Nicky.

"No. I wasn't saying th—"

"It's girl's night to The Man Trap then," Amina chirped cutting me off.

"Wait y'all. I don—"

"*Oow oow oow oowooooooo!*" Nicky howled over me as they smacked hands in agreement. "Don't stop! Get it get it!" She sang as the others joined in repeatedly.

Oh lord.

18

Yasmin

I stared at the front door of my home nervously as the Uber slowly exited my driveway. It was a modest 5-bedroom, brick front, two-story home with a finished basement and backyard patio. I remembered the day Malik and I saw it and instantly fell in love with every inch.

It was nice enough weather to only need a heavy sweater, a knit hat, jeans and UGG boots with my cross-body Coach bag on. Pausing at the threshold, I held the keys in my clammy hands and fumbled with the lock like it was a Rubik's Cube. I hadn't been inside since Malik left me for dead in the spare bedroom, and my nerves hadn't forgotten that.

"Hey! Yasmin. How are you?" My portly next-door neighbor Gerald greeted from his porch, startling me as a lit cigarette dangled from his fingers.

He was a nice older white man with gray hair, thick glasses and an eternal smile. He didn't have a wife and I didn't know which side of the fence he played on, but I'd never had anything but pleasant exchanges with him. He was as neighborly as they come, and you could count on seeing him at least three or four times a day smoking a cigarette and people watching from his porch.

"H-hey Gerald."

"I'm glad to see you looking well. I see your dad sometimes when he comes over to get your mail. Are you thinking about moving back in?"

"Uh… yeah I might. It was nice seeing you," I stammered with a fake smile, anxious to get inside without having to answer any questions. Today wasn't the day for that and I rushed inside with a wave.

Pains in my abdomen kept me moving slowly until that brief encounter. I quickly opened the door to the slightly warmer air and shut the door behind me before turning off the alarm. I glanced around at the sunlit foyer and living room illuminated by the rays streaming in from the high windows and sighed. The home I once thought of as a sanctuary, now felt haunted with the spirits of what used to be. And I felt like a ghost lost in limbo.

My eyes fell to the carpet and an instant chill pricked my spine as I gazed down the hallway to the spare bedroom. Despite being cleaned twice, I could still make out subtle dark spots in the plush crème carpet where either my blood, or Malik's, stained it.

I made a mental note to have it replaced soon after I purchased a new car. Fingering the bannister to the stairs, I flipped the switch to light the upstairs and looked up. Per doctor's orders, I wasn't supposed to be climbing stairs or lifting heavy objects, but the unfinished nursery was on the second floor.

When Malik and I first started trying for kids, we jumped the gun and began converting one of the bedrooms. We hadn't done much. We only purchased a rocking chair, a changing table and a couple of wall decorations to start. After so many additional failed attempts at motherhood, neither of us bought anything else or entered the room much.

Having little to do while on bedrest at Daddy's, once I knew I was having a girl, I started ordering everything under the sun online. Thankfully, Daddy had brought the boxes upstairs to the nursery like I asked when he checked on the house. There was no way in hell I would have been lugging boxes back and forth today.

My goal was to put together the unassembled crib and set up whatever else I could to be ready for my daughter's homecoming, God willing, in a couple of days.

My cell rang in my back pocket at the same time I set foot on the bottom stair, startling me.

"Hello," I answered brusquely.

"Aye Shawty. I'ma be round there as soon as me and Tez finish this lil bidness we handlin' right nah. I ain't want you sittin' round waitin' on me and I ain't say I'm runnin' late."

"Running late? Negro, by *four* hours? You were supposed to be there this morning when they discharged me. Thank God my father was already there seeing Sophie because I sure couldn't depend on *you*."

"Chill out. I figured you be there wit' the baby anyway. I ain't know you was rushin' to leave."

"Are you kidding me? You got me at odds with my daddy because of you, so yes. I'm rushing! I'm trying to move back into my house and I *told* you that. Our daughter might be coming home in a day or two and nothing is put together at my house yet. Nothing! What *'bidness'* did you and *Tez* have Dwayne? Huh?" I spat flailing my hands and pacing the foyer.

He sucked his teeth but didn't reply, infuriating me further.

"That's what I thought. Some dumb shit is what. Do you think it's right that I'm over here, just hours after being discharged, about to put together a crib *by myself?* Do you know how *stupid* you've been making me look for sticking up for you? How stupid you *keep* making me look to everybody? To my father?"

My father and I had gotten into a huge argument the night before at the hospital because of the way he kept coming at Dwayne. Stupidly, I called my self defending Dwayne, who wasn't even there, because it *did* seem like Daddy was picking fights with him unprovoked. If I wanted Dwayne to be around more, I knew Daddy was going to have to cool it.

Still, my father felt entitled to say how he felt regarding Dwayne, when he felt it, with absolutely *no* filter. We argued, and I let my father know that I didn't appreciate how he was acting now that Dwayne was with me. He was certainly less dogmatic when Dwayne was just Tamika's baby's daddy. It was the truth.

Before I knew it, my dad and I were having one of the biggest arguments we've had since I became an adult. By the end of it, he was adamant that I should rely on Dwayne to pick me up when I was discharged, since he felt like I was siding with him.

Shocked, but not wanting to back down, I arrogantly agreed. Idiotically, I thought it was possible since Dwayne's license suspension was over December first, that he might actually do what I asked.

His car had been out of impound for months, so all he needed to do was get his license reinstated again and everything would be good. That's what he was *supposed* to be doing most of the day yesterday when we'd barely spoken, and he hadn't been to the hospital to see me or Sophie.

What I absolutely *was not* going to do, was be anywhere that Cortez was *ever* again. At least, not if I could help it. That carjacking bastard would not be chauffer to me or my child anywhere, and I let Dwayne know why the day after Cortez had been in my room too.

Of course, Dwayne thought I was being absurd and that I was letting my loathing of the man cloud my memory. He was convinced that my ID of the clothing and scent of his cologne was purely coincidental. Even when I told him that I recognized his voice, Dwayne's countenance was fully doubtful.

"Why would he do all that?" Dwayne had asked with certainty that I was mistaken.

"I don't know! I don't have any idea *why*. Maybe he just doesn't like me for you that much. I don't know. But I'm telling you, it's him."

"So, you expect me to believe my boy jacked you, but ain't neva' done nothin' to my baby's mom? C'mon Yas."

With that, I clammed up and had little to nothing to say to him the rest of the the day. Now that Dwayne didn't need Cortez to take him anywhere, I fully expected him to make Sophie and I a priority, but he kept making a fool out of me.

"Shawty, if anybody's makin' you look stupid, it's you. I'm doin' what I can do. You ain't the only important person in my life. I gotta juggle you, my boys, and chasin' this paper. I ain't yo' kid to be bossin' around."

I was angry enough to smash my phone, but that would have only made things worse. Maybe if he acted like a responsible adult, I would have to boss him around.

"Then why don't you act like an adult and do what you say you're going to do Dwayne?"

"Nobody ain't forcin' yo' hardheaded ass to do that. You got one of them bassinette thingys at yo' pops house already anyway. You just impatient Shawty. Sophie ain't even out yet. Nah I got the addy in my GPS, and as soon as I finish up what I'm doin' wit' Tez, I'm gon—"

I pressed end on the call as water salted my eyes in anger. I wasn't going to waste another minute bickering with this fool. I wanted to get as much done in Sophie's room as possible by six o'clock, which would give me almost four hours. Then I was going to head back to Piedmont and stay with my daughter the rest of the night.

Everybody thought I was doing too much right now, but *nobody* wanted to help. Daddy was still salty with me over our argument and refused to drive me over to the house, so I just took an Uber. I didn't even bother to call any of my family. For as much support as they had of me in the hospital, I didn't trust it to be genuine.

Wiping my tears, I sniffled and put my phone back in my pocket as I sluggishly ascended the stairs. Passing a linen closet and the room I used as my home office, I entered the master bedroom and looked at the mess with narrowed eyes.

Because Malik and I were sleeping separately before the stabbing, he had free reign of the master while I stayed in the room on the first floor. The clothes on the floor and disheveled sheets and comforter bunched up on the bed reminded me of what I wouldn't miss about Malik. The slob.

Impulsively, I picked up two of Malik's shirts and a pair of his boxers. Tossing them into the hamper by the closet door, I made another mental note to gather all of his things and donate or trash them. Malik didn't live here anymore, so his things didn't need to either.

Wincing as a stabbing pain bit me from bending and standing too quickly, I closed my eyes and tried to breathe the aching away.

"Get it together Yasmin," I told myself aloud with a slow exhale.

"Yeah. Get it together Yasmin," a deeper and alarming voice concurred behind me.

Snapping my eyes open, I stood dumbfounded in the middle of the bedroom. Hoping, praying I was imagining things, I listlessly rotated around. My heart fully halted a beat as I stared into the face of my wet, shirtless spouse with a gun aimed at my head.

"M-Malik?" I squeaked confusedly.

Like an idiot, I left myself open to this by not changing the locks or at least the security code to the alarm system. Still, with my hawkeyed neighbors and the periodic police patrols, I didn't expect him to chance it.

"If you scream, I'll put a bullet in your head before you close your mouth."

Crazy enough, I hadn't even thought about screaming until he said it. My mind was on Daddy's gun which I'd slid in my purse before leaving the house, and how I might be able to get to it. That, and the fact that my psycho husband was looking like he was going to be somebody's prison bae.

He didn't look anything like the Grizzly looking homeless man I viewed through the kitchen window that night. Nor did he resemble the slightly out of shape, perfectly groomed man I used to call my husband. Maybe if he looked more like *this* before, I wouldn't have strayed at all.

His head was shaven clean for the first time in the history of our relationship, and he was sporting a long scar under his jaw that almost made me cringe to view. Is it possible to loathe and lust for a person at the same time?

His biceps bulged tautly from his arms, and his once flabby chest had transformed into sculpted pecks. Most impressive were his abs. Chiseled and glistening with water, they looked hard enough to grate cheese on. I hadn't seen his body look this good since college. In fact, it didn't even look this good then.

"P-please don't hurt me."

His deadpanned gaze only increased my anxiety as he stood less than three feet from me with water dripping from his torso and arms onto his dark sweatpants. He must have been showering in the master bathroom, which explained how he easily got the drop on me from behind.

"I didn't think you would be back here until after the baby was born. But I guess that already happened," he said noting my deflated stomach.

"Yes. She was early. A preemie."

"She."

I nodded.

"Give me your phone," he ordered outstretching a hand.

"You don't have to do this. I won't... I won't say anything. You can just... Lock me in the bathroom or something and leave. I won't say a w—"

"Woman! *Shut up* and give me the damn phone," he yelled stepping closer and leveling the gun between my eyes.

I couldn't have blinked it to him any faster after that if I were a genie. Seeing it was locked, he demanded the passcode, which I begrudgingly, but quickly recited. I watched him perplexed as he swiped through my phone with one hand.

Glancing from me to the phone repeatedly, I had no idea what he was looking for. I was just grateful that he hadn't pulled the trigger yet and I hoped he wouldn't find anything in there that would change his mind.

"She's a tiny little thing. Looks a lot like you," he grinned as I realized he was looking at pictures of Sophie. "What's her name?"

"Uh... Sophie."

"Sophie," he repeated, his smile fading into revulsion. "You named her the same name *we* were going to name *our* daughter? Really Yas? You just..."

Insulted, I felt my face flush with vexation.

"Hold on. That was the name I was going to name *my* daughter, no matter who her father was. It was my great grandmother's name Malik. It's not like we came up with it together."

"Yeah, but I agreed that we would name our daughter that if we ever had one, didn't I? But here you go talking about... *No matter who her father is*," he grumbled mockingly. "You can't stop being a bitch even with a gun in your face, can you?"

"I didn't mean it like that," I recoiled regretting my choice of words. The last thing I wanted was to *provoke* him into shooting me. Sophie needed her mother, and I wasn't ready to die. "I just meant that... I-I didn't mean it like it came out Malik."

"I bet you didn't. I caught the tail end of your little squabble on the phone with that fuck-boy. What's the matter? Did the grass turn out to be browner on the other side after all?"

I didn't answer. I *couldn't* answer. Not truthfully. Swallowing to wet my current cotton mouth, I ran a shaky hand across my forehead and averted my eyes. He placed my phone on the armoire beside him and twisted his mouth while watching me in deliberation.

Afraid of what he might come up with, I decided to make my apologies now, in hopes of altering my fate for the good.

"I'm sorry Malik. I'm sorry that I didn't believe you when you said nothing more than a kiss happened with that woman. I was angry, and I was jealous. I'm sorry that I slept with Dwayne to get back at you, and I'm sorry that... That all of this happened. I just wish we could go back to how we were when everything was good. Maybe we could go to counseling."

He snickered pacing a small circle in front of me with the gun still trained at my head.

"I'm not crazy Yasmin, and I'm not *stupid* either. Don't try to placate me with bullshit. Teddy's smooth-talking ass probably tried the same shit before he got killed. There's no coming back from where we are right now, and I wouldn't want you back for all the freedom in the world. I tried to kill you for a reason, and the only thing *I'm* sorry about, is that you're not dead."

His eyes didn't even blink as he uttered the most malevolent words *I* ever heard him say with ease. His cousin Teddy was bludgeoned to death with a hammer a couple of years ago by the husband of the woman he was having an affair with. The mention of that gruesome murder sent chills up my spine.

"Okay. I know you hate me, and you have every right to. But Malik… I have a little girl depending on me now. I can't take back what I did. I can only apologize for it, but please. Please do—"

"Shut up Yasmin. Shut. Up," he ordered as tears drained my eyes. "And I don't want to see your fucking tears either. Go sit down over there and let me think," he instructed, waving the gun towards the bed.

"Plea—"

"I *said* sit down and let me think Yasmin!" he grit, making me retreat hurriedly to the bed.

My tears had been the antidote to his anger during our marriage. He used to soften like Pillsbury dough whenever I cried, but the Malik standing before me wasn't the Malik I married. Because of my actions, he was a changed man, and therefore, I might get a reaction I didn't plan on if I pressed him.

Choking down the cries I so badly wanted to expel, I thought about the lay out of the house and considered ways to escape or get help. He was watching too closely for me to get to Daddy's gun, but I wasn't going to let myself be an easy victim.

At some point, he put on a long sleeve shirt and socks from drawers in the armoire where his clothes still were. Minutes ticked slowly away like hours as I lamented on the things I did that got me here. Malik arbitrarily maneuvered around the room looking out the window, sitting, then standing, and mumbling to himself.

He noticeably favored one leg, and I wondered what he had done to injure it. Anxiety, silence and his incessant pacing was getting to me as I noticed the sun beginning to descend outside the window.

"Did you hurt yourself?"

"What?"

"Did you hurt yourself? You're limping and you have a scar on your chin," I stated timidly, stroking my own jawline where his was scarred.

He stilled like he was deciding whether or not to answer my question, then leaned against the door frame. Exhaling harshly, he wiped his nose with the heel of his hand and cussed under his breath while relaxing his gun hand.

"I wiped out on the motorcycle in the snow. I misjudged some black ice. It's nothing."

"You're limping."

"I'll live," he retorted dryly.

"You look like you've been working out a lot too."

"I got a lot of time on my hands these days. Might as well be productive. I can't spend my days following celebrities on Twitter, shopping and watching T.V. like some people."

I knew that was a direct dig at me by the way he said it, and that let me know he had to be monitoring my social media too. I wondered where he had been hiding all this time, because I was almost positive it hadn't been here. Still, I had an even better question.

"Where did you get that gun?"

"Why bitch?"

"I just… Never knew you had a gun before."

He huffed. "I didn't. You think if I had a gun, I would have chosen this rinky dink .38? I had to get whatever I could get my hands on for protection out here in these streets."

"Why are you still here anyway? I thought you were probably long gone to another state. I couldn't believe that was you in Daddy's backyard," I baited him, hoping to neutralize the air of animosity in the room.

"I *was* gone. But then my mother got sick. I had to come back to see her and I needed a way to get around that… Never mind. You don't need to know all that."

"Well, what's wrong with your mother?"

"Like you care," he huffed sizing me up and curling his upper lip in disgust.

"I *do* care. I've never had a problem with your mother. She even called to check on me while I was in the hospital. I didn't stop caring about her just because of what you… What happened with us."

"She has liver cancer. It's too aggressive for them to save her," he muttered somberly.

"My God. I'm so sorry to hear that."

I truly was sad to hear it. Malik's mom was an alcoholic for most of her adult life, but she cleaned herself up a decade ago, and hadn't had a drop since. At least, not that I knew of. I could only imagine how weak her liver already was after so many years of damage to now have cancer attacking it.

"Hmph. I'm sure you are. And she was sorry to hear that her son was on the run for attempted murder. But sometimes, that's the hand we're dealt. Get up," he suddenly commanded leaning up from the frame and using his gun to direct me to stand.

"Why? What are you about to do to me?"

"For the love of God. Just get up," he directed like I was annoying him to no end. "We're moving."

"Moving where?"

"To the basement."

The basement. Where there was only one window to let in light? Where the one door with a stairwell up into our backyard was partially blocked behind that damn deep freezer he insisted on buying two years ago that didn't fit anywhere? The one place where he could probably shoot me without anyone hearing it and leave my decomposing body for days if he wanted to? Hell no!

"Why? Why the basement? Malik, you don't have to do this," I pled.

"Shut up Yasmin. We're going to the basement," he insisted as I continued to plead with him against it. "And don't think of running either because you can't outrun these bullets."

The insinuation that I could run in my current physical condition would have been laughable if the situation wasn't so serious.

"If you do what I tell you, we'll both be alive at the end of the day. If you don't… I'll just shoot you and take my chances with whatever comes. Your choice. Are we clear?"

"Yes," I muttered

"All right C'mon let—"

"Ding Dong!"

Both our eyes widened at the sound of the doorbell and he was instantly on me, grabbing my arm with the gun in my face.

"Who's that?"

"I don't know. I don't know," I answered cowering under his grasp.

"Don't make me kill somebody today Yasmin."

"I swear, I don't know who it is."

Maybe it was my nosy neighbor Octavia, UPS with another package from Amazon, or maybe Daddy came after all. Whoever it was, they were either going to be my saving grace, or the last nail in my coffin.

"Yas! Yasmin! Open up Shawty!" Dwayne yelled banging on the door.

"I knew you were lying. That's your fuck-boy boyfriend. Illiterate muthafucker. You were going to have this bum up in the house I paid for?" Malik sneered.

Technically, it was the house *we* paid for. I was a partial owner of the firm and until my attack and later orders of bedrest, I was just as active in and outside of court in our business. I didn't think this was the right time to correct him, however.

"No. I-I wasn't. He was going to help me put the crib together but, you heard us arguing. I didn't think he was coming anymore," I whimpered.

"Well since he's here, why don't we just invite him to the party."

He flung me around towards the bedroom door, then shoved me in the back, making me stumble forward. Grabbing me by the collar of my sweater, he forced me downstairs with the gun in my back.

"Just open the door. Don't say shit else," he growled.

I nodded, still hoping without hope that Dwayne would grasp what was happening the instant I opened the door and overpower Malik to save me. Save us.

"Yasmin! C'mon girl! You wanted me here! I'm here! Stop playin' fo' somebody calls the cops on a nigga!" Dwayne yelled.

Malik released me and stood to the right of the door out of view with his firearm aimed.

"I-I'm coming."

My whole body tensed as I unlocked the door and turned the knob. Dwayne barged in too quickly for me to even attempt a warning, and before I knew it, Malik's gun was crashing into his temple repeatedly.

Frantic, I backed away, fumbling in my bag for Daddy's gun.

"Stop!" I cried training the Smith and Wesson on Malik.

His rage filled eyes met mine as he lunged at me like a rabid Pitbull. And I pulled the trigger.

19

Amina

The Jackson Five's "I Saw Mommy Kissing Santa Claus" blared through the house as I danced around in my bra and panties while sifting through clothes in the closet. In spite of all the turmoil lately, I was happy. Happy that nothing crazy had happened to me lately, happy Jamie hadn't rung or texted my phone at all today, and happy to have some semblance of normalcy with my cousins again.

I didn't have a plan yet to deal with Lala, Jamie or *whoever* from stalking or attacking me again, but I would figure it out... Later. Tonight, I was going to enjoy some much-needed girl time with my cousins and think about the shambles my life is in tomorrow.

The melodic chiming of my doorbell rang, causing me to jut out of my closet with a frown to see who it was on the surveillance television.

"What does he want?" I asked myself while viewing the uninvited guest on my front porch.

By the third ring, and second knock, it was obvious he had no intentions on going away, and I was kind of curious about what he wanted. Slipping into my robe, I checked my hair and face, dabbing a little nude lipstick on first, and headed downstairs.

Swinging the door open with attitude, I displayed an unwelcoming mien. I hate pop ups, but lately, everybody and their momma seemed to think it was a good idea.

"Donovan, is something wrong with your phone? Why are you on my doorstep without calling?"

"Well happy holidays to you too. These are for you," he beamed pushing a large bouquet of red roses towards me as his cologne beguiled my nostrils. "I didn't think you would answer my call, and I wanted to make a grand gesture."

Ignoring the flowers, I fought the urge to smile. I don't know why I was being so stupid. For all I knew, he was the one who broke into my house looking for the combination to my safe. My intuition told me that he wasn't, but either way, he was owed the cold shoulder.

"I'm in the middle of something. What do you want?" I probed standing in the opening.

"You're in the middle of something?" He asked giving me a once over and gazing past me curiously. "Oh. I'm sorry. Do you have company?"

"Does that matter?"

"That depends on you. It will if you're not going to take these roses and let me in."

"What are the flowers for?"

"You. Beautiful roses, for a beautiful woman," he grinned stepping closer.

Rolling my eyes, I snatched them and held them in my hand against the door.

"Okay. I have them. Thank you. Is that all?"

"No Ms. Meany, that is not all. I haven't been able to stop thinking about you since I saw you at *Starbucks*, and I felt like I owed you an apology."

I continued to stare blankly at him, but my insides swirled with excitement. As much as I didn't want to care, I couldn't help myself. His entrancing eyes, boyish smile and full lips made me want to leap in his muscular arms and devour his mouth. But I wouldn't dare. This negro bailed on me like a bucket full of water and never looked back.

"That's sweet, but it's too late for all of that. Thank you for the flowers, but I have to go." I stepped back to shut the door.

"Wait!" His hand shot out, stopping its close and Linx came from behind me with his head lowered and growling.

"Oh shit!" he drew back and retreated two paces. "Where did he come from?"

"Heel Linx," I commanded smugly, and Linx instantly sat by my leg, still eyeing Donovan threateningly.

"You uh… You got a dog."

"Congratulations. You can see," I teased.

Despite his obvious caution, he came closer again. His eyes surfing between Linx and I.

"If you don't have company, other than the dog, can I come in and talk to you? I'll even sit on the bed and help you pick out an outfit while you get dressed like I did last time."

My spirits had been low the morning of Uncle Vernon's funeral, but he managed to make me smile with comforting words and long embraces as we chose my outfits. He had been with me in my closet then. Was it possible he noticed the safe behind my clothes then? Was I being naïve?

"No, you *can-not.* But you can come in for a few minutes to talk right here in the doorway. *A few minutes,*" I reiterated. "Linx, kitchen," I commanded.

Linx didn't budge, still fixated on Donovan like I hadn't even opened my mouth. I wanted to put my foot in his stubborn ass.

"Linx, *kitchen!*"

He barked defiantly at Donovan but went down the hall and laid across the kitchen threshold facing us. As a guard dog, he was taught to stay close and keep me in his view. So, he did that without pause. I could have let Donovan get acquainted with Linx like I had Val, but I chose not to.

"Whoa. You're not going to let him bite me, are you?" Donovan asked slyly.

"Not unless you earn it. Say what you came to say so I can finish getting dressed," I ordered leaning my back up against the closed door.

He licked his full lips and peered with mock gloom at me.

"I missed you."

"You said that already."

"Did I? Did I also say that I'm sorry? I'm sorry I didn't stick around to hear you out that day or take any of your calls afterwards. We talked about the craziness I dealt with when I was with my last ex. I just saw the drama, the red flags and… I bailed. I may have overreacted."

"You *may* have overreacted? I think that's more than an understatement," I huffed tossing the bouquet on the bottom stair and posting a hand on my hip.

"I mean, you have to admit that was a lot Amina. You were already shot not long before that. Somebody spray painted your garage with threats, broke in your house, and played a *porno* of you with some guy. Is there protocol for how I was supposed to react to that?"

"First of all. It was *not* a porno. I never knew that video existed, and neither did the man in the video with me. And no. There is no protocol, but I'm sure if there were one, it would include hearing me out before storming off and erasing me from your life," I objected crooking my neck.

"Probably," he replied ruefully. "In my defense, I was overwhelmed. Porno. Not a porno. Whatever you want to call it. There was a video of you, half naked with a whip in your hands, and some old white man eating you out. I was traumatized. I didn't know what to think."

"I understand that it would be a lot for anybody, but you didn't even want to hear me out Donovan. I know we hadn't been seeing each other that long at the time, but in that time, we shared a lot with each other. Or at least, I shared a lot with you. I thought we were building something solid, but you rolled out at the first sign of imperfection.

I was shot *before* you started dating me. You knew that person was still on the loose, and you knew from our conversations that I was still afraid they would do something else. What happened to, 'Nothing else is going to happen baby. Not while I'm here'? Isn't that what you said to me?"

His guilt riddled face looked to the floor, then back up at me.

"I did say that. I'm sorry I didn't keep my word."

"Maybe you are, but if you hadn't seen me in Starbucks, would we even be having this conversation? You were fine with letting me go on about my business and vice versa before that. I've moved on."

"Moved on how?" he asked placing both hands in the baggy pockets of his cargo pants. "Are you seeing somebody else?"

"I was."

"Why aren't you seeing him anymore?"

"It's not important. My point is, I let any hopes I had for you and me go. Now you show up with a bouquet talking about you miss me, and you want to know what happened. What are you expecting me to do with that?"

He closed the distance between us. His face only a few inches from mine. The minty smell of his breath wafting from the slight gap in his lips."

"I was fucked up for bailing on you like I did. I was. I know that. I know it seems like I didn't want anything to do with you until I saw you again. But the more time that passed, the harder it got to humble myself to contact you.

At first, I convinced myself that I had a reason to be mad at you. But after a while, I wasn't even sure what I was mad at you for, because I didn't know the whole story. I've been on a few dates since that day, but none of them kept me from thinking about you.

Then when I saw you in Starbucks, I didn't want to let you get away again, just because I rushed to judgement before. I realize that you don't owe me anything. But I really would like to know from you, what that was all about that day. What happened?"

"Why? So I can open myself up again for you to turn right back around and tell me it's too much? No thank you."

"I won't."

"You can't promise me that. You don't have any idea what I'm about to say."

He threw his head back and expelled a harsh breath before focusing on me again with a contemplative stare. I just wished he would back up.

His close proximity was starting to melt my bravado. I hadn't been able to erase him from my mind or heart either, as much as I wanted to.

In the short time we dated, he managed to awaken feelings in me that had been dormant or nonexistent before him. I had only had two serious relationships in adulthood, but none since I started escorting.

It was like, once I opened my heart to him, I couldn't close the portal. What I had with Cedric was a fling to pass the time, and as much as I wanted to fight this wanton feeling I had for Donovan, I couldn't.

His eyes slowly left mine and trailed downward to the slight opening of my robe, exposing my ample lingerie clad bosom. Biting his lower lip sexily, he gazed back up at me.

"Okay. Let me just ask you this. What was going on in that video? Was that an ex? Because honestly, that's the thing that had me stuck. You told me you used to model and be a decoy for a P.I. firm, but what was that?"

Folding my lips under, I decided I didn't have anything to lose by telling him the truth. Well, the majority of it anyway. I groaned and fluttered my lids in frustration. I was sick of feeling like I had to lie or be secretive about who I was and what I used to do. What I did for money was more legal than not, and my life choices made me self-sufficient and rich enough to stop working at 29 years old. I was my own woman and my own boss because of it. Not many other people my age could say that, and that wasn't anything to be ashamed of.

"He was an ex-client," I answered tautly scratching the tip of my nose. "Look, let me just cut to the chase because I don't want to waste your time, or mine, and there's nothing to lose between *us* at this point anyway. I was honest with you when I said that I used to model and that I was a licensed decoy for a P.I. firm. What I didn't say, is that I also worked for a high-end escort agency for seven years.

What you saw in that video, was one of the services that I provided for one of my regular clients. He liked to be submissive, and I was his dominatrix. Somehow, his wife got hold of *that* video, found out who I was, and vandalized my house. She didn't have any reason to, since I'm not escorting anymore, and wasn't going to see her husband again. But I guess she didn't know that."

His chiseled jaw went slack, the color drained from his face, as his eyes pled with me to recant my disclosure. I stoically awaited his verbal response and my insides imploded with anxiety. Shifting in place, Donovan's hands found their way inside of his pants pockets as the information sunk in.

"I don't know if you know what a dominatrix is, but..."

"I know what it is," he replied insipidly. "You control, degrade and humiliate men during sex."

"Umm… Close enough I guess, but not entirely. I didn't have to have sex with them to dominate them. The ones who wanted that kind of service I mean. He was a rare client. It's really just about being controlled, and he wanted me to control him."

"Wow. I don't know what I expected you to tell me, but that wasn't it. An Escort. For seven years."

"Among other things."

"But that was your primary way of making money, right?"

My face flushed as I groaned and fluttered my lids in frustration. He was probably trying to calculate how many dicks had been in my vagina over seven years. Honestly, I probably had sex with less people in the years I was escorting than most single people do who aren't. Funny thing is, men are rarely held to the same standard. Most women, myself included, could care less how many women a man slept with as long as he wasn't diseased.

"Yes. Being arm candy and good conversation for the wealthy was a big chunk of how I made my money. Not being a dominatrix or having sex. I was an escort. Not a prostitute. I was also a licensed decoy for *Femme Fatale Investigations* like I told you before. But you can think, or call it whatever you want. I have a clean bill of health and I haven't run out of fingers or toes to count how many people I slept with on them. It is what it is."

His brow raised and his long tongue swabbed his bottom lip in thought, and I faked an apathetic stance. I felt judged and I hated it.

Even though I just finished telling myself that I had nothing to be ashamed of, his troubled expression had me second guessing my own affirmations.

I pursed my lips and nodded ruefully.

His lips buckled under in dismay, and his judgmental eyes looked like they were teetering between two verdicts.

"Amina, this *is* hard to hear. I'm glad you aren't a... *Porn star* or a prostitute. But this isn't that far off," he snickered pretending to find it funny, though the tension in his face read differently. "You're not still escorting though. Right?"

Shaking my head slowly, I watched him with trepidation, waiting for him to wrap this up and make his exit. He was probably wrestling with the imaginary count of partners I slept with in his head too.

"So, did your occupation have anything to do with you being shot?"

Clasping my hands together, then rubbing my palms flat against each other, I let the words fall in as vaguely honest a fashion as I could muster. I didn't know where we were going from here, and I wasn't about to drop even more reasons for him to run into his lap.

"It could. I'm not sure. It's complicated, and from the look on your face, finding out I was an escort is complicated enough for you. Believe it or not, I totally get it. Which is why I never intended to tell you about it," I spoke honestly.

Silence befell us as we fixated on each other without words and The Temptations, "*Give Love on Christmas Day,*" played through the house.

"Well, I answered all of your questions, and I really *do* need to finish getting dressed." I broke our gaze and turned to open the front door again.

I wasn't about to sit here in my feelings while he dissected my life and determined if he still wanted to deal with me or not. No ma'am. He could figure that out somewhere else, and if I didn't hear from him again, so be it.

"Can I ask where you're headed out to?"

"To *The Man Trap.*"

With enlarged eyes, he cocked his head back and smirked.

"The strip club?"

"The strip club. My cousin Val dances there now."

"The twin that danced for Alvin Ailey?"

I nodded.

"Wow. Career change huh?"

"Umm, I'm not trying to be rude or anything, but I'm in my robe with the door open in the middle of winter," I gestured with my hand for him to leave.

"Can I see you again tomorrow?" he asked invading my personal space and bringing his face so close to mine that I thought he was going to kiss me. I was shocked by his abrupt movement, but I actually wanted him to.

That charming grin was back on his face again and despite the cold wind blowing through the door, my body was suddenly hot.

"I'll think about it."

"You think about this too," he counseled, capturing my lips with his and pinning my body against the door.

20

Vanessa

"Aiight Vix. I'm out," Gavin said as he crossed in front of the TV, looking at me with displeasure. "You good?"

Keeping focus on the television, I blew ringlets of smoke into the air and repositioned myself on the couch. I was slightly tipsy and very agitated after a long day of sulking and sleeping all day without an ounce of comfort from him.

"Just go already. I don't even know why you're faking like you care."

"That's how you feel? Hmph. Well, if that's how it is, I don't know when I'll be back, so you might as well go chill at your own place."

Grunting, I leaned forward to tap ashes from my cigarette into the tray on the table. He had nerve, and like it or not, I wasn't leaving. Not tonight anyway.

"What's new? You don't need to be here for me to be here. I have the keys and the codes. I know you're not trying to tell me to leave on some petty shit."

"I'm telling you to leave on some *real* shit. No reason for you to be sittin' up where I rest my head and pay the bills wit' a stank ass attitude. You can do that where *you* pay the bills."

Glaring at him threw slits, I cleared my throat and downed my glass of Grand Marnier as I soaked in his appearance. He was drenched in Givenchy and jewels with a fresh cut and smelled like heaven and orgasms, looking like a *whole* snack. If I wasn't so mad, I would have pulled his jeans down and blown him before letting him loose into the world of groupies.

"Don't play yourself. First of all, it's raining. So I'm not going anywhere unless I have to. Second of all, get out your feelings. I'm the one who's been suffering, and you haven't shown an ounce of compassion for me.

I did my thing at the video shoot Thursday *and* I drug my ass to Kingdom's Christmas party last night. I put up with all those cameras in my face and I even answered some of those tacky ass questions the press lobbed at me with a big ole smile on my face! Can you give me a fucking break today?

I'm just asking for this *one* day to wallow in misery by-my-self. Since my so-called man, has been too preoccupied to offer me any comfort, at the very least, you can let me lay around here where I have unlimited access to alcohol, a big screen tv and a maid to wait on me hand and foot. These are real life problems I got right now," I spat swiveling my neck.

"This *one* day is costing me money. Canceling studio sessions and appearances for you to take a break is bullshit in this business. Everybody has *real life problems*," he mocked. "I got guys on my *label* that's facing possible penitentiary time right now and they're still grinding. Ain't no taking a break because your feelings got hurt."

"Go to hell Gavin. You know It's not just because my feelings got hurt. You're not even *trying* to understand," I scoffed, gulping down the rest of the Grand Marnier from my glass and slamming it on the table.

"What don't I understand? You did some grimy shit to people before you got famous, and now everybody wants to tell all your dirt. I understand perfectly. That comes with the territory. Hiding out ain't gonna change the facts. Just be happy people still care. When they don't, that's when you have a problem."

"That's *sooo* easy to say when you're not the one everybody is dogging out. I got your baby momma lying on me, the police questioning me, social media trolls dragging my name for old shit when I already got my *own* man. I mean… C'mon! I got a thick skin, but I'm human Gavin.

How do you think I feel that my *own* man isn't even trying to comfort me through it? What's up with that? You see me here miserable and you're about to go to the studio?"

"I got work to do. And if you want to stay on Kingdom, you'll remember that *you* got work to do too. I let you take this day off, and I let you get what you felt off your chest Wednesday when you told me what happened at the hospital.

I'm not a coddler though Vix. I didn't think you were the type to need coddling either. What happened to the unapologetic boss chick I thought I had? You wasn't hiding behind shit while you was fuckin' Brand Beats or your sister's dude. Right? You was out there bold and brazen. So why you all ashamed and trying to hide out now?"

I jerked my head back in offense.

"You trying to be funny?"

"Nah. I'm just keeping it a hunnit' Babygirl. You ain't nobody's victim. If anything, you out here making *other people* victims. Until recently, I ain't have no reason to care about who you messed with before me or how you made your choices.

Your music was dope, your look was dope, and your confidence was sexy as fuck," he said raking his teeth against his bottom lip sexily. "You had the total package for what Kingdom needed in a new artist, and what I needed in a new woman. But this ain't you. Mopin' around lookin' for sympathy. Tomorrow, put on your big girl panties and get back to work."

"You're so supportive," I groaned cynically, leaning back on the couch.

I needed a shoulder to lean on. *My man's* shoulder to lean on, and this bastard was busy giving me the third degree. Where was the love? What happened to the guy who was so into me that he wanted me to move in with him a few weeks ago? This man. This man acted like I was expendable *and* replaceable.

He hadn't done or said anything remotely sympathetic to me since news spread of my affair with Brent. I was starting to feel like he was judging me like everybody else was, when he was supposed to be having my back. Lately, he had little or no reaction to the things that upset me and I felt like he was on everybody else's side but mine.

"As soon as somebody else fucks up, that'll be the new news and people will move on to that. At the end of the day, this is the brand *you* created for yourself. If you don't like it, change it. But listen, I gotta roll. I'm out," he replied bopping coolly towards the arched doorway to the foyer.

"Be out then!" I spat brattily.

Leaning over the couch, I launched a throw pillow at the back of his head with all my might. Halting, he turned halfway toward me with clinched jaws. Crooking my neck defiantly, I waited for him to say something or maybe even rush me. To show me some kind of emotion other than indifference. But he didn't. He looked me up and down, swabbing his bottom lip back and forth with his tongue before bending the corner out of my sight.

A few seconds later, the front door slammed, and I was left to swallow the lump of embarrassment and tribulation I was feeling by myself. Infuriated, I tossed another pillow from the couch across the room and spun back around to the TV in a huff. Sounds of women screaming and scuffling on an episode of *Black Ink Crew* filled the room as I buried my face in my palms.

My world was falling apart. Even the damn IUD that boasted 99% pregnancy prevention I've had in for two years failed me. Ninety nine percent effectiveness my ass! I knew I was pregnant even before I copped the test from the drug store this morning.

Last night I was struggling to stay awake past midnight at the party. Coupled with my weepy mood swings and the soreness I had begun to feel in my breasts over the last week, I figured out last night that there was a bun in my oven.

I was glad Gavin decided to stay when I took the car service we had for the night back to his place instead. I had the driver stop at Kroger and paid him to pick up a Clearblue test for me. No way in hell was I going to let some random catch me out here in these streets buying a pregnancy test.

I cried myself to sleep after the digital screen on the test confirmed that I was pregnant. I decided then that I was taking a mental health day off for myself. I didn't get up until after noon, and Gavin still hadn't come home. So, by the time my 2 pm studio session came around, I was already resigned to chilling in the house.

He came in around three-ish, talking about he stayed over Drizzy Dre's, another Kingdom artists' house, after they partied all night. I wouldn't have cared about him staying out all night if not for the way things had been going with us already. Other than having good sex and making good music, we couldn't get along for shit this past week. I know a week isn't long, but in the celebrity world, every day together was the equivalent of dog years.

The timing for this baby was terrible for my career, for my relationship, and for my current mental state. Plus, I need cigs and alcohol to cope with all the stress I'm dealing with and being pregnant wasn't conducive to that. No way in hell was this accidental impregnation about to make me stop cold turkey. As soon as I was able to, I was going to have this little mistake vacuumed out like it never happened. And I was definitely going to visit my doctor to see why this IUD was on bull.

Composing myself, I moped into the nearest bathroom and relieved myself since I hadn't been off the couch in hours. While washing my hands, I eyed the new gray 24-inch lace-front I was rocking and the expensive mink lashes that made my hazel eyes pop even without make-up on. Gavin was crazy if he was going to let a stunner like me go.

I heard my cellphone ringing and sighed, drying my hands. My bare feet sank into the plush carpet as I trekked back to the living room without haste. By the time I reached for it on the coffee table, the ringing had stopped.

The number didn't link with anyone in my contacts, but as quickly as I put it down, it started ringing again. Same number. I answered, picking up my cigarette from the ashtray and toking as I flopped down on the couch.

"Hello,"

"Holla Vanessa?"

Pulling the phone from my ear, I looked at it like a foreign object, then brought it back with a frown. Uh uh. It couldn't be.

"He-llo?"

"Nessa, it's Delia. Can you hear me?"

"Uh, yeah. I thought… Your number didn't come up in my phone. I… What are you doing calling? I mean… I can't believe you're calling. How are you?" I babbled, probably sounding like a complete fool whose brain wasn't synced properly to her mouth.

"Well. I'm alive. So that's something. Recovering slowly but surely. Trying to get back into the real world, and back to myself. God saved me so, I'm going to make the best of the life he blessed me with."

"I hear you."

"But by the grace of God, there go I. I guess it just wasn't my time yet."

Everybody wants to go to heaven, but nobody wants to die. I don't care what anybody says, God does make mistakes. There was absolutely no reason for her to be breathing right now after taking a bullet and falling damn near three stories through trees and rocks in the woods. She didn't sound anything like the blathering idiot I expected her to after coming out of a coma for so long. This wasn't nothing but the devil!

"So, I know I'm probably the last person you expected to hear from."

"Definitely. Of course, I'm *happy* you called. But yeah. I'm definitely surprised. I heard they had you stashed away in some secret rehab center and that they weren't even sure if you were talking yet or not."

"You know how the media likes to exaggerate. If they don't know where you are, you're automatically at some "secret place". Some of my motor skills aren't right just yet, but I'm doing good. I've been rehabbing at one of our summer houses since I got discharged with an on-call nurse and physical therapist."

Last time I checked, she wasn't married to Brand yet, so I'm sure the "our summer house" she was referring to actually belonged to him, and not *them.*

"I'm glad to hear you're doing well. Believe it or not, I did try to come see you in the hospital, but… That didn't work out."

"I know. Brandon and Rachel both told me you did and I was happy to hear it. I'm sorry my Brandy-poo was nasty to you if he was. I'm sure he was just being protective of me."

I gulped down half of the full glass I poured, rolling my eyes at her stupid pet name for him, and poised myself to sound sincere.

"I can understand that. You know, the media has been saying *all kinds* of ugly things about my relationship with you. You have no idea. So, I guess Brand thought it was best to keep me away. I knew it was a long shot anyway, with the way things were left the last time you and I spoke. But I regret how I handled that meeting with you and I didn't want *that* to be our last memory together."

The pregnant pause was so long that it could have given birth in the time she took to respond. I wondered if Brand was in the room with her, but I dared not ask. Sucking in the last bit of my cigarette, I eyed the phone lying on the table in the dead silence before mashing the bud into the tray.

"My memory's still pretty hazy about all that. I don't have any memories from anything that happened almost that entire month. I'm working with a therapist, but they say the loss is 90% permanent. I'm lucky to have *any* brain functions at all, let alone *memory* given the severity of my head injuries. But I've been having dreams about you."

My breath hitched in my throat as I anxiously rubbed the newly formed tension on the back of my neck. She was still speaking evenly, so I took that as a good sign. I swallowed hard and walked my words to the cliff of my tongue and let my question free fall.

"What kind of dreams?"

"Weird ones. My most vivid one was where we were at the mall and a sniper started picking off shoppers from the food court. I kept wanting to hide, but you insisted we try to escape. The sniper shot at me and you dove in front of me, taking the bullet instead. I was hysterical, and when I turned you over to see if you were still breathing, you had a clown mask on and you kept telling me to save myself.

It was one of the craziest dreams I've ever had. But then I've been having a lot of crazy dreams since I've been on these prescriptions. At any rate, it's kept you in my thoughts and in my heart. Even in my dream you tried to save me. I don't care what the blogs or anybody says about you. I know the real you."

"I'm glad you do."

"I know you've done some trifling things before. We both have. But we've been friends since middle school. Best friends. Sure, we were going through a rough patch because of Brandon, but I will never believe you would be ruthless enough to try to kill me and my unborn child just because he chose me."

I exhaled all the breath in my body with relief, despite her misguided belief that Brand didn't want me anymore at that time. If I told her how many times we screwed behind her back before the day she and I met up, she would slit her own throat.

"Listen Dee, I've had a lot of time to reconcile how Brand and I ended, and I'm entirely over it. He's your man now. Soon to be your husband, and I've moved on. There's no reason for us to be at odds over something that isn't even a factor between us anymore.

Besides, you probably don't remember this, but my father's home going services were the same day you were shot. You and Rayche even sent a reef to the funeral. You know how much I loved my daddy. I was such a mess that I don't even remember most of the service. It's not only absurd, but it's cruel for gossip trolls to insinuate I would attempt to murder anyone, let alone on the day I was burying my father."

"Oh, Nessa. I'm so sorry about your dad. You know my memory all around that time is still fuzzy like I said. Yes, that would be crazy. How did he die?"

"Heart problems," I revealed, feeling genuinely weepy about it as I watched the droplets of water pelt the outside glass of the huge picture window overlooking Gavin's manicured lawn.

"Miss Vixen, I'm leaving now. There is pot roast, yams and green beans in Tupperware in the refrigerator if you're hungry. Did you need anything else before I go?" Mrs. Cox poked her head in with a forced smile on her elderly face as she stood with her coat over her arm, and a firm grip on her handbag.

"No. I'm good," I answered apathetically waving her off.

"Good night then."

I nodded.

"Who was that?" Delia asked.

"Gavin's maid. I'm over his house."

"Gavin? Gavin who? You got a new boo?"

"Gavin The God."

"*Ooooh*. That Gavin."

"Yeah. We're a couple now. Have been since June. I'm also a Kingdom artist now too. I thought it was best that I distanced myself from Brand and Brand Good. He needed to be able to focus on you without the rumors and drama that came along with me still being there, and I needed a fresh start."

"Ah," she replied breathily as I smirked to myself. She may have had Brand, but everybody knew he wasn't banking it the way Gav was. "So, Nessa, I called for two reasons. One is because they just confirmed today that they're moving me to a new facility tomorrow, in California. My doctor's feel I would have a faster recovery if I went there.

I know this is really short notice, and you're busy and all, but I was hoping that you would come see me before I left."

"Tonight?" I bristled.

"Yes. I know it's getting late already, but if I'm being honest, I've been preoccupied with so much else, that I just got the time to contact you myself. I didn't want anybody else to do it for me. My flight leaves early afternoon and I know I'll be pulled every which way but loose the whole morning."

"Ohhhh… I don't know Dee. I *do* want to see you, but I'm already supposed to be going to the studio; and if you think it's late now, by the time I get dressed, it's gonna be *hella* late. Besides, I don't want any mess with Brand. I really do want to see you and everything, but I've got enough bad publicity following me right now."

"C'mon Nessa. For me. Brandon won't be here, so you don't have to worry about him. I sent him to the studio for a change instead of being up under me every minute of the day," she chuckled. "He's barely left my side since I got released. He's such a good man. I know he's been neglecting business because of me and I made sure he left me tonight. So yeah. He will be gone."

I sighed and made a gagging motion. Good man my ass. Good men don't rape people.

"Vanessa Aria Vincent, if I learned anything during this ordeal, it's that no one is promised tomorrow. Fences need to be mended between us while we're both still around to do it. Look how quickly you lost your dad. In the blink of an eye, I lost my baby, parts of my memory, and I almost lost my life.

I know *you* haven't lost *your* memory, and you may still have an axe to grind with me over Brandon, but *I* just want to make up. We used to be *sisters* Vanessa. We can even take selfies together and post them on Instagram if you want to.

I haven't let anybody take a picture of me since I got out of the hospital. Not even Brandon. You say you've had bad publicity, maybe people seeing us together will create some good instead."

I was surprised she was laying it on so thick. I ran both hands down my face and stared at the phone, weighing my options. Lightening flashed outside making me cringe at the thought of driving in that mess. I had no interest in re-friending this turncoat, but posting exclusive pics with her *could* do wonders for my PR.

But what if my being in her face triggered some latent memory that landed my sneaky ass in the clink? She was already having dreams about me. What if her memory wasn't totally erased and seeing me brought it back? Then again, she did say the doctors told her it was probably permanent. I exhaled loudly and waited a beat longer to give my final answer.

"Okay," I nodded as though she could see me. "Text me the address. How far is this place from the city?"

"Not that far. Maybe an hour and a half drive towards North Georgia"

"North Georgia? Aww hell. Where in North Georgia? The mountains?"

"No, it's not the mountains. C'mon Nessa. I'm leaving tomorrow. I'll make sure it's worth your while."

"Umm hmm,"

"Listen. I'm texting you the directions now. GPS won't work the closer you get to the house, so I'm going to give you the address to a Walgreens close by. Then you'll have to use the directions from there."

"It's *that* far out that GPS doesn't work?" I huffed. "What if I take a wrong turn after the Walgreens and get lost? I won't be able to call you and ask for directions."

"You won't get lost. Just get a full tank of gas," she chirped. "It's almost a straight shot once you pass the Walgreens. I'm sure you can go 15 minutes without phone service Vanessa."

"You want me to read directions from a text message while I'm driving in the dark? You sure we can't just face time? By the time I get there, it's gonna be like... Like almost 11 o'clock. We can have this *same* conversation from the comfort of our dry homes on facetime right now. Can't we?"

She sighed impatiently.

"No, we can't. Plus, I didn't tell you what the second reason was for why I want to see you."

"Why?" My interest peaked.

"Because it's almost Christmas and we won't see each other then. I have a gift for you. It's custom. You *have* to come get it in person though. I'm not mailing it and if you don't come get it, I'll just give it to Rachel or my mother or someone. Even though it's special for you."

"Well why didn't you lead with that?" I grinned recalling the expensive gifts she and I used to exchange when we were tight. She was the only person I knew besides Amina whose taste in clothes, shoes and jewelry rivaled mine.

"Now stop whining and get ready. I'm not worried about the time you'll get here. I need to lay down anyway. PT was a killer today."

I brooded a while longer and then gave in. I needed to get out of Gavin's house tonight anyway, and using Delia for good PR, *plus* getting a gift, was a win win. Things may have been looking up.

She texted the directions right after we hung up and my lips pressed together miserably when I punched the address into my GPS and saw how far it was. My stomach grumbled and I lifted my shirt to examine my non-existent baby bump. Delia wanted a baby so badly and here I was pregnant when I didn't want one at all. I almost felt bad for her... Almost.

21

Valerie

Money rained over my bare legs as I gyrated my hips on a handstand to Jeremih and J. Cole's "Planes". V-103 had been promoting a football player from the Falcons' party all week, so TMT was packed like a can of sardines with stripper poles inside. I was having a great night. These ballers were helping me make up for all the nights I took off, and I wasn't complaining.

Tamika and Nicky cheered me on with cat calls and money tosses during my first set. By my second, they were entertaining themselves with drinks, food, other strippers and thirsty men. I never knew how freaky they were until I saw them in action. I was happy they were having a good time regardless and even more so that they were there supporting me.

For the first time since the first week I started stripping, I didn't need liquid courage to get me through my performances. I wanted to make sure I showed up and showed out for my cousins, and partly because I was starting to worry I might be becoming an alcoholic. I wasn't giving up drinking, but I was going to wait until after I was off the clock. At least for tonight.

It was my last set, and I usually walked around to customers after each one to solicit lap dances and the like. But tonight, I was going to hang with my cousins in the VIP section I secured. If not for the sprinkle of strippers throughout the place, TMT could have been mistaken for a nightclub.

There were just as many scantily clad hoes in here trying to nab a NFL player as there were girls who were being paid to be here. Twenty minutes later, I was changed into sequins shorts with a sheer off the shoulder shirt over the matching tube top, and six-inch rhinestone platform pumps. I still donned the gray wig I wore with the metallic outfit I performed in since it went with what I had on too. Of course, Courtney had a helping hand in styling me.

"Have you heard from Amina yet?" I asked in Nicky's ear as we watched Tamika twerking like a professional on a tall slender guy who looked on the verge of busting in his pants.

She nodded and spoke back into my ear as I noticed a tall Tyra Banks looking chick eyeballing me in disgust. There was sometimes an element of hate that came along with the occupation, but I wasn't here for it tonight. So I turned my back to her.

"She texted that she was on her way. Somebody came by her house and slowed her down."

"Who?"

"She didn't say. Must've been a man."

We both chuckled before the feel of two large hands on my waist caused me to spin around faster than a Tasmanian devil.

"Boy! You scared me. You know how these men can be in here," I kissed Maaco on the lips.

"Hey Maaco," Nicky greeted.

"My bad baby. Sup Nicky. I'm on my way to Platform but I just wanted to stop through real quick, and check on you on your first night back. You good?"

I nodded and smiled at how handsome my man looked in his black suit and black button-down shirt. Unlike my cousins, I can't call out name brands off the top of my head, but he looked and smelled superb.

Nicky made her exit to the couch and Maaco pulled me closer to talk.

"Can you come by my place when you leave? I might be at the club late tonight trying to clean up some bullshit Jamie got me into, but I have an early Christmas present for you that I need you to get ASAP."

All 32's graced my face, and I mashed my breasts into his chest, looking up into his face and placing my arms around his neck with glee.

"Do you now? It might be the only Christmas gift I'm going to get this year, but I can wait until Christmas day."

"I got a call that I had to pick it up early so, I thought you might as well get it early. If you come over, I won't be able to hide it from you anyway. Plus, I like seeing you in my bed when I come home. Don't you like being in my bed when I come home?" His lips were on mine, parting them with his tongue before I could answer, rising my temperature a notch.

"I do," I answered breathlessly when it ended. It must be a huge gift if he wouldn't be able to hide it from me. I could use a new car, but I didn't think he was balling like that.

"You'll probably need this then," he held a key up between his index and thumb.

"Ohhh," I beamed. "Are you sure you trust me with this?"

"Why wouldn't I? You've never given me any reason not to trust you have you?" I shook my head no. "Okay then. You now have full access to me. I'm making us official, and I don't want to hear any excuses about why it shouldn't be. You love me and I love you. I don't want to fight about dumb shit with you and I want you to know you don't have to be insecure with me."

I shrugged coyly, plucking the key from his hand and placing it in my tube top. There was no reason for me to protest or question his declaration. I had been fighting a losing battle against my feelings for him for months anyway.

The giddy way I felt about him when we dated the first time was multiplied now, and I loved that he was finally taking charge. I wanted to be my own woman, but truthfully, I needed him to take charge of this relationship. I wasn't going to on my own.

"All right. You're not going to get any argument out of me. I'm through with the mixed signals and the game playing. I'm still a little afraid to open my heart again, but I'm willing to do it with you."

"That's all I'm asking for. That, and a taste of that honey pot when I get home tonight."

"Well, since you put it like that. I don't know when we're leaving, but I'll be coming straight to your house *with* my key when we do."

We grinned suggestively at each other and he stroked my backside with his huge hands as I swayed my hips to the song playing overhead.

"How'd you get here? I don't want you driving drunk."

"I took an Uber, but I can have Amina drop me at your place tonight since she lives near you."

"Okay. Well look, I gotta go baby. Be good," he reminded me kissing my forehead. I nodded and lifted my chin to kiss his lips again. I needed something to tide me over until tonight. I watched him part the patrons suavely towards the exit until I couldn't see him anymore.

Evil Tyra Banks caught my attention again as she held her cellphone in my direction with a mischievous grin. Who was this broad and why was she all in my business? This was

exactly the type of attention I was afraid of getting after my outburst with Vanessa.

"What's wrong?" Nicky asked when I sat down next to her on the couch.

"Nothing. Just some woman staring me down."

"Who?" she probed. Neck craned to see through the crowd.

"Damned if I know. I think she was taping me too."

She looked a second longer than gave up.

"Girl I don't know who you're talking about over there. Taping you doing what?"

"Talking to Maaco I think."

She cocked her neck back and waved it off.

"Forget these hoes girl. Tonight, is our night!" she whooped and bounced while handing me a prefilled glass of Ciroc.

I took a sip and decided she was right. I needed to stop letting what other people did and thought puppeteer how I moved. This was my life, not theirs. In fact, I was a little envious of how my sister remained driven no matter who said what about her.

"Can I ask you something?"

"What?"

"How long are we staying mad at Vanessa?"

I raised a brow.

"What do you mean how long?"

She gulped down the rest of her drink and put the glass on the table.

"Listen Vee. I was the first one to want to put my foot up Vanessa's ass when I found out what she did, and I kind of still want to. But it's almost Christmas. I know it's gonna be hard for her to get through the holiday without Uncle Vernon here just like it will be for the rest of us. That was his favorite holiday and he always made it big for everybody.

Now I'm not saying what she did was okay, but she's our blood. Since you found out about him, Brent has shown himself to be a stalking, crazy, womanizing fool. I see the shit they've been posting about him in the news. And I'm still mad you weren't going to tell any of us that he put his hands on you up here if it hadn't gotten out either."

I sighed and looked down at my drink in shame.

"You don't have to flat out forgive her, but you *should* talk to her. I understand why you fronted her up at the hospital, but I think she might have been trying to apologize before that. Maybe it's the holiday spirit getting to me or whatever, but I think y'all should try to end this.

We already have Yasmin and Tamika on the war path and what if Yas would've died in labor? Then they would never even have the opportunity to make it better. I'm going to work on them next, but you... I think you know Brent wasn't right for you anyway. You were just going through the motions, and we all knew it."

I tossed my drink back and nodded considering her words. I was still mad at Vanessa, but Nicky hadn't said anything that wasn't true, and that somehow made my anger feel a little forced.

"Come on," she said grabbing my hand and leading me to Tamika who had shed the tall guy and was dancing with her hands in the air. Misty Rain was doing her thing on the main stage to some trap song I hadn't heard before, but the crowd was hype anyway.

Amina tapped me on my shoulder with a big grin on her beautiful face and Nicky pointed her to the drinks on the table. We gossiped about Amina possibly getting back with Donovan, teased Tamika about Dean, drank, danced and laughed the rest of the night.

By one o'clock, Tamika was toasted, Nicky was sloppy drunk, Amina was barely drinking, and I was barely sober. Amina agreed to drive me to Maaco's and Tamika and Nicky had taken Uber to the club in anticipation of inebriation, so they were taking it back too.

Even though the rain had stopped, it was still cold outside, so Amina and I waited with them in the entrance way for their ride to arrive.

"Somebody stole my panties," Nicky griped feeling up under her dress drunkenly while Amina tried to help her put her coat on.

"Stop it," Amina scolded, swatting Nicky's hand down. "Nobody stole your damn panties. You didn't wear any. Put this coat on girl."

"How do you know?" Nicky slurred. "You been looking up under my dress?"

"I don't have to look up under your dress because I already know, hoe," Amina giggled inciting the rest of our laughter as Nicky finally allowed her to slide her arms into the sleeves of her leather coat.

Nicky sucked her teeth and grinned, falling up against the wall where we left her to lean. I had changed back into my sneakers but still wore my club gear under a long wool coat. Everything I needed for the night was in a duffle bag hung over my shoulder, and I was anxious to go see my man.

"You, are embarrassing us," Tamika joked pointing at Nicky as she teetered on her own wobbly high heels with her messy locks obscuring the view of her face.

"Look at you stumbling," Amina laughed.

"A total mess," I cosigned.

"All of them should be embarrassed," a snide female commented, causing our heads to snap in her direction.

"Silly ass hoes," her friend concurred.

Evil Tyra and another modelesque female with dark brown skin, jet black shoulder length hair and a body to kill for mused. What the hell was this girl's issue with me?

"Bitch. Why are you even talking to us?" Tamika bucked steadying herself on Amina's shoulder. "Because my hands like to talk too."

"I wasn't talking to *you*. I was talking to my friend. It's not my fault you want to be trash canning around town with my baby daddy's stank hoe girlfriend," she sassed eyeing me at the same time.

Her baby daddy? Lord. Please tell me this wasn't another one of Maaco's long lost baby momma's coming to confront me again. If it was, I was about to be done with Maaco. I was resigned to handling one baby momma, but two was just too much for me.

"You calling us trash?" Amina frowned. "Honey, don't get slapped in here tonight. Judging from that Versace knockoff dress your friend is wearing, *you're* the one out here hanging with trash."

"This is genuine Versace you knock off version of Kenya Moore!" Dark Brown retorted.

"Genuinely fake," Nicky garbled, still coherent enough to throw shade as Amina sniggered waving the girl off.

"We'll see who's fake when Gavin gets in your ass for tonguing down another man. *Yaaaaaas* bitch. I posted the video on my IG for him and everybody else to see how disloyal you are. You're welcome," she taunted dipping her hand in my face with every word until I slapped it down.

"I don't know who you are or what your crazy ass is talking about, but I *do* know you better keep your too big for a lady's hands out of my face."

"Or what? I already owe you a beat down as it is. Don't make me act out of character to give it to you tonight."

She slung her long weave around her shoulders and got closer to my face.

"Step back broad!" Tamika barked shoving her back.

"Don't touch her!" Dark Brown got in Tamika's face.

I knew it was coming the way you could see it coming when Ms. Sophia balled up her fist in *"The Color Purple"*. Tamika's head tilted to one side just before her fist rocked the other woman's head to the other side. I opened my mouth to say something, but Evil Tyra jabbed me in it before I could speak.

I dropped my duffle and let all my pentup aggression loose on her five-head. I wasn't the same Valerie that Vanessa pummeled six months ago. My hands were on autopilot as I tagged, slapped and grabbed at the woman who assaulted me first.

I felt my wig being ripped off as we bounced off the walls fighting and the sound of my cousins scuffling with her friends resonated in the background. Security was on us quickly, but I got one last punch in before I felt Jake's big hands pulling me off of her.

It took three to separate us and their threats of having us all locked up acted like an instant tranquilizer. Luckily the officer who was usually on the door wasn't at the time, or we likely would not have had the option.

Mikey strong armed Dark Brown and Evil Tyra mutually outside as they continued spitting expletives back and forth with us. Jake and Franky let us pick up our stuff and ushered us out the doors as well.

"That's okay bitch! I posted a video of you kissing that guy on my IG! Talk your way out of that! You'll get what's coming to you! Watch! You think this a game? Watch how fast Gavin cuts you off! I ain't letting him see his son again until he does either! Bitch!" Evil Tyra screamed walking backwards towards their car in the lot.

"Is this hoe off her meds? Gavin *who*?" I grumbled to anyone who might have a clue.

Nicky giggled, stumbling up against Tamika, who was already unsteady and enlightened me.

"That's Vanessa's man. Gavin The God. That dumb hoe probably thinks you're her."

I frowned, putting my wig back on my head under Jake's scrutinizing eyes and took my duffle bag from him.

"I should have known," Amina spat.

"All right Angel. Get your people and go. You know I can't let you stay after fighting," Jake chimed in eyeing all of us.

"We were leaving anyway," Tamika complained. "Can we just wait for our ride? Damn."

"I'm sorry Jake. You know I don't fight. Me and my cousins were just minding our business, and they started with us. Can we please just stay until their ride gets here? I swear we won't make any more trouble."

He looked towards Mikey walking back from the lot where he left Evil Tyra and her friend at their car, then back at me. Frank left us all by the curb after a nod from Jake and went back inside.

"You're not driving yourself, are you?"

"No. I'm riding with her," I gestured towards Amina who was inspecting a broken nail with displeasure. "She's good to drive. I promise. And like I said, my other cousins are just waiting for their Uber. That's it."

Jake and I had a few friendly conversations on slow nights from time to time and I believed his concern was genuine. He stared contemplatively at me for a few seconds and sighed.

"Okay. Y'all are lucky Gene went to the bathroom or he would've had all y'all in cuffs."

"I know. And we don't want that."

Tamika rolled her eyes at his back as he retreated through the doors of the club and I released an exasperated breath. This wasn't the ending to our girl's night I had hoped for. My phone vibrated and I looked at the text message from an unknown number.

678 555 8789: Nobody will love you like I love you Angel. I'll always be here for you. Don't fight it.

Frowning, I closed out of the message and exhaled. Was this some crazy customer who got my number or was this Brent calling me from a new phone number? Either way, I was creeped out by the message.

"That trick isn't even here and she got us fighting for her," Amina griped about Vanessa. "Look at my damn nails. I just got them done and now look at them! How much longer on your damn Uber."

She was holding her hand splayed out in front of Tamika's face to show the broken tips on her ring finger and thumb before Tamika shoved it away.

"Why're you getting snippy with me? I didn't break your damn nails."

"Yeah, but *you* started the fight because you swung first. You *always* swing first."

Tamika withdrew her phone from her coat pocket.

"Of course, I always swing first. What am I supposed to do? Let bitches tag me first? Stop whining. You look okay to me."

"That's not the point. I'm okay because I was trying to break it up instead of wilding out here like a bunch of unruly drunk bitches. You can't afford to get arrested again and none of us wanted to get cuffed either. You need to do something about those anger issues."

Tamika sucked her teeth and dropped her head back in aggravation.

"Shut. Up. I have anger issues because these hoes keep trying me and mine," she yelled clapping between syllables. "No, I don't want to get arrested. But if that's what has to happen for me to get these hoes all the way right, then it is what it is.

I bet you don't think I should have slapped Yasmin's disrespectful ass either huh? Right? It's not my fault her fragile ass can't hold water. That's my niece she was carrying. I didn't mean for that to happen. I'm not heartless like that and you know it."

We all stared dumbstruck at her impromptu confessional, watching her pace in place. I felt bad for my cousin. I understood the anger she was feeling towards Yasmin because I had a similar anger towards Vanessa. Tamika played tough all the time, but I knew she was more hurt than she was angry.

As different as they were, Yasmin and Tamika used to be close. We all were. And Sophie's birth was only going to make it harder for Tamika to continue to hate and avoid Yasmin, especially if she and Dub were going to be a couple.

"Calm down. Nobody thinks you meant to send her into labor. That liquor has you in your feelings. I'm sorry," Amina apologized trying to hug Tamika.

Tamika playfully shoved her as an older black lady in a Hyundai Sonata pulled to a stop at the curb.

"I don't want your stinking hug," Tamika laughed wiping the tears that escaped away. "You're damned right it's the alcohol. I ain't out here crying naturally. Bring your drunk ass on Nicky. This is our driver."

We said our goodbyes as they got into the car and Amina and I got into her Jaguar shortly after. I put Maaco's address into her phone and sat back in the low riding leather seats.

Amina chattered some about her encounter with Donovan earlier, but I was only half listening. I leaned my head against the window and stared out thinking about my broken relationship with Vanessa. Toting around this anger was probably harder on me than it was on her, and I needed to find a way to get rid of it.

In the midst of thinking, I must have drifted off, because I didn't even know I went to sleep until Amina shook me awake.

"This is his house, right?" she asked nodding towards the two-story brick home with a well-manicured rectangular lawn in front of it.

"Yes," I yawned, disappointed that Maaco's car wasn't in his driveway yet. "Looks like I beat him here. Are you going to be okay driving home by yourself?"

"I'll keep her awake," a baritone voice startled me from the speaker.

Amina grinned coyly. "That's Donovan. You fell asleep on me, so I called him to keep me company."

I pursed my lips and grabbed my duffle from the backseat. Playfully nudging her, I opened the door and slung my bag over my shoulder.

"Good night girl. *Goooood* night *Dooooonovan*," I cooed childishly.

"Good night," he answered as Amina and I laughed.

"You're stupid. I'll call you tomorrow. Tell Maaco I said hello."

I nodded getting out and closing the door. I gave her a last wave and started sleepily up the walkway. Unzipping the side pocket, I dug around for his house key, then realized I put it in the other pocket once removed from my cleavage.

Drearily, I twisted the bag to reach the other pocket, with thoughts of laying across Maaco's king-sized bed and going back to sleep. For all that talk I had for him earlier, that little bit of sleep on the drive over reminded me of how much I needed it. Once I took a shower, I knew I was going to be out like a light.

Amina waited until I finally got the door open, honked and drove off. Leaving the door ajar to allow the streetlamp and Christmas lights on the house to illuminate the foyer. I stood at the threshold and ran my hand against the wall in search of a light switch just as an arm clamped around my neck.

Shrieking, my first thought was that it was Maaco being funny, but the compression against my throat brought quick realization to it being someone else. I reached back over my head, trying to claw his face and eyes, but my fingers barely grazed the wool of his mask before he tightened his hold using his other arm as a vice against it.

Slinging me sideways, I quickly lost my footing while he dragged me backwards, nicking behind my ear with the knife I didn't realize he had in the hand of the arm around my neck. Tears blurred my vision and Maaco's doorway got further away, as my nostrils filled with the scent of Brent's cologne and my lids involuntarily shut.

22

Yasmin

I came to with an excruciating headache, a bloody nose, swollen mouth and missing teeth. My ankles were bound to the legs of the metal folding chair I sat in with rope, and my wrists were tied behind my back with an extension cord. My efforts to shoot my ex-husband had failed miserably. I never took the safety off, giving Malik time to overpower me and take the gun away.

Of course, he didn't let me off easily either. I was backhanded in the face with the butt of the gun with such force that a few of my now wobbly teeth cut straight through my upper lip. I marched in front of Malik as he forced me down to the basement, and the next thing I knew, I was waking up like this.

I assumed he drug Dwayne's dead weight down the stairs after knocking me out cold. Dwayne's scarcely moving mass hung limply from the exposed pipes across the ceiling. His extension cord bound wrists dangled him mere centimeters from the floor as barely audible ragged breaths escaped his bloodied lips.

His formerly brown dreads were drenched in his plasma and the amount of blood soaking into his black Tommy Hilfiger snorkel coat made me wonder how much longer he would survive like that. I was nodding in and out of consciousness myself from the blow to the back of my head Malik administered, and I worried about the long-term effects of that too.

My hands were getting numb from being tied up so long in the same position and I already soiled myself from his declination to take me to the bathroom. Now, a bowel movement was knocking at my backdoor and I was going to beg for bathroom mercy a second time.

"I have to go to the bathroom Malik," I whimpered.

"You already went right there. Just do it again."

"No. I have to… I have to go number two."

"*I have to go number two*," he mocked sitting deeper into the recliner he occupied in front of the flat screen. I couldn't see the screen from where I sat, but I knew it was sports by the commentary. The basement had been his man cave during our marriage, despite its dual capacity as the laundry room and toolshed. There was also a loveseat, a few metal folding chairs when he had guests and a four-foot chest with his football memorabilia on it beneath the window.

"*Please* Malik. I'm serious. I know you don't want to smell me crapping on myself."

"Yasmin, I literally don't give a shit," he laughed, sipping a beer from a six pack beside him. "I've smelled worse. What you don't understand is, the more you're humiliated, the happier I'll be. You *and* your street thug."

Water weltered from my eyes yet again as my mind tried to work a way out of this. I couldn't die like this. My dad was too old to raise Sophie on his own and no matter whose hands she might fall into in my family, no one could love her like me.

"Malik, you know my daddy has a key. He's going to come looking for me when I don't show back up at the hospital, or answer any of his calls. Everybody knows I've been by Sophie's bedside from the time I could see her. Why don't you just take me to the bathroom, lock me inside and go?"

"Always trying to negotiate. You know what Yasmin? You ruined us," he answered with his own agenda. "Our marriage wasn't perfect, but we had a good thing going. We were almost better than the Huxtables on *The Cosby Show*, except we didn't have any kids and we were both lawyers. If you would have just been a little more patient, Sophie could have been yours and mine instead of this piece of shit's."

He stretched out one leg and kicked Dwayne's hanging body with a look of disgust. Dwayne's head fell lazily to the side as he emitted an indecipherable groan and I flinched. Not wanting to watch my daughter's father in that state.

"You awake yet Fuckboi?" Malik taunted.

"Malik. Please."

"Is that all you know how to say now? 'Malik. Please.' You begging for this no good nigga now?" he affronted with disgust. "Please what? All I ever did was try to please you, and look what happened. Everything I ever strove for in life, I got it. I wanted to go to Morehouse College. I got in. I wanted to be a Kappa man. I did it. I wanted to be a lawyer. I did that too. I wanted the prettiest and smartest girl I ever met to be my wife," he gulped down the beer and cut his eyes at me. "And you turned out to be the worst thing that *ever* happened to me."

"I'm sorry. I never meant for any of this to happen."

"I know you didn't. You never mean for anybody to find out the sneaky shit you do behind their backs. Do you? You're better off that way, because when people find out, they want you to *pay* for what you did. I'm glad Tamika whooped your ass too. How is she these days? I hope better off."

I stared back at him without a word. If this fool thought I was going to update him on Tamika right now, he was more delusional that I thought. He and Tamika were both psycho.

"You know, I didn't even come back here until I saw you at your father's house. I figured if you were staying there, nobody would know I was here. I didn't have anything left to live on. I was desperate that night. No more car. No more money. No more support from my sister or my mother. I was bled dry trying to stay free. But I didn't want to jeopardize their freedom for helping me anymore.

So, I came to get my motorcycle and sell it for some cash to help me eat and plan my next move. I'm not cut out for jail Yasmin. I'd rather die, than be locked in a box with all the kinds of people I've been keeping at bay my entire life. I'm not like them. And I hate that you forced me to act like I was."

"If it's money you need, I can get you money. I can go to the ATM and take out as much money as my card will let me. Cash. Whatever you need. I'll help you. Just please. Please let me go."

He snarled and stood up, approaching me as I recoiled the best I could while bound to the chair. I feared he would strike me again with Daddy's gun in my already throbbing face, but he left it on the armchair. Still, I didn't know where the .38 he had was. It was much smaller than Daddy's, so it could easily have been on his person.

"You can't talk your way out of this Yasmin. I'm a smart man. I know my luck has run out. I don't have nowhere to go long term anyway, and no way to get there if I did. It's only a matter of time before the cops pick me up or pick me off out there," he gestured outside. "I just want to live long enough to see my mother one last time. And since she won't be back home from the hospital until tomorrow, I might as well torture you and your bae until then."

"What time is it?"

"I forgot there's no clocks down here. Don't worry your pretty little head about the time. I'll let you live long enough to watch me torture your boyfriend to death and make you sorry you ever cheated on me."

I gasped. There was a time when Malik used to love me, and I hoped he still had a shred of it left. Surely somebody would look for me before then. Daddy had to know that I wouldn't have missed seeing Sophie on purpose. I hoped and prayed he would come to the house to see what was wrong. Pease God. Let *somebody* come to the house!

"No," I shook my head feverishly. "No Malik. Don't do this. I'm already sorrier than I've ever been in my life about anything, for making you do the things you've done because of me. But please. Please Malik. For Sophie. I'm all she has. Please don't kill me."

A ringtone blared behind us, and Malik snapped his neck around, then stormed over to Dwayne's person, searching his pockets. Coming out with keys first, he shoved them in his own pocket, then hastily retrieved the cell. He looked down at it, then back at Dwayne's semi-conscious groaning body.

"Who's Cortez?" he grumbled.

"Fu-fuck y-you," Dwayne muttered.

Malik's eyes bucked in amusement and he grinned, tapping the screen.

"Oh, you want to talk slick do you? I see you got this shit on fingerprint lock. Maybe I should cut one off with my pruning shears and see if it opens up this phone."

"You don't have to do that Malik. Just press a finger against the phone until it opens."

He rolled his neck around to glower at me and exhaled harshly.

"Was I talking to you? I know I don't *have to* cut his finger off. I said maybe I should. You're an attorney. You should be a much better listener than this Yasmin."

I swallowed hard and dropped my eyes, intimidated by his gaze. Instead, I tried to concentrate on not pooping my pants for now. My only immediate concern was being saved. At the very least, being taken to the bathroom.

"Well, well, well. Let's see what your Fuck-boyfriend has been up to when he's not with you. Shall we?"

He held the phone to Dwayne's hand and unlocked it, all while looking into the one bloody eye Dwayne lethargically opened and closed. He shoved Dwayne's body hard again after getting the phone unlocked, causing Sophie's daddy to grunt louder. Malik claimed another folding chair from the wall and pulled it closer to me, opening it and sitting.

Hunched over with his elbows on his knees, he inspected the cell with both hands as I continued trying to loosen the binds from my wrists and legs. Whatever apps he went to first must not have held much interest to him, because he kept making annoyed faces each time he tapped in and out of things.

"All right. Let's get to the text messages. Everything is always in the text messages. This, is going to be hilarious. I can't imagine this dumb nigga even knows how to spell correctly. It's probably all in ebonics the way he talks."

"Please Malik. I really have to go to the bathroom," I begged trembling while his interest remained buried in the phone.

"*Shhhhh.* This is going to be good. Just wait on it. We already covered that topic anyway. Shit on yourself or hold it in. It doesn't matter to me one way or the other. I can always move my chair further away. Damn. You two argue a lot for a couple. I don't see not one love text sent between you in the… Ohhhh. I see. All the nasty stuff was sent before you got pregnant."

I gulped self-consciously, and my anxiety intensified again. Breath hastened, I wasn't sure what messages he would come across, but our pre-pregnancy conversations were definitely more risqué than those of late. Raunchy even.

"You know what he got you stored in his phone as? Yasmonster. Hmph. How accurate. March 19, 2015.

Dub: I've been thinking about that pussy all day

Yasmonster: I can barely concentrate at work. I'm so wet right now. I want you badly

Dub: Show me how much that pussy misses me.

And then you sent this nigga a picture of your fingers spreading it open," he sneered turning the screen for me to see. "Wow. I don't think you've ever sent me a picture like this before. Not even when we were dating."

Dwayne was obviously coherent enough to snort a short laugh, garnering nothing but venom from Malik.

"Bruh. If you're laughing right now, I swear to God…" Malik warned tilting his head towards his hanging nemesis only feet away.

"Pussy," Dwayne burbled through what I assumed was a bloody mouth full of broken or missing teeth.

Surprisingly, Malik didn't react. Instead, he pressed his lips together tersely and went back to thumbing through messages. His jaws tightening, and his eyes narrowed, he cracked his neck from side to side with ire visible on his face.

Minutes passed as he read more messages, and with his attention away from me, I managed to free my right ankle, though the rope remained loosely around it. Startling my internal celebration, Malik lurched from the chair, toppling it and stalked to the La-Z-Boy to guzzle from the open bottle like a parched man in the desert.

A different ringtone chimed from the phone, which I knew was Dwayne's text message notifications and Malik's scowl blossomed. My eye's shifted to Daddy's gun lying unattended as I twisted my wrists back and forth trying to free myself.

Suddenly, spittle and beer flew from Malik's mouth and he grabbed the gun with fervor. Cringing, I feared he saw what I was doing and was going to handle me, except he didn't come to me. He was in Dwayne's face pressing the barrel under his chin, huffing and puffing like a big bad wolf in a heartbeat.

"So, tell me. *Dub*," he snarled as if each syllable was rancid. "You been on the down low? Huh?"

"I'll k-kill you," Dwayne rasped, and Malik pressed the gun harder into his jaw.

"With what? How? How exactly are *you*, going to kill *me*? Cause last time I checked. I was the one with the gun in my hand. But don't try to change the subject. You and this Cortez dude on some gay shit?"

Happy his attention was on Dwayne and not me, I worked harder on getting my wrists free, all while shaking my head in disbelief. Malik was definitely reaching now. Yes. Dwayne and Cortez were too close for my comfort, but gay? No. I needed receipts to believe that.

"I know you probably don't read too well, but I do. Your boyfriend here seems pretty upset that you haven't come back home yet. Did you know he had a boyfriend too Yasmin?"

I instantly froze under his gaze and shook my head.

"He's not."

"*Ohhhh* yes he is. This two timing, menace to society, is an under-cover booty banging piece of shit."

"I still stole yo… Yo bitch anyway. P-pussy. Fuck you," Dwayne rattled despite looking and sounding like death warmed over.

"Nah. Fuck *you*," Malik spat.

Ominously glancing at me, he pulled the trigger, blowing pieces of Dwayne's skull and hair out through his jaw. I shrieked louder than the emergency brakes on a freight train as he pulled the trigger twice more until it was empty. Daddy's gun wasn't fully loaded.

Disappointed, Malik tossed the gun on the floor and reached under his shirt, retrieving the .38 from his waist. He let off three additional shots into Dwayne's already limp body, then watched with depraved pleasure. This man was no longer the man I once loved. The man I wanted to have children with once upon a time. This man was a monster.

Blood splattered everywhere. On the wall. On the floor. On the ceiling. On Malik. On me. I started hyperventilating. Malik's pitiless eyes regarded me with depraved indifference before he was on me, thrusting the phone's screen into my face with agitation.

"Bitch! Are you crying for him? Huh? Read this. Read it! Read it and let me know if you still have any tears left for him. Never mind. Let me read it to you."

Cortez: Why where are you? You better not still be over there playing house with that fish when you got sausage waiting for you over here. You promised you were only gonna co-parent with her. You're my man. Not hers. If I find out you're playing me, we're gonna have to throw hands again and I'm gonna be done with you. You got 10 minutes to call me back or I WILL be at that bitch's doorstep. Try me!

"Looks like your man is his man too. Were you doing us at the same time?" Malik fumed standing to his full height again to looking down on me with disgust.

"No. No! I didn't. That's how I knew Sophie was his. We weren't… you and I … we weren't sleeping together then."

"You're probably lying. Dick sharing whore."

He wiped blood from his face with the forearm of the hand holding the gun and spat onto the floor. At the thought of Dwayne sleeping with Cortez, my organs twisted with the urge to vomit. He was probably cheating on Tamika with him all along. *That's* why Cortez hated me so much. *That's* why he wanted me out of the picture.

The scent and feel of Dwayne's blood dripping down my cheek was enough to wrench my innards and send puke spewing from my lips in a stream. Tears raced down my face in succession and Malik's scowl said 1000 words plus a postscript, as he glowered between me and Dwayne's corpse.

"I know I didn't have to kill him. But I figured I should practice the feeling before I got to you. See what it felt like to take a human life. And you know what? It felt good as hell. Like a weight was lifted off of my shoulders. Retribution granted."

"Please don't kill me," I muttered. "I swear. I hate me too for what I've done. For what I've put you through. And if it makes you feel any better, I think Cortez is the one who carjacked me the night I was late getting home. I recognized his voice and his cologne at the hospital. So you see, karma was already punishing me."

Yet again, he grinned and shook his head incredulously.

"I told you before you can't talk your way out of this Yasmin. I'm just trying to think of a better way to make you suffer than shooting you. It's so cliché anyway. Don't you think?"

I know he said I couldn't talk my way out of it, but it was the only tool besides my tears that I had at my disposal.

"I know it's too late for forgiveness. But please. For my little girl. She's innocent. She doesn't deserve to be punished for what her parents did Malik. You've already killed her father. I just want to see my little girl again. Please. Please Malik. I just want to see my little girl again."

Regarding me with a deadpan expression he closed his eyes annoyedly and shook his head. I was going to have to speed up my concentration on freeing my wrists.

"You're driving me crazy with all this crying and whining. You're just making me want to kill you even more," he admonished with a cynical laugh.

"Cortez said he was coming over if Dwayne didn't call him back. He'll probably be here any minute now. Are you going to kill him too?"

At this point, I was just talking. I would say anything to distract him from shooting me. He squinted suspiciously at me, then gazed down at the phone as I continued rotating my wrists and inserting my fingers as far as they would go between the extension cord to loosen it.

Ironically, I hoped Cortez would do what he threatened. I was even hoping nosy Octavia would ring my doorbell and save me. Somebody needed to come to my rescue. He couldn't kill everyone.

As if awakened from a trance, Malik's eyes suddenly lifted towards me with a pensive stare. I froze, staring back with wide eyes, hoping it wasn't because he saw something that made him want to blow my head off immediately the way he had done Dwayne.

His sanity was teetering, and that meant my life was on the verge of being snuffed out with every passing second. Dropping the phone to the floor, he got up and loomed over me with a foreboding smirk, scanning me from head to toe with contempt.

"I have keys to a car now, thanks to Dub, so I don't have to stick around for his little *butt buddy's* arrival. Unfortunately for you, that means I'm going to have to cut this little reunion of ours short. And I know exactly how I'm going to leave you."

He used the barrel of the gun to lift my chin up and smirked. I didn't say anything, because there was obviously nothing left to say. His mind was made up. Putting the gun back in his waist, he walked over to the La-Z-Boy, retrieved the remaining unopened bottles in the case, and sat them down on the bottom stair before bounding the steps in twos. Where was his damn limp now?

Choking down my tears, I wriggled, twisted and writhed with determination, ignoring the aches in my body and the rawness of my wrists until I finally freed one arm, then the other.

My heart palpitating and adrenaline rushing, I quickly massaged my wrists, then worked on untying the ankle that was still bound. I could hear him lumbering around the house, jogging up and down the stairs to the second floor, and rummaging in the kitchen. I could only speculate that he was gathering things to take with him on the run, but what he had in store for me, I didn't know.

Trying to escape upstairs where Malik was still loitering was 100% out of the question. He still had that gun, so he could shoot me before I ever turned a knob on the front door. At this point, I was mentally preparing myself to either move the deep freezer from the door or go through the window. The window was my best bet. It was easier to get to and climbing through it would put me at ground level.

Finally loose, I stumbled towards the window, but heard Malik barreling down the stairs just as I reached the La-Z-Boy. Why God? Why? I shrieked and spun around with my hands up as a bullet whizzed past my head. He wore a coat and a ski hat now to match his cold mien.

"I guess that's what I get for never paying attention when I was in the Boy Scouts huh? I knew I didn't tie those ropes right," he quipped from the bottom stair.

My eyes were glued to the cardboard box he held close to his chest more than they were to the gun though. Registering my gaze, he set the box down on the floor as I spied the things inside of it.

The remaining five bottles of beer were joined by six more that must've been in the refrigerator, and the tops had already been removed. Two, quart sized bottles of cooking oil were open beside them. One half full and the other must've been previously unopened. The last thing was the red grill lighter we used for barbecues, and that's when I realized what he was planning.

"Malik, please don't do this. You can just leave me here."

"You wish," he sneered plucking a bottle from the box and taking a sip before spilling the rest out on the floor all around the stairs.

He then went bottle for bottle, walking around with the gun pointed at me and hurling beer onto everything within reach. The walls, furniture, floor, and me. He saved the full bottle of oil to douse me and the La-Z-Boy, then poured a trail to the stairs from me to the steps with the half full one, all while I took the abuse and stood sniffling. I gave up on begging him. It was clearly too late.

He was going to burn me alive. Hoping that God wouldn't let this be my fate, I steepled my hands in front of me and began to pray aloud for God's forgiveness and his mercy on my daughter.

The sound of his gun going off sliced my words in midair as an excruciating pain soon followed. Falling back into the La-Z-Boy, the bullet pierced through my right forearm and into my left collarbone, making my body vibrate like a tuning fork in agony.

Shock and pain paralyzed my vocal cords as I watched Malik's finger pressing the trigger repeatedly with no result. My mouth gaped open and closed like a fish out of water with fear as we both realized he was out of bullets simultaneously. Instinctually, I used my good hand to press against the wound on my collar while Malik leered at me caustically.

Sucking his teeth, he pulled the lighter from the box and flicked it on, holding it to the cardboard until a quarter of it was aflame. Flinging it, the box landed a few feet in front of him into a puddle of the beer and oil he poured out. As the fire caught, he pitched one last detestable glower my way.

"Burn in hell bitch. Don't worry. I'll probably see you there soon," he spat, and head up the stairs.

I wiped the dripping oil and beer from my face with the back of my left hand and tried to think straight. It was too late for me to try to put the fire out, so I had to get out or incinerate. Forcing myself from the chair, I lifted my right arm to inspect the damage as I pulled off the scarf from my neck.

I was bleeding like a stuck pig from both holes, but I could only attempt to nurse one. Nearly biting through my bottom lip, I held in the scream aching to escape as I tied the scarf around my arm to stop the bleeding and stumbled to the window.

The concrete floors were a blessing in that it didn't allow fire to sweep across the way carpet would have. Despite his dousing everything with beer and oil as accelerants, the fire was still burning relatively slow. The consolation prize was more smoke than fire. Both were deadly though.

Resigning myself to ignoring the pain, I swiped Malik's football memorabilia off the chest and grabbed the last fold up chair from against the wall. Smoke stifled the air as the fire crept up the walls and Dwayne's corpse hung in the path of destruction. God knows I didn't want to smell human flesh burning.

I used the chair to step up on the chest so I could reach the window. The oil and beer had my hands slippery, so my first attempt to open the window after unlocking it failed. Frantically wiping my hands on my jeans, I finally slid the glass to the side, pushed out the screen and screamed out for help after exhaling the cold, but fresh air.

If by some lucky twist of fate someone was around, I wanted them to know there was a life to be saved inside this house. I was tall enough on the chair to open the window, but not to climb through it. Coughing, I grasped the back of the chair and tried to bring it up with my good hand, but I almost toppled over for my efforts.

"Uuuuuugh!" I grunted, squatting and lifting the chair with both hands as my arm and collarbone throbbed with pain. There was just enough space to squeeze the chair up on the chest with me on it, but the front legs were slightly over the edge. One wrong move would send it … and me … toppling over.

Holding on to the sill for support, I stepped up on the chair and tried to thrust myself through the window and onto the grass. Managing to get my upper body out, I used my elbow against the outside of the window to keep me from sliding back through and dug into the grass with my right hand.

"Raaaaaaaaaaaaaaaaaaaaaah!" I screamed as the pain surged through my forearm and my collarbone in concert. It was immense, but if I was going to get myself out of this, I was going to have to grin and bear it. Or should I say, grit and bear it as saliva and tears streaked my jaws.

I heard the chair fall as the smoke billowed out and the flames and heat built behind me. The bite of the cold air aided in keeping me alert as I clawed at the grass and tried worming my torso the rest of the way through. I was tired and weakening. My body wasn't built or prepared for this kind of endurance.

I took a moment to catch my breath until I was shocked into action by the searing sensation of fire burning my left foot. My upper body drenched in beer and oil, I knew if it traveled up much further, I would be engulfed in flames in no time.

Without hesitation, I lunged my left arm out with everything I had and dug my fingers into the grass like I had my right. The earlier rain had loosened the dirt for me to grasp, and I was holding on for dear life. Screaming as my injured limbs stretched to capacity, I pulled myself the rest of the way through, beating my boot against the window and the ground simultaneously.

Flipping onto my back, I kicked the enflamed boot against the grass before shooting up to pull it off with my hands and other foot. Tossing the scorched boot to the side, I mashed my now singed and throbbing hands into the grass hoping to sooth the pain. Inadvertently, I sucked in a lungful of scorched air, and instantly began coughing uncontrollably.

Lightheaded, tired and aching, I fell back, listening to the sound of sirens amidst the crackling of the fire eating through my house. I couldn't tell how close the firetruck was, but I could only hope they were close enough to save me.

"Yasmin! You back here?" A gruff voice shouted.

"He-Here!" I squeaked. The smoke strangling my voice.

With me down in the grass and the smoke mushrooming the yard, I was probably hard to see in the darkness.

"Oh, dear God," Gerald's fearful face, one hand covering his mouth with a cloth, suddenly appeared over me. "It's okay. I've got you. I've got you"

In oversized pajama bottoms, bedroom shoes and a big T-shirt, he bent down and scooped me up, staggering a bit under my weight. At more than 60 years old, I was just happy he could still pick me up without breaking his back.

Hacking from the smoke, and probably the stench of defecation on me, he paused briefly, then rushed through the yard with my left arm around his neck and my head and blood-soaked sweater pressed against his chest. A firetruck halted in front of the house as Gerald struggled with me toward it and several firemen jumped out to help.

23

Amina

Still laughing at something Donovan said, I glanced in my side mirror and almost swallowed my tongue. A silver Aston Martin was suddenly angled in front of Maaco's house behind me and its occupant dashed towards Val leaving the driver's door ajar.

"Oh shit!" I slammed on my breaks and threw the car in park, franticly rolling down my window and screaming out. "Val! Val! Turn around!"

"What's going on? What happened?" Donovan questioned as I popped my glove box and snatched my gun out.

"Hang up and call 9-1-1. Somebody's attacking Val."

"Wait! Wait! What's the address?"

I pulled up Google Maps and rattled it off, kicking off my heels and leaping out of the car. I bolted down the street like Denzel Washington in the movie "Ricochet", except I was wearing a red Gucci thigh high dress instead of boxer shorts.

God knows I haven't exceeded more than a jog since high school, but I was channeling Jackie Joyner-Kersey with everything I had.

"Let… Her go… You sick fuck! Or I'll blow… I'll blow your fucking brains out!" I growled trying to catch my breath as I drew on him from the lawn, too unsteady to fire. "Now!"

He pivoted slowly towards me, dragging Val in a choke hold with him. His crazy eyes made contact with my pistol and then to me. Then he glanced both sides of himself and back to me as if expecting more people to ambush him.

"Now!"

He hesitated, eying my gun again, then released her, tossing his hands up in compliance. I noted the large knife in one hand as my eyes darted anxiously between him and my cousin, now lying limply on the ground. God please don't let him have slit her throat.

"Val! Val, get up baby! Val!"

The multi-colored Christmas lights blinking on and off over the yard distorted my vision too much to see if she was bleeding in the darkness. I hated that I didn't get the contact lenses the eye doctor recommended at my last visit.

"Back away from her mother fucker! But if you run, I'll shoot you in the back in a heartbeat!"

He backed up a few paces and I stepped closer, squinting down at her with worry and darting my eyes between the both of them. I thought I saw blood on her neck, and I was going to shoot this dude on GP if she was dead.

"Val! Val, can you hear me?"

Seconds later, she groaned and sluggishly rolled onto her side.

"Yes," she replied thinly. "It's… It's B-Brent."

I knew whose Milk Dud head was under that mask, but I was happy she was alive to confirm it. If nothing else, that car and those ironed creased Balmain jeans gave his ass away. Criminals rarely drive million-dollar cars or take the time to iron creases in their kidnapping jeans. Cornball. It had to be him.

His crazy ass just stared at us wordlessly as the whirr from his still running car resounded behind me. Val pushed herself up and stumbled to her feet, resting her hands on her knees first, then rising to her full height and sucking in a deep breath of air.

"Why won't you leave me alone? Let me live my life."

His face was covered, but his eyes gave away the smile I felt like he was wearing under that mask. He robotically shook his head from side to side and lowered his empty palms to half mass.

"Don't move douche bag! Val. You're bleeding. You sure you're okay?"

Blood trickled down her neck and I could see the inflammation in the skin around her nose and mouth when she reached me. This douchebag really did a number on my cousin.

"He cut me, but I don't think it's serious," she answered touching her wound and wincing.

We sneered at him and I considered letting off a shot on GP but didn't. People were starting to exit their houses now and for all I knew, we were being recorded.

"What were you going to do to her, you sick fuck? Huh? She doesn't love you anymore. She's with somebody else!"

"I knew you had to be the one following me," Val followed.

"You're mine," he uttered dissonantly as sirens approached in the distance.

"Are you on something? He's got to be on something," I surmised.

Brent's eyes shifted from her to me as I steadied my aim and re-planted my bare feet in the cold, damp grass praying he'd make a move to make me shoot him. Sneezing, I used my bicep as tissue but kept my attention on him.

I wished I hadn't taken my coat off in the car. I hated cold weather, and the low temperature in the wee hours of the morning solidified that. I needed a triple, venti, half sweet, non-fat, caramel macchiato. STAT!

The police arrived with guns drawn and ordered me to drop mine immediately. I didn't want any mix ups, so I did as I was told while Val and I blurted out that the masked man was the one they needed to cuff. Not me.

Brent didn't resist the arrest or removal of his mask, but he was an otherwise, unresponsive puppet once cuffed. His expression was empty, but his psychotic eyes were fixated on Val's every move. Either this negro had totally lost his marbles, he was high off his ass, or both.

He couldn't contain his frown when they roughly forced him in the back of a cruiser though. For the first time in my life, I was wishing police brutality on a black man.

Twenty minutes into the police questioning me, I saw Maaco pushing through the developing crowd of neighbors before an officer halted him. His face was etched with worry as he volleyed animated words back and forth with the cop until they finally let him through.

I was detained and questioned for almost an hour while they took my statement and checked on my gun permit. The ambulance came but Val refused to go with them, though she did allow the paramedics to assess her. I was all too happy to oblige when the police finally said I could leave. She had Maaco with her now and I was exhausted. Though they let me retrieve my shoes and coat, I still couldn't shake the cold I felt coming on.

I texted Donovan that I was okay and would call him later, but he called me anyway. He said he couldn't sleep until he knew I was okay, and that made me happy. I talked to him the entire short drive home and promised to call him when I woke up. The sun hadn't come up yet, but my eyelids were going to be going down as soon as my head hit the pillow.

The minute I opened the kitchen door from the garage and turned off the alarm, Linx padded up to me wagging his nub. I set the alarm back, dropped my bag on the island, kicked my shoes off and carried them to my bedroom.

A half hour, one shower and a cup of green tea later, I was knocked out beneath my Egyptian comfort, 1800 thread count sheets and comforter. My phones ringing woke me up with a start. I silenced it with hella attitude as soon as I saw Jamie's name and buried my head under my pillow.

Linx's black ass was next to annoy me not long after, standing at my bedside whimpering and galloping in place wanting to go out. I was tempted to make him hold it, but the last time I shirked my dog walking responsibilities, he left me a little brown gift on my living room carpet.

"Okay. Okay," I garbled kicking my feet over the edge of the bed and sliding on my slippers.

Grabbing my thick robe from the back of my room door, I followed him downstairs with the enthusiasm of a woman being led to her death. I got the retractable leash off the hook by the door, fastened it to his collar, disarmed the alarm, and wiped sleep from my eyes.

This kind of stuff early in the morning is why I questioned whether I would ever want kids or not. If I didn't even want to fulfill my dog mommy duties, I certainly wouldn't fair well fulfilling an actual crying baby's needs in the a.m. The sun doesn't even rise until about seven and I don't like being up before the universe says I should be.

What I was sure about, was that his demanding ass needed to find a place to poop and pee quick, fast, and in a hurry, because my patience was thinner than tissue paper right now. I didn't have a bag to pick up his poop with me, but I doubted my scattered neighbors would be up patrolling my poop pick up diligence around my own property this early in the morning.

I stood at the end of my driveway with my robe's collar pulled up and Linx's leash extended to capacity. I was dozing again when Linx's barking and yanking drove my lids open.

"What's up Beauty Queen?" Jamie asked exiting a black Ford Explorer parked a few feet from my mailbox wearing a tan Shearling coat with the hood over her head, sunglasses, and gloves.

If she hadn't spoken, I wouldn't have recognized her, and that was a red flag. She paused just outside of Linx's reach as he patrolled the curb protecting me and issuing a low growl. My shock at seeing her was upstaged only by the memory of a black Explorer creeping by just before I was shot. I've never seen her driving anything other than a royal blue Yukon.

"Uh… Jamie. What are you doing here?" I cleared my throat trying to mask my alarm by glancing at my watch, which I forgot I was no longer wearing.

She smirked, adjusting the shades on her face as I inched a step backwards. Damn it! My gun was still in my bag.

"You're not answering my calls. You okay?"

"I've been... B-Busy?" I stammered.

"With Lala still on the loose, I thought maybe something had happened to you. So, I took a shot in the dark and came to check," she noted side eying Linx with one hand in her pocket while the other flicked the tip of her nose.

She winced noticeably and grit her teeth in pain while I stared at her curiously. My expression must have been incredulous because she glanced both sides of her before I could answer and revealed a weapon.

"All right. I'm done with the games Beauty Queen. I ain't got time for it and we both know what it really is. Let's take this inside so we can make this fast and painless for both of us.

Even in the dark, the extended silencer attached to the tip was grossly evident. Linx increased his growling and tugged towards her as if he sensed her threat.

"Don't even think about letting that leash go. I guarantee you I'll shoot this mutt before he can make it to me, and I'm gonna be mad you made me do it. I'm here for one thing and that's it."

Fear gripped my heart like a vice, and I almost forgot to breathe as she pointed the chrome at Linx. What did she mean by fast and painless? Lord knows I didn't want to die like this. I closed my eyes briefly and exhaled warm breath into the cold.

"Beauty Queen, don't make me wound you first. Reel that motherfucker all the way in and let's go inside. And by all the way in, I mean he better not touch me. If he does, I promise you I'll kill him and shoot you for allowing it."

Heeding her warning, I retracted the leash in where Linx had no choice but to walk directly by my side. Jamie trailed closely behind us into the house, and my eyes went straight to my purse. Even though she was in back of me, she was apparently still two steps ahead.

"Uh uh uh," she chastised in a sing-songy tone. "Don't even think about going for the piece in your bag. You're not fast enough. Now lock the mutt in the basement and turn around. You're lucky I like dogs."

I wanted to scream out so badly, "He's not a mutt you cunt! He's a purebred, AKC certified Doberman Pinscher!" But I kept my mouth shut. I must have been deliriously tired, because I was worrying about the wrong thing. I opened the basement door and released Linx from his leash at the stairs.

"Good boy. Go to bed," I told him with a pat of his head as he descended the steps with a whimper to his dog bed.

I fumbled with the lock before closing the door but didn't lock it. Turning to face her, I was startled by what the bright kitchen light exposed. Jamie's hood was dropped, and her sunglasses removed, revealing her long braids twisted atop her head and a battered face.

Both eyes were red, sunken and glassy, but her right one was black and blue. Her ashen face gave way to a nose that looked freshly broken and the right side of her upper lip was swollen. Somebody kicked her ass.

"Oh my God. What happened? Were you in a fight?"

She smiled bizarrely, licking the corner where her lip was split and sniffled.

"Aww. I'm flattered to know that you care," she laughed. "I wasn't in the type of fight you're thinking about. I fought a couple of money bouts is all. Believe me. They look worse than I do. Much worse. You still got bandages and shit from when you got shot around here don't you?"

She unzipped and removed her coat one grimacing and careful arm at a time, switching the gun between hands as she did. I wondered if her gambling debts had anything to do with her fighting again. She told me once that she stopped because it was hard on her body and she wasn't a spring chicken anymore. I guess the season had changed.

"I still have a few things. What's injured?"

"You let me worry about that. I'll take it with me when I leave."

"Okay. So what's this all about Jamie? Since when do you need a gun to talk to me?"

"Since you got too smart for yourself, and since I started running out of time to make up shit and play games with you to get that money."

I crooked my neck. "Too smart how?"

She snorted flicking the tip of her nose a second time, then winced. It had to be broken. I mean, I'm no doctor, but the way her nose was mangled, it had to be, and she must've kept forgetting.

"Game recognizes game Beauty Queen. I know you're on to me. So we can bypass the bull and go straight to the safe. I got a plane to catch and a bunch of loose ends to tie up before I catch it." She waived the gun towards the hall and nodded for me to walk.

"The safe? What are—"

She spazzed, smacking me hard with her free hand. The stars I saw cosigned her earlier assertion that she was still a beast with her hands.

"I would hate to have to smash in your pretty little face Beauty Queen. I always liked your face and your ass the most. Now you know, that I know you have a safe. Stop fuckin' around and take me to the money."

I stumbled, steadying myself with the top of the counter and touched my face where it stung. My narrowed eyes met hers as she cocked her head and shoved the barrel against my temple.

"Capiche?"

"Yes," I grit as Linx began whining and scratching at the basement door, jiggling the knob.

She eyed it suspiciously, then discounted it, pivoting to the side for me to pass. I swallowed hard and she lifted the gun, again waiving it towards the hallway, and that time, I walked.

"Uh uh uh," she scolded, pressing the metal into my back. "Wait for me."

"I don't understand why you're doing this Jamie. I thought we were friends."

"We were. Until you decided to double cross me and go into business for yourself."

"But I didn't. I serviced Todd a few extra months, but that's it. When I said I was getting out, I meant it."

"Shit. That counts. I should have got a cut of that too."

"So you were gonna kill me for skimming an extra three months from a client that was already mine after I gave you seven years? Really?"

"Actually, no. I mean, yeah, I did drop dime on you to Todd's wife and offer my PI services so she could blow up y'all little arrangement.," she cackled, gaining a sneer from me as we neared the stairs.

"It took me till that night to get an inside bitch at the hotel to set up the cameras. I didn't know that was y'all last night trickin' til you hired me after his wife had already tore your shit up. All I did was give her your address. She staked out your spot for when to tear it up all on her own."

"So, you're saying his wife was the one who shot me?"

"Naw. That was Lala. I ain't lie when I told you she reached out to me about Kev's murder. I just didn't tell you that I pointed her in your direction. I damn sure wasn't gonna fess up to doing the shit myself. Once I put these lips on her cat, she ate up everything I fed her, including my pussy."

I snapped my head around so fast that she pushed me roughly up the last stair and warned, "Don't try me Beauty Queen."

"I wasn't going to try anything. I just can't believe you killed Kev. Why?"

"What you mean why? Because that nigga was talking too much like he was running shit, and because his and Lala's share gave me three times as much as I already had. Keepin' it 100. If you hadn't already left before I came out of the bathroom that day, there was gonna be two bodies on the reserve. You just got lucky."

"So then why are you doing this now if Lala's the one who shot me and put cameras in my closet?"

"I ain't say she put cameras in your closet. I said she was the one who shot you. Dumb broad got high as fuck staying at my place and used my back up truck to do a drive-by on you while I was at the club. Picked up in the middle of the night and ran her ass back to Miami. She ain't even tell me she did that shit till I asked her about it after you called me from the hospital. Messed around and got knocked the same week for beating her steady."

We paused at my bedroom door for me to turn the lights on. She nudged me towards my closet with the nozzle in my back and kept talking.

"So, she didn't come back to Atlanta for me?"

"Nah. She actually came back to Atlanta for me. All that time in lockdown must have gave her time to think more clearly. She came back. Confronted me at my own house. But she was a stupid hoe. Brought a knife to a gun fight and died with two bullets in her temple. I left her body dead and stinking in the brush behind a park in Bankhead, just like I did her brother."

I did not expect her to say that. There was no way that she was going to let me live after robbing me now and I knew it. She wouldn't be telling me all of this so freely if she planned to let me live. She might have been sloppy lately. But one thing she was not, is stupid.

"I see your little eyes dissecting everything I say just like they were when we met up at that Mexican restaurant. I knew then that you probably weren't buying anything I told you. But I had to commit. Right? I was already in too deep. I guess I taught you too well when I let you work with me. Huh? You didn't trust me?"

"Are you surprised?"

"Nah. Nobody should trust nobody. As much as I love my brother, I don't trust his ass either. Nigga tried to check me about money I've been taking from my club I let him partner with me on. You believe that shit? Ungrateful fuck. If it wasn't for me, his ass would still be driving bitches to get screwed and bouncing at clubs instead of partially owning a club."

"Can I ask you something?"

"What?"

"How did you get the alarm code to my house to get the camera set up in my closet anyway?"

"From you."

"Me? I never gave you my alarm code?"

"Yeah, you did. You punched it in right in front of me the last time we met up over here when you came in with the groceries. Then while you were out jet setting with your old sugar daddy, I let myself in and searched your place for the stash. I knew you stayed caked up. I just didn't know where you kept it.

Once I found the safe, I set a camera up to catch you punchin' in the code. I was gonna come back later and bust that shit open, but your lucky ass spotted it, so I had to come up with a plan B.

Unfortunately for you, you're too smart for your own good. I could see it in your eyes that you wasn't buying my story. Pssshhh, hell. With all the trouble I got going on right now, I was tripping my own self up trying to remember it half the time," she laughed. "So, when you started dodging me… I knew I was gonna have to go to plan C. Get-this-fuck-ing-money."

"And after you get the money, then what?"

"Then I get the hell out of town. I got some people who want to meet up with me real bad to collect on a little debt I got with them. I ain't got it to pay, and even if I did, I wouldn't hand that kind of money over to nobody else. So what I'm gonna do, is take whatever you got in this safe here, and burn rubber. I know you don't put the majority of your cash into banks like I taught you to avoid getting taxed for money you shouldn't have."

"And what are you going to do with me?"

She looked me up and down like she was thinking about sexing me, and licked her lips.

"Well, Beauty Queen. That's gonna be up to you. I don't know what it is about you that makes me hesitate to blow your brains out. Maybe it's because you remind me of my first girlfriend. I loved that chick, but she got killed in a shootout between her brother and the cops back in Detroit when I was 17.

Even though you ain't never give me the pussy and you're stuck up as hell for a bitch who ain't never go to college or make paper off nothing but laying on your back. That's another reason I was salty when you double crossed me with Todd. I was starting to like you.

Now, you ready to open the safe for me or am I gonna have to go back to my car and get the explosives?"

"How do I know you won't shoot me in the back of the head as soon as I punch in the code and unlock it?"

"You don't. But I can assure you I'll shoot you in the face if you don't get to opening that safe right fucking now."

I glared at her with the ire of a thousand haters and went to the hanging clothes in front of the safe without another word. Swiping them to the side, I stared at the gray square with the keypad in the wall for a few seconds before lifting my hand to punch in the code.

Just as my finger tapped the second number, Jamie bellowed a curse and a shot went off, lodging into the wall mere inches from my head.

I spun around with my mouth agape as Linx's growls rumbled through my closet and Jamie pounded his writhing face. His jaws were clamped down on her wrist and he was shaking her with so much ferocity that his entire body wriggled.

"Fuuuck!" she hollered trying to fight him off as I eyed the gun she'd dropped inches away.

My ear drums ached from the deafening shouts and cusses Jamie released as Linx tore into her flesh and blood poured out onto my carpet.

"Neck bite Linx! Neck bite!" I screamed lunging for the revolver.

Mark and I had taught him the kill commands ourselves since my friend that sold the dog to us wasn't in the habit of training dogs to murder. Linx already knew that "bite" meant to attack, and once he learned what "face" and "neck" meant, all we did was combine them with "bite" to get results. He was here for my protection, and part of that entailed him sending anyone who threatened my life out in a body bag.

He freed her bloody arm from his mouth and immediately went for her throat. Anticipating it, she crunched her shoulder up protectively and swung at him with her right. Connecting and backing him up a second, he shook it off and attacked again, just as I stood to my feet and unloaded a single bullet into her snarling face.

I ordered Linx to heel by the bed as I stood in my closet beside Jamie's lifeless body with blood trickling down my face. Looking into her vacant eyes, I felt nothing but relief. Ding Dong the witch is dead. Without my knowing, she had been the bane of my existence this entire year. She orchestrated every bad thing that happened except my uncle's death, and I had no remorse for ending her.

The surveillance cameras on my property would show her approaching me outside with the gun and following me inside. As far as I was concerned, this was about to play out like a simple attempted robbery.

The fact that she drove the black truck I told the police about when I was shot could only add more credence to my version of the events. This was undeniably self-defense. They didn't have to know anything about Miami, Lala, Todd, or any of that. My past was finally about to be buried. With Jamie.

When the police arrived, I was sitting on the bottom stair with Linx on a leash sobbing. It would have looked suspicious if I wasn't emotional, and suspicion is the furthest thing from what I wanted.

I knew they were going to make me put Linx up, but until they got here, he was going to be cuddling with me. As much as I complained about how hardheaded he is, his disobedience literally saved my life. He was my hero.

One thing's for certain though. I could go the rest of my life without having to see, call or talk to another police officer ever again. I stopped escorting because I wanted to live a simple life, and my life had been everything but since.

24

Vanessa

Two hours and 20 minutes later, I passed Walgreens and was following the directions Delia texted me to their property. I was glad the rain hadn't lasted long. Atlanta's weather is so bi-polar. One minute there was a monsoon, the next minute there were clear skies everywhere.

The radio stations I liked were staticky for the last hour and I absentmindedly left my iPod at Gavin's, so I opted to ride in silence. I took a long drag from my cig and glanced the directions on my phone propped on the dashboard.

The quiet forced me to toil with my thoughts for lack of anything better to do. I mulled over ways to build my celebrity, how I was going to confront Val about that bullshit she pulled at the hospital, and the pros and cons of having Gavin's baby. Surprisingly, the pros outweighed the cons.

Nothing would hurt Daphne's feelings more than knowing Gavin had a child with me. That alone would be a win against her. Besides, with the way he treated Davin, my child, ergo *I*, would be taken care of for life. Whether we split up or not, my name would be bonded with his forever like Toya Wright, Kim Porter, Amber Rose and Blac Chyna's are with their famous baby daddy's.

Regardless, I was still going to smoke and drink as much as I felt like it until my second trimester. I wasn't ready to quit yet, and plenty of kids whose parents smoke and drank in the early months of pregnancy came out fine. I could always fake like I didn't know I was pregnant until it was too obvious to hide.

Yawning, I sipped my bottled water, wiping my sleepy eyes with my sleeve and blinking back at the road. I had been off the main strip for a while now and I was traveling down a windy dirt road with my high beams up, looking for a turn to come up on my right. Why the hell did they buy a house way out here? I prayed a deer or some other animal lurking in the trees aligning the road wouldn't gamble with life and jump out in front of my BMW. The last thing I wanted was to have myself and my car mangled in an accident out here in hillbilly country. If *this* wasn't east bubble-fuck, it had to be the same road you would take to get there.

Finally, I came upon the large cast iron gates to their property. There was a security box planted in front of it for car riders to let themselves in or push a call button.

"Hello,"

"Hey. It's Vanessa. Buzz me in."

"Follow the trail passed the mansion on your left until you come up on the guest house on your right. You can park directly in front of it."

A second later, a loud extended beep emitted from the box and the gates cranked open. I rolled my window back up and eased my car through, taking in the massive grounds, illuminated by tall iron lamp posts along the path.

This place was plantation style huge. Why the hell was she staying at the guest house when she had that huge mansion to stay in? There were four cars parked in the round-about and the house and surrounding trees were beautifully lit with Christmas decorations. I wondered who was in there if she was in the guest house.

I squinted at the cabin style guest home when I arrived through the downpour and parked in front like she said to. It was twice as small as the manor, but still bigger than my Aunt Pam's house, except it was only one story.

The light streamed so brightly through the windows over the cobblestones that it almost looked like early evening. I stuck my phone in my back pocket and grabbed my Louis Vuitton bag from the passenger's seat. I brought an extra change of clothes, shoes and toiletries because after driving this far, this late, I was damn sure staying.

I slung the bag over my shoulder and jogged the short distance to the huge oak door. I rapped hard on it with the knocker and drew my body close in anticipation of it opening. The wind was blowing like it had a vendetta against me and the sounds of nature were creeping me out.

I got impatient after a couple of minutes passed and no one came to the door. Craning my neck to look through a window on the side, I impatiently banged the knocker again like I was Atlanta PD. Why didn't these fools have a doorbell and what was taking so long?

"Delia! It's cold as a witch's ti—" my words caught in my throat as the door swung open and Rachel's apathetic eyes gawked back at me.

"Hey."

"Hey. You didn't hear me banging?" I frowned striding in.

"Sorry. We didn't hear you."

"Where's the maid?"

"They're all in the main house," she answered with a mocking tone.

"It's not like I didn't *just* call from the gate"

She shrugged and swat the air in front of her grimacing.

"You must have been smoking the whole drive. It's like a cloud of cigarette smoke followed you in."

"Don't start Rachel. We're not that cool again yet. I thought Delia said you left already."

"I'm not starting anything. I was just making an observation. I spent the weekend, so maybe you heard her wrong. You know I'm always available when a friend is in need, and there's no way I wasn't going to be here for this. That's how I am, and how I'll always be. Loyal."

I looked her up and down again, completely unimpressed with her assertion. She didn't have to remind me of her loyalty to the bitch who stabbed me in the back. I was well aware of it.

"What does she need *you* here for? Doesn't she have a nurse, her mom, Brand, and God only knows who else to wait on her hand and foot?"

"She does, but I'm not here to wait on her. I'm sure that's not why you're here either. Is it? I'm here as a friend."

Her saccharine tone didn't match the smug expression on her anorexic little face. In my new celebrity role, I was not only good at faking friendly, but I could also read when someone was blowing smoke up my ass. Either she was better at it at the restaurant, or something changed since then. Whatever the case, I wasn't here for her.

I surveyed the simple dark wood interior, country style decor and rustic furniture with a raised brow. It wasn't at all what I expected. It felt like a luxury version of the *Little House On The Prairie* cabin to me. The strong scent of lemon scented Pine-Sol wafted through the air like it had been freshly cleaned, but it didn't feel homey at all.

"Good talk. You gonna lead the way to *our* bestie now, or what?"

She tilted her head with a disingenuous Stepford smile, and ambled passed me in jeans and an eggshell, destroyed wool-blend sweater that I recognized from Kanye's tacky fashion line. I wanted to cup my hands to my mouth and boo her entire wardrobe.

"Right this way. Your highness."

I fluttered my long lashes mockingly and kept in tow behind her. We passed a scarcely decorated room and a bathroom before she turned into an open doorway to my left.

"Look who's here," Rachel introduced rapping on the open door.

It took every ounce of my willpower not to gasp and react when I finally saw the guest of honor... Or should I say *horror*, sitting in a wheelchair by the window. I wasn't prepared at all for the disfigured mess that made up her grinning countenance. The poor attempt somebody made to spruce it up with makeup only succeeded in making her look like a wheelchair bound corpse bride.

"Not what you expected huh?" Delia asked shifting her lean to the right arm of her chair. "Imagine how *I* felt when I saw myself for the first time *without* make up. Those fucking tree branches and rocks got my face looking like a jigsaw puzzle."

"It ... It doesn't look *that* bad. I mean, you don't look like yourself, but you look way better than I expected," I lied wishing I could unsee the keloidal scarring that laced the right side of her cheek, jawline and part of her forehead like fleshy ropes.

She wore an auburn turtleneck sweater with red pajama bottoms and bedroom shoes, looking like the poster child for disabled Walmart customers. I could only imagine what disfigurements her clothes were shielding me from. Not that her face wasn't traumatizing enough.

Her right eye looked lower than the left now, her once long hair was lopped off and shaved low on the right side like she was trying to pretend the style was intentional. She could easily have been a character in the movie *The Hills Have Eyes* and I didn't want to look at her anymore. Let alone touch her. But I gave her a weak hug, and quickly stepped back, noticing that Rachel had left the room.

"You don't have to lie. I have a mirror. We both know I need reconstructive surgery, and I'll get it. I've just got to conquer these milestones in rehab first. Get myself back to at least 80%. Then I'll tackle getting my face back pretty," she said humorously.

"I hear you. By the way, this place is far as hell. This will be my first and last time visiting you here." I was anxious to change the subject away from her creepy face. "Are we even still in Georgia? Why the hell would y'all buy a house this far out? This looks like some place stupid teenagers go to sleepaway camp and get killed in horror movies."

We both laughed.

"It *is not* that far. Okay. Maybe it is, but you wouldn't have come if I would have told you that. He had it built for his mom and his little sisters, but when his mom remarried, she moved back to SC. Now it's just a getaway house for the family or for him to work in the studio reclusively.

You can't find a place more peaceful and beautiful at the same time than here in the daytime. Nobody's around trying to get a picture, wanting to be in your business, and you can be one with nature."

"One with nature? *Chiiiiiile.* Don't nobody care about that. I'd rather be one with Starbucks, WIFI and civilization. How far is your next neighbor?"

"Probably about two miles. You can scream your head off at the top of your lungs and nobody would hear you."

My brows knit together. "What?"

"That didn't come out right," she giggled eerily. "I didn't mean *you* as in you specifically. I meant you, as in anybody. Sometimes this physical therapy is like murder. If we had close neighbors, they'd probably think someone was killing me the way I scream sometimes."

I twisted my lips wondering where Rachel disappeared to since she hadn't come back. I wasn't particularly thrilled to have her here with us, but she wasn't acting anything like the groupie she had been at the restaurant.

"What's up with your girl? She was all friendly when I saw her at the restaurant, and now she's acting weird. Where'd she go?"

"Weird? Why do you say that? She's probably just trying to give you and I time to talk alone. She knows how much we need this, and I've had her this whole time."

"Hmph. I guess. *Soooo,* what's going on over at the big house? There were a lot of cars out there. Or are those all yours and Brand's?"

"I don't know girl. I haven't been over there since I got home. I told him to go to the studio and he probably went to one he had built in the house instead of the one downtown. He's probably got people over there."

"Speaking of which, why are you over here instead of over there? Not that this isn't a nice place, but isn't your full staff and what not in the big house?"

I plopped myself and my bag down on the ugly flower quilted queen-sized bed just as a thunderous clap rumbled outside. I grabbed my chest with a start and snickered.

"I hate this kind of weather. It just stopped raining. Now it's about to start up again. This property is above flood level, right? You know I swim like a rock, and after seeing what happened with Katrina and all those other national disasters, I don't like to take chances."

"Nessa, it's just a little storm girl. Yes, we're above flood level," she snickered shaking her head like I was foolish for even thinking it. Whatever. It could happen! "Anyway, I'm over here because it's more peaceful. Everything I need is on one level and the doorways and halls are wider for me to wheel around. There's no stairs to maneuver except the ones to the lower level and I can always take the elevator if I want to go down there."

"Elevator? I thought this was one level?"

"Uh… It is. Kind of. It's built on an incline so there's a drop in the back of the house. I'll show you later what I mean, but the elevator also goes to the roof. There's a balcony up there and a lounge area that's great in the summer."

"That's crazy that you would have an elevator in the guest house but not in the main house."

"We do."

"But you just said that you're not staying over there because of the stairs. Didn't you?"

She stared at me and darted her eyes from me to the floor, then back again. "Did I say that? That's not what I meant. I get mixed up when I'm talking sometimes. My brain doesn't always catch up with my mouth," she giggled and tapped her temple. "I see you brought an overnight bag."

"It's late. I figured you'd have an extra room for me to crash in until morning."

"Yes, of course. There are two other bedrooms. I knew you wouldn't be leaving the second you agreed to drive out here," she smirked.

"Oh. You just know me like the back of your hand huh?"

"I'd like to think I still do. It was already late when I called and we have so little time tonight, I wouldn't have let you leave even if you wanted to."

I faked a smile and averted my eyes to every drab piece of furniture and picture in the room to avoid looking at her mangled face. Actually, I was hoping this night would be over sooner rather than later. I just wanted to get a few "ussies" in, see what gift she had for me and go to bed. This baby had me so sleepy that I stifled a yawn as she spoke.

"Are you hungry? Thirsty?" She asked taking a sip of something inside of a 64 oz metal thermos.

"No. No, I'm good."

"You know I love hot cocoa, and it's almost the only guilty pleasure I can have right now. I'm still having a hard time digesting. This thing keeps it warm for hours. It's a new product Brandon is looking into representing."

"So, what is this gift you have for me?"

"Later. We'll have plenty of time for you to see it. I swear you haven't changed a bit," she chuckled.

Well, *she* sure had. She started probing into what I had been doing over the last six months. There was no way around talking about my new-found celebrity, which led to talk about my songs. She brushed over the subject matter of the song that put me on top, "Take Your Man", but said how happy she was for me finally getting the props I deserved in the industry.

Rachel joined us for a few short minutes, never leaving the doorway and observing the conversation more than adding to it.

The two of them must've been talking about me before I got there because they kept exchanging weird looks. When I called them out for it, they both acted like it wasn't happening and I was being paranoid. Maybe I was, but I doubted it. I felt like I was on the outside looking in and they were on the inside plotting.

Rachel eventually excused herself, claiming she had to finish up some project for work on her laptop. I was happy to see her go. After a while, my prior apprehension and defenses were down. It felt like old times again and we were joking and laughing like the good friends we used to be.

"All right. Why don't you leave your phone and stuff in here and let me take you on a tour of the house before it gets too late. It's fabulous for a guest house."

"I don't go anywhere without my phone."

"There's no service here anyway. You might as well leave it for now. I'll get the WIFI password for you later. I don't want to disturb Rayche asking her for it. Actually, I don't even think she knows it. I think Brandon entered it on her laptop for her."

"It's fine. We can still take pics or whatever. I'll just upload them later."

This heifer was tripping if she thought I was going to leave my phone unattended. I don't do that for anybody. She stared at me like she wanted to say something else, but changed her mind.

"Let's go then."

She was rolling before I could open my mouth, so I followed without protest. The guest house turned out to be a lot bigger than the outside led me to believe. The additional bedrooms were minimally decorated, but they were large, and there was a fully equipped gym that I guessed to be four or five-hundred square feet.

She pointed out which equipment she was using for her therapy to help with her mobility and joked about how much she hated it. Honestly, she was way more upbeat about this whole thing than I expected. I wouldn't be nearly as cheerful if I were the one wheeling around looking like a horror movie villain. She was probably faking it for my benefit, but I let her do it anyway because frankly... I didn't care.

We peeked in on the elaborate rec room and lingered in the distressed wood kitchen with timber, brick and vintage appliances in it for a good while too. She rambled on about the décor and how it didn't compare to the kitchen in the main house, but that she couldn't wait to get back to being able to cook when she wanted to. She had me doubled over with laughter talking about the tiny kitchen in our first apartment and how I almost burned the building down trying to cook a fried turkey.

Honestly, I was kind of glad that I came to see her. Besides hanging with Red, I hadn't had anybody to girl chat with since my cousins were being asses. I needed these laughs. We even took a few pics together.

"Last but not least, we have the sauna and an underground lap pool down here," she gloated pushing the button to the elevator which was directly beside the staircase near the kitchen.

I yawned and looked at my Michael Kors watch.

"It's late Dee. I'm getting tired. How about we skip seeing the sauna and the pool, and you show me the gift you got me instead."

Her grin matched mine, but the shaking of her head declined my request.

"Not yet. Don't worry. You'll get it soon en—"

She stopped talking and brought a hand to her forehead, squeezing her eyes shut.

"Are you okay?" I touched her shoulder concernedly.

"Yeah. I'm okay," she replied patting my hand and forcing a smile. "Sometimes I get these paralyzing migraines that come on out of nowhere. I saw pictures where they actually had me in a helmet for months to protect my skull and brain after surgery. It's frustrating not knowing who did this to me or why. I don't know why anyone would want to kill me."

All I could do was gaze at her sympathetically. I didn't feel bad for shooting her. It was the karma she and Brand brought on themselves by the way they treated me. But as long as she never remembered I was the one who shot her, I could live with her recovering and maybe rekindling our friendship. Hell, I didn't want Brand anymore anyway.

"You know we already had a name for our son."

"No. I didn't even know you knew the sex."

"Yeah. I was 13 weeks. Brandon Gregory Davis II. It's hard to believe someone could be heartless enough to shoot a pregnant mother in the stomach. I may have survived that day, but a part of me died along with my baby. Then when the doctors told me I'll never be able to carry a pregnancy to term again because of my fractured pelvis, I died again."

The elevator came and she rolled in first with me behind her. It wasn't large, but maybe one other person could fit in with us if they needed to. We descended to the lower level in silence as she stared straight ahead, and I watched the cranks lower us through the glass ceiling.

I got out of the elevator and she rolled out behind me onto what looked like a granite floor. It was decorated with tropically tiled walls, and the ritzy orange and white wicker chaises, chairs and tables aligning the elongated pool that was less than 10 feet from us. The entire back wall was a floor to ceiling window which reflected off the mosaic tiled pool.

There was a sliding glass door to the right of the pool which transitioned perfectly from the window. It conveyed a feeling of bringing the outside indoors since the view was of a vast clearing.

I wasn't sure how I was going to manipulate our friendship to my advantage just yet, but I needed to get her to trust me again until I figured it out, so I mustered up the sympathetic response she was fishing for.

"It's not the end of the world. Maybe you and Brand can adopt. There's a lot of orphaned babies out there waiting on a mommy to love them."

She sucked in her cheeks with an air of frustration and slowly rotated her neck towards me.

"I know there are. But I wanted my own baby. My own flesh and blood. And somebody stole that away from me."

"Okay. Maybe you can get a surrogate to carry a baby for you then. If you still have your ovaries, they can probably take your eggs and make it happen. I saw something on television about that once. All hope isn't lost girl."

I put a caring hand on her shoulder again like I had upstairs, but this time, she eyed it before looking back at me with a blank expression. Then she rolled her wheelchair right up to the edge of the pool.

"Isn't it beautiful? I would swim in it every day if I could. It's too deep for us to do physical therapy in it, but I can't wait to get back to myself so I can enjoy it again. Brandon let me design it myself."

Well, that explained why it looked like a crayon box exploded over expensive furniture down here. That must've been her Puerto Rican heritage shining through.

"Uh… Yeah. It is beautiful."

"It's 40 by 20 in length and 10 feet deep. The tiles were flown in special from Dubai. The sauna and changing rooms are there," she gestured passed the sliding glass door with her head. "But this… This will always be the gem of the house if you ask me. An indoor pool with an outdoor feel. Rain or shine. Winter, spring, summer or fall."

I let her have her moment without response. What would a person who can barely swim care about a pool with no shallow end? I was already over being her "Yes" woman for the night. I was sleepy. I just wanted to see my gift and go to bed.

"Come here. Let me show you something," she coaxed waving me closer to the pool.

"You're mighty close to the edge Dee. You better roll back before you accidentally roll in. We both know I won't be able to jump in and save you if you fall in."

She guffawed.

"Don't worry about me. I can still swim. Now come look at this. You can't see it unless you're in the pool or right up on the edge. No other pool in the world has it. I promise you won't be disappointed."

I ran both hands wearily over my jaws and brought them to a steeple in front of me. Me and water did not get along. Sure, I would get in a bikini and go to the beach or any pool party I was invited to, but I rarely put more than my feet in it.

When I was nine, I almost drowned on a family trip to the beach and I've had an aversion to deep water ever since. I *was* curious however, to see what Delia had convinced Brand to pay for that nobody else in the world had. Reluctantly, I stepped beside her, my eyes downcast, scanning the sides and bottom of the pool.

"Okay. Kneel down and look right there," she pointed. "You can't see it properly standing all the way up."

I frowned, but bent over, resting my hands on my thighs and squinted into the water where she pointed. Within seconds, I was reeling forward, and H2O instantly inundated my mouth and nostrils as my lungs constricted and I sunk to the bottom mid scream.

My heavy winter clothes felt like weights pulling me down as I fought against the depth of the pool to resurface. Each time I broke the surface, I became acutely aware that no one was going to save me, as Brand and Delia's leering eyes looked on. I didn't know where he came from, but he must've been lying in wait for me this whole time.

My heart hammered in my chest with each gasp for air as I frantically flailed around, trying to reach the edge. A sliver of hope baited me when one flailing hand smacked against the window. Grasping for anything, my fingers found the narrow sill where the pool tiles met the glass and latched on. I tried supporting myself with the soles of my sneakers against the tile grooves, but they slid repeatedly until I was finally successful.

Craning my neck above the water, I coughed and gasped my plea for help. It didn't take a rocket scientist to figure out that this was planned, but I still wanted to live.

"Please. Please. Help me. I'm… I'm sorry."

"Yes you are," Delia taunted. "And we're not leaving until you're dead. Just like my son."

"W-Wait. I'm pregnant. Dee. I'm pregnant."

Now that it was painfully obvious that they knew I was the trigger woman, I had to pull out all the stops. I didn't want to die, and if I had to, I didn't want to die like this. It might have been useless to beg for *myself,* but begging for my baby, might work.

She threw her head back, laughing loud and maniacally.

"You're pregnant? Did you hear that Brandon? The *wittle baby kill-wer* is *pweg-nant,*" she parodied in baby talk, holding her fists in front of her disfigured face and twisting them back and forth in feigned weeping.

"I heard her," he answered tugging the brim of the black baseball cap further down over his face and folding his arms. "She's probably lying."

"She fucking better be. God wouldn't dare bless the bitch who murdered my child with a baby. I know he wouldn't."

"Dee. Don't do this," I begged struggling to keep water out of my mouth. "You'll... You'll get caught. They'll look for me and Rachel is rig—"

"*Rachel*," Delia grit ominously. "Is probably halfway through South Carolina in your BMW right now. They might start looking for you, but it won't be *here*. Brand called you on three-way with me from a burner phone, so they can't trace that call, *or* your phone's signal anywhere near us.

You see *Sweetheart*, I remember exactly what happened the day I was shot. I always have. I dream about it every night. Your beady little eyes staring back at me before you shot me over the edge into those trees. The burning pain in my stomach. The branches ripping me apart before I hit the bottom and passed out."

Her voice trembled, and I knew she was crying now, even though I was focusing more on keeping my head above water than on looking her way.

"Do you know why I never told the police? Huh!"

I didn't bother answering, I knew she was going to say either way. I tried calculating the distance between the window and the adjacent edge of the pool instead. Maybe if I pushed off from the wall, I could repel myself close enough to grasp it with a few strokes.

"Babe. Calm down. We got her," Brand pacified.

"Because I wanted to watch you die myself!" She ignored jutting a finger at me. pay for it the same way my son did. "You're a murderer! You killed my son and you tried to kill me too! And for what? For what? All because *my* man chose me over you? You-fucking-jealous-bitch!"

Anger fought its way through the terror I felt of dying and reared it's ugly head through words I knew might very well be my last.

"He raped me! I shot you because he raped me for telling you he was still sleeping with me and…" my foot slid from it's placement and I lost my grip, causing me to sink underwater before fighting my way back to the surface in a frenzy.

Coughing and blinking water from my eyes, I managed to clench the ledge again and hoist my head above the water.

"Please! Please don't let me die!" I cried out fearing the watery grave I was submerged in. I was already tired, and my grip was weak.

"She's lying! That bitch will say anything right now! I never raped nobody in my life. I ought to jump in there and drown your fucking ass myself!"

"No," Delia grumbled. "Stick to the plan. No contact with her until she's dead. What if she scratches you? Just… Just leave her. She can't hold on forever."

"*Pleeeease*," I begged, my saliva and tears rinsing each time the water rippled. "I'll confess. I'll confess everything to the police if you want me to. I'll… I'll give you my baby. You can have my baby. You can have whatever you want. Just please don't let me die. Not like this. I'm so—" the pain was instant as metal connected with my forehead causing me to again lose my grip and footing.

Delia's thermos sunk beside me as my vision blurred and blood dyed the surface. Still, the instinct to hold my breath until I could get air kicked in as I futilely flapped upwards.

Every second deprived of oxygen made me weaker and more frantic. I felt my eyes bulging from their sockets and every cell in my body on fire before my mouth involuntarily snapped open and I inhaled a flood of chlorine and H2O. My body instantly spasmed, my fingers clawing at my neck in an effort to force air that didn't exist into my lungs.

"Die bitch! Just die!" Delia's hate filled words rippled through the water with peculiar clarity.

Agony and terror swaddled my twitching limbs as I prayed forgiveness from the heavenly father for the things I've done. I may have betrayed my sister, killed a man in a fire, attempted to kill my former best friend and her baby, but they were all with good reason. Still, I was sorry for the terrible things I'd done. Because now I was living long enough to regret them.

25

Valerie

"We don't have to stay here if you don't want to."

"I know," I sighed burying my face into Maaco's chest and wrapping my arms around his waist. "I just want you to hold me right now if that's okay."

"Whatever you want baby," he confirmed squeezing me tightly and kissing the top of my head. "Whatever you want. How's your neck?"

"It's fine. It hurts a little, but this mega band-aid is doing its job," I smiled.

I was emotionally numb and drained. I just wanted to be in the only place I felt safe nowadays. In his arms. We hadn't moved from that spot in the foyer since the police and paramedics finally emptied out. Our coats were hung on the coat rack and my duffle was on the floor beside it with my sneakers.

"What about you? Are *you* okay?"

"Me? Don't worry about me. Aside from being mad I wasn't home before you got here so I could've bodied that sucka, I'm fine."

Looking up at him, I could see the anger brewing behind his weary eyes, but I also felt like something else was going on.

"Are you sure that's all that's wrong with you? What BS did you have to handle with Jamie?"

He licked his lips and sucked them in in thought before answering. "She's back on that coke hard. She's been gambling everything she owns and shit *we* own together away. Threatening staff and management. Using money from our business account for personal stuff.

She showed up tonight high as a god damned kite, getting in my face, cussing and puffing out her chest. I don't even know who she is anymore. I almost put my hands on her stupid ass. Can you believe she forged my name on..." he grimaced, ran both hands down his face, and sighed.

I placed a loving hand on the side of his cheek. He was trying to be strong, but it was obvious he was deeply pained by the extent of what Jamie had done. This was a side of him I hadn't seen before.

"Look baby. This isn't the time for us to talk about this. You've been through a lot. It's late and we're both tired. This is my problem to resolve. Not yours. I got this. And I got you."

"We're supposed to have each other. Wait. Did you hear that?"

"Hear what?" he questioned.

"It sounds like… Like something yapping."

"Oh," he grinned. "That's your Christmas present. I almost forgot about him. He's upstairs."

My eyes saucered and the tears instantly stopped with anticipation. "Who's upstairs?"

"Your puppy. What else would be making all that damn noise?"

"My puppy? My puppy!" I bounced up and down and raced up the stairs with him in tow. "Where is he? What kind of puppy is it? Oh my God. Did you really get me a puppy?"

The pup must've heard me coming because his little barks became more erratic. I passed Maaco's bedroom and into the spare where the noise was coming from. On the floor, in a cage twice as long as he was, was a tan Pomeranian leaping around.

Maaco laughed behind me as I knelt to unlatch the cage door with squeals of joy. My dad was allergic to dogs, so we never had one growing up, and I've always been too busy and traveling to keep one of my own.

Brent said animals were too messy and needy, so I never even broached the topic of getting one when we were together. I doubted

Courtney was going to welcome the little fox faced fella I was gawking at either, but I already loved him. We would work it out, or I would just have to get my own place.

"He's *soooo* adorable! I can't believe you did this. How long as he been locked up in here?"

A bowl I assumed was for his food was flipped over, the water bowl was still half full, and pee stains and a couple of turds were on the other end of the cage.

"About four or five hours. I left him food, water and a wee-wee pad. You should check his paws before you let him run all up on you like that. It looks like he was probably walking on the pissy side of the pad too. The little sucker peed on me the first time I picked him up," he smirked watching me fawn over the little fur ball as he leapt and licked at me excitedly.

"Puppies do that sometimes when they're happy. They can't help it. They're like little babies."

"The breeder was supposed to keep him until Christmas eve for me, but he had a family emergency and had to leave town yesterday. I wasn't ready for his little crybaby ass yet. He whined all through the night."

"Awww," I cooed holding the pup in front of me as he squirmed and licked the air rigorously. Finally, something that made me happy in my life. "Courtney's going to kill me. She is not a dog person."

"Well, he can stay here with me. With us."

I gazed up at him with an eyebrow raised, still grinning.

"With *us?* Babe. We just made it official between us tonight. I know you're not asking me to move in with you. Are you?"

He shoved both hands in his pants pockets and offered a weary smile. Exhaustion was written all over his face, but the sincerity and love he felt for me was just as apparent in his eyes.

"I am. Shit baby. I could have lost you tonight. You can't imagine what I was thinking when I came home to police cars and EMT's. The whole time you were sitting in the back of the ambulance, I was going crazy. That motherfucker's lucky the cops hauled his ass off before I got home, or he would've been leaving with the coroner."

I shook my head listlessly and glanced the ceiling. I didn't want to think about that anymore tonight. I was sure I would have nightmares about it anyway, so there was no need to revisit it now. This puppy was bringing me a little bit of joy at the moment and I wanted it to stay like that. For me and for him.

"Let's not talk about that right now. We're talking about us, and this cute little guy. Let's stay on topic."

He sighed and his eyes dropped to the puppy I was cradling like a baby as he barked and nipped up at my face until I put him down.

"Okay. Let's talk about us then. Move in with me."

I watched the dog scurry around and ran through a few names in my head that might fit my new pet. Bear? Chico? No. He seemed like a Max. I was going to call him Max.

"Is that a no?"

"I didn't say no."

"You didn't say yes either."

"May, what's the rush? Don't you want to wait until we can settle into some form of normalcy before moving me in with you? Your crazy ex is claiming you have a child together. My crazy ex just tried to kidnap me in front of your house. My crazy sister is the reason I'm in the blogs and my business is all in the streets. You just said *your* crazy sister is tying you up in a bunch of shady shit right now. Our lives are literally… Full of crazy people and crazy things," I laughed solemnly. "Now, what do you think about Max? For a puppy name."

He scratched the top of his head and glanced the dog as I stood, then back to me. I could tell he didn't want to drop the subject, but was tired of pushing the issue.

"It's your dog. If you want to call him Max, call him Max. He's supposed to be housetrained already, but he's only two months old, so I'm not sold on that yet."

"He's so cute. It's the best Christmas gift I've gotten in a long time. Thank … Thank…" Suddenly, my head ached like someone was twisting my brain and everything looked distorted, as though I were viewing it underwater. My chest tightened so savagely that it buckled my knees while my stomach wrenched in unison, and my breath wedged in my throat.

I wanted to scream out in pain, but no voice escaped me as Maaco rushed to my aid.

"Babe! What's wrong?"

I clutched my chest with one hand and his arm with the other as he pat my back like he thought I was choking.

"Damn. What's happening now? Breathe baby! Breathe! Shit! I knew you should have gone to the hospital."

He started to scoop me up, but I fought him to remain on my feet, shaking my head and sucking in every ounce of oxygen like a vacuum as the feeling began to subside.

"You need water? Are you having a panic attack?"

"No," I eked through ragged breaths. "No. It's my sister."

Something was wrong. Vanessa and I always had an inexplicable molecular connection between us that transmitted intense emotional and even sometimes physical reactions. Whether I liked it or not. Whether I like *her* or not, we still had it. A dark sense of trepidation invaded my gut and twisted it into knots as goosebumps rose on my arms. Something was *very-very-wrong* with my sister.

He watched me worriedly as I recomposed myself and the pup leapt around at my feet.

"I know you're going to think I'm crazy for what I'm about to tell you, but Vanessa's in trouble. I don't know where and I don't know how, but something is wrong with her."

His expression converted from that of concern to one of apathy.

"Val, what are you talking about baby? I know something is wrong with your sister. She's crazy as fu—"

"No. You don't understand. Something is happening to her *right*-now. Or it did. I don't know which but, I can feel it. I can't explain it but it's a connection we have to each other that we've had since we were kids. It only lasts a few seconds. A few minutes at most, but we can feel it when it's bad enough.

When she was six, she slammed her thumb in my grandma's car door and damn near filleted the flesh off of it. I was in the house sleeping and work up screaming. When I was 12, I broke my arm jumping on our neighbor's trampoline. Vanessa was in the car with my dad when it happened, and he said she screamed so loud about her arm hurting *out of nowhere* that she almost made him crash.

Same thing when I tore my Achilles tendon on stage. She was in the studio recording when it happened, and she *felt* it. I can tell you so many more times it happened. We always know when something *really* bad happens to the other one. It's one of the only things we're equally connected by. We legitimately *feel* it."

"What about when y'all fought? Did you feel each other's pain then too?"

"I'm serious," I snapped knocking both his hands from my arms.

"I'm serious too. It's a legit question."

I don't know if I was more pissed at the fact that he would bring that up at a time like this, or because I didn't have a definitive answer for him. Considering that I was the one who took the ass-whooping, I guess Vanessa would have to answer that.

"I'm-telling-you this is real, and if something *is* really wrong with her, it's going to devastate my mom. We're all she has left. I'm not forgetting why we're not talking but... this feeling was really intense. Like, *really* intense. It's never been this bad before. It actually felt like I was going to die. I couldn't breathe. It was sort of like how it was when she almost drowned, but way worse."

"Babe. That sounds like a panic attack. After what happened tonight, and maybe my asking you to move in just... I might have sent you over the edge. Vanessa's probably out there doing whatever she's always doing. I'm sure she's fine."

I sucked my teeth, rolling my eyes simultaneously and picked up the dog. This is the very reason why I never shared this part of me with him before. The last person I told was my college roommate and her treatment of it as some type of mystic bull is why I never told anyone else.

Of course, all of our close family knew about it, but even they were skeptical at times when they weren't there to witness how we're affected. I tried moving past him, but he towered over me with a penetrating gaze grabbing my free hand.

"Okay. All right. Just, relax a second. I'm on edge. *You're* on edge. You had a long night, it's almost the crack of dawn, and we were outside in the cold for hours. Let's just go to bed."

"I'm going to get my phone and check on my sister. Even if it's just to have her tell me to fuck off, I just need to know she's not lying in a ditch somewhere or in a car accident or something. I'm not going to be able to rest until I do."

He looked at his watch, ran his huge palm over his face and pivoted for me to step around him. Downstairs I got my phone and realized I didn't even have her damn number. Thinking, I called somebody who did.

"Hello?" Nicky answered like I woke the dead.

"Hey. I need Vanessa's phone number."

"What?"

"I need Vanessa's phone number. I never saved it in my new phone. It's important."

"Girl. What time is it? It feels like I just went to sleep. My head is killing me."

"I don't know. Still early. On second thought, I need you to call her for me," I replied impatiently, secretly second guessing calling her. At least she didn't still sound as hammered as she was after the club.

Was I overreacting? What if whatever happened to her was just temporary, like when Brent tried to choke me out, and she was fine now? What was I going to do either way? Hell, I'd be lucky if she even answered the phone for me at all.

"Why? What's going on? Is Aunt Di okay?"

"Yeah, I guess so. This isn't about her. You know how sometimes me and Vanessa can feel each other's pain?"

"Uh huh."

"Tonight, I felt it again and this time … this time it was scary. I just want to make sure she's still breathing."

Maaco wrapped his arms around me from behind and I sunk into his embrace with little Max now cradled and docile.

"Oh shit. It was that bad?"

"It was that bad. I couldn't breathe or anything. Something like the time she almost drowned at the beach but worse. Way worse."

"Hold on. Let me three-way you."

I glanced up at Maaco's consoling eyes with the phone pinned to my ear and leaned my head back into his chest. I couldn't quell the dreadful feelings swelling in my gut that Vanessa was in dire need of help.

I heard the phone ringing when Nicky connected the call, but just as I feared, it went straight to voicemail. Maaco kissed the top of my forehead and I cleared my throat.

"Hey, Vanessa its Val. Umm … I know we're not cool right now, but… I had one of those pain attacks we get. It was *sooo intense*. Like, worse than I ever felt before between us. So, I just wanted to find out what happened, and see if you were okay. Call me at my new number, 678 555 2352 or call Nicky back at least. Okay? Bye."

"You done?"

"Yeah."

"Hold on while I disconnect."

"Okay."

"Maybe it's not as bad for her as it felt Vee," Nicky said coming back on the line. "Have y'all ever had a false alarm? You know, where it was a fluke feeling? A bad dream maybe?"

"No. Never."

Whatever happened to her was bad. Very bad. And I wasn't sure I would ever see my sister alive again.

26

Epilogue

May 28, 2016

Yasmin

"Let me hold my Niecey-Poo," Nicky beamed taking Sophie from my arms.

I grinned, playfully rolling my eyes and straightened the top of my dress as Nicky rested Sophie's sleeping head on her shoulder. My baby girl looked like a doll with her frilly light blue dress on and matching bows throughout her hair.

Orchestra music played through the speakers as we stood in the lobby along with numerous other wedding guests, waiting for the event planner to open the doors for seating.

"Aunty missed her pretty little baby," she sang with a pout, leaning in to kiss my cheek in greeting. "How was your flight?"

"Not too bad. I just hate going through TSA. Some of them take their job *way* too seriously. I love this dress by the way."

"Thank you. I thought I'd give you a little summer yellow," she cheesed. "Anyway, you should have drove. Trying to be all fancy shmancy," she joked.

"So, you say. I do not miss driving in this Atlanta traffic. Especially not on Memorial Day weekend. Picture me stuck in the car for four hours with Sophie's little spoiled behind hollering the whole way. I can barely put her down now without her throwing a fit."

"And whose fault is that?"

"Her Papa's. He's the one who carries her around like she's glued to his arm every time he comes to visit."

"Umm hmm," she groaned dubiously swaying back and forth in her stilettos while rubbing Sophie's back. "Well Auntie Nicky wants time to spoil her too. You need to come visit us more."

"I'll try. You know I'm still getting acclimated to Charlotte. I got a new house. A new job. It's not easy being a single mom."

After everything I went through in Atlanta, I just wanted a fresh start for me and my daughter. Besides my wayward family, there was really nothing left in Atlanta for me, so I left. The insurance company refused to pay for damage due to arson. Definitely not when the arsonist was also a named insured on the policy.

In the end, I just took the loss. I sold it for next to nothing, as is, and used partial proceeds from the sale of the firm Malik and I owned to pay off the mortgage balance. I hated the idea of working for someone else after so many years of being my own boss, but it was something I would have to do again.

Luckily, I was able to get veneers to repair the damage Malik did to my mouth, which made my job hunt a little easier when I had to go on interviews. I landed a senior position at a firm in Charlotte in March and found a house for me and Sophie two weeks later. I made sure to get acquainted with my new neighbors as soon as I moved in too, because you never know when one of them could save your life. Daddy wasn't too happy about the move, but my mind was already made up. Even though Malik was no longer a threat to me, I just didn't want to be anywhere that reminded me of him anymore.

An officer spotted Dwayne's car in the parking lot of a Walmart just two days after the fire and discovered Malik with a self-inflicted shot to the head in the driver's seat. I don't think he ever got to see his momma after her left the house, and frankly, I hope he didn't. I hope he suffered before he died too.

"Are you staying at Daddy's tonight or are you flying back?"

I frowned. "Girl, please. I am not doing a turn-around flight with a baby all by myself. Plus, Aunt Di already threatened to whoop me if I didn't let her keep Sophie over night the next time I visited. My plane doesn't leave until Monday."

"Oh okay. Good."

"*Heeeey* good people," Amina tapped me from behind and I spun to hug her with a grin. Things between myself, my sisters and my cousins had improved tremendously since I almost died. Again. "Oh my god. Look how big she got. What are you feeding her?"

"My baby is average weight. Thank you very much," I cheesed.

"Your cousin is a hater sweetie. Ignore her," Nicky pretended to whisper to Sophie.

"Nobody would ever guess this little rolly polly was a preemie," Amina laughed, gently squeezing Sophie's fat foot.

"Where's Donovan?" I questioned taking in how stunning she looked in her turquois and black off the shoulder shift dress.

I envied her ability to look magazine worthy every time she was out in public, and wished I had the time to care as much about my appearance as I used to. With everything I was juggling on my plate these days, everything under mommy duties and work was secondary.

Don't get me wrong now. I was looking damn good today. I dyed my hair a sandy blonde and had it flat ironed bone straight now that it had grown to shoulder length. All my baby weight was gone, and I was filling out my money green wrap dress in all the right places. On my feet were a simple pair of black suede ankle strap pumps, because on mommy duty, too high heels can be a disaster. Nevertheless, if I had been looking for a man, which I wasn't, I could definitely pull more than my share of the crop.

"He's parking the truck. Have you seen my mother? She texted me to bring her some earrings like I'm her personal jewelry store."

"Haven't seen her," Nicky answered.

"I just got here, so I haven't seen much of anybody yet."

"Oh okay. How long are you staying this time Yas? I'm having a Memorial Day barbecue at my place tomorrow if you're going to be here."

"I'm not leaving until Monday."

Nicky balled up her face. "Umm... nobody told me about that."

"We just decided to do it this morning. You know I don't grill. Donovan is going to come over and cook. It's going to be my first big thing at my house. Anyway, I'll catch y'all later. Let me find this woman and give her these earrings I brought for her."

She strode off in some to-die-for ballerina style turquoise pumps with black ribbon laced up to her calves, and I peeped both men and women sneaking peeks at her.

"So how have you been? I know I haven't been keeping in touch as much as I said I would, but I've really been struggling trying to get through this registered nursing program. This is probably the first weekend I've had off all month."

"I'm fine. Really. Don't worry about it. I completely understand what you're going through. You remember how I was in law school. A mess," I snickered. "You just do what you have to do to succeed. It's hard now, but it will be worth it later."

She nodded, shifting Sophie to her other shoulder when she stirred. "You want me to take her?"

"Did I ask you to take her? No, I do not. This is probably the most time I'm going to get to spend with her by myself. As soon as the rest of the family sees her, it's going to be a free for all. I'm glad Tamika's busy doing the bridal party's hair or else she'd have her grubby little fingers trying to snatch my Niecey-Poo too."

I smirked, knowing she was right. As tragic as Dwayne's murder was, I'm not sure Tamika and I could have gotten to this point we're in now had he survived. The pain, anger and heartbreak our betrayal caused her was replaced with grief and concern after the fire. Even *I* was surprised when she arrived at the hospital in tears, glad I hadn't been killed too.

Dwayne's death and the truth about his history with Cortez sent both of us reeling. The last time I saw him, was at Dwayne's closed casket funeral and that was one time too many. At the end of the day though, Tamika and I are family, and we're both raising Dwayne's kids. Siblings. Two things that won't change no matter how we act. Before I moved to North Carolina, we agreed to attend five counseling sessions together to give us some tools to use going forward.

I have to admit, those were five of the most grueling sessions I've ever experienced. The anger, hurt, jealousy and resentment we both carried around towards each other ran deep. Deeper than my sleeping with Dwayne. It hasn't been easy for either of us to rebuild our bond, but the way she's loved on Sophie, and the way I love my nephews has helped a lot. I'm just glad she's let me back into their lives again.

I also think her new-found love with Dean, Brent's older, richer, and obviously saner brother made her more susceptible to forgiveness. I don't know about anybody else, but I never saw that one coming. Anyway, you know how the saying goes. If you want to get over someone, get under someone else. I'm happy for her. I'm happy for me too. We both got what we wanted. Love. Except mine is for Sophie.

***

Amina

"We cannot have sex in this bathroom right now," I chastised Donovan demurely as he pinned my body against the wall with his and hovered his lips over mine.

"Why not?"

"Because the wedding is going to start any minute now. Plus, somebody could walk in on us?"

"How can they walk in on us when the door is locked?" he grinned running one hand up my thigh and under my dress.

He had been insatiable since I shared the big news I discovered Monday night with him, but had yet to divulge to my family. He greeted my mom and aunt when he saw us talking in the lobby and excused both of us shortly afterwards to "show me something." Leading me by the hand to a door marked as the Family Bathroom, he quickly locked it behind us and proceeded to molest me.

"You are crazy. You can't expect me to do this right now with all those people out there. We just did it before we left my house."

"And. I want to do it again. And again. And again. And again," he muttered, tugging my panties down while kissing and licking his way from my exposed shoulder, to my collarbone, all the way up to the nape of my neck.

He wasn't playing fair at all because there wasn't a pleasure point on my body that he didn't know how to manipulate anymore. The first time we had sex was New Year's Eve, after he brought me to a climax during the peach drop countdown with his mouth.

"I want you so bad right now baby," he whispered in my ear before sticking his tongue inside of it and guiding my hand to the bulge in his pants while keeping my other hand pinned above my head. "Can I have you?"

"The wedding is supposed to start in 15 minutes," I whimpered, not being able to resist stroking the monster behind the fabric of his slacks.

"We can be done in 15 minutes," he assured me with a smoldering gaze as he leaned in, placing his pillow soft lips on mine, then lustfully invading the space between them with his tongue.

He had my little kitty as hot as an inferno and there was nothing else for me to do but give him what he wanted. What *we* wanted. Still engrossed in our kiss, I stepped out of my panties and tugged at his belt, signaling my utter consent. Thank god for swing dresses. Though I had worn this one to conceal the slight bulge in my stomach from the suspicious eyes of my nosy relatives, I appreciated the easy access it was providing at the moment.

He released my hand from the wall as I turned to face it while he unbuckled his belt. Sweeping my hair over one shoulder, I hiked my dress up over my bare bottom and his large hands gripped my waist. His girth filled me up in seconds as I braced myself with one hand on the wall and he let out a guttural hiss.

"Y'all better bring y'all nasty asses on out here before Ma finds out what you're doing," my brother bellowed amusedly at the same time he banged on the door. "No but seriously. The wedding's about to start in a minute and they're going to close the doors. Hurry up."

If my brown complexion could flush, it would have. Of all the people to catch us in the act, my brother was one of the most mortifying. Donovan didn't break stride at all, instead gripping me tighter and plunging deeper and faster into my peach.

"Oh… oh… oh…" I stammered as my orgasm neared.

Moving one hand to my throat, he pulled my back into him, turning my face to ravish my lips with his own. Seconds later we were both coming. Groaning into each other's mouths as he drowned my pussy with his seeds.

When I was able to catch my breath again, I leaned against the wall, slightly moving forward as he withdrew himself from behind. We grinned impishly at each other while maneuvering to the sink to quickly wipe ourselves down.

Two minutes later, we emerged hoping Mark was the only one who knew we'd just had sex and hoping we didn't look like it. Thankfully, the doors were still open, so we crept in and made our way to the row beside my brother and his girl. His girl that Mark still hadn't revealed used to be a man to the family.

Honestly, I don't think he's ever going to tell them unless they find out somehow, and if they do, it won't be from me. As it stands, Donovan's the only other person that knows Dana used to be a man, and I swore him to secrecy when we started dating. It's not our secret to tell and as long as it's not hurting anyone and my brother's happy, it will remain so.

Hell, I had my own secret to worry about, and my momma was not going to be happy to find out I was pregnant out of wedlock. Though I'm sure she'll be ecstatic I'm going to give her her first grandbaby. I wasn't even sure if *I* was happy when I initially got the news.

I certainly hadn't planned for kids in my immediate or distant future for that matter, and Donovan and I's relationship was still fresh. Luckily, he was surprised, but cheery when I shared the news. It will be the first baby for both of us, and we eventually agreed that whether we work out or not, this is a good thing.

I'm not even going to lie and say we were practicing safe sex as often as we should have been, because that would be a bald-faced lie. After we viewed each other's clean bills of health, we had been a little less than responsible with where and when we got it in. Sort of like how we ended up in the bathroom screwing right before my cousin's wedding.

I was on birth control a week after we started getting physical, but my OBGYN said I was approaching 11 weeks, so it must've failed me somewhere. I truly had no idea until I went for my annual checkup and my doctor came back with the news.

My menstrual cycles have always been light, and once I started on the pill, they got even lighter. I just chalked the missed cycles and day long periods up to my body getting used to the birth control. But look. We're grown as hell, so I'm not making any excuses, nor do I feel like I owe anybody an explanation for what we do. I'm simply stating the facts.

He may have left me hanging the day he saw that video of me, but since this whole thing with Jamie unraveled, he's been by my side the whole way. I hate that I can never tell him the full truth about my relationship with her, but some things are better left in the past.

The shooting was deemed justifiable after they saw the video of how she approached me on my property, and it didn't hurt that she had an undisclosed amount of cash, explosives, guns and forged passports in suitcases in that Explorer either.

I felt bad for Maaco, because despite the things she did that caused her death, Jamie was still his sister. She was going to leave him in the lurch anyway, had she been able to get away with it. Turns out she cleaned out her accounts and those of the clubs she owned too. As karma would have it, the million-dollar life insurance policies they both had on each other paid off in a big way for him. Plus, he got all the money she was going to smuggle out with her as the next of kin.

Of course, I didn't go to her funeral, but Val attended with Maaco, and she said only 22 people showed up to pay respect. I guess who you are in life, will be reflected in your death. Personally, I'm just happy I won't have to look over my shoulder anymore the way I had to this last year.

Things between Donovan and I were going great, and though this pregnancy thing isn't exactly what I wanted for my life, it was happening now. I've had two showings at a gallery downtown since January, and I sold three of the six pieces I presented. Most of my days are filled with painting when I'm not with my man or hanging out with my family whenever I can. I've had enough excitement to last me a lifetime already, so all I'm looking for now is happiness.

***

Valerie

"You may now kiss the bride," Pastor Watts told Victor and Zaria as I dabbed a wad of tissue at my eyes.

Maaco smirked at me and wrapped an arm around my shoulder. I smiled embarrassingly at him and leaned into his chest.

"Weddings make me cry."

"Big surprise there."

Everyone stood for their recessional song as "Spend My Life With You" blared in surround sound and the new Mr. and Mrs. Victor Vincent walked down the aisle.

Zaria was a beautiful bride. Her hair was swept up into an elegant bun with a single Swarovski crystal bridal comb on the side. The spaghetti strapped, lace bodice, mermaid style dress flowed down into a long train. Simple, but elegant.

My brother reminded me of my dad in the wedding album my parents kept in their living room. He wore a white-on-white three-piece suit with a white tie that accented his coffee complexion. The deep waves in his hair were thick enough to make you seasick as they faded into a sharp cut.

It was a lovely and intimate ceremony with only 50 guests in a small room at an event hall downtown. Liking things to be simple is something my brother and I have always had in common.

Following everyone out onto the huge outdoor patio where the reception was being held, I spotted my cousin and her man in conversation with my mom, Aunt Pam and Uncle Derrick, who I hadn't seen in over a year. I glanced at Maaco and saw that he was looking in that direction as well.

He and Amina hadn't been in the same room since she shot and killed his sister in her home, and I wasn't sure if he wanted to be. The two of them had their own friendship separate from me, so I knew it was difficult for him to determine how he was going to handle her.

On one hand, he understood that it was in self-defense, but on the other hand, it didn't make sense to him that Jamie would go through so much trouble to try to rob her. Not unless she anticipated there being a big score, which judging from Amina's occupation, shouldn't have been possible.

"How much money did she think Amina had?" he had questioned one-night scrolling through pictures of his sister.

"She was desperate. Desperate people do crazy things sometimes. You said yourself she owed a lot of money to somebody. And she was high on coke. She might not have been thinking rationally."

I wanted so badly to tell him about the theft and murders Amina told me about in Miami, but she had sworn me to secrecy, and I was a woman of my word. That was the kind of secret that could put people behind bars if it ever came out, and I didn't want that for my cousin.

"We don't have to go over there if you don't want to."

"I'm good baby. I told you before we came that I was good."

We were walking arm and arm. Me in a red knee length sheath dress and he in a tailored dark blue two-piece cadet blue suit. My hair was in tight coils, swept up into a frohawk that took me a half an hour to style right, and he rocked a freshly tapered fade and goatee like a model fresh out of GQ Magazine.

"There's my girl," Uncle Derrick greeted me with a big hug and a kiss on the cheek.

He looked a little older, and grayer than the last time I saw him but being the baby brother to my mom and Aunt Pam, he still looked young for his age.

"Pretty dress," Aunt Pam offered with a smile.

"Thank you. Uncle Derrick, this is my boyfriend Maaco. Everybody else has met him before."

Maaco shook my uncle's hand and said hello to everyone else as Amina and I exchanged glances. She looked just as uneasy as I suspected Maaco felt.

"How long are you in town for?" I asked grabbing hold of my uncle's arm lovingly.

When I lived in New York with him, he was like a father to me, and even though he was almost 15 years younger than my real father had been, I still thought of him that way.

"Till Monday. You know school in New York doesn't let out until June."

"Yasmine and the baby are going to be here until Monday too," Amina interjected.

"Good. I haven't seen that little munchkin in weeks," my mother cooed.

"Say what you want about how she was conceived, but they sure made a pretty little baby. If I still had my ovaries and a man to fertilize them, I would be trying to make me a little baby myself since my own kids ain't trying to give me no grandkids"

We laughed and Amina and Donovan exchanged a strange look.

"Be careful what you wish for," Amina retorted flinging her hair sassily. "I don't want to hear about how busy you are when I give you your first grandbaby and you don't want to babysit."

Aunt Pam sucked her teeth and waved her off.

"Girl hush."

"So, Valerie. When does the play you're in open? What's it called again?" my mother asked.

"*Birds of A Feather.* It opens June 15th at the Fox Theatre."

"I'm glad you're back to working on the big stage," Uncle Derrick nudged me. "I've always thought you had too much talent to do anything else. I was hoping that if you didn't find anything here in Atlanta, you would move back up to New York again. I miss you."

"Noooo, I'm sorry Uncle Derrick. I'm sorry. Can I call you that?" Maaco asked smiling slyly.

My uncle laughed. "As long as you're with my niece you can."

"Thank you. But I'm sorry to tell you, Valerie won't be moving back to New York again. Not as long as we're together she won't. Now that I have her all to myself, I'm not going to let her go again."

I blushed and bit my bottom lip bashfully as the brows on all of the women raised.

"Is that so?" Aunt Pam caricatured cheekily. "Umph. Well, you sound like somebody who needs to be going ring shopping soon then since you're over here claiming where folks can and can't live. Ain't y'all already over there living in sin at your place anyway?"

"Ma!" Amina scolded with a chuckle.

"She is," my mother nodded.

I might have taken offense, if my Aunt wasn't a known pot stirrer, and most of what she says is usually meant in jest anyway.

"Y'all need to stop," I giggled.

"You might be right though Aunt Pam," Maaco replied.

"Well now *I* didn't see you could call me Aunt. I'm too young and beautiful to have anybody who isn't biologically my niece or nephew calling me Aunt. And don't call me Ma'am either. Ms. Pam will do just fine."

"I swear I don't know what I'm going to do with her," Amina shook her head.

"The same thing I'm going to do with you after you and this little chocolate drop were around here having sex in the bathroom at your cousin's wedding," Aunt Pam said placing a hand on her ample hip.

All mouths dropped as Donovan's eyes nervously shifted from person to person and Amina clutched her chest in shock. Nobody said anything for at least 30 seconds before Aunt Pam finally broke the silence.

"Boom!" She said slicing her hand through the air like she dropped an imaginary bomb and laughed. "I bet that'll teach you to come for your momma."

Everyone laughed, including Amina and Donovan as she hid her face shamefully in his chest.

"Oh boy. How do you transition from that?" Uncle Derrick asked grinning. "Back to you being in this play. So, is it only going to be here in Atlanta? Or will it be in different states?"

"Well yes. If it does well, we may be hitting a few more cities with it. We've been preparing for the last two months for this opening. I'm excited."

I really was too. I hadn't been back to The Man Trap other than to get the rest of my things out of my locker since the night Brent tried to kidnap me from Maaco's house. Ultimately, though dancing there opened me up to another side of myself, I didn't love what I did. Any occupation that led me to self-medicate in order to perform wasn't right for me.

What it did do, was gain me a little local popularity which I capitalized on with my new IG page. So far, I had over twelve thousand followers, which I hoped would ultimately result in large ticket sales to my play.

Granted, a lot of my followers were probably people who followed my career with Alvin Ailey, which I was proud of, and people who found me by association with Vanessa's social media. No one has seen or heard from her since December 17th, the night I had a pain attack.

Since then, there's been a lot of conjecture, both plausible and far-fetched, about where she is and what she might be doing. An investigation into her disappearance revealed that Gavin The God's housekeeper was the last known person to see her alive.

She stated that Vanessa and Gavin had an argument earlier in the day, after which he left for the studio. The housekeeper later heard Vanessa on the phone with a woman before leaving her in the home alone. That lead to speculation that she was kidnapped by somebody holding her for ransom, or that she was so distraught by all of the bad press, that she went underground.

The police then dropped a bombshell that they were looking into my sister as a suspect in the murder of some producer whose house was set on fire last year. That, in addition to them seriously considering her as a person of interest in Delia's shooting.

The most far-fetched theory I've heard thus far, is that *I* and my family have been harboring Vanessa to keep her from being prosecuted, and that we take turns leaving the house pretending to be me.

As wild and disturbing as all of those theories have been, the most palpable one to me, is the one I find to be the most harrowing. The belief that she may be deceased. Of all the things people have said, the thing that can't be denied, is what I felt that night. The pain, the fear, and the feeling of finality that resonated inside me was real.

I knew when it hit me that something was terribly wrong with my sister. That she was severely hurt or worse, and the fact that she's been missing for *five* whole months, only confirms that I was right.

She hasn't used a credit card, made a phone call, posted a social media status, or been seen by anyone in five months, yet the police have been treating her case like she's a fugitive rather than a missing person.

My mother chooses to believe Vanessa has disappeared of her own volition. I told her about my pain attack, because if anybody knows how real they are, my mom does. Even with that and the knowledge of her last activity, she claims she doesn't believe Vanessa is dead.

I believe it's what she tells herself to keep from breaking down. For her, to accept that Vanessa may be dead somewhere, is to acknowledge that she will never have closure with the daughter she already feels like she failed.

Understanding that, I've made every effort to mend fences between us. I love my mother with all my heart, and I know she loves me, Vanessa and Victor just as much. I can't imagine losing my husband, and then my child in the same year.

So, if it makes her life easier to pretend Vanessa is somewhere gallivanting in the world under an alias, so be it. It's not like I *want* her to be dead. I just know in my heart that she is. Dreams of her decaying body lying in a field, talking to me from a grave with no coffin have haunted my nights at least twice a week since her disappearance. I wish I could remember the things she says when I wake up from them. But I never do. Maybe I never will.

Whatever happens, Brent won't be around to see it. I was afraid his money would get him off, even after stalking and trying to kidnap me, and I was right. His attorneys claimed mixing anti-depressants with Ambien and alcohol made him psychotic and his actions were not in his character. It was all a bunch of bullshit, but they let him bond out anyway.

I was on edge for days after, even with a restraining order on him, because I felt like his money was long enough that he might try something again and expect to get off. New Year's Day I got the both the shock and relief of my life. Tamika called to tell me that Dean received a phone call that Brent was dead.

Apparently, he OD'd at a friend's party off a combination of cocaine and other drugs mixed with alcohol and it sent him into cardiac arrest. His so-called friends didn't want to get arrested for drug use and waited over an hour before finally deciding to take him to the hospital, where he was later pronounced dead.

***

Vanessa

I'm not sure what happens to most people when they die, or if there really is a purgatory for the ones who've done wrong on earth or not. All I know is, I'm in a world of darkness with no, up or down and no left or right.

The last thing I remember is feeling like I was having an out of body experience. I watched from above as Brand pulled my limp body out of the pool and hurled it into a big dirty wheel barrel like I was a pile of trash.

"Are you sure everybody who's supposed to be here tonight is already in the house? The last thing we need is for somebody to catch you wheeling her body out into the woods," Delia questioned.

"*Nobody's* going to see me. Even if they did leave the house right now, they won't be able to see out this far. Not in the dark. It's almost three o'clock in the mornin' baby. Your mother, your brother, the staff... everybody's asleep in the house right now.

Now I left John John and Steelo in the studio at about one when I came over here. I told them I was going upstairs to check in on you and catch some z's for a few hours while they worked on that track.

We got a full house of alibi's tonight if we ever need it, and the Paps will be chasing your every move in California after tomorrow anyway. You heard from Rachel yet? She was supposed to be back here an hour ago."

Delia glanced at her cell phone, then back at her partner in crime.

"Yeah. She texted. There was an accident on the route she was supposed to take, so she had to take an alternate one. She lost her signal, got lost for like a half hour... whatever. She's switched cars and she's on her way back now with Vanessa's license plates."

"Well we're gonna have to bury those in a different spot later then. I don't want to wait too long to put her in the ground. The longer we keep her out, the better chance of somebody seeing us."

"Okay. I agree with that. How much did you say you had to pay this guy to crush her car again?"

"Just a thousand," he waved her off dragging the barrel over to the sliding glass doors. "Money talks baby. He didn't care where the car came from or why I wanted it crushed. All he wanted was that green. All right. Let me wheel this bitch out there now before it starts raining again or something."

"Wait. You almost forgot her bags," Delia reminded him, spinning her wheelchair around and heading to the elevators.

"Aww shit. Yeah. You need me to do that?"

"No. I got it. I'll be right back."

She returned with my belongings not long after and maliciously tossed them on top of me. Seeing myself like that was freakish and if I had a mouth to throw up from, I would have. My eyes and mouth were wide open. My lips were blue, my skin pale and my pupils looked like dilated marbles.

I kept trying to close my eyes so I could reopen them and wake myself up. But nothing was happening.

Delia wheeled herself over to Brand and pecked his lips as he adjusted the fit of the gloves he wore on both hands.

"It shouldn't take me more than forty-five minutes out there. The grave's already dug, so all I gotta do is roll her up to the edge of it and dump her. The dirt is already in the tractor waiting for me to dump it back in."

"And you're sure it's deep enough?"

"Baby! Stop questioning me god damn it! Hell yeah it's deep enough. In fact, it's deeper than deep enough. It's eight feet deep instead of six. Now we've already gone over this a hundred times."

"Okay," she rolled her eyes indignantly. "I'm just trying to make sure we didn't forget anything."

He shot her a look and slid the door open with power. She wheeled her chair around to go back upstairs as my ethereal body seemed to be hovering over my human one.

Yelling and screaming didn't do me any good, as I quickly found out on the trek through the woods. Brandon couldn't hear me, and I was powerless to stop him from reaching his destination. It took at least 10 minutes to get to the large hole in the ground in a clearing in the middle of the woods.

He must've dug that thing with the jaws of the tractor too because it was far from the rectangular grave I expected to see when we pulled it. It was more of an oval shape, at least three times wider than my petite frame required. But the one thing that was evident was the depth.

As promised, he wheeled my body to the edge of the hole and dumped me in. Instantly, the only things I could see were dirt and the sky above. I was no longer levitating above myself. If my eyes could cry, they would have. Soon after, the tractor roared to life, piercing the silence. The last thing I saw was a load of dirt being dumped on me. And after that... complete darkness.

And that's how it's been ever since.

THE END

Enjoyed This Book?

Please leave a review on Amazon or Goodreads to share!

Other releases by K.F. Johnson:

BEHIND CLOSED DOORS: LOVE HURTS
LIAR'S BALL: BEHIND CLOSED DOORS 2
WHEN I'M BAD I'M BETTER
WHEN I'M BAD I'M BETTER 2
WHAT I'D DO FOR LOVE
WHAT I'D DO FOR LOVE 2
LOVE HURTS: SERIES COMPILATION
WHEN I'M BAD I'M BETTER FOREVER: SERIES COMPILATION
STABBED THIS CHRISTMAS: A NOVELLA

Join my mailing list and be the first to get sneak peeks, giveaways, contests, new release info, learn event appearances and more!
http://www.kfjohnsonbooks.com

"The Empress of romantic, murder, suspense", **K.F. Johnson** is a Queens, New York native residing in Atlanta, Georgia. As a child, habitually failing to make curfew before the streetlights lit, earned her numerous occasions on restriction where reading & writing became her main form of escape. Later, K.F continued to develop her talent while obtaining a B.A. in Psychology at Spelman College & acquiring an MBA. In 2012, she published her 1st book for her social media friends & family to see. To her delight, it went viral, repeatedly reaching #1 on Amazon's top 100 for its genre. Since then, K.F. has published multiple books, started One Ironwoman Publishing, been featured in magazines & nominated for numerous awards, both for her books & as an author. With her fan base cheering for more, this mother & wife has blossomed into a witty & cunning author, penning spicy, realistic & deadly tales of African American life to remember.